STAR CURSED

STAR CURSED

Book Two in the
Curse of the Beast Series

By
Ashley Lavering

Star Cursed

Edited by Mystic Manuscripts LLC, Diana Yerka, Lydia Ross, and Holly Millett

Cover Design: Misty Polish

Interior Design: Misty Polish

First Edition: 2013

ISBN-13: 978-0-9855703-3-0

Library of Congress Control Number: 2013900649

Also an E-book: 978-09855703-2-3

"Standing before the mirror of reality, it is sometimes hard to see hope and happiness through the struggles and sorrow that cloud our vision. But life has taught me that they are there if we are brave enough to reach for them."

~Tayla Jonas

A GEOGRAPHICAL NOTE ABOUT THE DESCRIPTION
OF CODY, WYOMING:

While I strived to keep true to the wonderful city of Cody, there were times when I changed small aspects for the needs of my book. I sincerely hope the residents of Cody will excuse the fictional liberties I took in adding more foliage to City Park and around Cody High, and changing Cody High's football stadium. Plus, all street names, and restaurant names mentioned in the book are purely from my imagination.

1

SPUDS AND PANCAKES

Tuesday, April 10

I groaned. My whole body ached, as if every cell was bruised. Exhaustion weighed on me like an x-ray blanket. With effort, I lifted my arm and rubbed my eyes, blinking the room into focus. The rosy light of morning filtered through the gossamer curtains covering the French doors. Embers from the previous night's fire lay cool in the soot-stained hearth.

I was in Beast's room. In his lodge. In the middle of nowhere.

I shifted uneasily under his comforter. Why had he let me continue to sleep in his bed? He could have easily carried me back upstairs to my room, but he hadn't. He had willingly given up his bed for me, and my chest tightened. He was very possessive about beds, and the implication of his action wasn't lost on me, warming my heat. I wrapped myself tighter in the blanket, accepting the protection he offered.

A mist of doubt clouded my peace. Had he done it out of guilt? My temples throbbed from the simple thought and I rolled over to my side, burying my head in the pillow. His musky woodland scent infiltrated my senses, transporting me back two nights ago—the night of the full moon. I could hear the terrifying sound of wolves pounding the ground as they chased me. I felt again the razor teeth sinking into my calf, ripping it open.

I jolted to a sitting position, my leg pulsing with sharp pain from the memory. I gripped the comforter as I rode the flashbacks that assaulted me. My breath hitched. I was back on the kitchen rug in a pool of my own blood—bleeding to death.

But I hadn't died.

I held my throbbing, bandaged finger close to me as the memory of Beast's fang slicing it open sent new pain through it. I'd never forget the way the fiery-liquid of his venom had spread through my body—changing it, forever.

If Beast was right, a month was all the time I had to rid myself of the poison in my blood and stop the transformation. Beast wasn't even sure it would be a cure. It was just an old worn piece of paper he found in the alpha logs that said something about true love and a human. Finding true love was daunting, even when I was normal and had all the time in the world. Now I had to find it in a month, with one werewolf for a shadow and another inside my own head. *Yeah, no problem, right?*

I groaned and swung my legs over the edge of the bed. My calf banged the wooden frame and I bit off a curse. This whole thing sucked. How was I going to find a guy to fall in love with me in time? And I with him?

What worried me the most was the prospect that Beast might be wrong and I would be a wolf forever, or that the change would kill me.

I shivered and wrapped my arms around my chest. The impulse to lay back down and let despair swallow me was tempting, but my mind flashed with the faces of my family. Aunt Lily, who had raised me from infancy; my two cousins, who I thought of as sisters; Grandma Jonas, whose spunk was contagious; and Uncle Stan, whose memory still weighed heavily on us all.

I won't lie down. I won't let this beat me. I owe it to them and to myself to fight until there is no hope left.

I clamped my jaw tight. There was still hope and I wasn't alone. Beast was willing to help, and I was surprised to find how much I had come to rely on him. He was taking me home, back to my family, and that alone was a miracle.

My eyes flicked toward the nightstand where a fluted crystal vase cradled the infamous rose. The vivid scarlet petals flamed with yellow at the base. Its sheer beauty and symbolism stole my breath. How could something so beautiful represent the transformation into something so hideous? A single petal rested on the cherry wood stand, taunting me.

My shaky fingers plucked the petal from the polished wood. Breathing became difficult as I looked at the withered edges of the petal. My precious time as a human was already ticking away. How many petals were left? I tried to count them without touching the delicate rose, but it was impossible to tell.

I pressed the petal tightly to my chest. *Please let there be a guy out there who can love me.*

A sneeze brought my gaze sharply to the bedroom floor, where Beast lay curled in wolf form on a massive area rug. His silver eyes zeroed in on the red petal showing through my fingers. Rising, Beast closed the small gap between us until his moist muzzle touched my arm.

Memories of his concern and tenderness the night before threatened to break my brave façade, but I resisted the impulse to throw my arms around his furry neck. I'd never forget the way his hands had moved so gently to bandage my leg and how his caramel eyes had enveloped me in a warm cloud of protection.

I could've lost myself in those eyes, but I couldn't think of that now. I had to stay focused on my cure.

Taking several deep breaths to steady myself, I crawled out of bed and tested my wounded leg. To my utter surprise, I could stand without crumpling to the floor in agony. Tentatively, I shifted my weight. My leg was still tender and stiff, but the sharp pain from yesterday had ebbed to a bone-deep ache, something that should be impossible. Half of my calf had been ripped off. I shouldn't even be able to use it. I slumped back onto the bed. Trembling, I fingered the back of my calf, feeling the mended and whole flesh.

Dizziness spun my vision and I closed my eyes, slowing my rapid breathing. I thought Beast had said it was only a drop of venom. That I wouldn't change so fast. My eyes flew open and I inspected my index finger, praying that I was just hallucinating. Where an angry gash used to be, there was now only a faded pink line. My breathing picked up and full panic began to set in. Beast jumped on the bed, knocking me onto my back. His head nuzzled my face. I curled into him, digging my fingers into his shaggy coat as I sobbed in despair. It was happening. I could see it with my own eyes. I was changing, and the fullness of that truth overwhelmed me.

I cried until my eyes closed in exhaustion. I woke to the bright rays of mid-morning. Beast had stayed with me, sharing his warmth and reassurance. My fingers glided across his soft coat. It was like his very presence was telling me it would be okay, and I held onto that like a life line. Slowly, I unraveled myself. His eyes watched me.

I gave him a weak smile. "Thanks."

He licked my hand and jumped off the bed. It was time to fully test my leg. I stepped gingerly across the room, wincing each time I flexed my calf. My damaged leg ached and burned like fire ants were biting it. I guess it wasn't as healed as my finger, but I could use it, and that alone was a magical feat. I continued my slow journey across the room to the bathroom.

By the time I reached the vanity, sweat glimmered across my brow. A large mirror reflected my oily brunette hair, knotted in a messy nest atop my head. It was in need of a good washing with some salon-grade shampoo. My stomach gurgled. I guess my hair would have to wait.

Before I rejoined Beast in the bedroom, I heard the distant *clink*, *clink* of dishes. Shaking my head muted the echoing noise, but it came back the instant I stilled. Could I hear what was going on in the kitchen? The thick log walls should have blocked all sound, with the kitchen two rooms away and down the hall. Besides, Beast was in the next room, so there should not be anyone around to make clattering noises.

Curiosity tugged at me. I exited the bedroom, leaning heavily on the walls. Beast followed on my heels. Once in the hallway, the sound of clanking dishes intensified and I could make out the sloshing of water and the soft breathing of someone or something in the kitchen. My eyes darted to the wolf beside me, making sure it was really him and not another from his pack. But there was no mistaking his silver-dusted brown pelt. Whoever was in the kitchen wasn't Beast and couldn't be another wolf, unless my mother had learned to wash dishes with her paws. *Highly unlikely.*

So was it a thief? I had no doubt Beast could handle a burglar, but his hackles weren't up. He must know who the intruder was. I cocked my head at him.

"So who is it?" I asked. "Why are they here?"

He snorted and butted his head against the back of my good leg, as if impatient with my caution and questions. I would have my answers soon enough. I inched my way down the hall and pushed the oak door open. Rounding the fridge, I froze and blinked hard, unable to believe my eyes.

"Grandma?" My shocked voice vibrated through the kitchen.

Grandma dropped a plate and suds flew, splattering the general area and blending in well with her paint-splattered outfit. Grandma swiveled around, and her turquoise eyes locked on me.

"Tayla!" She wrapped me in a crushing, wet hug. My tender flesh shrank from the embrace, but the rest of me wished she'd never let go. Snuggling my face into the nook of her neck, I breathed in the faint scent of paint mixed with a tiny hint of her favorite lavender perfume. I sighed at the little piece of home. I hadn't realized how much I'd missed her. She had a way of easing my worries, just with her presence.

"You sent my heart racing, sneaking up on me like that," she said, gripping my arms to look at me. "Next time make some noise."

I still couldn't believe she was here. But no one else could make those camo-green pants and paint-splattered brown shirt look cool.

"How?" I asked, my throat tightening in emotion. I took a deep breath and forced the question out. "How can you be here?"

"That is a long story, dear." She rubbed her neck as if she wasn't sure where to start.

I tried to focus on her, but my eyes blurred. I sagged forward. The little strength I had was spent. I'd have hit the floor if not for Grandma's quick reflexes.

"You should be resting," she said with concern in her voice. "But I guess you couldn't resist my cooking." She winked. "Come. Let's feed you before I force you back to bed."

I gave a small chuckle. "You won't have to twist my arm."

Wrapping her arms around me again, she guided me to the dining room table. I sank into the chair, my limbs like jelly, and laid my head against the back of the carved chair.

The smell of blueberry pancakes wafted through the air, making my stomach rumble so loud that the room seemed to vibrate. I blushed and rubbed the noisy nuisance.

"Pancakes coming right up." Grandma loaded my plate with a stack of her homemade pancakes drizzled in maple syrup.

I watched her stride back to the stove on the kitchen island, slapping pancakes onto a second gold-rimmed plate for herself.

"Am I dreaming?" My voice came out small, afraid everything would shimmer and disappear if I closed my eyes again.

"No, Tayla." There was sadness in her voice.

"But how—" My unfinished question hung in the air as her plate hit the table with a clunk.

"Eat. There's plenty of time for talking later."

Without waiting for Grandma to say grace, I shoveled one bite after another into my watering mouth. Grandma would normally slap my hand if I took even one bite before she'd thanked the Lord for our bounty. A moment later, my food was gone and I wished for more, but the cooling griddle was empty. Downing two glasses of milk, I was more satisfied. Grandma gathered my dishes, but before she could move away from the table, I caught her arm. She stiffened.

"Grandma," I said.

She shook her head, the first sign that she wasn't handling everything as well as she portrayed. I studied her more closely. Dark circles shadowed her eyes and her hands shook.

"Do you know how I was wounded?" I let go of her and picked at the sleeve hem of the robe I was wearing, unsure about her reaction.

Resigned, she sat back down, placing the dirty pile of dishes in front of her. "I guess the dishes can wait."

Drowsiness weighed down on me, but I pushed it away, needing to hear her answer. Leaning back into my seat, I waited for her to speak.

"Did Beast call you?" I asked. Her silence was killing me. The lines in her face sagged in a sadness that was almost palpable. In that moment, and for the first time, she looked weary and old.

"Sort of." She glanced at the wolf lying beside my chair and back up to me before she continued. "Last night, he sent Rose to me with a soggy message clutched between her teeth. She emerged from the shadows like a bullet, scaring the breath right out of me."

I was riveted to the spot at the mention of my mom's name. "Was the wolf gray?"

"A soft slate, yes."

My lips tilted. Grandma's artistic vocabulary, of course, just had to find a better word than gray.

So, it *was* my mother who'd protected me that terrible night of the full moon—the night I was bitten. My heart warmed. She loved me enough to have fought off the whole pack *and* endangered her own life by standing up to Beast. It was still crazy to think she had been a wolf my whole life and I had never known, never known that she hadn't wanted to abandon me.

Then something important occurred to me. I quirked an eyebrow at Grandma. "How did you know it was Mom?" I hadn't even known it was Mom when I'd first met the gray wolf.

Grandma took a deep breath before answering. "I was never certain until last night, but I knew my little gray wolf was different. I've been tracking her for years. She would venture much closer to me than the other wolves, but it wasn't until Beast sent her with the message to my campsite that I knew for sure." She shook her head. "Not that she didn't scare me plenty, coming out of the shadows like some grizzly bear."

I nodded. I knew that feeling well. "What did the note say?"

"That you were hurt and to follow the wolf." Grandma chuckled humorlessly. "Honestly, I thought I was hallucinating. I'm still not sure what to think."

A rueful smile tugged at my lips. "Yeah, I tried buying into that theory, but the hallucination doesn't go away. It just gets worse and worse."

"Oh, Tay." She reached over and captured my hand.

I squeezed her fingers. "Is it wrong of me to be glad you're in this mess with me?"

"Family sticks together, no matter what form we take." She patted my hand with her free one.

I grimaced at her choice of words. "So Beast told you?"

"Beast was in his human form when I finally arrived." She shifted, releasing my hand to run her fingers through her spiked hair. "He explained what had happened to you and to...to Rose."

Her voice was tainted with sadness. "Tay, I'm not sure what I can do. I failed Rose, and the only positive thing I can scrape from this whole thing is the twisted logic that you will finally be with your mother again." A deep loneliness filled her eyes.

My gaze fell to my hands gripping the robe's thick fabric, pulling the seams to bursting.

"Did he tell you how long I had left?" I could hardly speak the words as emotions clogged my throat.

"Yes," she said.

A high-pitched scratching on the sliding glass door echoed through the room like squealing tires before a crash. I winced and clapped my hands over my ears. Grandma looked at me with a raised eyebrow before turning her attention to the source of the noise.

"Rose! There you are." Grandma's voice filled with excitement, cutting through the residual sadness hanging in the air. Her crestfallen expression transformed into a brilliant smile, and she yanked open the door.

A gray wolf stood patiently on the other side, staring straight at me. Her eyes enveloped me in a warmth I can only describe as my mother's love, and a tingle shot down my spine.

How did I ever doubt my little gray protector was anyone other than my mother? As if answering my unspoken question, Beast nosed the back of my hand, encouraging me forward. My mother stood so close to me, just on the other side of a door, but I couldn't close the distance. I sat paralyzed.

Through the open door, a gush of cold wind poured into the kitchen. Hugging my fluffy robe closer to me, I watched my mother's eyes flicker to Beast's as if asking permission to enter his house. Some unnoticed approval must have occurred, because she placed a tentative paw on the tiled floor. My hands felt slick, and I fumbled for words as I watched her slow progression across the room. Here she was, and I didn't know what to say. Countless times I had imagined meeting my mom. I had even planned out what I would say and the answers I would demand. But never had I imagined her as a wolf, unable to answer any of those questions.

She halted next to my chair. I still hadn't moved an inch. Shyly, she nuzzled the hand resting on my thigh. My fingers curled into the gray fur around her ear. It was as soft as a rabbit's coat. I bent forward, gazing intently into her brown eyes.

"Mom?" I breathed, unable to hold back the question in my voice. It was still hard to believe she could be a wolf, even after seeing Beast change multiple times.

Mom's tongue slobbered the side of my face. I jerked back against the chair and wiped the saliva from my cheek.

"Gross," I complained lightheartedly. I smiled at Grandma's laughter and Mom's wolfish grin. Her tongue lolled playfully to one side. I was grateful for the unexpected laughter. Apparently my mother didn't know how to act in this situation anymore than I did.

I tried batting her head aside, but she dodged out of my range, and I almost fell from the chair.

"If I could run, I would so get you back," I teased through my laughter. My chest burned from exhaustion, but I didn't care.

Grandma's amusement died at my comment, and she looked at me as only a grandmother could. "How's your leg doing?"

"It's fine, I guess. Beast cleaned and wrapped it last night." My brow puckered. "He might've slipped me some pain meds in my drink. It doesn't hurt as badly as I remember."

"Hmm."

After grabbing a couple of steaks from the fridge, Grandma tossed them to Mom and Beast. Mother waited to eat hers until Beast turned his back on the other offered steak. It was odd to see them acting human one moment and pure wolf the next. I turned back to Grandma while they devoured their breakfast, so I wouldn't lose mine at the sight of the bloody meat.

"He said you would heal fast," Grandma said.

"Did he say that this was normal?"

Grandma shrugged. "He wasn't really specific, but he did warn me that you might not wake at all today. Guess you smelled my famous pancakes and just couldn't help yourself."

I smiled at her attempt to lighten the mood, but my mind was still strained with the fears Grandma couldn't ease. Only Beast could answer the questions that plagued me like a waking nightmare. Was my body changing too fast? Was my time as a human shorter than we thought?

I sighed and lowered my forehead into the crook of my arm resting on the table. Beast's dark snout snuffled around my face. If I'd been feeling better, I might have laughed, but my eyelids were losing the battle to sleep now that my hunger was sedated. Beast prodded my arm, demanding I look at him. When I didn't, he grabbed the baggy sleeve of my robe with his teeth, and pulled, indicating that he wanted me to go back to his room to rest.

"He's right, you know, Tay. You've already nodded off twice," Grandma said.

She came to my side and looped a supportive arm under my shoulders. Beast padded along in front of us, skillfully opening doors in our path with his paws. Suddenly, I realized someone was missing—my mother.

"Mom? Mom!" My heart beat frantically, and I forced my sleepy eyes to scan the room. Had Beast made her leave? A wave of panic raced through my body. I couldn't lose her again. I sucked in quick breaths. I couldn't. I'd just found her.

A few moments later, a gray wolf entered my line of vision and my heart rate stabilized. I took a deep calming breath. "Don't leave me."

Mom gave me a sharp nod and a low ruff of reassurance. Grandma led me to Beast's bed and tucked me into the thick comforter. With my hand curled in the silky fur of my mother's head, I drifted off to sleep.

2
MORE
HUMAN

I blinked at the shadows shifting around me like streaks of
liquid mud. The trees swayed in the eerily soundless breeze,
and I shivered. A sense of danger triggered the urgency to
escape an unseen foe. My legs jolted into a run, and I felt my way
through the blackness. As I shifted from pine to pine, my hands
scraped bark, and the undergrowth grabbed at my legs like skeletal
fingers. But I didn't stop. I couldn't.

A howl echoed close behind me, and my heart slammed
against my ribcage in fear. A root snagged my foot, and I tumbled
onto a dimly moon lit path. I scrambled to stand, but my arms felt
wrong—they were paws. On all fours, I felt a bloodthirsty howl
vibrate up my wolf throat. Shock rocketed through me only to be
displaced by a raging hunger.

I jerked my head at the thrum of running feet. A slender
woman in a flowing white dress ran from me. Her sun-dipped hair

glowed in the dark like a thousand fireflies. Her blood smelled honey-sweet with power, and I licked my lips. My hind legs pushed into a sprint. Soon the woman was mere feet from me, her scent so thick it coated my tongue. Saliva pooled around my teeth, and I lunged for the kill. I sailed through the air just as a gray wolf slammed into me. We tumbled, biting at fur, until I kicked her away. Snarling, I looked into the warm chocolate brown eyes of my mother. A jolt slammed into my chest, and I was once again human, lying in the tall undergrowth.

My mother's snout nuzzled my cheek. My hand slid through her fur. A woman's ethereal laugh sang through the air with a haunted edge. Then, daggers of heat sliced up my calf. I screamed. My eyes locked on a wolf so black that only his yellow eyes were visible. He squeezed my leg harder between his massive jaws. I screamed and his eyes laughed.

Frantic, I reached for Mom but she'd vanished. I grabbed at the foliage around me, but the plants ripped out of the ground as the wolf tugged me into his black abyss

"Mom!" I woke screaming, and sprang to a sitting position, but a strong hand pushed me back down into the cloud-like pillows. I struggled to find my mother, grasping blindly for her. The bed bounced and a warm muzzle burrowed into my chest. My arms encircled the gray mass of fur as shuddering breaths passed my lips. I sucked in sharply. "A dream, just a dream," I mumbled into her fur.

"Tayla?" Beast's voice was full of worry.

My eyes drifted up to meet his. He was standing by the end of the bed, dressed in his normal black clothes with white linen wraps thrown over his broad shoulders. The room was once again dark with only the dim lamplight illuminating it.

I shivered as the last drops of terror rolled off me. "A nightmare." I softly answered his unspoken question, and his eyes softened with compassion. I scratched the velvety fur behind mother's ear, focusing on anything but the eerie dream. A contented rumble vibrated the bed. I smiled down at my mother, still awed by her presence.

"I need to finish undressing your leg," Beast informed me.

Beast grabbed hold of my calf and elevated it enough to continue unwrapping the blood-soaked cloth. That must have been the tugging I thought was dragging me to my doom in the underbrush.

"You really need to wake me up before you start that. I thought a wolf was dragging me off to devour me." I sagged back into the pillow feeling tired.

Beast smirked. "I'll keep that in mind."

My gaze flowed up his arms and over his short-sleeved tee pulled taut around his chiseled biceps and chest. The strong contours of his jaw looked broader under the half inch stubble growing only in the area of a typical full beard, instead of encompassing his whole face like it had before. He was ruggedly handsome in a strong, alluring way I had never encountered before meeting him. He was definitely no high school boy. His hands rubbed a salve into my calf, sending pleasant warmth up my leg. An increasingly-familiar heat stirred low in my abdomen.

"You look...different." To my horror, my voice came out soft and with a hint of sultriness, and my face flushed.

A slight twitch of his full lips was the only indication that he had noticed my desire. Thankfully, he didn't bring it up. If he had put it into words, I would have died from embarrassment, especially with my mother next to me.

"Right after a full moon, I have more control over my wolf, regaining more of my human form. I'll slowly lose that control as the next full moon approaches." His voice was full of sadness.

I remembered too clearly his beastly appearance that dark night in the park when the curse tethered us together. His hairy face, silver eyes, and sharp gleaming teeth.

"I bet I wouldn't have freaked out as badly if you'd looked like this the first time we met." I smiled, hoping to lighten the mood with humor.

His lips pressed together. "I only hunt when forced. Never would I do it willingly."

My plan had failed miserably. "Beast, I didn't mean..."

"It's fine." He moved his hands along my leg.

My heart hurt for him. How would it feel to live so long as a werewolf? Forced to bend your will to something else? I would find out soon enough if I didn't get his wolf venom out of my blood.

I would have to remember that right after the full moon was when a werewolf had more control over their wolf, just in case. I'd have to tell my family when the best day was to visit their wolf members. If they came at the wrong time... I shuddered. The image of them being ripped apart by my teeth was too horrible. The thought made my determination double in intensity. I *had* to find true love before the last rose petal fell.

Almost as if the rose mocked my efforts to defy it, a petal broke from the rose bud and fell slowly to the nightstand. I watched it settle on the dark wood. My vision blurred with tears, swirling the colors. I couldn't focus. My life as a human teetered on an almost impossible feat. How was I going to fall in love, *true* love, with someone in under a month? Finding a date was hard enough.

"You're healing well. Flex your foot for me a few times," Beast instructed, his voice breaking into my depressed thoughts.

I performed the task without thinking and was surprised when only a fragment of heat sliced through it, like shin splints after a long run. Was I really healed? Looking down at my now completely-unbound leg, I saw faint pink, irregular shapes of what was left of my once bloody wound. It was like months had passed instead of just two days. I got lightheaded. This couldn't be right.

"Good," Beast said as he watched the muscles in my leg move. "You'll be like new by tomorrow."

How could he say that? How could he not see it? This couldn't be normal, even for a girl becoming a wolf.

"You're wrong," I stated soberly.

"Oh?" he questioned, cocking his head slightly to the side.

"I don't have a month. I may not even have a week." My voice was inching toward hysteria. I couldn't lose my humanity! Not yet. Beast silently waited for me to compose myself. Several breaths later, I was calm enough to continue without yelling.

"I'm changing too fast. My hearing is too sensitive, and I'm healing way too quickly. You must have infected me with more venom than you thought." I shuddered at the idea.

He smiled kindly at me, like a wise mentor waiting for his student to pay attention.

"The changes you're experiencing are only the first to manifest. Your transformation to full wolf will be slower because you actually received a *tiny* amount of saliva in your bloodstream. Smell and keener eyesight will come late—"

"Slow? This isn't slow!" I cut him off.

"Yes, it is, Tayla."

I bit my tongue. "How can you be sure?"

He was silent for a long while, and the quiet stillness grew uncomfortable.

"I know my pack. I've seen enough men, women, and girls changed at my teeth and those of my alphas, that I know how it works. Plus, the alpha logs give detailed accounts of the change, trying to understand it." He swallowed hard before continuing.

"Most often infected people change that same night, and there are only a handful who've stayed human until the next full moon."

My mother gave a small whimper, as if reliving a bad memory.

"How did it happen for my mom?"

Shadows deepened in his tight face. "That horrible night is better left in the past. Your mother is lucky she survived." With his eyes downcast, he whispered, "her rose grew and withered that same night."

Sadly, I asked, "Does a rose grow every time?"

"No."

"Then why us?" I gestured to my mother and me.

His eyes met mine again. "Because you are bound to me through 'The Curse of the Beast,' as I call it. You and your mother were the purest descendants of Star, under the age of twenty, when it was time for The Hunting."

"The Hunting?"

"Every sixteen years or so, I'm forced to hunt for a girl that will be tethered to my wolf through the curse. I'm drawn to those of the star's bloodline, but one will call louder than the rest. It doesn't matter where in the world she is, whatever magic binds me to this form compels me to her side. And, well, you know what happens after that," he explained.

"So *The Legend of the Beast* is true, and the star really came to Earth?" I asked, awe evident in my voice.

His eyebrows rose. "You snuck into my study, didn't you?"

I ignored his question. "Did she?"

He nodded, humor playing deep in his brown eyes.

"But I don't look anything like her." I refused to believe I was a descendant of something ethereal.

He chuckled. "You *did* sneak into my study."

"It's your fault." I pointed an accusing finger at him.

He put a hand to his chest in mock offence. "My fault?"

"You're the one flaunting secrets, and then telling me not to look." I sat up. "You practically handed me an invitation to snoop."

He grinned. "Maybe that is reason enough for you, but to me it doesn't justify your actions."

"Whatever. I needed answers and you weren't going to give them to me anytime soon." I crossed my arms, refusing to feel guilty for invading his privacy.

His gaze dropped to my leg, and his smile faded. His fingertips brushed my leg. "I was hoping to have more time..."

Tingles drifted across my skin like sparks on kindling. I pulled my leg away from both his touch and the longing in his voice. His hand fell to his side. I couldn't look him in the face. My desire for him scared me. Was it the bond? Some trick to make it even harder to find a true love? The thought snuffed out the heat in my belly. I wouldn't let him distract me—my life depended on it.

I cleared my voice. "So the legend in that book really happened?" I asked, trying to break the awkward tension between us.

"Yes," he whispered, and it hurt my chest to hear the pain there.

I gripped the comforter in frustration. Everything was so messed up. I was paying for someone else's screw-up. Then the aged note claiming Star had descendants popped to the forefront of my thoughts, and I scowled.

"So I'm just her lucky descendant, cursed to pay for her mistake?" My voice hardened with sarcasm.

"You can't change your blood, Tayla," Beast stated simply.

I wanted to pout or sulk, to do anything but be reasonable. I wanted someone to tell me how unfair this was. But Beast wasn't that person, and I missed my best friend Chel all the more.

"Who else in my family are you planning to hunt?" I couldn't stop the hurt and anger from coloring my words.

His lips pressed into a hard line at my jibe. "The rest of your family doesn't have even a drop of the star's blood in them."

"How can that be?" Everything I had learned in genetics protested the statement. I could understand Grandma not having star blood, but what about Aunt Lily, Sarah, and Cammie?

His eyes drifted to the rose on the nightstand. "The star's bloodline must have come through your biological grandfather."

"What do you mean *biological* grandfather?" I demanded, offended. "Are you trying to insinuate that Grandpa Jonas wasn't my grandpa? That's just...just..." I trailed off, but a seed of doubt had already taken root.

"It can't be true," I breathed out loud, but my mother nudged my hand. She looked deep into my eyes, causing my resolve to waver. My world shifted again as another part of my foundation cracked with doubt. There were so many things I thought I knew about the world, about my family, and it shook me to the core to find out they were false. First, werewolves actually existed and my mother was one; second, I was turning into a werewolf as well; and finally, that Grandpa Jonas might not be my biological grandfather. It was too much to handle, and I pinched my eyes shut to block out the barrage of images.

"Your clothes are there," he said, pointing to the foot of the bed. I peeked at him, following his finger to a pile of neatly folded clothes, blue jeans and a t-shirt striped three shades of green.

"Get dressed. We'll leave within the hour," he commanded, and stood to go. But he paused before taking the first step. His gaze bounced between my mother and me. "I'll leave you to say your goodbyes."

"What!" My shocked voice reverberated around the room.

Turning around, Beast held me in the intensity of his golden-brown eyes. "Tayla, your mother has to stay here with the pack."

A whimper came from the gray wolf by my side, and Beast gazed at her. A moment passed as if a silent conversation had transpired, and Beast shook his head. Mom let out a whine that sounded so pleading that it hurt my heart.

"Rose," Beast rebuked. His hands went to cradle his head as if he had a migraine and he closed his eyes. Mom continued to whine pleadingly.

"What's going on?" I questioned, anxious to understand.

"Rose, stop it, or I'll block you out," Beast hissed through clenched teeth.

"Tell me what's going on!" I snapped unable to handle the growing anxiety building inside me.

They both turned their eyes on me. Beast relaxed once more, the look of pain no longer etched into his face, and my mother's heart-wrenching whine stopped, though she lowered her head in defeat.

"Your mother wishes to say many things to you, but in human form I'm unable to translate even half of it." He sounded tired.

My heart drummed in my chest. "What do you mean translate it? I thought you could talk to her?"

"It's not that easy, Tayla," he admitted. "She can understand us, but she can only communicate through images and relay basic emotions to me when I'm human. When I'm wolf, we can converse with images and words mind-to-mind."

"So you can't tell me what she's saying?" My voice sounded small, like a lost child. "I was hoping to speak to her..."

Beast captured my gaze with his tender one. "Her love for you coursed through my body so strongly that it was physically painful to bear it."

21

She loves me. I wiped at the tears falling from my eyelashes. Deep down I'd always hoped that she did, but having the fact validated to me made it tangible, something I could firmly hold on to. My arms fell around my mother's furry neck.

"I love you too!" My voice muffled by her fur.

She whined happily, rubbing her nose against my head. My chest ached with joy, as if my heart had swollen too large to hold it.

I sniffed. "I was so angry with you growing up, but I understand now. I know you didn't want to leave me." I let the tears slide down my cheeks and onto Mom's silky coat. She loved me, and for that moment nothing else was important.

Beast cleared his throat, but I didn't bother looking up. Mom nuzzled my neck with her wet nose and backed out of my embrace. My fingers raked through her fur, reluctant to let her go.

"It's time," Beast stated. "Get dressed and grab the rose. I have everything else in the truck."

I couldn't move my eyes from Mom.

"If you don't move quickly, we'll have to wait until tomorrow to leave." Beast stepped out of the room, shutting the door behind him.

I snapped out of my stupor and quickly dressed. I was going home. I would see everyone again. But my heart was torn. I'd be leaving Mom.

I reached for my rose and paused. What if I never saw my mom again? I just found her. For several seconds I debated my options, and then Mom yelped, motioning to the door. She was right. I couldn't give up my humanity, and I knew where she was now. I'd come back. And not even Beast would keep me from seeing her again.

With renewed purpose, I picked up the vase with my rose and walked to the truck with my mother trailing behind me.

Climbing into the truck, I felt like my heart would rip from my chest as I left Mom standing a few feet away on the bluegrass lawn. Her brown eyes glistened with sadness. I knew it had to be this way, but it hurt to leave her. Grandma sniffled from the backseat of the pickup and my heart squeezed even more. I could only remember seeing Grandma cry once, and that was when Grandpa Jonas died. I had been eight years old.

Now, it looked like he hadn't even been my grandpa. Mom had acted like she believed it, and my chest hurt all the more. How could Grandma cheat on him? How could she keep it from me? But most of all, I needed her to answer the *why*. Why would she do it?

Anger swirled like heat rays through my sadness. I opened my mouth only to shut it again. Before I could formulate a thought, Beast shifted the truck into drive, and we pulled away from the house. My eyes darted from my lying Grandma to the mother I was leaving behind. Pain ripped at my chest, and tears slid down my cheeks as I watched Mom and the cabin slowly disappear out of view. Roughly, I wiped the tears away. I would find true love at all costs. I would stay human. And I'd break this curse that had trapped my mother and me.

3

BEAST'S
STORY

A half mile from Beast's lodge we stopped and Grandma climbed out of the truck. "See you at home, Tay."

When I refused to speak, her brow lifted in confusion, but I held silent. After another failed attempt to get me to speak, she wandered off to her own truck parked by the dilapidated shack.

Beast and I drove down the dirt road with Grandma following behind us in her truck. My gaze kept drifting to the rearview mirror. I was so used to her presence being the only reliable one in my life after Uncle Stan died, that this stinging rift of betrayal between us crushed my heart.

I clenched my jaw and stared straight ahead, refusing to look back at her truck again.

"I know you are mad at her, Tay," Beast said, his voice soft. "But everyone makes mistakes."

Emotions clogged my throat, and I turned from him to glare at the dark shadowed trees out my window. *What did he know? He wasn't the one who had been lied to his whole life.*

Thankfully, he didn't attempt another word, leaving the cab silent.

I stared out the window and lightly stroked the soft petals of the flower in my hands. I shifted my gaze to the scarlet rose, taking in its every detail for the hundredth time. My white fingers contrasted sharply with the rose's vibrant red and ethereal glow. *Human fingers forever destined to be wolf paws? Is that what it will be like when the last petal falls?*

"Beast." I looked meaningfully at him. "What's the change like?"

He gave me a sidelong glance. "Painful."

That conclusion was obvious from his nightly morphing ritual. "What happened the first time you changed?"

His hands flexed on the steering wheel, but he stayed focused on the road illuminated by the truck's lights. His reaction was hardly comforting. I shifted my gaze from his stiff form to the glowing neon-blue console. The time ticked by slowly: 9:24...9:25...

Still Beast said nothing.

I shifted uncomfortably in my seat. I popped open the glove compartment to distract myself. My eyes zeroed in on the operator's manual and the words "Toyota Tundra." I tried to swallow my mirth, but it came out as a cough-like snort that broke the silence.

I must've been out of it not to notice the silver lettering on the outside of the truck. It was ironic that I would be sitting in one of the few trucks I knew something about. Kyle had talked of nothing else when I'd first met him last November, before he turned from charmer to stalker. His father had bought him a Tundra for their hunting trips, and he loved to show it off. It felt like a lifetime ago that I'd played hide-and-seek with Kyle in the Cody High School hallways as I desperately tried to avoid his possessive demeanor and leering eyes. It had been a time when my problems were significantly smaller, and even the thought of Kyle didn't scare me like it once had, though I wasn't in any rush to see him. My life was complicated enough. I didn't need the headache of dealing with Kyle's weirdness.

I shut the glove compartment and turned toward Beast. I'd felt him staring at me for the last five seconds after I'd snorted.

"Is something funny?" His eyes searched mine for answers.

I shrugged my shoulders and looked back at the center console. "Not really."

"Hmm." He didn't sound convinced but left it alone. "How well do you know U.S. history?"

"History?" His question grabbed my attention, and my eyes met his pained ones.

"I was a foot soldier in WWII." His face hardened in a scowl.

I angled my body toward him as much as my seatbelt would allow, waiting for him to explain, but the silence continued until my impatience won.

"And?"

"I don't think you should hear this, Tayla. War is perhaps the ugliest thing in the world, and werewolves are a close second," Beast said.

His caramel eyes held no mirth. He wasn't joking. But I would risk a queasy stomach. I needed to know what to expect if I failed, so I nodded.

Resigned, his eyes shifted to the road, and his chest expanded with a deep breath. "Shortly after Pearl Harbor was bombed, I joined the army. I was eighteen."

I lowered my eyes to my lap, unsure what to say in memory of such a tragic day. Thankfully, Beast saved me from speaking.

"My platoon fought in many places, Africa, Europe, but my final stand was in the Battle of the Bulge." He stopped speaking, and I looked up at him. His expression was tight with pain. "Blood flowed like rivers. Everywhere there were explosions, gun fire, men freezing to their guns. There aren't words to describe the despair that choked us."

Grief clutched my heart, and I stared at Beast, unable to remove my eyes.

"As the battle continued, we were slowly pushed back. One night, the Germans pushed us hard in our retreat. The darkness was lit by deafening explosions." His voice echoed with the faraway sound of memory.

"Shrapnel ripped into my leg, and I couldn't keep up with my platoon. My good leg buckled from exhaustion, forcing me to hide in the underbrush. The night grew still as the fighting moved away from me, leaving me among the dead. I knew I was going to die, and I hated that it would be on foreign ground. Soon after, I lost consciousness with my pistol in my hand."

My lungs burned, reminding me to breathe, and I sucked in a breath.

Beast glanced my way. "I'll stop."

I shook my head.

"You'll regret it," he said.

"It doesn't matter. You can't stop now." I wouldn't let him wriggle out of telling the rest.

His hands rubbed the steering wheel, like he was trying to wring the polish from the leather. Seconds ticked by until finally his lips parted. "I awoke to pain so fierce it felt like a fire consumed me. Something tore at my body. It was dark, but there was enough light from the full moon to see a wolf's green eyes glowing like haunted orbs over me. He was huge, with a bloody chunk of my flesh hanging from his teeth. I thought I'd landed in Hell. Terror engulfed me, and my finger twitched automatically on my pistol's trigger. Out of dumb luck, the bullets hit him square in the chest. The wolf dropped to the bloody ground next to me, and I blacked out again."

Beast cleared the emotion from his throat. My fingers ached to touch his arm, to comfort him, but I was afraid of the intimate gesture and sat on my hands instead. He continued.

"It wasn't long before I felt the moonlight burn my skin, bringing the change with it. It was like lava replaced my blood and hot tar seared my skin." The steering wheel squeaked its protest at Beast's strangling hold. "The next thing I knew, I was on all fours, a wolf." He looked at me, gauging my reaction. I nodded, even though my stomach twisted from the emotions seeping through our connection and the vivid details of the story.

"The hunger I felt was so intense I couldn't help myself." He faced forward, his knuckles white. "I ate the wolf that had attacked me, tearing into his flesh like it was my favorite flavor of jerky."

Nausea overwhelmed me, and I placed a hand over my mouth. I turned to face the road, trying to control the feelings of revulsion that leaked through our bond.

If he noticed my disgusted facial expression, he didn't react, like the memory had captured him as well. "Later that night, I discovered the wolf I'd killed had been the alpha of all alphas, and I had replaced him. I wasn't a werewolf for more than a few hours before I heard the voices of the other wolves in the pack. I had leadership over every alpha throughout the world and they all pledged their loyalty to me. It was overwhelming, so I ran. But it didn't take long to understand that no distance would release me from what I was, so I found a cargo ship and sailed home, back to America, smuggling my personal pack on board as zoo animals."

My mind struggled to understand. "So you inherited a pack because you killed the alpha wolf?"

"That and I ate the largest portion of him. Power transfers to the werewolf who consumes the most. But I didn't know that at the time."

I gagged again at the image of him feeling compelled beyond his control to rip into a carcass. At least I wasn't forced to eat helpless animals. Not yet, anyway.

"Isn't there another way?" I asked, trying to distract myself from the reality of my potential future.

"The alpha's blood calls to male werewolves. I didn't have a chance." His voice was solemn.

After the realization came that my future eating habits would be changing, I was done with the story. Why hadn't I realized this before? Vegetarianism for wolves probably wasn't a biological option. And, on top of that, I'd have to kill the poor creatures myself and eat them raw. I cradled my sour stomach and glanced in the rearview mirror, making sure Grandma's truck was still behind us. When I was satisfied that she was there, I turned to stare out the side window and settle my stomach, but Beast wasn't finished telling his gruesome tale.

"Almost sixteen years passed before the curse—that I didn't know existed—forced me to hunt a young woman of Star's bloodline. It only happens to the alpha of the alphas, you know. I hate seeing the girls cry out in fear, only to have their memories hidden from them. It was like hauling away toddlers. It took months, sometimes years, before all their memories resurfaced. I have no idea why you were different, Tayla. Maybe there's more to this curse than we understand."

The memory of when he had stepped out of the shadowed trees in the park was too vivid for me not to feel sympathy for the other girls before me—and especially for my mother.

29

4

TWO
MAGICAL
ENTITIES

I forgot how to breathe when Beast pulled right behind the navy-blue Civic parked in front of Grandma's lemon-meringue colored house. Had Grandma called Aunt Lily? I wasn't prepared to see her tonight. Heck, I wasn't even ready to see Grandma again. What was I going to do now? I was really hoping to have a day or two to prepare for Aunt Lily and figure out the whole Grandma cheating thing, but I knew I'd never be ready for either conversation, no matter how long I procrastinated.

And now Aunt Lily was here, and I was going to have to face her. But how could I? I'd failed to protect her. Beast had knocked her out cold, then forced me to leave with him. I felt horrible, even if I couldn't have changed what happened.

My door opened, and I jerked involuntarily, sucking in a breath. Beast stood with his hand held out as if he was nothing more than a chauffeur. I climbed out, wincing as the door snapped shut behind me. There was no backing out, but I wasn't about to be the first one through the door. No, I'd make Grandma the sacrificial lamb. She owed me that much.

"Hand me your rose." Beast stood with my purple duffle bag slung lazily over his shoulder. I did and Beast gently pushed me forward by pressing on the small of my back. I refused to move. What was taking Grandma so long anyway? Her vehicle was parked in the covered garage at the side of the house, the tail lights dark, but there was no sign of movement in the house.

A smug grin pulled at Beast's lips as he noticed my inert form. That he could find this amusing was irritating. He should be hanging his head in shame right now, not laughing like a teenage boy about to pull a prank. My emotions swirled inside me as I gazed at the front door. What if I broke my aunt's heart all over again?

Beast guided me forward. His hand never left my lower back, steering my reluctant body up the cement path towards the house. My skin warmed under his touch, but it wasn't enough to distract me from how close we were getting to the porch.

Frantically, I searched the shadows for my wayward grandma. I'd never forgive her for leaving me to face Aunt Lily's wrath alone, not with everything else I was still mad at her for. We neared the porch and I dug my heels into the ground, trying to halt my forward progress.

Beast gave me a knowing look of pity. "Let's get this over with."

"No." I folded my arms. "I refuse to go in there first."

His face lost all traces of amusement and his voice sounded tired. "Tayla, it has been a long day. The faster we get in there, the sooner we can sleep. Now, up you go."

Somewhere in my mind I knew I was tired as well, but I was way too keyed up to feel it. He prodded me forward again, and I was no match for his strength. I lifted my foot to put it on the lower step when Grandma strode up to us. Relief washed over me, and I planted my foot back on the cement. But the good feeling dissipated as Grandma also pushed me up the steps.

"Hey, stop it!" I twisted out of their grasps.

"Tayla, you're acting like a child." Grandma's hand found her hip.

"Don't you dare turn this back on me." I stepped toward her with an accusing finger pointing at her. "You, my own grandma, lied to me."

"What?" Grandma's eyes popped wide.

"I know about Grandpa. How you hid your shame behind lies. But you couldn't quite hide it well enough." I scoffed. "No, you had to sleep with a cursed man."

"Watch your tone." Grandma brushed my finger out of her face, her eyes fierce. "And now is not the time to discuss this." She turned the glare on Beast. "You couldn't have waited for *me* to tell her."

"My apology, ma'am. I shouldn't have let her bait me." He nodded his head in respect.

"Don't you dare take her side!" I yelled. Their buddy-buddy act was making me sick.

"It was not my place to tell you." He looked at me with apologetic eyes. "I should have been more careful."

I snorted. "So it's better to let people lie to me?"

"I was going to tell you, Tay," Grandma said, placing a hand on my shoulder.

"Yeah? When?" I shrugged off Grandma's hand. "You know... never mind. I don't want your excuses." I hiked up the stairs, and pointed at the door. "Now, you get in there."

Grandma shook her head like she was disappointed in me. "You're not seeing the bigger picture."

"Maybe I don't like the picture." I clenched my jaw.

"Tayla, things will be okay. Lillian loves you like her own child, and she's worried about you," Grandma said. "She needs to see you."

I knew that was true. That was why this was so hard. I had hurt her, leaving her just like Mom had, and it tore at me. But the prospect of giving her false hope made me want to hide. And how would she handle seeing Beast in his human form? A sideways glance at Beast gave me a tiny bit of hope. If she got to know him, surely that would help her see that the curse was to blame, not him.

Beast twisted the knob, and I turned to flee, but he caught me with one arm.

"TayTay, it'll work out," Grandma whispered in my ear.

They were conspiring against me, and it pricked me with betrayal. Working as a team, they opened the door and shoved me into the lion's den. I wasn't supposed to have to do this alone. I wasn't even supposed to be the first one through the door!

I threw a wounded look on Grandma.

"Don't look at me like that. If she sees you first, it will save us all a lot of yelling."

I was about to tell her what I thought of that when Aunt Lily's voice echoed through the hallway. Grandma pushed me further down the hall, trailing behind me like I was her body shield.

"Mother?" Aunt Lily sounded tired, and I winced with guilt.

"It's me," Grandma called back.

"I've been calling you, and all I get is a text!" Aunt Lily's voice swelled with anger as she moved toward the hallway. "She's been kidnapped! And I need your help to find—"

Grandma squeezed my hand before shoving me around the corner and into the direct path of my rampaging Aunt Lily. Our eyes met, and hundreds of emotions flashed instantly across her face. They felt like physical blows: anguish, shock, love.

Before I could catch my breath, she crushed me in a vice-like embrace. "Tayla."

"Mom," I croaked, hugging her back as our tears mingled on our cheeks. Though I had my real mother back in my life, Aunt Lily would always be my surrogate mother.

"It's a miracle." Her voice broke, and she squeezed me tighter, as if I would transform into mist and evaporate. "I thought I'd lost you."

I sniffed. "I'm so sorry, but I'm here now." I rubbed her back in circular patterns.

She stroked my hair, pulling slightly away to look at me. "How did you escape?"

I could clearly see the dark circles under her usually bright eyes. Her skin was too pale—sickly. My insides felt like they were being shredded with guilt.

I hung my head. "I didn't." My voice was so low even I had a hard time hearing it.

Aunt Lily stiffened in my arms, her head jerking up. "Is that filthy wolf here?"

"He's out front," I whispered.

"Lily," Grandma said, stepping around the corner. "Let's sit down. We have a lot to discuss."

"You..." She pointed her shaky finger at Grandma, releasing me and advanced on her. "You knew about all of this, and you never told me?" Her voice climbed in octaves. "How could you!"

"Oh, put that finger away." Grandma brushed Aunt Lily's finger out of her face. "Yes, I had my suspicions, but you always mocked me when I talked about the legends. So don't go accusing me." Grandma put her hands on her hips. "But that isn't the point right now. Tayla needs us. So put a lid on your childish tantrum."

I squirmed under the guilt. How much more would my family suffer because of me? Aunt Lily's rigid pose slouched in defeat.

Five short steps, and we all found seats on the couch and recliner. The cushions were too squishy for the tension in the room.

"There is one more thing, before we get started." Grandma sent me a pointed look, clearly communicating it was my turn.

"Mom, I'm going to bring him inside. Just don't freak out when you see him, okay?"

She shot to her feet. "I refuse to be around that wolf. I still have a bump from that mangy mutt!" She touched the spot on her head where she'd been hit.

I rested my hand on her arm in an attempt to calm her. "He isn't in his wolf form."

"What?" Her eyes bulged and she stumbled back, falling hard on the couch.

As if on cue, Beast stepped slowly out of the hallway. His head was bowed under his hoodie to keep his face hidden. He stopped and leaned against the wall, lounging with hands in his jean pockets as if waiting patiently for a late bus. He was trying to appear less threatening, and I gave him an appreciative smile.

Aunt Lily's eyes went wide, and I slipped my hand into her clammy one. I stepped toward Beast, until my arm was stretched back holding Aunt Lily's. "Mom, this is Beast in his *human* form."

Beast lifted his head, and Aunt Lily gasped, an appalled look on her face. If she was religious, I swore she would have crossed herself to ward off evil. The yellow light illuminated his strong jaw, stubbled cheeks, and flat canine-looking nose. His huge frame coupled with his wolfishly-deformed face made him look fierce.

His whole essence radiated power, and something inside me howled with delight.

I stiffened, unnerved by the new sensation. Was I feeling my wolf? *Please, no! It's too soon. She can't already be manifesting herself?*

Aunt Lily's fingernails bit into my hand, diverting my panic attack. I winced when her fingers squeezed harder. I was sure she drew blood.

Beast's gaze flicked from my face to my hand and back again. "Tayla?"

I opened my mouth to reassure him that I was fine, but Aunt Lily snapped, "Don't you dare speak to her, not after what you did to her, to *Rose*. You're nothing but a monster!" She released my hand and strode forward, blocking me from Beast. I rubbed the blood back into my hand.

Beast growled menacingly and glared at Aunt Lily.

"You know nothing." He bit off the last word with a snarl.

Her hand flew out and struck his face, flat-handed. His head barely moved. I sucked in a shocked breath and stepped closer. A flicker of silver shot through his eyes and my heart stopped.

I placed an open palm on his chest, pleading with my eyes for him to relax. Why hadn't he blocked her slap? His lips pressed into a tight line, but he didn't yell or hit her back. Aunt Lily's face was scarlet, and a crazy light danced in her eyes as they zeroed in on my hand on Beast. She reared back again to land another blow.

"Mom!" She didn't seem to hear me. She swung, but I caught her arm. Beast was tolerant, but his wolf wasn't. Her glare was like fire licking my sore heart. I held her anger-filled eyes until I saw reason start to peek through her blind hatred.

"Don't blame him. He was forced to take me and M—" I stumbled over referencing my biological mother to my aunt, who I also called mom. Feeling awkward, I simply ended with, "Um..us."

It was the wrong thing to say, and she ripped her arm from my grasp and stepped back.

"Forced," she spat the word. "You're defending him?" She thrust a finger at Beast without looking at him. Her eyes bored into mine like a rattler about to strike. I stilled, afraid to even breathe. But her eyes demanded an answer, and I managed a subtle nod. Her expression turned aghast. "He stole my sister—*your* mother. And you're defending him! For all you know he killed her!"

A threatening growl rumbled in Beast's chest. My gaze darted to Beast, but everyone's eyes stayed on me. My eyes widened a fraction. *They couldn't hear it.* Before I could start hyperventilating over my own problems, I looked meaningfully at Aunt Lily.

"He didn't kill her," I said. Aunt Lily gave a disbelieving snort. She thought I was lying, which irritated me. "She's alive. *I* saw her."

Aunt Lily staggered to the couch and dropped into the cushions as if the strength was suddenly zapped from her limbs. Her eyes could no longer veil the raw pain that plagued her from her sister's disappearance. I felt as if I couldn't move.

"Why didn't she come back like you did? Why isn't she here?" Aunt Lily's voice was hollow.

Grandma was the first one to respond. In two powerful strides, she was out of the room and in the hallway plastered with her paintings. As quick as she departed, Grandma was back, holding a canvas painting of my mother as a wolf. Grandma had captured her soft brown eyes perfectly. It was almost like my mother was here with me, giving me strength.

Aunt Lily's eyebrows puckered as she looked at the familiar painting.

"This *is* Rosalyn," Grandma said, handing her the painting.

"No." Tears glistened on Aunt Lily's cheeks, and disbelief was apparent in her eyes.

Grandma sat next to her, wrapping an arm around her. "My Lily, I haven't been honest with you about why I moved here."

All our eyes were on Grandma. It was so quiet I wasn't even sure anyone was breathing. I braced myself for a second round of hysteria from Aunt Lily. She was in for another shock.

Grandma inhaled deeply. "Rose left a trail for me to follow. I found hidden letters in my painting supplies, and for three days after she disappeared, I received phone calls from strangers sharing messages on her behalf. But the trail ended here in Cody, where she was said to have had a fight with her boyfriend, but I knew that was a lie. So I moved here, hoping another clue would be revealed. Years passed, and I lost hope. I honestly thought you had gone crazy after dear Stan died, thinking someone was stalking you." Grandma gave a humorless laugh. "I should have listened to you, Lily. Now, because of me, the curse has claimed Tayla as well."

I sat, close-lipped. It had been Grandma's fault. As the thought crossed my mind it tangled in guilt. I knew it wasn't all Grandma's fault, but I wanted her to feel the sting of her actions. She had yet to explain why she had cheated, and because of that action, my mother and I were cursed.

"There has to be a way to break his hold on her." Aunt Lily eyed Beast with contempt. If I didn't know better, I'd swear she was longing to sprint for the kitchen knives.

I sat next to her on the couch. I wasn't so sure about true love breaking the curse. I knew so little about the whole wolf thing, but I prayed it would work and break the wolf inside me, stopping it from consuming me.

"There is a way." I paused, knowing how pathetic it would sound. "Well, more of a lead."

"Get on with it, Tay." Grandma shifted impatiently in her seat.

"I have to find true love," I spilled it out in a rush.

Aunt Lily gave a mocking laugh. "So when did this horror story turn into a fairytale?"

"I'm not making this up!" I crossed my arms simultaneously mortified and peeved. "Don't you think I know how lame this sounds?"

She shifted in her seat. "I'm sorry. It just sounds…so…*Sleeping Beauty*."

I rolled my eyes. "If only a single kiss could get me out of this, I'd sneak attack every boy in town."

Grandma smothered a startled laugh, and Aunt Lily gave me a stern look clearly communicating how not funny that line was.

"Well, if you only had a month to get someone to fall in love with you, your mind would've gone there too," I told Aunt Lily.

"Only a month? Why so short a time?" Her voice was hedged with caution.

I inhaled through my nose. I so didn't want to tell her what would happen if I failed, but she'd find out eventually. Better to shock her system all at once and get it over with.

"I've been infected with werewolf venom." I swallowed the lump of fear. "Even now, I'm turning into a—werewolf."

"What!" She sprang from the couch. This time, I was sure she'd head for the cutlery.

"Wasn't Rose enough for your harem? Now you have to prey on her daughter! You are *disgusting*." Her voice lashed out like a whip, and Beast flinched as if the words sliced his cheek.

His eyes clouded with sorrow I was only starting to understand. "The curse commands me. I have no choice but to hunt Star's bloodline. I warn them to follow the rules while at my house for their own safety and protection from the pack. But this time, the bond was too strong for her to comply." He hung his head. "She's lucky to be alive. Rose and I barely saved her."

"You mean you almost killed her?" Her hands balled into fists.

My hands flew out in exasperation, propelling me from the couch to take up my station between them.

"Stop shouting at him," I pled with my aunt. "We need to focus on getting the wolf out of me. It doesn't matter whose fault it is. What's done is done. I only have until the next full moon to break my wolf's hold, or it'll own me and I'll end up just like her." I pointed to the painting of my mother.

Oh, geez. Did I just say 'my wolf' out loud? I felt a little queasy, as if speaking of her would bring her out faster.

"I'm sorry, Tay." Aunt Lily's hand found my shoulder and squeezed, tears hanging on her eyelashes. "So, who's this Star?"

Aunt Lily sat back down. Grandma took over from there, retelling the *Legend of the Beast* as only she could. Her voice rose and fell as she told how a Star fell from heaven to save her beloved human from ravenous wolves, only to have him cast her aside years later when her youthful beauty faded with age. Heartbroken, Star had cursed him to wolf form, creating a monster. Trying to undo the great evil she had brought upon the Earth, she sacrificed herself to give him a sliver of humanity back. With lowered eyes, Grandma ended the retelling.

"You're telling me that a star actually fell from heaven?" Aunt Lily scoffed.

"Really, Lily!" Grandma threw her hands up in exasperation. "Can you be more blind? A werewolf is standing right there, your sister is a wolf, and your niece is becoming one." She jutted a finger at Beast while still addressing Aunt Lily. "And you can't believe that a star fell from heaven and cursed the first man to become a werewolf?"

40

"Don't you yell at *me*, Mother. Weird isn't my specialty. It's yours." She cradled her head in her hands. The seconds ticked by as we gave her time to process everything.

"Fine." She sat up straight. "So I'll accept that somehow this is real. Now what?"

Grandma and Aunt Lily batted around possibilities, until my head swam. When the questions about Mom began, I felt exhaustion settle over me like a heavy blanket. I began to nod off, so I pinched myself awake. I had to make an important call before I fell asleep. Lifting my lethargic body from the couch, I let out an unfeminine grunt. Aunt Lily raised her eyebrow.

I gave her a tired smile. "I need to go to bed."

"I'll drive you home." She stood, grabbing her denim purse from the end table.

Alarmed, I sought Grandma's help with a worried glance her way. I didn't want to be the one to tell her I couldn't go home.

"Lily," Grandma said, drawing her daughter's attention. "I think Tayla should stay here."

"What? Why?"

Grandma sighed, as if explaining something to a child. "Do you want Beast in the same house as Cammie and Sarah?"

"He can stay somewhere else, can't he? I'm sure another stray mutt wouldn't mind sharing a dumpster." She glared pointedly at Beast, who hadn't moved from the wall during the whole conversation.

I shook my head sadly. It was stupid to think she would ever like Beast.

"No," Grandma explained, rubbing her tired eyes. "They are restricted by distance—about twenty yards to be exact. Any farther and it causes them both unbearable pain, and might kill them if they are forced apart."

Aunt Lily didn't look like she minded picturing Beast dead, but when our eyes met, her look of loathing morphed to anguish. Then a spark of understanding lit her eyes.

"That day, the picnic, you were in pain. I was hurting you..." The turmoil churning in her eyes was unbearable. "Because of this bond?"

I nodded, and her face paled.

"But it wasn't your fault. You didn't know." I closed the small space between us, wrapping her in a soul squeezing hug. "I love you."

Aunt Lily trembled. "I love you too."

Ending the embrace, Aunt Lily hastily wiped away her tears. She tucked a lock of hair behind my ear before turning her eyes on Beast. All her tenderness vanished.

"You harm her, and I'll personally lead a hunting party after you. I know some doctors who'd jump at a chance to have a wolf pelt in their den." Her voice was like steel, and the coldness in it made me shiver. The fire in her eyes didn't belong to the depressed aunt I'd known for years, but to someone that was lashing out, fighting for control. I was glad it wasn't directed at me, but Beast didn't seem fazed by her hate-filled glare. His face remained emotionless, but he gave her a curt nod of acknowledgement. He was the master of camouflaging his feelings. I'd never seen this intensely angry side of my aunt, and frankly, I was glad it disappeared when she turned to kiss my forehead goodnight. But, for all of her bravo, I could see her trembling, and a scared, slightly haunted look entered her eyes as I turned from her.

It was hard to step away from her. I knew she was slipping, but I couldn't wrap my arms around her and tell her it was going to be okay. Because nothing was going to be okay again. Even if I freed myself from my wolf's hold, I still had the curse to deal with. And how does a mere mortal fight a celestial magic like that? No, I didn't have the strength to fight off both of our depressions and still have enough strength to breathe. She would have to learn to fight her own demons without me, and from the way she'd stood up to Beast, I thought she would be okay.

I headed down the hall to the spare bedroom. Beast took the cue to leave as well, and followed me. With each step, my feet dug into the carpet more and more, like they were slowly sinking in a bog. My legs crumpled in the hall, and I felt reality floating by, but Beast's arms caught me before I crashed into the floor.

"You've overexerted yourself," he chided.

I ignored his reprimand and sagged into his side, happily giving him my weight. He opened the door to Grandma's spare bedroom where he had slept only days before.

It looked just the way it had when I'd arrived with Beast. I was puzzled. I expected my tie-dyed comforter to be rumpled with the sheet hanging lopsided underneath, but it was so crisply made that I wondered if a quarter would bounce off it. Once I thought about it, I realized it shouldn't have come as such a shock. Everything in Beast's house was neat and orderly. A little too orderly. Did he have OCD or was it his military training?

The room was small, with only a daybed and tall white dresser, but I gratefully slumped onto the soft mattress. Beast plopped my duffle bag next to me and gently placed my rose on the dresser under the window. A halo of moonlight framed the brilliantly colored rose, adding to its stunning beauty.

I shifted my eyes to Beast and the world seemed to freeze. His powerfully built body was framed just as perfectly by the silvery light as my rose, two magically alluring entities side by side. The moonlight folded around every dip and curve of his biceps as he leaned against the window. I cleared my throat, hoping to clear the butterflies climbing my torso. "Where'll you sleep?"

My chest tightened, nervous for the answer. Despite my attempt to squash it, my abdomen fluttered like a thousand caged hummingbirds. I wanted time alone, but anxiety accompanied the thought of him leaving my side, leaving me alone. Could he feel it? Memories of us lying next to each other, watching the meteor shower, brought more waves of heat. It was the best night of my life, followed by the worst day ever.

Without a word he strode back to the bed and knelt down. His strong arm brushed against my leg. Pleasure jolted through me, and I jerked my knees up to my chest, stifling the impulse to tackle him and snuggle up cozy in my bed. Beast's lips twitched in amusement, and I was sure a wave of my desire pushed through the bond. My cheeks warmed.

Effortlessly, he pulled the trundle out from under my bed and proceeded to haul it into the hallway.

With his hand on the doorknob, he said, "Sleep, Tayla."

"My aunt—"

"Is leaving." He finished my sentence.

I was about to ask how he knew, when my ears instinctively shuffled through the hum of noise to focus on footsteps. Concentrating, I could hear Aunt Lily and Grandma whisper an emotional goodbye. I followed the sound of her footsteps out the door and to her car. When I heard her Civic drive away, I stared at Beast.

"How do you live with all this noise? My head feels like an out of tune radio," I said, rubbing my temples.

He gave me a crooked smile. "You'll learn to decipher which noises are important and which ones to block out. Now, sleep." He shut the door.

Earplugs would be easier, but unfortunately I couldn't stand having them push against my ears while I slept. Then again, having all this noise in my head was pretty miserable, too.

The bed beckoned to me like a long lost friend, but I still had to call Chel. Fishing my phone out of my duffle bag, I ignored all the missed texts and looked at the time: 11:40. *Good.* Chel rarely went to bed before midnight, even on a school night.

I hit speed dial. Within two rings, I heard Chel's voice. "Finally!"

My heart warmed at her voice, even if she was clearly irritated. It was my Chel, and I missed her. "Hey, Chel."

"Don't they have cell reception in the woods? I was ready to call the rangers when you didn't show for British Lit today!"

Chel knew I loved Tuesdays, when Mrs. Lannic took us to the library to perform research for our essay assignments. It was the only day of the week that made avoiding Kyle almost effortless. The library wasn't anywhere near Kyle's classes. What would it be like to turn back time and only have to worry about avoiding Kyle? It felt like a different lifetime.

"Chel, some things have come up with my aunt's health, and she needs to pull me out of school."

"What?"

I hated the lies, but I certainly couldn't tell her about Beast. He'd probably burst through my door and confiscate my phone, or Chel would snicker at me and think I'd lost it. Both options weren't appealing.

"Grandma will be helping with my aunt, but she'll need help with her painting business to do it. So I told her I'd help between my online homeschooling."

"Are you crazy? I can't believe you are just dropping out! Not to mention you are totally ditching me. Do I mean so little to you?"

"Chel, of course you matter to me! We'll still hang out. But I can't come back to school. I'm sorry." I felt like a serious loser.

She began to protest, but I talked over her, before I started choking up. "This wasn't the reason I called. I need an unrelated favor that only you can pull off."

"I'm listening," Chel said, disappointment lingering in her voice.

"Well, since I'm going to be out of a social life—" Chel snorted, interrupting me. She knew I had no social life to begin with. "Chel."

"Okay. Sorry."

"I need to meet guys. Blind dates. Parties. Anything. I'll do it all."

She paused, as if waiting for the punch line to my joke. When I didn't speak, she said, "Did those woods frazzle your brain?"

"Are you going to help me or not?" I demanded.

Thankfully, she realized I wasn't joking. "Of course! So when do you want your first hot guy lined up?"

"Tomorrow."

Chel was so silent I could hear her favorite Goth rock band playing in the background.

"Chel?"

"Who are you, and what have you done with my best friend?"

"I'm serious. I had a lot of time to think, and you're right, I do need to date more." I thought it best to stroke her ego. "Especially if I'm going to be stuck at home."

"I'll say. Only one date in your seventeen years? That's appalling."

I ignored her playful jab. "So are you going to help me change that?"

Chel squealed. "You're really serious! Leave everything to me." And without another word the line went dead. I smiled gratefully down at the phone. A slight ping of guilt coursed through me, but it wasn't like she'd believe the truth anyway.

With the phone call taken care of, I finally gave into the draw of the bed, kicking off my shoes and pants before sliding under the chilly covers in my t-shirt. My face burrowed into the pillow and instantly, the musky, woodsy smell of Beast enveloped my senses. I breathed it in deeply, and my head swirled with guilty pleasure as I drifted off to sleep.

I woke to the buzz of a text message. Throwing off my covers, I stumbled out of bed and my hand found my phone on the moonlit dresser, next to two shriveled petals. I ignored the petals and the pang of panic they threatened to bring on. Instead, I focused on the text from Chel: *Party Saturday. Hot guys. No Kyle.*

Hope bubbled in my chest. Chel had come through, and even found a way around Kyle. But I couldn't keep my gaze from returning to the deep crimson of the wilting rose petals. Dread seeped into my happy bubble. Four days. How many petals would wither before then?

5

MIDNIGHT VOICE

Wednesday, April 11

The next day, anxiety raged through my body like a thunderstorm. I paced the house until Beast nosed me onto the couch, before forcing a book on the coffee table in my direction. But I couldn't sit still long enough to breathe deeply, let alone read a book. I resumed my half marathon, and Beast found solace in the backyard.

I should be looking for guys right now! But all the ones my age are in school. I messed my hair in frustration. *Should I drive to Powell and walk the college campus?* The thought made me want to dive under my bed covers.

Let's face it. I needed Chel's charismatic personality to outweigh my desperation, and she was at school right now. If I went out alone, in my current state, I'd scare every man that looked at me. *It was just four days of wasted effort, surely it wouldn't matter that much?* But the knots in my stomach wouldn't ease.

I felt like I was in a stupid hourglass that some laughing giant was shaking while my life crumbled around me. I pressed my pounding head to the sliding door, ready to self-combust.

I glared at Beast who was lounging happily in the afternoon sunshine in the backyard. *How can he be so calm?* It wasn't fair. He was the one that did this to me and there he was, the picture of ease. My teeth snapped shut in anger. His ear flicked in my direction, but he didn't bother lifting his head.

Am I invisible? Or does no one care that I only have a few weeks to save myself?

My chest felt heavy, like a lead ball had replaced my soul.

Who am I kidding? Haven't I always been alone?

I frowned. Relying on myself was good, right? No one could hurt me that way. But the sadness wouldn't leave. I strode from the backdoor, and my gaze fell on a small picture perched on the bookshelf: Grandpa Jonas leaning on his walking stick in his beloved Allegheny Mountains.

Under his leather-brimmed hat, his sky-blue eyes twinkled jovially. His long, withered face held a golden tan acquired from long hours in the backcountry. Grandpa Jonas had worked for the Virginia Department of Game and Inland Fisheries as a resource educator. My index finger lovingly caressed the photo, remembering all our hiking expeditions while Grandpa lectured away about the local flora and fauna. Those trips were the few times when I hadn't been so alone. Another pang of loss pricked my heart.

How could Grandma cheat on him?

Anger simmered in my veins. *He was the best of men! She didn't deserve him.* With the picture in my hand, I strode into the studio. Grandma's wild mess of bleach-tipped brown hair was easy to spot over the white edge of her current canvas.

"I need to talk to you." My voice was stiff. I marched up to her side.

Grandma continued her paint stroke, not looking at me. "Hmmm."

"Why did you cheat on Grandpa?" I demanded.

Her hand jerked, sending a blue streak of paint above Beast's wolf face on the canvas. She heaved a shaky breath before looking at me. "It was an accident."

I snorted. "No, an accident is slipping on ice. Affairs are never accidental."

She tossed her brush into the cup of water, her lips thin. "It wasn't an *affair*. I loved your Grandpa with every fiber of my being."

I stared at her, unable to speak. A geyser of anger and hurt exploded inside me. "How can you even say that? You slept with another man!" My voice was raw. "How can you sit there and call yourself my Grandma? He's the only Grandpa I've known, and now that's been stolen from me. And with who? Do you even know the man's name? You and Mom are so alike!"

Grandma swiveled toward me on her stool, fire swirling in her eyes. "That. Is. Enough!"

Mom's soft brown wolf eyes flashed in my mind. The gentle love radiating out of them caused me a moment of guilt. I hadn't meant to bring Mom into this. Maybe, subconsciously, I was still angry at her as well.

I thrust the picture into Grandma's hands. "He was a good man." I bit my lip to keep the hot tears at bay. "Why? Why did you do it?"

She gripped the frame with trembling fingers. "Yes, he was, and it has killed me a thousand times over that it even happened.

What I did was unforgivable, but Grandpa will always be your grandfather. Not even blood can take that away from you." She went to brush a strand of hair from my cheek, but I jerked backwards.

"Don't touch me." I glared at her, not caring about the pain in her eyes from my rejection. "Because of *you* and that *man*, my mother's a wolf and I'm fighting for my life!"

Grandma reared back like I'd slapped her. The old grandfather clock in the hall ticked by for what felt like hours before she spoke. "I can't change the past. No matter how much I want to." Her teary voice matched the moisture in her eyes as she caressed the picture of Grandpa.

"Did," I cleared my emotion clogged throat, "did Grandpa know?"

Suddenly, her answer meant everything to me. Had he died unaware that Rose and I weren't his blood?

"Yes."

"And he was okay with it?" I asked incredulously. How could she say it so calmly? Grandpa was all about family. This would've crushed him.

Grandma smiled sadly at the picture of her deceased husband, and the impulse to rip it from her hand was overpowering. She didn't deserve to look at him like that.

"Jimmy loved his mountains, but he loved his family more." She sniffed, wiping her nose with the back of her hand. Tears clouded my eyes as I thought of my grandpa patting his knee for me to climb up.

"I'll never forget the crushing guilt I felt after I woke up; hung-over, and in another man's arms." Her voice shook.

I felt queasy, unsure if I was going to make it through this confession without sprinting to the toilet.

Grandma continued in a whisper, unable to take her eyes off the picture. "It was the busy season at the park, and he couldn't come with me to my grand opening art exhibit in New York. The opening was a bigger success than I could've ever imagined, and my heart ached not to share it with him. Many of my old college friends were there. We went out for a few drinks late that night. I had one too many." She laughed harshly and looked up at me, regret shining in her turquoise eyes.

That's why she's so against drinking.

"Telling your grandfather was the hardest thing I've ever done, but keeping it a secret wasn't an option. I broke his heart. Being buried alive would have felt better than seeing the earth-shattering pain in his eyes."

Tears rolled down her cheeks, but I couldn't bring myself to comfort her. It was like my heart had turned to glass and the hammer of Grandma's confession shattered it. I couldn't look at her. My gaze went to the canvas where Beast's silvery-blue eyes stared back at me. Starving for comfort, I surrendered to the desire to drink in the sight of Beast captured perfectly in paint. But it couldn't quench the fierce need I felt to curl my fingers in his dark pelt. Need flamed through me, and my wolf hummed as my eyes roamed over his well-defined canine muscles, sending a flood of hot desire pulsing through my blood like molten lava.

Jerking my eyes to the floor, I shivered with the effort to keep myself from running to Beast in the backyard. Disgust cooled my body as I realized I was lusting after a wolf right after my grandmother confessed to cheating on the man I thought was my grandfather. *What was wrong with me?*

Everything. And now Grandma wasn't even the person I thought she was.

Grandma's gentle hands cradled my face, bringing it up so our eyes met. "I'm sorry that you had to find out from Beast. Lily and I were going to tell you when you were older."

"Older, huh." I brushed her hands away and stood, walking from her comforting arms that I so badly wanted around me. "I don't think you ever intended to tell me."

"Tay." Her voice broke, tearing at my soul. "I'm so sorry..."

I turned my back on her and ran from the room.

Throwing myself under my covers, I sobbed until I drifted off to sleep.

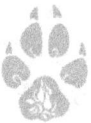

A sound startled me out of bed, and I stumbled to my phone, anxious for a text from Chel, but the home screen was blank. My head still pounded from my endless tears, and I staggered toward my bed, intent on going back to sleep.

Then, the sound of my name fluttered into my ears. My darkened room made the glowing numbers on my phone easy to read. *1:30 in the morning?*

"Tayla..."

I strained to make out the distant voice that sounded like Beast's. Listening more closely, I felt a consciousness slip underneath mine. My senses heightened, and I knew it was my wolf fighting for control. I clenched my teeth and pushed back at her presence, but she resisted, and my hearing suddenly magnified.

I could hear Beast's heart thump several rooms away. I could even hear the swoosh of his breath as he inhaled. *How dare he purposely call my wolf out! And in the middle of the night.* I fumed in his general direction, and my teeth groaned under my growl.

"You're going to grind them into sand if you keep it up." Humor played on every word he said.

I wanted to flay him, but I had a wolf to put back in her place. So instead of marching into the living room, I decided to ignore him and climb back into bed. I continued to push at my wolf's essence while stuffing the thick pillow over my ears, drowning out Beast's whisperings.

"Don't you dare go back to bed! We have work to do." His voice grew louder through the muffled pillow as if he was yelling right next to me. Was there no way to escape him?

"Leave me alone!" I shouted. I didn't want to deal with anything more tonight, but too many things were working against me.

My wolf quivered with excitement, and the longing she pumped through my blood rolled me toward the edge of the bed. I grabbed my headboard, resisting the impulse to run to him. I pushed her back inch by inch into the imaginary cage I formed for her. She resisted. Waves of her irritation slammed into my mind, and fear trickled through me. One day, I knew she would be stronger than me. My concentration faltered, giving her ground to push her presence through.

"Come here, Tayla," Beast called, and my wolf used the distraction to push further into my mind.

"No," I said aloud, fighting her and Beast's call. I held the pillow tighter around my head.

"I thought you'd say that." His voice was like a silky whisper.

I groaned. Angrily, I threw the useless pillow across the room.

I jolted upright at the sound of Beast's stealthy footfalls sprinting toward my room. My door flew open, and he scooped me into his hairy arms before I could blink. My wolf's heart fluttered with excitement, and my hand splayed across his chest, moving in a tiny caressing circle. I watched it as if my hand was possessed. My fingertips tingled with warmth, aching for more. Horrified, I pulled the hand back and clutched it in a tight fist, stuffing my wolf back into her cage. If Beast noticed the brief moment of exploration, he didn't show it. His face was set and determined as he bolted through the shadowed house and out the back door in seconds. Suddenly, I was dumped unceremoniously on the grass, still wet from the midnight sprinklers.

I jumped to my feet, trying to wipe the moisture from my silky shorts in a useless effort. "What's wrong with you?" I hissed, glaring at him.

His lips quirked in a sly smile. Anger boiled inside me. My wolf had exerted her will over me, and it was all his fault! I stomped past him, intent on going straight to bed before she made me do something really stupid. But his vice-like arms wrapped around my waist, pressing my back against his chest. His fire-like warmth licked my skin, consuming my previous thoughts in flames. I melted against him, aching for more, needing his touch like nothing else mattered.

His lips were inches from my ear, and his breath made my skin vibrate with excitement. "I have much to teach you."

My wolf panted, and a lump formed in my throat, but I couldn't gather the strength or will to pull away from him.

"Teach?" My voice came out breathless. My heart throbbed against his taught muscles, and my wolf thrummed contentedly.

Beast inhaled slowly. I felt his arms flex invitingly before he let go and stepped back. The pang of losing his embrace stung my flushed skin in the chilly spring night. The shock gave me enough clarity to push my wolf firmly back into her cage. But the doubt remained; had those feelings come only from her or was I really falling for a mythical beast? For the first time, I wished, for just a moment, that it wasn't a human I had to fall in love with to break this body-snatching wolf.

He cleared his throat, and my eyes eagerly found his. "You need to learn to protect yourself."

I arched an eyebrow, unsure what he was getting at. Did he know my wolf had taken over my body for a brief second?

"If the change does come, you need to be prepared to face it alone if I'm not close enough to help." His face was expressionless, everything mine wasn't.

"What?" I exclaimed. I winced at the volume of my voice. The thought of standing alone on the dreadful night of transformation hadn't entered my mind. Would the other wolves try to kill me? Did he really expect me to fight them? Fear quivered up my spine. There was more to being a werewolf than he was telling me.

"Won't you defend me?" I hated the plea that entered my voice.

He glanced up at the moon. "There are times I might be unable to protect you."

The night of the full moon flashed back into my head, the snarling blood-thirsty wolves ready to rip his throat out, my throat out. I shivered, and goose bumps rose on my skin.

"Come. We will practice some basic defense techniques."

"What good will that do when I won't be in the same form?"

Beast ignored me and continued. "First, we will hone your senses. Close your eyes. The night is rich with sounds, but you've been blocking them out." He closed his eyes as he instructed me to do, but I just stared at him.

This couldn't be happening. There was no way I'd help the wolf inside me grow stronger. She was already becoming a prominent presence in my head, and I couldn't risk losing all control to her, no matter what skills I might learn. I crossed my arms, unwilling to participate. These lessons he'd planned were a waste of time. I was going to break the wolf's hold on me, not encourage it. Beast seemed oblivious to my rebellion. "Sounds are layered. First, organize them according to frequencies and then duration—" he said.

I hummed to myself, trying to ignore his calm hushed voice, but his words initiated an eager response in my wolf. She pushed against her cage like a puppy wanting to follow her master. Her yelps of frustration made me nauseous. It was like my very body revolted against me.

I had to drown out their voices. "Pelvis, femur, tibia, fibula..." I listed aloud, working my way through naming the human skeleton. Beast arched his brow, but when I didn't stop, his eyes flashed with determination. He repeated everything three times, so I was sure not to miss anything.

"Focus on just one sound. The wind through the trees..."

I clenched my fists. *I won't hone my wolf senses!*

"The day was cold. The windmill was old. So it didn't fold."

Dang, what else rhymes with cold?

Beast's voice filled the silence. "The wind through the trees is a large sound. Go smaller. Find the one leaf that is flapping in the wind."

I felt myself complying as if my ears had a mind of their own.

No!

Out of desperation, I recited the only poem I could remember from English, "The Road Not Taken." I focused so hard on Robert Frost's words that my day old headache morphed into a full-blown migraine. But even poetry had pauses, and his voice trickled into my ears like water, saturating me with meaning. There was nothing else I could do—but learn. The massive hum of noise around me shifted with his instruction as my wolf applied the lesson. I felt as if my ears were suddenly unclogged, clarifying the jumble of sounds around me, relieving my headache completely.

I sighed.

Maybe a few lessons wouldn't be too bad.

6
WARM DREAMS

Thursday, April 12

Due to the early morning lesson and being emotionally drained from Grandma's confession, I was sleep-deprived and grumpy when I woke around noon. I was exhausted, but I needed to see if Aunt Lily and the girls were all right, so I texted her.

Want 2 come over 4 games later? I bet Cammie would love 2 beat me at Chutes n Ladders. How r they n u?

Everything had been so crazy the last two nights that I'd forgotten all about inquiring about Sarah and Cammie. What had Aunt Lily told them? Did they think I was just staying at Grandma's? Was Cammie mad at me for not stopping by and playing Barbies with her? That reminded me of a promise to stargaze with them which I still needed to fulfill, but I didn't want to push Aunt Lily too far, too fast.

My screen lit up with a response: *We r fine. The girls r at Jill's. Working late, sorry. I'll c u on my day off.*

I noticed how she didn't include the girls coming. Would she keep them from me now that I was tainted? That I was only half blood related? Anger at Grandma stung my heart anew, and I snapped my phone shut without responding.

Disappointment sunk my soul to ocean depths. Was she avoiding me? Wouldn't she want to make time to see me? Wouldn't the girls? Why had I come back if they didn't want me? Tears stung my eyes and I clutched my phone harder. No, I was here to save myself. Aunt Lily was just scared, too scared of Beast, of the wolf inside me to even see her daughter—well, niece. *Her loss.* A lump formed in my throat, and I bit back a sob. I wouldn't cry.

Feeling the strength to fight wane, I buried myself in blankets, trying to suffocate the emotions swirling in my chest. My aunt's rejection. My Grandma's confession. My mother being a wolf. All of it blurred in my watery eyes. I closed them, blocking out the painful truths, sinking deeper into my mattress, and was asleep before I could count to ten.

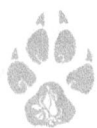

My teeth chattered, and I rubbed my arms, but I couldn't get warm. The dark icy mist crashed down on me. Grandpa's smiling form materialized in front of me. He laughed. Confused, I laughed

too. Suddenly, his eyes focused on me and hardened. His lips curled into a sneer. "How dare you infect this family with your cursed blood! You're nothing but poison."

I gasped as if struck across the cheek. "Grandpa," I sobbed. "Please, I love you."

I reached for him, but he backed up.

"You're not mine." He dissipated back into the mist, but his words stayed like a rusty knife in my heart.

I crumbled to the rocky, barren ground.

I am a curse.

"I'll leave." I whispered.

Dragging my feet under me, I stood and trudged into the darkness, hoping a crevice would swallow me. Just when I thought my blood would freeze, a warm breeze fluttered against my skin. I wasn't worthy of the warmth, but I couldn't help turning toward it.

With every step, the warmth grew around me, and a clump of light glistened on the now-sandy ground. It was like a cloud of sunlight, and my legs quickened to reach it. I curled on the ground next to it, pressing up against it. Surprisingly, it was solid under my touch. Heat washed over me, and my wolf shivered, like an excited pup. A deep sense of protection tingled deep in my soul.

Safe in the tentacle of light, my heartache poured out of me in waves of tears and sniffles. "Grandpa thinks I'm poison."

A deep rumble came from the cloud, holding me. "He loved you."

I shook my head against the warm cloud. "No, Grandma cheated on him, and it cursed the family. I am destroying them."

"No, if anything you held them together. They all love you, remember that," the deep voice said.

The words vibrated through me and images of my family painting, playing games, and hiking flashed through my mind. The smiles on their faces, and the warmth in my heart were evidence that they loved me as much as I loved them. Grandma was right, blood didn't matter.

"Thank you," I said, snuggling into the cloud, and it rumbled, sending a pleasant tingle across my skin.

My wolf whined with contentment as if the tingle was a hand stroking her fur. She stepped out of her cage, and I let her. I was safe, the cloud would protect me; besides, I was too tired to care. I let her control my hands. They played along the contours of the solid mass of light I was pressed up against. My hands slipped under a layer I hadn't known was there. The warmth turned to a fiery heat that didn't scald my hands, but raced up my arms before pooling in my gut. I groaned. Had that been me or my wolf? Shivers of pleasure ran down my spine, and I realized it had been both of us.

"Tayla." A gruff voice came from the cloud, and the tendrils of heat curled around my wrists, stopping their upward climb. "You need to wake up."

My consciousness stirred. Wake up?

My wolf growled as I pushed her back into her cage. My eyes fluttered open to the dim light of the moon, and I took several things in simultaneously. A mere inch from my nose was a t-shirt covered chest that smelled like musky woods with a hint of spice. My hands were slim bumps under the t-shirt, splayed on well-defined pecs. The length of my body was pressed up against Beast's, lighting my flesh with his heat.

Horror washed through me as understanding hit. Beast is in my bed!

I pushed against him, and he released my wrists. My momentum rolled me off the bed, and I hit the floor with a small thud. "How dare you climb into my bed!" I growled into the darkness.

He chuckled, and I sprang from the floor ready to smack him, but my eyes registered the trundle surrounded by the living room couches. Blood drained from my face, and my mouth opened in shock.

"You're sick. How dare you grab me from my bed just to share yours?" I turned, but a hand shot out and snagged my wrist, whipping me back to face him.

"Once again you are wrong." Silver shone in his eyes.

I glared. "Let." I tugged on his hold to no avail. "Go."

But he didn't release me, and tears of frustration stung my eyes.

"You walked in here and crawled into *my* bed," Beast said, the heat of his breath tickling my arm.

My mind flooded with the memory of my dream. Of the warm cloud that comforted me, that held me while I wept. My gaze flashed down the hallway and then back to Beast. "No, I never sleep walk." I shook my head. "You must have lured me out or...or..." I didn't want to contemplate the alternative.

"Hmm. And how might I have *lured* you?" The corner of his lips lifted. "And why didn't I figure it out sooner?"

Heat flushed my face, and I failed to come up with a retort. The silence felt fathomless, as his thumb stroked my wrist. The memory of his warmth, soothing my heart like a healing balm, was something I couldn't ignore. I had cried in his arms. *My tears.* I looked back at his shirt, but it was so black that I couldn't see if his shirt was wet. Avoiding his eyes, I pulled my wrist free and touched my fingers to his chest. They came back damp.

My questioning eyes flicked to his. I had walked to him in my dream, and his shirt was evident of the tears I'd spilt for Grandma's betrayal.

"I did sleep walk?" I said with a hint of disbelief.

Beast sat up, a concerned look on his face. "You were pretty upset."

Embarrassment tumbled through me, remembering how I'd pressed my body against his and run my hands up his hairy chest. But I refused to let him see it.

"Aren't you going to apologize for waking me up?" He winked, clearly enjoying my growing agitation.

"No." I folded my arms like a pouting child. I was so not saying sorry—not with him grinning like that.

"Then it's a good thing I didn't mind." His silver-streaked eyes danced with a hidden flame that made my knees weak.

I squeezed my arms tighter. "You're right...you do need your sleep, you look awful."

He chuckled at my poor attempt to wipe the smirk off his face. I turned on my heels and marched down the hallway with cheeks tomato red. I'd been in his arms—in his bed! Just remembering the fire his touch left in my gut was enough to falter my step.

"Tayla," Beast's soft whisper floated down the hallway like a wind chime.

He has got to be kidding me!

"Since we are both up..." His voice held insinuation.

Was he trying to kill me with embarrassment?

"We should practice."

I turned around with a groan. It would be better to just get this over with. He would just force me outside anyway, and being carried against his chest... I bit my lip and my wolf whined her disappointment. No, that wouldn't be good. I stomped back down the hall. I could see the faint smile on his lips as I walked straight past him and to the back door.

Over my shoulder, I tried for my best nonchalant expression and said, "So are you coming, or did you need to groom yourself before we continue this torture?"

He strode up to me and paused. My breath caught at his closeness, and I cursed my body for reacting.

"Nope." He leaned down, and my heart quickened at how close our lips were. "You already did that for me." He flashed me a wicked smile and slipped past me, brushing my flushed body with his.

I took a shaky breath, remembering the heat of his skin and the huskiness of his voice. Thankfully, the cool air helped calm my body. I couldn't let him affect me this way. I lifted my chin and took a deep breath to collect myself. Then I plastered on a disinterested expression, and stepped out into the night.

7

TORTURE DEVICE

Friday, April 13

Smell—that was the night's lesson. And believe me, some smells hidden from humans are less than pleasant. Who wants the odor of a thousand stink bugs in their nose? Thankfully, not all of the smells were unpleasant, and that was why I wanted my old nose back. During the lesson, the heart-pounding allurement of Beast's scent was too much for my overly stimulated body, and I couldn't help audibly sniffing in Beast's direction. It was humiliating.

Curse that she-wolf!

Lying in my bed, I growled as I wrung the bedspread covering my body. But even the distraction Beast held over me couldn't keep my mind off my quickly developing sense of smell. My inner wolf was that much closer to controlling me.

I couldn't sleep. Whatever wood the dresser was made of had a spicy tang to it that, when combined with the chemical smell of paint, made me gag. I pinched my nose closed from the sickening smell. It helped some but not nearly enough. If that wasn't bad enough, I could hear Grandma snoring in the next room. It rattled my ears like an old cranky heater. I glared at the window as Friday's sun rose from its Eastern bed. *This wolf stuff sucks.*

I flipped over onto my side, annoyed—angry even—and stared at the obstacle course of chairs blocking the way to my locked door.

Stupid wolf! How dare you use my dreams to lure me to Beast, I growled at her in my mind.

Just remembering waking up in his bed burned my cheeks with embarrassment, but there was a part of me that savored the tantalizing memory. I'd never been so mortified. And yet my skin tingled from the memory, my mind lingering on how his body heat had warmed mine. I sighed, before abruptly cutting it off. *She's distracting me! Again.*

I angrily threw off the covers, and grabbed my cell to text Chel: *Want 2 skip school n scope out guys in Powell?*

My fingers tapped impatiently on the screen. The seconds ticked by without a response. She couldn't be in school yet. *What is she doing!* I threw my cell on the bed with a growl. I stared at the phone as if willing it into flames, but the longer I stared, the more volcanic frustration built in my blood.

"Fine, I'll go by myself!" I jerked off my night shirt, threw it across the room and ripped my dresser drawer open. I looked at the slim wardrobe pickings, and slammed it shut.

Nothing! Not a thing to wear. And I'm supposed to get a guy interested in me with this stuff? All I have are crappy t-shirts!

Tears sprung to my eyes, and I was about to melt into an emotional mess when my phone chirped and the screen lit up.

I wiped my nose with the back of my hand and walked over to the bed, scooping up my cell. The text was from Chel: *I wish. It would beat taking a test in History! Excited 4 party tomorrow. Ttyl.*

Saturday was only one day away. What could I do to keep the manic feelings at bay? Maybe Aunt Lily had the day off? That thought warmed me, and I quickly texted her: *Want 2 come over today? How about bringing the girls 2. I miss u all so much.*

Minutes passed as I waited for a response. Maybe she did have to work this morning. I frowned and quickly put on a t-shirt and jeans. Needing to do something before I self-combusted from anxiety, I decided to put my nervous energy to work. I strode into the kitchen with Beast on my heels, no doubt hoping for a snack, but I wasn't in a kind mood. Yanking open the cupboard under the sink, I grabbed the cleaning bucket and froze.

"Grandma!" I yelled, and Beast scampered away and through the open back door. I glared after him. Irritation raged through me and I gave into it, wanting a fight. I stomped the whole way to the studio carrying the bucket of toxic chemicals.

"You promised to throw this out! You lied. Again."

Grandma hid behind her canvas. I slammed the bucket on her work bench, knocking over cups of paintbrushes that clattered to the linoleum floor.

"Oh, for heaven's sake, Tayla!" Grandma stood waving an angry paintbrush at me. "I'll use whatever I want to clean my house and you will not come in here banging my stuff around."

I stubbornly held my ground and yanked the bleach bottle out. "Are you trying to kill yourself and me? The vapors from this alone can poison you!"

She ripped the bottle out of my hand. "Then I'll open a window! Now get out and take your anger somewhere else. It's not like the paint I use is eco-friendly either, but even Chel uses them." She pointed a finger at the door. "Go, I have work to do."

"Fine!" I turned on my heel and stormed out, slamming the door. I marched out the front door to the garbage can and dumped the cleaning supplies.

There!

With a satisfied thump of the lid, I marched back to the kitchen and filled the bucket with white vinegar, lemon juice, and baking soda. I took a mental note to swing by the store and pick up some already-mixed natural cleaners. Maybe Grandma would use them if they were all she had available.

By evening, not even a dust-bunny hid under the sofa. The floors glimmered, and Grandma's usual haphazard pile of papers on the kitchen countertop was sorted and stacked. The sharp smell of vinegar and lemon permeated the air, giving the house a fresh new zeal.

I wiped my brow and stuffed the cleaning bucket under the sink.

When I turned around, Grandma was standing behind me.

"You've been cleaning a long time." Grandma walked to the stove and grabbed a pot. "You must be hungry."

"I'm fine." I glanced over my shoulder at her.

Grandma bit her lip and struggled to find her words. "Are we fine?"

I considered the question, realizing that the dream and Beast's arms had helped me work through the betrayal some. "I think so."

She dropped the pot on the stove and closed the gap between us, squeezing me into a hug. "I love you, my TayTay. I always will."

Moisture swam in my eyes and my heart lightened. "I love you, too."

"I'm really sorry I yelled earlier. I know you're dealing with a lot." She pulled away from the hug to look at me. "I'm sorry about Grandpa. I just wish I could fix all the wrongs plaguing this family."

"Oh Grandma. I'm sorry, too." I leaned into her. "I snapped and it was like I just needed to fight." I sighed, feeling the tension drain from me. My stomach twisted uncomfortably from Beast's hunger. "Poor Beast still hasn't come in from the backyard even though he's starving."

"A wise man." Grandma smiled. "Why don't we fix supper? I have barley soup and the fixings for a yummy salad. And of course a large roast for Beast."

A loud whimper came from the back door, where Beast sniffed longingly at the air. We both laughed.

"Maybe you should feed Beast first." I grinned. It felt good to laugh.

"You know. I think you're right."

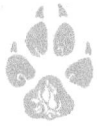

After dinner, I relaxed in my room. I was lost in a book when my phone chimed. Hopping up from my bed, I crossed the room. *I really need to get a nightstand in here.*

I grabbed my phone from the pile of petals on my dresser, and my heart stopped at Aunt Lily's name. She had finally texted me. With nervous fingers I hit the button to read it: *Not safe 4 the girls. I'll c u n Gran on Sunday."*

"Aw!" I growled, directing the pain into anger before I cried. "You gave up. Leaving me to care for the girls. Me! A child. And now you dare question if they are safe with me." I jammed my cell into my jean pocket. "What do you know anyway? Always too depressed to see any of us. Not safe for the girls," I scoffed, grabbing my keys. "As if I'd put them in danger!"

I stormed out of the house with Beast close behind me. Crossing the lawn in huge strides, I yanked the back door of my van open. "Get in," I snapped.

Beast growled at my harsh tone.

I inhaled, counted to ten, and then mustered a "please."

He leapt in, and I shut the door softly as an apology. It wasn't a great apology, but it was all I could manage at the moment. Starting the van, I only knew one thing: I needed to get out of town and the Belfry Highway was a long stretch of nothing. So I drove. Streams of tears blurred my vision and the darkness forced me to flip my headlights on, but I didn't stop.

The bone crushing sounds of Beast's change sent a slip of clarity into my mind, and I pulled onto the shoulder before the pain sent me crashing into a telephone pole. I braced myself for the onslaught, but was surprised when only a dull ache thrummed through my flesh, like pressing on a bruise.

Thinking back, I realized I hadn't felt his change for several days now. Was my wolf blocking it out for me? For a moment, I was tempted to be grateful for the she-mutt, but quickly changed my mind. I'd take pain over her body-snatching any day. My gaze slipped to my rearview mirror. Beast had already pulled on sweatpants from his emergency clothing stash and was bending down to pick up a shirt. Even with his skin raw from the change, my face flushed watching his muscles ripple as he tugged on his shirt.

Ah! It was happening again. Why couldn't I keep my thoughts from drifting back to him? Maybe he *was* dangerous, just not in the way Aunt Lily thought.

Aunt Lily. Her name slashed my heart and anger steamed from the inside out. I banged my head against the steering wheel—repeatedly—until a nice throb penetrated through the betrayal and calmed me a little. From the corner of my eye, I watched Beast crawl into the front seat fully dressed, but I paid him little heed. He stayed silent, and I was thankful for that, but I could feel his gaze on me. Aunt Lily's text played in my mind like a torture device.

"I'm sorry." Beast's voice was soft and low.

I knew he understood better than anyone, but if it wasn't for him, I'd be with her right now. Then again, I would still think my mother had abandoned me.

"This is so messed up." My forehead hit the steering wheel once again and stayed. "She's afraid of me. Of *me!* The person she raised and who's cared for her and the girls for how many years now?" A sob escaped my tightly pursed lips.

Fingertips brushed my arm, and I quivered with an intense need—a need to be comforted. I leaned into his touch, crossing a line I knew I'd regret, but I couldn't help it. I would've crawled into his lap and sobbed like a child, but I had enough restraint left in me not to take the leap.

"Walk with me." Beast slowly pulled his hand away and climbed out of the passenger side door without waiting for an answer.

He opened my door, and I climbed out too. I shivered from the cool night air. I hadn't thought to bring a jacket. Beast took one look at me and climbed back into the van, coming out with his trench coat.

"Here." He helped me into the coat.

It was heavy, and its smooth weave rested on my skin like a layer of protection. "Thanks."

He nodded. "This way." We walked down the highway for a few yards before turning on a dirt road. Rocks clattered as I kicked them, thinking about Aunt Lily. She'd been fierce and commanding when she'd fought to protect me from a supposedly wild wolf, but now that the wolf was a mythical werewolf and I was turning into one, her brave bubble had popped, leaving me with nothing.

"What are you thinking?" Beast's deep voice floated on the air like brass notes.

"Nothing." My voice was bitter.

"Not so. I heard you muttering in your room after you received a text. Not to mention the display in the van."

"You were eavesdropping. Is nothing private anymore?" I crossed my arms, thoroughly irritated.

He chuckled. "Tayla, have you not learned that there is nothing private about being a werewolf?"

I ground my teeth. "I'm not a werewolf."

"No, not yet," he said in a sad voice. "But I am."

"*No really*, I hadn't noticed."

"Tayla." He rebuked me with his tone.

I hung my head, deflated. "Can we just not talk about this?"

His hand found my shoulder and halted my steps. Turning me toward him, he said, "It will not go away. Family is family. As imperfect as they are, we still love them."

"But she's afraid of me." I rubbed at the tears rolling down my face. "I'd never hurt her or the girls. Never."

"Ah, but it is not you she is afraid of, but the wolf." He tilted my chin up with his hand and looked me in the eyes. "Her fear blinds her from the happy moments she could be sharing with the people she loves. You aren't the only one she is hiding from."

My cousins' faces flashed through my mind and sadness filled me. He was right. I breathed deeply, like I was inhaling his essence. His touch soothed my nerves and comforted me. "I don't think she will ever have the strength to see past the fear. What if I never see my cousins again?"

His hand dropped from my chin to hold my hand. His fingers intertwined with mine, and I felt anchored, safe. My wolf hummed with happiness and my agitation calmed. Was he that much of a calming balm to my wolf? To me? I looked curiously up at him, but his face was turned from me.

"Come sit with me. There is a story I want to tell you." He led me to a large rock that poked up higher than the sagebrush. My curiosity calmed me enough to want to listen. It wasn't often Beast told stories.

When we were both settled, Beast looked down at his hands now resting in his lap. "When I brought my pack over from Europe, we docked at Savannah. I told myself I could just pass through, but that was a lie." His lips curled into a humorless smile. I couldn't look away from his moonlit face.

"As if my feet had a mind of their own, they walked me right up to my home. I didn't know what I was going to say to my family when I arrived. The army would have already reported me dead or missing. And it was better that way." He paused, and I shifted, bringing my hand up to wipe the last trails of tears from my cheeks. "They wouldn't have recognized my beastly face, anyway." His jaw flexed.

"So, I hid behind a large oak tree, just so I could steal a glance of them. I kept my pack at a distance, but it was just a week from the full moon and their wills pressed on me, tiring my resistance. They were hungry and wanted to hunt. I wanted to hunt, too, but knew that if I waited just a little longer Richard would come out to stargaze. I needed to see my brother, if only for a moment."

Beast gazed off across into the darkness surrounding us. "While I waited, I fingered the letter I kept in my jacket pocket. It was worn and probably unreadable, but it was finally time to leave it. I peeled back the bark of the tree we had climbed together as children and wedged it deep in the tree. I wanted my brother to have it. I wanted him to know I'd fought bravely in his stead. That I'd done him proud."

Tears stung my eyes as I remembered the starry night he first told me of Richard and the polio disease that had crippled him. I touched Beast's arm, letting him know I was there. He turned his churning eyes on me, eyes filled with so much pain that I couldn't hold his gaze. I dropped my eyes to watch my hand stroking his arm in a gesture of comfort.

"He would've been proud," I said, my voice barely a whisper from the emotions clogging my throat. For a long moment the only sound around us was the crickets and the soft rustle of the wind blowing through the tall grass.

"He did come out that night."

"Oh?" My voice was ghost-like between us.

"I was about to leave when I heard the groan of his wheelchair in the house. Then the back door opened and there he was. He rolled his wheelchair across the lawn, craning his neck to see the stars. Not even looking where he was going. I smiled then as memories of us lying side by side on the grass came to mind." Beast's free hand slid over my small one still on his arm. Uncertainty gripped me and I looked up, but his gaze was heavenward. And I didn't pull my hand back.

"I wanted to run to him, but fear stopped me. I convinced myself it was my hunger I didn't trust, but really it was that I wasn't strong enough to have him run from me, and remember me as a monster—forever."

My heart hurt for Beast, but I had no words to offer.

"Tayla," His eyes found mine. "I almost denied myself a chance to talk to him, because of fear." For several seconds we said nothing.

"Luckily for me, fate had other ideas." Beast's oblique smile was full of secret amusement. "He wheeled his chair so fast that it tipped. I ran to him without thinking. I righted him, trying to hide my face, but he knew me and called my name. Our eyes met, and I watched as he took in my face. It was then that he gasped and I thought he was scared of me, that I was repulsive. I turned from him, telling him that I shouldn't have come. I tried to leave, but he grabbed my arm and asked what they had done to me."

Beast cleared his throat. "His words crumbled my defenses and I cried in my brother's arms, like I was seven again. I told him my tale of misfortune, and even to this day, he keeps my secret."

"Do you see him much?" As soon as I said it, I clamped my lips shut. If he was Beast's older brother, he was most likely dead already.

Beast shook his head. "It wasn't safe, but I've never forgotten that night we stargazed for the last time."

"You never saw him again?" This time I was shocked.

"No, but my letters still find him well enough for a ninety-one year old, even if he is starting to lose his memories." He gave me a small smirk before turning serious again.

He squeezed my hand. "No one can stop you from seeing your family. Only you can. Don't let that happen. You never know when it will be your last chance."

The sincerity in his eyes firmly clicked things into place for me. "Thank you." I stood and looked back at him, still perched on the rock, looking like a boulder himself. "You're right. There is a promise I made to myself up on that mountain, and it is time I made good on it. Let's grab Grandma."

8
STARGAZING

Saturday, April 14

It was one in the morning when I finally snuck into my home, if I could still call it that. Sorrow pricked at my heart, but I wasn't going to dwell on it. Tonight we were going to make new memories—happy ones. Stepping into the living room, I saw that everything looked just the way it had when I left. Sarah was asleep on the hide-a-bed. If Aunt Lily had really given up on me, she'd have given Sarah my bedroom. The thought warmed me with hope.

Making my way to my bedroom, I opened the closet and pulled down our family's most precious possession from the top shelf. The hard case was layered in dust, and I blew it off, revealing Uncle Stan's telescope case.

"You've been hidden too long," I whispered, sad that we'd let his death stop us from continuing his favorite family tradition.

On tiptoes, I entered Cammie's room, cursing as I stepped on the sharp edges of toys littering the floor to her bed. I shuffled to where she lay, barely illuminated by her nightlight. Cammie looked like a peaceful porcelain doll with her long golden hair fanned around her small face. I brushed a kiss across her forehead, emotions wound tight in my gut. Beast's sad account of his brother played in my head. What if this was the last night I had with them?

Then I'd better make it a good one.

"Cammie," I whispered as I gently shook her. Her blue eyes popped open, dazed and unfocused for several seconds before zeroing in on me. A smile lit her face.

"Tay!" She threw her arms around me.

I chuckled. "Shh. You don't want to ruin the surprise, do you?"

"Surprise?" Her eyes widened.

"Grab a blanket and I'll show you." I smiled down at her sweet face, now full of curiosity. "But you have to be quiet. We don't want to wake Mom."

"Okay," she said in an exaggerated whisper that lightened my spirits.

While she slipped on her fluffy dog slippers and grabbed a blanket from the foot of her bed, I listened to Aunt Lily's soft breaths from the next room over. She hadn't heard us.

So far so good.

We made our way softly to Sarah's bed in the living room. Her hand was curled in her hair as she slept. Fondness washed over me. Even though Sarah could be moody, she was still my little cousin and needed my love as much as Cammie did.

"Sarah." I shook her, but she didn't stir. I called her name again, but she still slept. She always could sleep like the dead. Then Cammie pinched her.

"Ow!" Sarah jolted up, rubbing the arm Cammie had assaulted.

It took her about one nanosecond to glare at Cammie. "That hurt! What is wrong with you?"

"Shh..." I put my finger up to my lips, and her gaze flashed to mine.

"And what are *you* doing here?" Her words were a slap in the face, rendering me momentarily speechless. "Did Chel forget to pack you along?"

"What?" I rocked back on my heels from the hostility in her voice.

"Mom told us all about you getting invited to 'save the turtles' in Costa Rica." She crossed her arms. "Well, I hope you enjoyed it, because we sure haven't! Mom totally lost it after you left."

I hung my head. "I'm really sorry, Sarah. I know how hard it must have been."

"What do you care? You got to go have fun."

I knew rebutting that statement wouldn't get me anywhere, unless I wanted to tell them the truth and that was something I wasn't ready for. What if they became scared of me too? I couldn't endure that. The telescope case was heavy in my hands, reminding me of my reason for coming. "Will you accept a peace offering?"

"What are you talking about? And why did you have to wake Cammie?" She tossed her bedding off and climbed out of bed. "Now I have to get her back to sleep." She grabbed for Cammie's hand, but Cammie dodged her grasp.

"But she has a surprise for us," Cammie pled.

Sarah cocked a brow at me. "Oh yeah? It better be Costa Rican chocolate or something really good to make up for abandoning us."

I rolled my eyes. "Just get your slippers and blankets. You are going to love this. But do it quietly. We don't want to wake Mom." With my foot, I scooted her ladybug slippers that Cammie had bought her last Christmas.

Sarah eyed me suspiciously. "Is it something Mom will yell at us for? Because I've had plenty of that to last a life time."

"Don't worry, I'll take the heat if she doesn't like it. Now move, we still have to set up, and Grandma is waiting." That piqued her interest.

"Grandma came too?" she asked as she slipped her feet into her slippers.

"Yeah, I needed a buffer in case Mom does wake up and I get fried." I threw Sarah a knowing smile, and she giggled. We made our way to the backyard where Grandma already had blankets spread out and mugs of hot chocolate waiting.

"Grandma," Cammie squealed, and squeezed her in a hug. Sarah followed suit but with a little less enthusiasm. Beast was staying in the shadows of the yard hidden from my cousins. He hadn't wanted to scare them. His thoughtfulness touched me.

I let them chat and got busy setting up. I laid the case down and popped the metal clasps with a click. The talking died instantly. I could feel everyone's eyes on me, but I didn't show it. I pulled out the pieces and assembled them.

"Tayla, what are you doing?" Sarah whispered as if just setting eyes on the telescope was taboo.

"Dad would have wanted this. To enjoy life and the things that he loved. It isn't fair that Mom has prevented us from stargazing." I looked straight into her aqua-gray eyes, misting with tears. "It's time we make happy memories again."

I screwed the last piece into the telescope and gestured Sarah toward it. "You want to focus? Mars is just over there." I pointed to the same celestial body Beast and I had looked at that night on the mountain.

Sarah stared at the scope as if it might bite.

"Go on." I nudged her, but she hesitated to touch it. "You remember how to focus, right? I can help you if you want."

Her eyes flashed with indignation and she grabbed the scope. "Of course I do."

I smiled at my small victory. Leaving Sarah to it, I scooted closer to Cammie and Grandma, claiming a cup of hot chocolate. "Do you see those two stars?" Cammie nodded. "Those are planets. Can you guess their names?"

And so the night continued with smiles and laughing. Grandma even told the milder versions of her fireside werewolf stories. I felt Beast's humor at some of the more interesting tales.

"Amused?" I whispered, just loud enough for him to hear.

"Very. You *do* know that those tales have been twisted over time?" He spoke so only my wolf senses could hear him.

"Oh, and you know the originals I suppose?" I felt my eyebrows rise, even though he wouldn't be able to see.

"Of course. Every alpha recorded their history. Some of them did a sketchy job of it, but I assure you our accounts are more correct than the ones I've just listened to." His voice held the humor I'd heard earlier.

"And yet she tells them so well," I said. He snorted and I giggled. "Anyway, would you like some hot chocolate? I think the thermos is still warm."

"No. I'm content just observing."

Grandma came to the scariest part of a legend and Sarah grabbed Cammie's sides. Cammie screamed, jumping right off the ground. Sarah rolled with laughter, and Cammie punched her in the shoulder. "You are so mean!"

Sarah flashed her a non-repentant smile, and Cammie tackled her in a tickle war. Grandma and I shared a smile. Then I heard a door opening in the house. My lips fell in a frown. Aunt Lily was up. I concentrated on her footsteps, praying she'd go back to bed.

"Shh!" I warned the others. "Mom's up."

The tickling war ended immediately and a solemn look overtook their smiles. I willed the steps to return the way they came, but more doors opened and I knew she had just discovered Cammie wasn't in her bed.

"Quickly, hide the telescope!"

Sarah and Grandma grabbed a blanket and threw it over the evidence.

"Tay, you need to hide, too," Grandma said.

"But I told them I'd take the heat."

Grandma grabbed my shoulders so that I could look her full in the face. "Lily is going to lose it already, but if you are here...she will know someone else is here as well."

Aunt Lily's footsteps were now in the kitchen. "Fine, but make sure she doesn't yell at them."

I ran to the shadows. Beast's hand rested on my shoulder, and I gripped his hand for support. Aunt Lily strode out of the house.

"What is this? And why aren't you girls in bed? It is four in the morning!" She swiveled around, her eyes stopping on Grandma. She crossed her arms. "Mother, explain yourself." Then her eyes fell on the lump under the blanket. "What is that?"

"It's nothing. I just thought the girls would like to have a midnight party with their Grandma." Grandma stepped in front of Aunt Lily, but she sidestepped Grandma and yanked the blanket off the object. The telescope wobbled and Cammie grabbed it just in time.

Aunt Lily's eyes popped open wide before narrowing at the girls. "You are never to touch that." Cammie and Sarah bowed their heads under their mother's anger. Aunt Lily turned her attention to Grandma. "And how dare you encourage this!"

"Now, Lily, we haven't done anything wrong. Stan would've wanted—"

82

"You have no idea what he would have wanted." She grabbed the girls by their arms and pulled them across the yard to the house. I could see the happiness seep out of them with each step, replaced by layers of heavy shame. I shook with the injustice of it, my grip becoming vice-like and even Beast's reassuring touch couldn't soothe the pain this time.

This has to end.

I stepped out of the shadows. "Dad would have wanted it, and you know it!" Aunt Lily stopped cold in her tracks but kept her back turned.

"So this was your idea? This midnight outing." She turned to glare at me, and it burned my heart. "That *thing* has already changed you. I can't believe you'd willingly endanger them and stir up such painful memories all in one night."

"They aren't in danger!" I shouted as hot anger pumped through me. The girls cowered from the fight, but Aunt Lily wouldn't let them go, so they hid behind her as much as they could. Their eyes were wide in shock from our fight—we'd never had one of this magnitude before.

"You know darn well that isn't true. That *thing* is around here somewhere."

"Leave Beast out of this. They deserve to be happy, even if you want to continue your selfish wallowing."

She snorted and I immediately regretted my choice of words. Deep gouges of pain radiated back through her bloodshot eyes. "Well, I guess I'll just continue my wallowing inside. As for Cammie and Sarah, they are *my* children and what *I* say goes."

I winced as if she'd slapped me.

"I'll put the girls to bed." Grandma stepped forward and Aunt Lily let them go into the house, her eyes never leaving mine. The door clicked closed behind them.

"So, what? Because you discovered my mother is a wolf and I'm becoming one, I'm suddenly no longer fit to be your daughter? I should just be happy with my future life and forget you, like you've forgotten me? Well at least I'll have my real mother back. And look how much I'm turning out to be like her."

"That's not what I meant." Aunt Lily dropped her gaze, but the feelings I'd bottled up since Aunt Lily's rejection bubbled out of my soul like poisonous vomit.

"You refused to come see me, lying about your shifts just so you won't have to face me again. And you wouldn't let the girls come over when you know I might not even survive this change." I stopped right in front of her. "Did you ever stop to think about me? The sacrifices I've made for this family since Dad died? When you needed me most, I put away my childhood and became mother to the girls *and* to you!"

I could see it coming, and knew I could block it, but I didn't. I wanted to feel the sting, the last thread snapping my heart. Her hand met my cheek in a sharp slap. My head moved only fractionally. My wolf growled and thrashed against her cage from the assault.

Beast stepped out of the shadows and touched my shoulder. "Tayla, it's time to go."

I jerked away from his touch, giving him his answer. I glared at Aunt Lily, anger consuming my soul and words pouring out of me of their own accord.

"Face it. You know what you're really afraid of. If it weren't for me, you'd have lost those girls long ago. You can't even take care of yourself. How do you expect to take care of them properly without me here?"

Aunt Lily hugged herself tightly, beginning to tremble under my rampage, but she remained silent.

"Did you think Grandma would raise them for you when you decide to check out? At least my mom didn't abandon me by choice."

Aunt Lily gasped, pain visible in her ashen face. Her whole body quaked and she looked like she would be sick. With my anger spent, a wave of guilt attacked me like an unforgiving frostbitten wind.

My heart sunk with horror at what I'd done and I froze in place. Beast pulled on my arm, breaking the spell. I tried to reach for my aunt, but she stumbled backward, falling hard on the porch steps.

"I shouldn't have...I'm...sorry..." I tried, but she scuttled into the house and slammed the door. I heard the latch click and my place in Aunt Lily's life closed with the sound.

9
TIED TO A CHAIR

Somehow I managed to get a few hours of sleep, but the fight with Aunt Lily still stung my heart when I awoke. Would things ever be better between us? Unable to think about the answer, I got ready for the dismal day.

I sat in the living room while Beast ate in the kitchen. It was noon, but food just wasn't appealing enough to grab some myself. I stared at my phone, lost as to what I was supposed to do. Should I call Aunt Lily? What would I say? My emotions clashed like opposing forces. I was hurt, angry, and felt tremendously guilty for lashing out at her. But she had lashed out, too. My cheek was still sore from her slap. I glanced at the blank cell screen. She should apologize first, but I hadn't received a single text. The pain was still too raw to think about it and not cry. So I gave into the anger, needing to feel it, to let it keep my eyes dry. I had to focus. There was a party to get ready for and a wolf to eradicate from my body.

"Are you ready to get out of here?" It wasn't really a question. I grabbed my keys and Beast followed me out with a steak hanging from his teeth. I turned from the sight, still squeamish when it came to his love of meat.

I drove out of town. The sun reflected brightly off my windshield, and I squinted to see the road. Chel lived east of town, and the morning sun was driving me nuts. Mile markers passed by and I counted the miles with them. If I didn't keep track, I always missed her turn. Finally, her mile marker flashed by, and a reflector atop a metal post marked the road. I hit the brakes hard, and Beast's nails gripped the floor as I barely made the turn onto the dirt road. It could have been described as a driveway since her family was the only one who lived on it, but I was still three-fourths of a mile from their home.

I serpentined around large potholes and ground squirrels darting across the road. It was almost time for Mr. Ruston to get out the tractor and grate the road again. Chel's father considered it a fun family outing and if Chel didn't make herself scarce after a rainfall, she'd get roped into the long, tortuous event of bouncing in the tractor for hours. Grating dirt roads really is as bad as it sounds. I knew first hand, having been roped into helping a time or two.

I could see the cluster of pine trees nestled against the hill, hiding Chel's house. As I approached them, I saw Chel's mica-red Lexus SUV through the trees.

Pulling up to her house, I cut the engine quickly. The Rustons were all about conserving natural resources, and always frowned at me when I left my van running just to drop something off. One time I even heard Mr. Ruston complaining to his wife that vehicles that old should be turned into scrap metal. We didn't all have the money to buy the most fuel efficient vehicles on the market, so I'd just let the comment slide. It was just the way the Rustons were, and behind their extreme behavior were people who really cared.

"Well we're here," I told Beast, whose head blocked most of my view of their eco-friendly home. It always reminded me of a hobbit's home, the way they had built it into the hill, with tunnel-like tubes for skylights for the parts of the home buried underground. The front of the house had large front windows to allow sunlight in the first and second story rooms. It looked very humble on the outside, with its roof topped with dirt and grass, but inside it was gorgeous. Railings were made of knotted wood that had been polished and stained to withstand the moisture. Their basement was used mainly as a root cellar. They even had solar panels and windmills for electricity. They had a well for water, but used rain barrels to wash their clothes. If elves existed, the Rustons would be instantly adopted.

We got out and Beast took off for the wooded back yard. He probably missed nature. I walked to the front door, knocked and let myself in. The house was very open with few walls. I could see the living room, kitchen, and the sitting room upstairs from the front door.

"Chel," I hollered.

"Up here," she yelled back.

I ran up the stairs made from polished split logs to her loft bedroom. When I finally reached it, she was on her bed, buried in her art portfolio.

"Chel!" I squealed like Cammie does when she hasn't seen me in a while. Crossing the room, I wrapped my arms around her.

"Tayla are you feeling okay?" Chel tried to get loose from my hug, but I tightened my hold. Tears leaked from my eyes.

"I've missed you."

She hugged me back. "What's wrong?"

"Nothing." My outburst embarrassed me, and I instantly released her. "I'm good." I turned to wipe the tears off my face before she saw.

"Tay, are you crying?" Chel moved from the bed to stand in front of me.

"Stupid, right?" I gave a strained laugh. "It must be that time of the month already again."

Chel looked at me with furrowed brows, not buying my excuse. "This is my fault, I shouldn't have been so hard on you about homeschooling."

"No, really, I'm just happy to see you." I gave her another quick hug before turning to the bed, needing a distraction. "These look good. I like the one of Fantasy Guy."

Chel frowned down at her painting. "He didn't turn out quite right. His nose is too big."

I laughed. "You are such a perfectionist."

"Hey, I just know what I want. And that big nose is a glaring blemish on his perfect face." Her lips formed a disapproving frown as she scrutinized the painting.

I knew I needed to distract her fast before I lost her attention to her painting studio. "Chel, I desperately need something to wear to the party tonight. Do you have anything I can borrow?" I plopped onto her couch that divided her sleeping quarters from her art studio.

"Duh, silly." Her eyes rolled like blue marbles. "I had outfits picked out days ago. I was going to call you, but you beat me to it." She looked at me with concerned eyes. "Are you sure things are fine?"

"As good as they're going to get," I replied, and a little bit of bitterness entered my voice as I recalled last night.

"Tay, you have always been a terrible liar." She sat next to me and put a caring hand on my knee. "Is it your aunt again?"

Tears stung my eyes, and I snorted, disgusted with my inability to control my emotions. "Not like you think."

"Then how?" Chel shifted so she could see me better.

"She slapped me." I wiped my nose with the back of my hand.

Chel inhaled sharply. "No way. Why?"

I closed my eyes as the night replayed in my mind. I wanted to tell her about the curse, Beast, everything, even my own cruel behavior to my aunt, but I couldn't bring myself to open that flood gate yet. "Can we please not talk about it?"

"Okay." She frowned. I could see it was hard for her not to pry. Then her smile came back. "I have the perfect distraction." Chel bounded to her closet and theatrically swung it open. I gave a shaky laugh. She smiled back at me and bowed.

I shook my head at her. "You're such a dork."

"But you laughed, so that makes me an adorable dork." She batted her eyes at me and placed a hand on her chest as if to prove her adorability.

I threw a pillow at her, still chuckling. She ducked into her closet before the pillow could hit her. When she stepped out of her closet she held a lightweight, turquoise shirt with droopy bell sleeves and sequined swirls on the modest neckline, something I imagined fairies would wear. It was gorgeous. She obviously thought so too, judging on her proud smile, but the shirt was not at all me, and not going to work for what I had in mind.

"Strip out of that hideous t-shirt and try this on." She held it out to me.

I shook my head. "Do you have anything more...provocative?"

Chel's brows crunched together like a train wreck, and her reddish-blonde hair fell into her face.

"Seductive," I added, to help with her confusion. My cheeks heated from what I was saying, and I fidgeted with my jean pocket.

Her eyes flew wide, and the shirt fluttered to the floor like a windblown leaf. Chel blinked several times, suffering from apparent shock. "That's it. At first, I thought I was finally getting through to you. But now, it's obvious. You've lost your mind!"

"Sorry, Chel. I just need them to be interested fast."

She look flabbergasted, then set her curvy lips in a hard line. "Even homeschooling wouldn't make you *that* desperate."

Her words stung, and I lowered my eyes, realizing I sounded like I wanted to score out of loneliness. But could she handle the truth? Could I handle seeing her repulsion? For a moment, I felt a drop of what Beast must feel when girls run from him. At least I didn't look like a wolf...yet.

"You'd better start talking or the party's off." She planted her hands on hips in her classic I'm-not-messing-around stance.

I stood and took a deep breath, exhaling slowly. My lungs constricted with fear. *What if she can't handle the truth?* "I can't."

"That's stupid. Am I your best friend or not?"

"Of course you are. I just...what if you are disgusted with me and never want to talk to me again? I can't lose you." I felt my eyes sting, threatening tears again.

She cocked a brow at me. I could see the wheels spinning in her head before landing on a conclusion. Her eyes flew wide. "Oh no, tell me you aren't pregnant! Not that I'd ever shun you for that. Just wow. That is huge! What are you going to do? I will help, but—"

"Whoa." I cut her off. "I am not pregnant."

"Then what's the big deal?" She looked confused.

I bit my nails. "This is a big deal."

Chel walked to me and put a hand on my shoulder, looking me in the eye. "Tayla, you're my best friend and that is not going to change. You can tell me anything."

91

Her blue eyes shone with sincerity and my anxiety lessened. "You can't tell anyone. Promise?"

"Promise," she said, waving it off like that was a given.

"I'm serious. You have to promise like your life depends on it."

She dropped her hand from my shoulder. "Tayla Rose Jonas, you know I keep your secrets. Now you'd better spill it before I get offended."

I winced at my full name coming from her lips. She reminded me way too much of Grandma in that moment. But she was right. If I was going to tell her at all, then I needed to just do it. Beast's warning came to mind. There was no way he was going to like this, but I needed Chel.

Words tumbled out of my mouth before my courage failed. "The dog—no wolf—you met in the park the other day was actually the guy Danny saw getting into my van after theater practice."

Her eyebrow rose in warning, as if saying, *You expect me to believe that?*

"He's a—werewolf," I blurted out. Beast's unease flowed through the bond like a tidal wave and a low growl of warning sounded from outside, just loud enough for me to hear. But I ignored him, too concerned about Chel's reaction.

I thought she might start yelling at me or cringe in horror, but instead she giggled. "Come on. It's not April Fools. And that isn't a believable joke anyway."

I didn't laugh. "I wish it was a joke." I sat on the padded bench by the bedroom window, staring out of the three foot tunnel to the trees. "That it was just a bad dream I could wake up from, but pinching doesn't work."

Chel pinched my arm.

"Ow!" I complained. "What did you do that for?"

"Just thought it might help get your mind off whatever fantasy world you're stuck in." She grinned like she was terribly clever.

92

"It's real." I rubbed my arm. "And don't you dare pinch me again."

"Okay. You want to play this game then prove it." She challenged me, a twinkle of mischief in her eyes. "Bring him in and have him change in front of me."

"It isn't that easy, and believe me, you don't want to see his transformation or hear it." I shuddered from the memory of the pain slicing through me.

She crossed her arms with a that's-what-I-thought look.

"I'm not lying. It's true." I was offended now. Did she think I just wanted attention?

"Well, how are you going to prove it then?"

I thought of the rose sitting at home, too far away to retrieve it. Next, I thought of Beast, but I really didn't want to wait until nightfall for her to get her proof, especially because it would mean seeing something no one should have to witness. Then a cold weight settled in the pit of my stomach, and I knew what I had to do.

"Fine, you want proof." My irritation at what I was about to do lashed out through my words. "Grab the belt from your robe and tie me to the chair." I threw myself into the chair that sat in front of her vanity and waited.

Chel's eyebrows shot up. "What!"

I gave a tired sigh. "Just do it. You're the one who wants proof."

I could see doubt and curiosity fighting for dominance on her face, but curiosity finally won. I let her tie my hands to the back of the chair, while my wolf made plenty of grumbling noises in my head about being restrained.

Chel finished and stood. "This is crazy."

I ignored her comment. "Go down to the basement."

"Now, I know you've lost it." She folded her arms. "How will this prove that your giant dog is the hot guy that got in your van?"

"I'll explain later. Just trust me."

One of her eyebrows rose.

"Please?" I waited for her to nod. "Once you're down there, I want you to whisper something. Then come back up."

"Whatever." With an eye roll, she left the room.

I focused on her feet thumping against the wood stairs and heard the change when they slapped across the tiled kitchen floor. Once the basement door closed, I strained to hear her, but all I caught was a beetle scuttling across the kitchen. Nerves tangled in my gut. Had I missed it?

"If this doesn't work, I'm calling the loony bin, Tay." Chel's voice rang so loud that I jerked back, toppling the chair. I hit the floor with a thud.

Beast's airy chortle resonated from outside the window.

"Shut up. This isn't funny," I told him.

Chel walked through the door. "Geez, what happened?" She hurried to me. "Are you okay?" She righted my chair with a grunt.

"That depends."

"On?" She cocked an eyebrow at me.

"On whether or not you're going to untie me."

"Oh my gosh. I'm so sorry." She scrambled to loosen the knots.

My hands slipped free and I rubbed my bruised arm. "What kind of friend are you?"

"What?" She startled.

I shook my head at her. "I can't believe you'd commit me."

"Wait, you heard that?" Her eyes widened.

I repeated it word for word.

"Whoa, that's, like, creepy and awesome at the same time. But I still don't understand how this proves your dog is a werewolf."

The dreaded moment had arrived and nerves attacked my stomach. "Because, Chel—he bit me."

At first her brows puckered together, and there was a vacant look in her eyes. Then suddenly, her eyes popped open wide. "You mean, you're a..."

"Not fully." Confusion crinkled her face again, and I continued. "I'm slowly changing, but I won't be a full werewolf until the full moon, or a little before. Beast isn't completely sure."

"You're really not pulling my leg?"

"No." My voice was sad. "Chel, I found my *real* mom."

"What?" Her voice rose an octave. "Holy cow! That is amazing. Where is she? How did that happen?"

I didn't know what to say. Chel's face fell. "Was it a good thing? I mean was she...was she happy to see you?" She swallowed hard.

"Yeah, it's just," I looked down, "she a wolf."

"Whoa. This is deep." And she sank onto her bed.

My lips cracked into a small smile at her statement. "That's the understatement of the year. I'm still tripping over the truth myself."

"Did she come with you?" Her eyes lit up with curiosity.

"No, Beast made her stay with the pack. It isn't safe to have werewolves around humans." My voice was sad.

"Am I safe? You're not going to freak out and attack me, are you?" She backed away in mock horror. I knew she was only trying to lighten the mood, but she didn't realize how true that statement might be.

I frowned. "Not at the moment, but when the full moon gets closer, the wolf part of me might have more power than the human part of me. So we'll have to be careful."

That stopped her, and she looked seriously back at me. "I'm sorry. I didn't mean to make light of this. It's just deep. You know?"

I chuckled, humorlessly. "Tell me about it. Try having a wolf in your head."

That's when the questions started flying. It took me a while to tell her the story, and that was the condensed version. I stumbled over my words as Beast's feelings of unease escalated through the bond, making it harder for me to speak, like a hand was squeezing my windpipe. Revealing his existence to yet another human caused him lung-crushing anxiety for the safety of his pack. I worried about my mom, too, but honestly, I had to share my secret with someone other than Aunt Lily and Grandma if I was going to have a chance to break the curse. And I needed Chel to help me find dates and not be weirded out when my wolf broke from my control—like she had already done, to my humiliation.

"Wait. If you're going to be a werewolf, doesn't that mean you'll get violent and have to eat—" Her face paled at the idea of me sinking my teeth into a dead animal.

"I don't want to think about it," I said, turning to gaze out Chel's gossamer curtains.

"Well, I guess other mythical creatures have become vegetarians. Maybe you could make it work with werewolves?" Her finger tapped her lips like this was a simple solution.

"Chel, this isn't some fairytale. It's my life, and the only solution is to find a way to stop myself from transforming into a monster." I looked back to see Chel's lips form a silent "oh."

"Beast said he found an old document talking about a human and true love breaking the curse, but he doesn't know for sure. It's the best I have to go on, right now. But the sucky thing is I only have until the full moon—maybe sooner." Beast's anger rolled through me, as I finished telling Chel the whole story. I had planned on taking my van to the party, but now I was afraid Beast was too mad to behave.

Chel chewed on her bottom lip, churning over the information in her mind.

"True love, huh?" Chel looked thoughtful.

I nodded.

"Well, then." She bounced off the bed, as if I'd just walked in with a triple-scooped ice cream Sunday. "Since men think with their eyes before their hearts, I have the perfect outfit to attract them. Then it's up to you to weed out the losers and reel in the keepers."

Chel flipped through the shirts in her closet, pulling out a multi-toned red, spaghetti strap shirt with a splattered print design. My brows furrowed. There was no way that shirt would cover even half of my torso.

"It'll fit," she said, reading the disbelief etched onto my face. "Gotta love stretchy material."

I still didn't think it would, stretchy fabric or not. I'd probably be more covered in my tank top than that shriveled excuse for a shirt. Nervously, I took it from her, already feeling naked. I wiggled into the shirt, unsure if it deserved the description. It felt more like lingerie. I gazed into the full-length mirror and heat flooded my cheeks. The v-neck plunged down to my black bra, exposing its lacy top.

"I can't wear this." I swallowed hard, trying to find my resolve to do whatever it took. But this was pushing it. "It's like I'm wearing nothing."

Chel shrugged. "I bought an undershirt to go with it, but you need to stand out, right?"

I glanced at the mirror again. *I can do this*, I told myself, but the uneasy feeling didn't lift. I nodded and Chel adjusted the shirt a bit before giving an approving smile. Her eyes then zeroed in on my blue jeans and frowned. Heading back to her closet, she tossed me a pair of slate grey jeans, whitewashed in the creases. The pants hugged my thighs like glue and rode low on my hips, exposing skin whenever I moved. I didn't even look like the same person. I looked...I looked...cheap.

I let out a heavy sigh. What was I doing? I moved to sit on the bed, but Chel stopped me and ran back to her closet. My heart skipped a beat. Maybe she'd changed her mind about the shirt? One could only hope. But then again, I had asked her for something provocative. And boy, had she delivered.

She crawled so far into the closet only her skinny white legs poked out. When she resurfaced, Chel held a pair of red stiletto heels.

I blanched. "You've got to be kidding."

She shook her head.

"I'll fall on my butt!"

"Then you'd better practice," she said, with a face that said she wouldn't budge.

I ripped the shoes from her hands and smashed my feet into the torture devices while Chel giggled behind her hand. I'd barely gained my balance before Chel pushed me back in front of her floor length mirror.

The colorful ensemble brightened my pale complexion. I could appreciate how the shirt slimmed my body, but I still felt naked. I wouldn't even wear a shirt like this to bed! Self-conscious, I crossed an arm over my chest.

"I need a jacket," I said.

Chel slapped my arm away. "I don't think so. Do you want to stay human or not?"

"Ow." I rubbed my stinging arm. I gave her my best puppy dog eyes. "Please?"

Her expression turned calculating, and I knew she was caving.

"Fine, but you better not wear it the whole night. Now sit. Time to do your face."

She forced me onto the stool in front of her small, wooden vanity. Makeup items littered the top like small mountains. I prayed they weren't all headed for my face. I'd been held at her mercy before and from the look of it, this would only be one step from plastic surgery. I closed my eyes; it was better not to see what she was doing to me. She pushed my head this way and that as she rubbed and brushed my skin for what felt like hours. Then, she attacked my hair with a curling iron that came way too close to skin for comfort.

"You can look now," Chel said, stepping away from me with a triumphant grin.

The reflection staring back was barely recognizable. She had transformed my ordinary features into something sexy and alluring. My eyes glimmered in shades of amber and autumn gold, making my jade eyes sparkle. My cheeks were skillfully bronzed and my lips outlined in a come-hither fleshy peach. Chel had blended the lip liner with a soft pink gloss, making my lips look plump and inviting. Even my hair looked amazing. It was pulled back loosely in a butterfly clip with a few wispy curls falling down the sides of my face.

I openly admired my new image, turning my head from side to side.

"You'll have to teach me how you do this." I pointed to my face.

"About time you asked." Chel grinned, obviously proud of her work.

We both giggled at the irony of the situation. Chel had tried forcing more than mascara on me since we'd met. With Kyle on the prowl, makeup was as dangerous as poison, but he was now the least of my problems, and I was feeling bold tonight knowing he was out of town.

But would it be enough to lure in a true love and break the wolf's hold? To get that she-devil out of my head? I took a deep breath. It was time to step out of the confinement of my self-made birdcage and into the lion's den.

10

GHOSTLY

CHUCKLE

"Let's take your car." I climbed in without waiting for a confirmation. Chel gave me a weird look but climbed in behind the wheel.

She hesitated to start the car. "Umm, Tayla, are you forgetting someone?" She scanned the shadowed yard eagerly for Beast.

"No, he can run there," I deadpanned. There was no way I'd let him near Chel with that much anger rolling off him. A good run would hopefully simmer him down.

"It's almost dark. I don't mind waiting for him to change." The hopeful note in her voice scared me.

"Chel, that isn't a good idea," I said, and the excitement in her face dimmed. "Just drive slow. I'll let you know if he isn't keeping up." She nodded, disappointment evident in her lack of wanting to talk.

Chel drove slowly, and we got passed several times by annoyed drivers, but we made it to Alex's house. He was in Chel's drama class and a pretty nice guy if you overlooked his fetish for neon colored clothes and weird hats. His house was outside of town, but it wasn't hard to find the place. It was lit up like a beacon with dozens of vehicles parked along the dirt road. He had just turned eighteen and his parents pulled out all the stops. Music blasted through the door as it opened before us, and I instantly recognized the distinctive sound of Daughtry. Seeing the throng of people stuffed inside, I froze, but Chel mercilessly pushed me through the doorway.

"Loosen up!" she hissed in my ear. "Pretend you're someone else if it helps."

"Who, a slut?"

"You are the one that wanted this!" Her eyes held indignation. "Now get in there and play the field. We need to get as many dates lined up for this week as possible."

I sighed heavily. "Sorry, you're right." I would never get a guy interested in me if I had "back-off" written all over my face. I took several deep breaths before I could relax my rigid stance into a more casual one.

"That's better." Chel didn't give me time to breathe before she started introducing me to every male she knew.

I tried not to notice the guys gazing at my plunging neckline and painted face. The attention was flattering, but it unnerved me a little that my heightened ability meant I could hear their breath catch and their heart rates speed up. That kind of attention was only flesh deep, but if I could at least reel them in, they could get to know the real me later, right? I tried to suppress my wolf senses, but I couldn't get them to go away completely. The cacophony of noises pounded in my skull, and the scents blended into a heap that burned my nose. Chel introduced me to more of her friends. My head swam with all their names and my cheeks hurt from smiling so much. Movement caught my eye. Natalie, my sworn enemy, advanced on me like an avenging angel. Her flaming red hair seemed to brighten her blue eyes like a lightning bolt.

I elbowed Chel, who quickly assessed the reason for my distress. Her eyes narrowed, but Natalie barely glanced her way and stopped in front of me.

"Prowling around like the whore you are?" she sneered.

I glared. Anger rolled through me, and my wolf growled. "As if you have room to talk. Haven't you slept with half the jocks in school?"

She took a step closer, her lips curling into a malicious smile. "What, are you jealous? Not like any guy worth talking to would look twice at a freak like you." She scoffed.

Chel stepped in front of Natalie's face. "Why don't you just admit what's really eating at you? Even with Tayla out of the picture, you still can't get Kyle's attention. Pathetic, really."

Natalie shoved Chel. With wolf speed, I caught Chel and swiveled her out of harm's way. I was sure Natalie's nails were only inches from my back now, but I never felt their sting. I looked back to find Danny, Kyle's best friend, with his arm around her, restraining her.

"Let go, Danny." Natalie's words were edged with danger, but Danny didn't seem fazed.

"Not until you cool down." Danny held tighter as she struggled in his arms. After a few seconds, she stilled.

"Fine." She twisted out of Danny's arms. "The slut isn't worth my time anyway." She cast me a glare that said otherwise and trepidation slithered down my back. "Go ahead and be a good little watch dog, Danny. You were always spineless."

I watched her leave. This obviously wasn't over.

"Don't let her get to you." Danny's masculine voice chimed behind me.

"Hard not to." I grinned ruefully back at him. He grabbed my hand and twirled me around. I laughed.

"Now that is what I like to hear."

I'd barely caught my breath when Danny stilled, staring at me with olive-green eyes. "Tay, you look amazing."

I blinked at him. Had he just dared to hit on me? Was he drunk? Maybe he thought I was fair game since Kyle wasn't actually here. Or maybe he was spying on me for Kyle? That thought made my skin crawl, and I tugged at my jacket, trying to cover my cleavage.

Unsure what to say, I simply thanked him and looked at the floor.

Chel jabbed me in the rib. "Whoops," she said, then winked at me. "I'd better go fix my shoe." She hobbled off to the side and slipped off her shoe.

"Sam," Chel hollered, waving her shoe at the thin Asian guy I vaguely remembered from theater. Catching his attention, Chel called over her shoulder, "See you in a bit, Tay." She slipped off her other shoe and weaved through the crowd to Sam, leaving me alone with Danny. I knew this was the plan, but I still felt pangs of abandonment. Didn't she realize Danny was dangerous? Any connection to Kyle was like playing with kerosene—it only took one match to make it explode. The temptation to run after her was hard to stifle, so I forced my eyes to leave her retreating back.

Swallowing my nerves, I gave Danny the warm, seductive smile I'd practiced all afternoon. It seemed to work because he returned it, grinning ear to ear.

I wasn't sure what to think of Danny. He was hot, for sure, with spiked blond hair and an athletic build, but I'd never really talked to him. Kyle always stole the spotlight when he was around. There were plenty of girls scribbling Danny's name all over their notebooks, and he had saved me at the theater the night Kyle attacked me. Could he be the nice guy stifled in the shadow of a jerk?

"Come on, there's a spot over there where we can sit," he said, taking my hand. Danny led me through the crowd to a cushioned bay window seat.

Focusing on Danny, I inquired about one of the only things I could remember about him. "So, how's soccer?"

His eyes lit with excitement as he filled me in on every single game they'd played this season. I learned more about soccer in ten minutes than I'd ever wanted to. I looked into his olive-green eyes, trying to hide the fact that my enthusiasm was fake. He was particularly proud about being a gifted center fullback and blocking the opponent's best strikers. Unfamiliar with that term, I made the mistake of asking. Thirty minutes later, I fully understood that a center fullback was a special player responsible for stopping attacks up the center, as well as exactly how he'd become so good at it.

"No one gets around me." Danny pointed at his narrow but well-defined chest.

"That's amazing," I said, keeping the boredom I felt carefully hidden. He seemed almost as cocky as Kyle. *Great.* But maybe that was normal for teenage guys. I had so little experience to compare it to, it was hard to know.

He leaned in a little closer, and suddenly, I was unready for what I found in his gaze.

"It's hot in here." I scooted back a little to remove my light jacket, thankful for the added space.

"Here, let me help you." Danny's hands were at my jacket collar before I could protest. His hand brushed my semi-bare shoulders slowly as he helped remove my jacket. I realized my mistake a little too late. He leaned down and brushed his lips over my shoulder. My wolf pressed against her cage, but I held the cage tight.

Danny's hands continued down my naked arms, finally slipping my jacket off. Heat rose in my cheeks and tingles raced down my spine. A faint tangy smell, like spikenard and orange, wafted off him and through my wolf senses. I didn't have time to process what it might mean when a growl sounded from the other side of the pane of glass. Fear rippled through me, and I prayed Danny hadn't noticed it over the music.

"Did you hear that?" Danny searched the shadowed lawn outside, and my hope shattered like brittle glass.

His expression changed from coy and flirtatious to that of a focused, avid hunter. My heart clenched. I couldn't let him find Beast.

"Sorry, I skipped dinner," I said, rubbing my flat stomach. "Do you mind getting me something to eat?"

He turned confused eyes toward me, and my lips curled into an alluring smile. I hoped. To cement the act, I traced from his square chin to his Adam's apple with my fingernail. "Please?"

Thankfully, he focused back on me.

"Sure, I'll be right back." His hand caught mine and squeezed it. Another growl came from outside, but this time it was quieter and more deadly.

I crossed my fingers and wished Danny away. He stood. Just as he was about to leave, he glanced back to the window, searching.

Curse hunters! Any other guy wouldn't have thought twice about the noise.

"Hurry back," I said, batting my long eyelashes to get him to leave.

He gave me a crooked smile, eyes flicking between me and the window. Finally, he headed toward the dining room where the food was laid out in all its junk food splendor. As soon as he disappeared down the hall, I snuck out the front door.

I felt a twinge of guilt at ditching Danny, but kicking a certain mythical creature's butt had jolted to the top of my priority list. I sprinted to the bay window near the front corner of the house, thankful no one was lounging out there.

"What do you think you are doing?" My voice was a harsh whisper as I approached the thick foliage.

There was no response, but I felt Beast watching me. I quieted my breathing, shuffling through the sounds of the forest. Crickets chirped and leaves rustled in the wind, but I couldn't make out the distinctive rhythm of Beast's strong heartbeat. I could hear the footfalls of a small animal nearby, but not him. *Stupid Beast.* He was exceptionally stealthy tonight. He must have masked his breathing and heartbeat with louder sounds.

"You're not going to hide from me that easily," I said with defiance. Irritation rippled through my bare arms, and I prepared to track him.

I resorted to the one sense that scared me the most—smell. Smells that had once been familiar but abstract now had become distinctive scents to my wolf-enhanced nose. I could even identify the difference between cotton and denim—cotton being a light sweet scent, while denim smelled heavy like forest fog.

Even though the sense wasn't fully developed, I was confident I could unmask Beast's familiar smell. I closed my eyes and sniffed the gentle spring breeze, leaning closer to the bushes where I assumed he was hiding. Slowly, I found his rich, musky aroma, but it was older than the concentrated strands to my left that streamed into the dense forest on the edge of the lawn.

My head snapped to the shadowy mass of trees. My developing wolf senses gave me better night vision. I peered into the tangled mass of branches and found him lounging against a pine, in the clothes I'd left on Chel's car hood.

A coy smile played on his lips. "Looking for someone?" His taunting whisper fell softly on my sensitive ears, like a wisp of vapor.

His playful banter lured my wolf out of her cage. She crouched low so as to not grab my attention until she had pounced, seizing control. It was like a puppet master commanded my limbs and all I could do was gasp in horror, thrashing to break free. My legs bunched to spring. A prickle of excitement—her excitement—zipped through my body at playing his hide-and-go-seek game. I advanced like he was my prey, leaving the house and party behind me.

His smile grew and anticipation lit his eyes; my wolf thrummed with eagerness. She lowered her guard just enough for me to overthrow her, successfully halting me in my tracks. I threw my wolf back into her invisible cage, slamming the door. Anger fueled my every muscle. That was never happening again!

"Don't. You. Ever. Call her out again." I advanced on Beast, my finger jabbing in his direction. "And just so we are clear, quit growling at every guy that touches me." I made sure my voice was firm.

All the playful vibes in his stance altered, and my wolf was sorely disappointed I had opened my mouth. Part of my human self was as well, but I stuffed that part in a locked box in my mind. I'd deal with it later.

"He isn't what you are looking for," Beast said.

"Like you'd know."

His caramel eyes hardened at the insolence in my voice. "I do *know.*"

"So you're a judge of romance, too?" He didn't answer me, and it fueled the flames of my anger. "Whatever. Just stay out of it. I can handle myself."

I turned to go.

"I won't let him touch you again, Tayla." A threat resonated through his growled words, and I felt the truth of it through the bond.

"You might have control over a lot of my life, but you don't have a say in who's allowed to touch me and who isn't." I took a few more defiant steps toward the house.

The sound of feet pounding the earth made me tense, prepared to be tackled by Beast, but I failed to notice with my ears what I saw with my eyes. Beast wasn't headed toward me, he was running down the tree line and away from the house. Caught off guard by this odd behavior, I didn't understand what he was doing until I was jerked forward by our magical bond.

"You wouldn't dare," I whispered through pursed lips, my eyes narrowing.

He plopped to the ground, challenging me to do something about the pain in my gut that made it impossible to reach the party without passing out. Finally, I sat down on the lawn, with my back to him. Frustration rippled through me. How was I going to get back to the party?

For the hundredth time, my sharp eyes traced the wood grain of the porch ten yards away. I hadn't moved from my spot on the lawn by the corner of the house and neither had Beast from his by the tree line. Where was Chel when I needed her? I wished I could telecommunicate right now. Why wasn't that one of the werewolf powers? It would make life so much easier, especially at moments like these.

I rubbed my arms for warmth. I'd been there for so long that boredom itched at me so badly even the occasional person leaving the party was no longer entertaining. They only looked at me like a freak for sitting on the lawn alone, in the cold, rather than in the house partying. I wanted to hide from their judging eyes, but running to the trees felt more like a form of defeat than a refuge. And I so wasn't going to let Beast have the satisfaction of seeing me hide.

I was counting the number of budding pinecones on a nearby fir tree when Chel's voice startled me.

"There you are!"

My head whipped around, and I watched Chel make her way across the front of the house to me.

"Why aren't you with Danny? He's been looking for you. I thought you two were hitting it off?" She gestured back to the house, still blaring with music, even though only a handful of people remained. I should've been one of those people. Irritation flared through me faster than I could breathe.

"Because *he* won't let me!" I turned and jutted a finger at Beast sitting cross-legged twenty yards away in his midnight trench coat.

Chel's eyes went wide. "Is that him?"

Reluctantly, I nodded and stood.

"Can I meet him?" The twinkle of excitement in her eyes was maddening.

"What?" I threw my arms in the air. "He's deliberately keeping me from the party, from finding any potential dates, and you want to meet him?" I let my frustration loose, hitting Chel with the brute force of it. "Sure, why not. Go meet the controlling jerk!"

"Geez, Tay. I didn't mean to tick you off. Besides, I thought you kind of liked him. I didn't think you'd mind." She shrugged her shoulders.

I crossed my chilled arms in front of my chest, looking at Chel. "Well, I mind!"

She glared at me and threw my jacket at my head. "I found this. Not that you care."

I caught it with a huff. We stared at each other before I could muster a bitter, "Thanks."

She crossed her arms. "Whatever," she said, her voice hard with hurt.

I lowered my eyes. "I'm sorry, Chel." I blew air through my lips. "Things just didn't work out the way I'd planned tonight."

"Just put on your jacket before you turn blue and I have to take you to the hospital." She gave a rude laugh. "I can just see your aunt's eyes when you go in looking like that." She gestured to my near naked torso.

"Yeah, I think we should avoid that." I threw on my jacket. It was still too soon to think about another confrontation with Aunt Lily.

"The party's dead. Think he might let you into my car?" She hooked a thumb back in Beast's direction.

She tried so hard to be nonchalant about it, but I could see her gaze at Beast with such longing that I caved. She had done so much for me; I could at least introduce her to the stupid werewolf.

"Fine," I said, catching her off guard. "I'll introduce you."

I grabbed the shocked Chel and marched her toward Beast, who met us halfway. I gestured to Beast without meeting his eyes. "Beast, Richele. Richele, Beast. Now, let's go."

I used her full name to show I was still annoyed, but her only response was a quick sideways glare, before focusing back on Beast.

"Call me Chel." A warm, flirtatious smile spread across her lips as she held out her hand. Did she have to hit on every male, human and mythical?

He took her hand and planted a kiss. A stabbing pain zinged through my body as Beast smiled back with sincere charm. "A name as beautiful as the woman who bears it."

Chel blushed and shied under her eyelashes. "The pleasure is all mine."

I gagged and my wolf snarled. It was like I was in a bad *Gone with the Wind* remake.

"You've met, now let's go." I jerked Chel across the lawn so fast she tripped over her feet, but I kept her upright.

"Whoa, Tay. I wasn't done looking," she whispered, glassy eyed.

I snorted with annoyance. She wasn't supposed to be attracted to him! Then I caught myself. What did it matter to me if she flirted with him or not? I was trying to get out of this stupid curse. They could do whatever they wanted. Maybe if Chel kept him busy I'd actually get some dates lined up. I aimed to convince myself that Beast was nothing to me, but I couldn't untie the aching knot of jealousy in my chest.

Chel took advantage of the pause in our sprint across the lawn to stare back at Beast. "Wow, what a body..." She licked her lips. "Yum. You're totally right, a good wax job and he'd be steamy!"

"Shh!" Heat burned my cheeks. "He can still hear you."

Her eyes went wide and she slapped a hand over her mouth. "Oh yeah," she said through her fingers, "werewolf hearing. Oops." She giggled and peaked over her shoulder to get another peek at Beast, who trailed us in the shadows.

I groaned. "The car's this way." I prodded Chel away from the ghostly chuckle behind us.

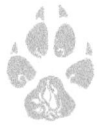

By the time Chel dropped me off at Grandma's, I was still mad enough to slam the front door and stomp into the house.

"You promised you wouldn't interfere," I seethed under my breath, knowing Beast would hear me. My hands wrung the trench coat I carried. Beast had launched it at Chel's windshield from the cover of the trees, before turning wolf, ready to run again. We were now home and he was no longer a wolf. Anger steamed out of me and I threw the wadded coat at the hall closet. It hit with a satisfying thud.

Marching down the hall, I barely registered Grandma peeking out of her studio room only to hastily shut it again. She knew this fight was between Beast and me and she'd already had her fair share of my temper lately.

I hadn't wasted a week waiting to meet guys at this party just to have him rip my chance from me. I rounded the corner and collided with Beast's broad chest. I staggered back, stunned by the electrifying contact that had my wolf gnawing at her prison. He was still too close.

I took a deep breath to shake the effect his body had over me. Big mistake. Instantly, his intoxicating scent filled my nose and lungs, smothering my roaring anger into ashes.

The living room felt smaller than usual as I held my breath and tried to find my anger again, but it was useless. The magnetic pull he had over my wolf made my body limp. He was strong and capable, the leader over all the werewolves. My wolf whined with the need to touch him—to stake her claim. It took all my willpower to keep my fists by my side, especially when his naked chest was only a hair's breadth away. The heat from his skin warmed my face like a loving caress. My fingers ached to touch him, to feel the tingling electricity that had flooded my body when he'd cradled me against his bare chest the night he'd found me half-naked and bleeding on the kitchen rug.

My heart hammered at the thought of him running alongside Chel's car, muscles flexing in his powerful wolf body. An appreciative smile curled my lips and my hold on the wolf's cage slackened. She shoved out of it and seized my consciousness.

Instantly, my hands found their target and traveled up his chest, reveling in the dips of his muscles. Desire seeped into my bones, and a soft moan escaped my lips. His caramel eyes found mine, enveloping me in their endless depths. My heart stuttered under the need radiating through his intense gaze, igniting a fiery heat through my body. But he didn't move to touch me.

Startled by the intensity of my wolf's passion mingled with my own, I tried to take a step back, but my legs refused to move. I knew which half of me wasn't going to allow my retreat. I pulled my fingers from his chest and crossed my arms to keep them from sliding back up his muscular chest and tangling into his dark wavy hair. Finding my voice, I whispered, "You had no right to interfere with Danny."

"He wasn't right for you, Tay." His deep voice sent tingles through me, and his hand brushed curls out of my face, leaving trails of fire where his fingers touched my cheek. My wolf drooled inside my head.

I leaned in, stopping just before my lips skimmed his deliciously hot skin. Breathing slowly, I mustered all the strength I could and took a step back, glancing away from him. I tightened my arms around my torso like a vice, creating bruises that I'd definitely feel tomorrow.

"And you're an expert on who's right for me and who isn't?" I forced steel into my voice.

"I could smell his arousal." His voice was hard, and he shifted away from me to look out the darkened window. "He wanted you for more than your *personality.*"

I blushed at his comment. I hadn't wanted him to witness my flirting.

"You can smell that?" I said, curiosity evident in my voice. What other emotions could he detect? I was suddenly very nervous. What did I smell like right now?

He turned around so fast, I stumbled back, breaking the spell. "You could too, if you'd use your senses the way I trained you to."

"You know what? It doesn't matter what you smelled or sensed or thought was right for me. Have you forgotten there's a wolf growing stronger inside me?" I snapped back. "I need them to be interested fast. Don't you want me to find love?"

"Lust isn't love, so it wouldn't have worked anyway. That boy—" He cut himself off and took a deep calming breath, silver shining in his eyes. "You deserve someone who loves you for your heart, not because of how revealing your clothes are or how fast he can get into your pants."

I winced. Waves of emotions swept over me as I recalled the stories of my mom partying at my age and then getting pregnant with me. I felt dirty. But what other choice did I have? I had to break the bond.

"I wish I had time to find someone like that. But I don't." I pointed to the waning moon through the window.

His balled fists relaxed, and weariness shadowed his eyes. "I don't want to see you hurt."

I lowered my eyes to the ground and bit my lip.

"I'm already hurting," I said, my voice small. "What's a little more pain?" I was turning into a monster, and I'd do anything to stay human—anything.

He didn't comment, but I could hear him shifting his weight.

I looked up. "I need you to let me do things my way, like you promised. Please...just leave me alone."

Pain flashed across his face so quickly it could've been the lights playing tricks, or maybe I transposed my own aching loss onto him. I knew keeping him at arm's length was necessary if I wanted to find true love, especially in light of tonight's escapades, but I wished there was another way. Beast was only trying to protect me. A horrible ache seized my heart as I realized how much I was hurting him. Why couldn't I find a human that made me feel the way Beast did? Why couldn't Beast be human? Then, I remembered, if it wasn't for him and his stupid curse, I wouldn't be searching in the first place.

"I'm trying to honor that promise, Tayla." He swallowed hard and the next words were but a whisper. "But I don't know if I can." He turned and walked out the sliding glass doors and disappeared into the shadows of the backyard.

11
GOTCHA

Monday, April 16

"Well, since Saturday's party didn't work, you'll just have to meet me at school in one hour." Chel's voice was bright and cheerful over the phone, while my chest squeezed in anticipation.

"Why? What's going on at school?" I asked. Beast's ear flicked in my direction. He lay curled up on my bedroom floor, but he clearly wasn't sleeping.

"Prom committee is meeting and there are some nice guys there. I think you'll be able to snag a date from at least one of them." Chel's voice became muffled like she was dressing while talking to me. Chel had been on the Prom committee two years in a row; she oversaw the use of materials. That girl could take trash and transform it into a masterpiece without spending a dime.

I looked out the window where the last rays colored the evening sky. In one hour it would be dark and Beast would be human. This could work.

"All right. What room are you in?"

"The gym," she said. "That way we can really visualize our creation." Her voice got that far-off sound it always did when she slipped into her creative mode.

I chuckled. "Fine with me. I'll meet you there."

I was about to hang up the phone when her voice stopped me. "Oh, and Tay. Don't you dare wear what you have on right now."

"What?" I sputtered. "How could you possibly know what I have on? It might be a new blouse."

Chel snorted. "Tay, don't make me laugh. I've known you long enough to know you have some revolting t-shirt on with either blue jeans or sweats."

I picked at the hem of my favorite green shirt and looked down at my black running pants. *Okay, so she had a point.* I sighed. "You win. I'll go change."

She laughed, and I hung up the phone.

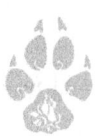

Beast was quiet on the drive. I didn't know what to say. I parked and he slipped out of the van with his trench coat on. I walked ahead of him, scouting out ways to get him into the building without being seen. Luckily, there weren't many people here tonight.

"Over here." I motioned for Beast to hide in the boy's locker room.

His lips curled in disgust, but he pushed the door open and stepped through. My heart filled with gratitude. Maybe I had been a little too hard on him last night. I stopped the door with my hand. "Beast. I...I just wanted to say thank you."

He gave me a slight nod. His eyes captured my gaze, and a mischievous glint flashed in them. "At least this time you have more clothes on."

I slugged him. "Shut up."

But we were both smiling. "Now, if I could just do something about the dirty sock smell in the room, this evening might be bearable."

"I'm sure you'll figure out something." I grinned, relieved that the tension had lessened between us.

I entered the gym, and Chel wasted no time introducing me to the others before she got down to business. It was 6:30 pm and she only had two hours to iron out the details of prom decorations. She was the head of the committee and she took it seriously. Dividing the group in two, she sent me with two boys, while she went with the three other girls. Her slick move was duly noted with a wink as she walked past me.

I followed the boys to the bleachers. We all sat down and they pulled out paper and pencils from their backpacks. The short, chubby one, Conner, sat down and started labeling the map Chel had given them of the gym and two adjacent rooms. He was too preoccupied with his task to even acknowledge my presence. Not that I was concerned about it. Conner didn't interest me at all. There was absolutely no chemistry between us. Kevin on the other hand was tall with dark hair and had an easygoing personality. Too bad he was already dating a girl from his band class. This was a waste of time. Gloomily, I stared off into space while the boys discussed the dimensions of the map.

I looked over to see what Chel was doing, hoping that she might want to ditch early and grab some ice cream, but she was busy arguing about decorations. Some wanted the stars gold while others wanted them silver. When they finally decided that they could have both colors, I was a yawn away from clamping my hands over my ears. I thought the girls were finally finished, and I could talk with Chel before heading home, when they launched into whether bubbles were better than balloons.

"Kevin, I'm telling you we need another pair of speakers right here." Conner pointed to the paper. I leaned over and saw that he was pointing to the chairs lining the wall.

"If we do that no one will be able to hear," Kevin pointed out. I agreed with him.

"That's the point. If we put it there, then we can't hear our dates whine!" Conner chuckled and Kevin followed suit.

I rolled my eyes and turned toward the door. "And Chel called them nice," I whispered to the only person who could save me from my boredom. "Honestly, Beast, I'm surprised they even got dates."

Beast chuckled. "They are normal teenage boys." His voice floated to me from the locker room where he was hiding. "That's what you wanted, right?"

I snorted and he laughed. "Hey, this isn't funny," I said, but couldn't keep the amused tone from my voice.

A few seconds later, a click-click of boots hitting the floor caught my attention. It wasn't coming from this room but the one next to us. Snapping my head up, I watched as the reason for the noise walked through the gym doors. Dressed in Wranglers, boots, and hat, walked in the hottest cowboy I'd ever seen. That was saying something since cowboys usually didn't do it for me.

He scanned the room, thumbs tucked in his Wrangler pockets, with disinterest bordering on total boredom. A belt buckle advertised his rodeo win in team roping. He was lean, but walked with a confidence that spoke of strength. How had I never seen him before? But a better question was whether or not he was available.

"Yo, Brayden!" Kevin motioned for the cowboy to come over.

Brayden walked toward us, his coffee brown eyes landing on me for only a second, but long enough to send moth wings to tickle my stomach. The night had thankfully become much more interesting.

Kevin slapped Brayden on the back. "About time you got here, man."

Brayden's slim lips spread into a grin. "What? There's something you can't handle?"

"No," Kevin said, pretending to be affronted. "But this doofus is arguing with me over where to put the coat rack. So now that you're here you can side with me and we can be done with it."

Conner stood. "No way, man. Brayden's on my side. You'll see. He'll pick the exact spot I did." He held out the self-drawn map for Brayden to see.

"You guys are fighting over a stupid coat rack?" The disbelief in his tone was amusing, and they both threw him a contemptuous glare.

"Just pick a spot," Conner commanded Brayden.

"How about by the door?" he said drily as if the answer was painfully obvious.

Conner slugged him in the arm. "We know that, smartass. But Chel wants to have an exact spot picked out, not too close but not too far away, and insisted we draw it on this stupid map. So I say we put it here." He jabbed the paper with his finger. "Or if we go with Sparky over there," his head jerked in Kevin's direction, "it can go here." He flicked the paper so hard I was surprised he didn't poke a hole through it.

Kevin gave Conner a dirty look, and I giggled into my hand, trying to smother it but failing miserably. Three heads turned my way.

"And what are you laughing at, *girl?*" Conner snapped, obviously finished with this business.

I blushed and had every intention of ducking from his displeasure, but my wolf slammed against her mental cage. I could feel her anger and lust for his insulting blood. I tried to hold her back but her anger was making her stronger. She wasn't going to stop until I put him in his place. *Crap.*

I stood. I couldn't keep my eyes from narrowing at Conner. I was having a hard enough time keeping her from taking full control and hitting him. Beast's worry skimmed across my conscience, but I couldn't lose focus now. Conner took a step back, and my wolf loosened her hold enough for me to lighten my glare.

"This *girl* just thought it was funny how indecisive you're being for a *boy.* Or are you just too worried about impressing Chel to make a choice?" I crossed my arms.

Conner's face reddened with embarrassment, or was it anger? His heartbeat spiked, telling me I'd hit too close to the truth for his liking. "You shut up."

I was making enemies, not friends, and certainly not finding a date. With my wolf placated and back in her cage, I tried to smooth out my blunders. "Not that I care, but I think she'll think you're at least trying if you put them here and here." I pointed to spots on both sides of the door, a few feet down the wall with enough room to enter the gym without running into them. When he just stared at me, I added, "There are two of them, aren't there?"

His face softened some. "We thought we'd only use one, but having two isn't a half bad idea," he reluctantly said, and penciled it on the map.

"Yeah. I like it," Chel said from behind us. We whirled around. "See, I knew you guys could figure it out."

I peeked over at Conner, who beamed like a teacher's pet. He handed the map over to Chel. "We hoped you would like it."

When their eyes met, his heart slammed so loud in his chest I was surprised no one else could hear it. I bit my tongue to keep quiet. *Oh, man, he likes Chel.* Doesn't he know that making her best friend mad would hamper his chances with her? Not that he had any chance to start with. It was clear that he wasn't the observant type.

"It looks good. I'll just show this to the girls. Can you guys clear out a spot in the closet there?" She pointed at an open storage closet. "I have two boxes that need to go in it."

"Sure." Conner was on it faster than Kevin and Brayden, who had knowing smirks on their faces as they trailed after Conner.

Chel quickly turned on me and whispered. "Now, which one caught your eye?"

At her words, my eyes shifted involuntarily to Brayden. Chel followed my gaze and smiled. "Oh. I didn't think cowboys were your type, but if you have to make an exception, that one is yummy *and* single."

"Shh... What if he hears you?" Heat flushed my cheeks, and my wolf paced with displeasure in her cage. *That's right, your days are numbered*, I told the she-wolf. She bore her fangs in a mental assault that stung my mind. I winced. Maybe antagonizing my inner wolf wasn't the smartest move, but it felt empowering.

"I hope he does. You don't have time to hide. You have to act!" She turned and I knew something embarrassing was likely to happen next if I didn't stop her.

I grabbed her arm, and frantically whispered. "Chel, please don't. I'll—"

"I'm not going to watch you get in your own way." Her glacier blue eyes flashed with determination. "And I'm not going to lose you to a wolf!"

Struck speechless, I let go of her arm and she called after the boys. "Hey, Brayden."

He swiveled to look over his shoulder. "Yeah?"

"Would you mind helping Tayla carry in a few boxes from the car?"

His brown eyes looked in my direction and his lips tugged into a small smile. For a moment I was lightheaded, and all I could do was blink back at him. That smile was dangerously potent. I didn't dare hope that this guy might be able to love me and cleanse my body of the wolf.

"Sure," he answered Chel. When I still didn't move, his brow rose, like he was questioning my intelligence.

"Oh, and I'll need you to organize them a bit. I was kinda in a hurry and just threw the decorations in." Chel winked in my direction before Brayden turned to look at her.

"Fine." He held out his hands as if waiting to catch a football. "Throw me the keys. We'll have it finished in no time."

"Thanks. You guys are awesome!" Chel fished her keys out of her pocket and had them sailing through the air before my paralysis lifted. Chel had already disappeared, leaving me staring stupidly at Brayden. He flashed me a friendly smile that threatened to turn my knees into jello. My wolf snarled at the happy buzz in my chest.

"So I guess you're with me." He jerked his head toward the door. "Let's get this done."

That shook me out of my stupor enough to respond. "Okay."

I followed him outside in silence. The night was calm and the stars were out in force, twinkling like fireflies. Needing to say something, I offered directions. "Her car is this way." I pointed to her SUV only two parking spots down. "It's the red one there."

I finished speaking about the same time he hit the unlock button on Chel's chain. Her lights flashed on and off and he chuckled. "I see that."

I wanted to hang my head. Could this night become anymore disastrous? Could I have sounded more stupid?

Needing to get this over with, I stepped closer to the SUV. My gut clenched in pain—a warning. I was at my maximum distance from Beast. Thankfully, Brayden kept walking, unconcerned with my failure to follow.

"Beast," I breathed too low for normal humans to hear. "You have to give me a few more yards."

I strained my wolf hearing for his response. "Can't. The hall is blocked with two boys moving coat racks."

Well, crap. What if Brayden asks me to grab a box from the back?

Panic threatened to rob me of thought, and just being around Brayden affected me enough. An image of my wilted rose at home jolted me back to my task. I wouldn't fail because I froze. *Just act like you've got this under control.*

"So how did you get roped into prom committee?" I asked, watching him from my position on the sidewalk.

He came around the car with a box. "Chel convinced me it would look good on my college apps." He chuckled. "I think I got had."

"Yeah, probably. Chel needs to go into politics. She'd have the whole Senate following her in a month." I held out my arms for the box. He brought it over to me and our fingers touched. My heart pounded. This guy couldn't be real. He was too nice. For a second, a sense of uncertainty hit me along with a pang of loss. Loss? The feeling didn't make sense, until Beast's face flashed in my mind. Would Beast disappear after I found a human true love and broke my wolf's hold? Would the curse break too? If he was free, why would he stay? The questions didn't lift my spirits.

Brayden went back to the car for his box. Shutting the back, Brayden said, "True, but sales might be more her speed. I swear she can sweet-talk anyone into doing something for her."

He joined me with the other box, and we relaxed into a conversation about schools where he wanted to study while we walked back inside. He was energetic and funny, and it took everything I had to keep my nerves from showing. I didn't want to mess this up. My whole future hinged on a love some people spent their whole lives searching for and never found. And I had only three more weeks. I bit my cheek. I had to stop thinking that way or I'd start hyperventilating and curl into an inert ball inside the box I carried.

We set the boxes close to the closet Kevin and Conner had cleaned out. I laughed. "Seems they just took out the coat racks."

Brayden passed me to peek inside. "Yup, those lazy culls."

I giggled at his reference to ranch animals.

"What?" He feigned a confused expression. "It was the nicest way to put it, without my Ma threatening me with a bar of soap."

"Come on, people don't do that anymore." I sat down next to my box, still grinning.

"Oh yes they do," he countered, and I looked up. "My Ma's favorite weapons are cocoa powder, soap, and rope. And there's no chance of running. She's one of the best ropers I know. So we learned to watch our language around her if we didn't want to be hog-tied and get something nasty stuffed in our mouth." He bent to drag his box closer to mine.

I laughed out right. "Oh man, your mom sounds fun."

His lips quirked into that heart-stopping smile and winked at me. "Yup. So where should we start?"

"I think we should unload them first," I suggested, barely able to draw breath from his closeness. Our knees brushed where he sat next to me. When I finally took a breath, I instantly wished I hadn't. My wolf nose was underdeveloped but he was so close it didn't matter. His rugged cologne couldn't mask the smell of cow manure and the tinge of something rusty and metallic that could only be blood. I moved like I couldn't reach an item from the box and scooted away, holding back a sneeze, but the awful smell clung to my nose, scraping away at it until I couldn't hold it any longer. I sneezed and to my horror that wasn't the only thing to come out. Snot dripped down to my mouth. I shifted forward, hoping he hadn't seen.

I heard him say, "Bless you," but I was frantically looking for a tissue in the box and didn't respond. There was nothing to of use in the box unless I wanted to use a paper doily. I paused for only a moment, before wiping my nose on it and shoving it into my pocket. I'd buy Chel another one.

I heard Beast chuckle and knew he was closer than the locker room. My head jerked up in time to see him duck down from one of the door windows.

"Shut up!" I hissed, mortified that I'd had a witness. It even felt like my wolf was laughing.

"What?" Brayden asked, bringing my attention back to the handsome cowboy.

"Umm. I was just thinking this was nice." I picked up a glittering silver streamer from the box, careful to keep my distance from him. If I took shallow breaths and sat a good yard away, the pungent scent was bearable. That got me wondering. Maybe this was an old scent that still clung to his skin. Nothing a good shower with lots of soap couldn't cure.

"I guess it's okay." He eyed me with a curious brow. He probably thought I was nervous, or worse, that I wasn't all there. Ah! Everything had been going so well until my nose kicked in.

You have to fix this, I chided myself. I couldn't afford to let this one escape.

"So what did you do to win the buckle?"

He pulled out tablecloths from the boxes. "I was the heeler for a roping team that placed last summer."

"Where did you come in?"

"First."

"Wow. I bet your mom was proud."

"Yeah. She taught me everything she knew, and I picked up a few new tricks from chasing my younger brothers." He grinned and his brown eyes lit with pride.

We talked about the rodeo until our boxes were unloaded and sorted into piles. Well, he talked about the rodeo and I pretended to know what he was talking about. I knew less about rodeos than I did about soccer.

"Put the wall decorations in my box and we'll put the table decorations in yours," I directed, needing a subject change before he discovered how much I didn't know.

"Here." He handed me bags of balloons.

A few minutes later we had the stuff organized, back in the boxes and in the closet. My time to act was dwindling. If I didn't ask him on a date now, I'd miss my opportunity altogether.

"So..um. I was wondering if you like the movies." I fidgeted with the bottom of my shirt.

He cocked an amused brow at me. "Who doesn't?"

"Yeah..." I stumbled over my words. He wasn't going to make this easy on me. "You want to catch a movie tomorrow with...um, me?" My nerves made talking almost impossible.

"I can't tomorrow." He shut the closet door.

"Oh." The outright rejection stung. I thought we'd hit it off. I heard Beast growl, no doubt from my pain. "That's okay." I turned to flee, but his hand shot out to catch my arm.

I looked over my shoulder in surprise, and he spoke. "But I can do Wednesday."

I couldn't help the smile from spreading across my face. "That would be great. I'll even let you pick the movie." I cringed visibly, and he smirked. "I'm not good at this."

He softly chuckled. "So where do I pick you up?"

"Give me your number and I'll call you. I think Chel wants to double if that's okay?"

"That's cool. But my truck can't fit more than three people. So we might have to take her car." His tan arms flexed as he dug his cell out of the Wranglers that clung snugly to his long legs.

"That's no problem. Chel won't mind." I pulled my cell out of my not-so-tight pants.

He handed me his phone. "Here, program your number in."

I did and he called my cell, so I had his number also.

"Well, I'll catch you later then."

"Yeah." I smiled after him as he exited the gym.

After he left, Chel came up and squealed in my ear. "Tell me you landed a date."

I blushed. "Yeah. Wednesday night we're going to the movies. Can you get a date?"

Her hand found her chest as if affronted by the question. "Of course."

I smiled. "Okay, I'm going to head out. Talk to you tomorrow?"

"Yeah," Chel replied, as she walked back to her committee members.

Beast was more than ready to leave. We drove home in silence. I wasn't sure what was eating at him. Brayden didn't smell tangy with lust, so why was Beast frowning? If anything he should be happy. It seemed like my nose was going to keep me from getting too close for very long. That thought made me frown as well. How was I going to control my sneezing, and my wolf, long enough to get a kiss?

I looked over at Beast, who was still not talking to me. "What's wrong with you?" I asked as I pulled up to the curb in front of my Grandma's house.

He looked at me with those piercing honey eyes. "Am I supposed to be excited about having been stuck in a smelly locker room for two hours while you flirted with cow manure boy?"

Guilt attacked my chest. I hadn't given much thought to Beast's comfort lately. "I'm sorry. I know I've been snappy lately." I bit my bottom lip. "But thank you Beast, for letting me come home, for putting up with my craziness, and well for everything."

Beast grunted to acknowledge that I'd spoken. He climbed out of the van and threw a glance over his shoulder. "Rest well. I won't be getting you for lessons tonight."

My heart ached. Would things never be right between us?

"Beast," I called after him, not caring for another rift between us. But he didn't stop or turn. He kept walking until he disappeared around the corner of the house.

12

SNEAK ATTACK

Tuesday, April 17

The next morning, I slumped over my cereal bowl, feeling lost. Beast hadn't come for me last night, and my wolf had whined half the night because of it. Now, I had a colossal headache to go with my depressed feelings. Beast had entered the house only to eat and then trotted back outside again, avoiding eye contact with me. Loneliness pricked my heart, making me melancholy.

I growled, "This is stupid!" I dropped my spoon back into my cereal. Milk splashed everywhere. I had a date with Brayden tomorrow and that was something to celebrate. If true love was possible with anyone in three weeks, it was with him. And I was going to be happy!

The front door clicked open.

"Grandma?" I turned in my seat. I didn't expect her back from shopping so soon. She'd only been gone thirty minutes.

"No. It's me." Aunt Lily rounded the corner. Emotions swirled in my chest, and I held my breath to stem the tears from flowing at the memory of her heartless slap. Clenching my teeth, I held onto the anger and turned around, showing her my back.

"What are you doing here?" I jabbed my spoon at my cereal. "Aren't you like in mortal danger just being so close to me?"

"Tayla," she drew out my name like it was painful, "please. This is hard for me."

"Hard for you?" I barked out a laugh bordering on hysteria and dropped my spoon. "You have got to be kidding me." I stood and turned on her, stabbing a finger at my chest. "*I'm* the one who has a bodysnatching wolf inside me." I snorted. "And you have it hard? Please, spare me the sob story."

Our eyes met and for the longest time no one spoke.

"You're right," Aunt Lily finally whispered, tears swelling in her eyes.

"What?" I blinked, preparing for an onslaught of her famous manipulative guilt-tripping.

"You're right." She reached out and tentatively touched my shoulder. "About everything."

Emotions clogged my throat and tears stung my eyes. "So you came by to say goodbye?"

Aunt Lily stared at her ragged, bitten fingernails, a habit she'd picked up after Uncle Stan died, but didn't speak. I couldn't move as the seconds ticked by. Her next words would either heal me or shatter me.

"No, I came to say..." She swallowed with discomfort. "Tay, I never should've hit you."

I bit my trembling lower lip, struggling to keep my emotions inside, and nodded.

"I'm *so* sorry. I promise." Her voice hitched. "I promise I'll try to understand you better. Just please say you'll forgive me?"

I felt my emotional shield lower, and I wrapped her in a hug. With a tear-strained voice, I said, "Oh, Mom. I never should've said those terrible things to you. It was beyond hateful."

"Shh." She pulled away and brushed my hair out of my face. "Tayla, you are the bravest, strongest person I know, and I'm proud to call you my daughter." She squeezed me into another hug.

"I love you," I mumbled into her shoulder.

"I love you, too."

We held each other for several seconds, before she pulled away to wipe her wet cheeks with her sleeve. "I'm still having a hard time with this whole body-changing thing."

I chuckled and wiped at my cheeks. "Tell me about it. At least you don't have a wolf prowling around in your head." I plopped back down, feeling more exhausted than I had in a long while.

Aunt Lily sat next to me. "Can you really feel it inside you?"

I nodded miserably. "Yep. And she hasn't been on her best behavior."

"What do you mean?" Her brows crunched together with worry.

"She just likes to exert her will every now and then, but I don't want to talk about it." I looked at the cereal I swirled with my spoon. "I do have some good news."

"Oh?"

"Yeah. I have a date tomorrow with a really nice guy. He's a cowboy. I never thought I'd fall for one of them." I gave a short laugh.

"Tay, I don't know if all this dating is going to work." She took the bowl and spoon away from me, forcing me to look up. She took my hands in hers.

"It has to." My voice shook. "The alternative is too scary."

Aunt Lily swallowed hard. "You mean turning into a wolf forever?"

"Yeah, but there's another way it could end." I lowered my eyes.

"What other way?" she asked, her voice full of apprehension.

"If I don't break the wolf in time and the wolf takes over, there is a chance I might not survive." I gripped her hands so tightly she pulled them from my grasp.

"No," she breathed out in haunted torment. Her arms wove around me in an instant and mine around her. "I can't lose you like that," she whispered into my ear.

I inhaled shakily. "I'm doing everything I can to fight her off, but she is just getting stronger."

There was silence for a few moments. "You really believe that true love will save you?"

"It's the only hope I have." I leaned out of yet another hug. "Hence, the reason I have to date. But I'm really hopeful about Brayden."

"Then he better treat you right." She gave me an encouraging smile. A twinkle entered her eye. "I have a surprise."

I cocked an eyebrow. Surprises weren't my aunt's strong suit. "Oh?"

"Well, more of an apology." She went back to the front door and when she returned she was carrying Uncle Stan's telescope case. She tapped it. "You were right. This was his favorite thing to do, and we all loved it. I had no right to take that away even if it was painful to remember."

I stared back at her in shock. "Do you really mean it?"

"Yes." Her eyes clouded with more tears, but they didn't spill. "You never know how long you have with those you love."

Emotions welled up in me, and I choked on my words. What do you say to the family you might never see again? How do you say your goodbyes when every fiber of your being screams *don't leave me*? But I wasn't saying goodbye yet, and if I had it my way, I never would.

She wiped her cheeks and tried to smile. "I thought tonight we could all stargaze as a family. And Grandma can make up some of her famous pancakes for a midnight breakfast."

I grinned and squeezed her into a hug. "Thank you. Thank you so much."

She chuckled unsteadily and squeezed me back.

"Oh, but what about Beast? You know he will be there, too."

She shifted uneasily. "I was hoping he could stay hidden." She gave me a shameful look. "I'm still not comfortable with him around, so maybe if I can't see him, I can ignore his presence."

"I think that can be arranged." I bit my lip. Thinking about Beast caused feelings of sadness to wash over me. I'd been able to mend one relationship, but I didn't know how to stop offending Beast. Would he talk to me? Would we keep cycling through our yo-yo act?

"Tay, is everything okay?"

"Yeah. Just thinking." I forced a smile. "Tonight will be perfect."

And it was.

Shortly before my family arrived, I talked with Beast, explaining Aunt Lily's request. He gave me a curt nod after I'd explained everything and strode off to a shadowed place in the backyard. His disinterested demeanor tore at my heart. But no matter how hard I tried to get him to talk he wouldn't say more than what was necessary.

Aunt Lily and the girls came with blankets and enough marshmallows to give everyone a sugar high for days. We stargazed for hours, quizzing each other on the constellations. Cammie drifted off to sleep around two in the morning, but the rest of us stayed up another hour playing Name that Tune until the tunes became more like lullabies and we all drifted off to sleep under the stars.

13

JELLO CAKE

Wednesday, April 18

My phone rang at 3:30 p.m. the next day.

"Hello?"

It was Chel. "Tay, I have the best news!" she squealed. "I've found dates for you for the rest of the week."

"That's great." I couldn't quite match her enthusiasm. I prayed I wouldn't have need for more guys after tonight, that somehow Brayden would ask me on another date.

"You don't sound excited." Chel's voice was sour from the lack of appreciation showing in my voice.

"I am excited. Thanks, Chel. You are the best of the best." I paused, waiting for a response and only got a huff. "Come on. I'm just nervous about tonight."

"Well, I guess that is excusable, but you'd better sound more excited next time," she chided me. I could imagine her shaking a finger at me. "This isn't easy, you know. Not only do I have to find dates for you, but I have to snag me one as well."

"But I thought getting yourself a date was the easy part."

"It usually is. But you are cutting the numbers in half."

I chuckled. "Oh, Chel, I'm sure they would rather be going on a date with you than with me anyway."

"That isn't the point, and so not true." She paused dramatically for emphasis. "I expect you to at least act excited even if you are about to puke. Got it?"

My grin was so large my cheek muscles ached. "You got it. Exclaim gleeful happiness before puking. Anything else?"

"Nope, that covers it," she responded with humor in her voice. "Now get over here so I can curl your hair!"

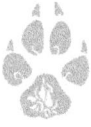

Brayden held the door open for me as I climbed out of the car. I tried not to cringe seeing the movie house again, but I couldn't stop my lips from pulling into a hard line. My wolf felt my unease and paced in my mind, adding to my nerves. I knew Brayden was different from Kyle. There was no comparison, but that night still haunted me, and seeing the place where Kyle had assaulted me left me a bit unnerved.

"Are you okay?" Brayden's hand rested lightly on my lower back.

"Umm." I shook the bad memories and turned a smile on him. "Yeah. Sorry. It's been awhile since I was here last." Like months. He looked confused, so I lied, "It just looks different. That's all. Why don't we get our tickets?"

"All right." He still looked unconvinced, but let it go.

We arrived at the ticket booth and both spoke at the same time, "Two for *Lights and Brimfire.*"

"Oh, I'm sorry." I looked off to the side of him. "I just thought, that well, since I asked you and all…"

He chuckled. "Tayla, it's okay." I looked up at him and the smile on his face tugged mine back into place. He continued, "And I always pay, even if the girl asked me." He winked at me and my knees wobbled from the fuzzy warmth creeping into my stomach. A rumble of agitation pushed through from my wolf, but it only gave me more confidence that this guy was it.

We picked the seats right in the very middle. To me they were the best seats in the house. I wasn't sure about the movie. It was some war movie. I felt bad that Beast had to be subjected to it. At least he hadn't had to run here. He had insisted on driving his own truck.

I felt Beast slink in behind us. He was a few rows up, wearing his trademark black trench coat and kept his head low. As people filled into the theater, they gave him a wide berth. I didn't blame them. Honestly, he looked like the grim reaper or something.

The lights dimmed in the theater and the previews started. I offered Brayden a licorice. He smiled, and my heart stuttered. Even in the dark, his smile lit the world.

"Thanks for coming," I whispered.

"No problem." He grabbed another licorice. "Thanks for the invite."

"Hey." I shouldered him. "That's my licorice," I teased.

He shoulder knocked me back. "Then you shouldn't have given me the first one. Now I'll eat the whole bag."

I made a great show of hiding them in my jacket and we both chuckled. He was easy that way. I didn't feel like I had to be someone else. Not like with Kyle.

Why am I thinking of him?

I mentally scolded myself and relaxed back in my chair, leaning close to Brayden. He didn't scoot away and hope warmed my chest. I was careful to only breathe through my mouth and had practiced clamping down on my wolf senses, not wanting a repeat of the gym scene. The heat of his arm against mine was comforting, and the way he periodically gave me sideways glances made my heart flutter.

The movie started but I was too focused on Brayden to watch. That was until the battle scenes demanded my attention. My wolf was riveted to the carnage on the screen and, to my horror, was licking her lips. I almost dry heaved right then. I shrunk from the movie and from her. I covered my eyes with my hands, praying it would stop her blood lust and my rolling stomach. I'm sure I whimpered or something equally as embarrassing, because Brayden lifted the armrest and pulled me close. I snuggled into his chest.

"We can leave," he whispered, tickling my ear.

"I don't want you to miss your movie," I responded, trying not to breathe as I was happily surrounded by his strong arms.

He squeezed me close. "All right."

My nose pressed up against his shoulder, a potential happy place for me if it wasn't for my wolf. I was too close and could taste the tang of animal blood on my tongue. I quickly closed my mouth. When I was forced to breathe, the smell of farm animals was strong, but not as strong as the metallic smell of blood. It all reminded me of the first time I met him.

The smell overwhelmed my senses and I felt my control slip. I closed my eyes, focusing on restraining the wolf struggling against her cage. She wasn't going to ruin this for me. I refused to pull away, but the thought of dead animals was too disturbing, and the smell was stronger than that day in the gym. My mind wandered from its task. Had he killed an animal today? But the horror that should have washed over me was replaced with a heady need. I breathed deeply and pressed my body closer, quickly losing control. The smell was delightfully tantalizing and my stomach grumbled, transporting me to a childhood memory of Aunt Lily's jello cake.

My mouth watered, as I pictured the cake. It smelled so real that I could almost taste it. I opened my mouth and skimmed the cake with my lips, biting down softly. My teeth met more resistance than I was expecting. I was about to bite down harder when large fingers slid between my teeth preventing me from my dessert. I growled and threw my head back, only to have Beast's strong arms capture me in a vice grip around my torso.

"What the—?"

Brayden's voice snapped me out of my delusion of a childhood dessert. My eyes flew open and I took in his disgusted expression as he rubbed his neck. His hand came away wet with my saliva. His gaze darted to his left shoulder where his shirt was several shades darker, thanks to my drool. Horror washed through me, but before I could utter a word of apology, Beast tugged me out of my seat and hauled me out of the theater. I could still hear Chel and Brayden.

"Oh," Chel said. "Eww. I'm so sorry. Maybe her blood sugar was low."

"What?" Brayden's disbelieving voice sliced me. How would he love me now?

"You know people do all sorts of weird stuff when their blood sugar is low," Chel explained.

"Oh, like biting me?"

I could imagine his eyes narrowing in anger.

"Umm," Chel hesitated, obviously surprised I had actually bit him. "Was it just a nip? I don't see any broken skin."

That news sent a trickle of relief over me. At least, I hadn't drawn blood.

"That isn't the point. She bit and slobbered all over me. My animals don't even get me this bad!" he hissed back. His voice sounded like he had stood and was walking out of the theater as well. Chel didn't respond. I'm sure she was trying to process the whole thing.

"And who was that guy?" Brayden asked.

"Oh, just a friend."

"She has some stalker friend to pull her from dates when she starts biting them?"

"No." She giggled nervously. "I guess you smell so good she just wanted a taste."

I cringed, mortified even more than I already was. *Way to go, Chel, now I really want to hide.* The night air hit my face as we exited the theater house. Beast strode a few yards more before depositing me against the wall, where I slumped down to the ground and hugged my knees.

Almost too low for me to hear, Chel's date, Dalyn, responded, "You can take a taste of me anytime you like, Chel."

"You're all nuts," Brayden said.

"Wait, I'll drive you home," Chel called after him, her voice getting louder as they neared.

"Don't bother. I'm safer walking." He pushed open the door. Our eyes met for a moment before he stormed off.

I hung my head. "Oh, Beast," I whispered. "What have I done?"

To my surprise, he chuckled. "So you nipped him?" He shrugged his shoulders but the mirth was still there.

I glowered at him. "Then why did you swoop down and carry me off if you didn't think it was a big deal?"

"The nip wasn't what I was worried about, but the real bite you were going to give him next would've drawn blood, and then it was unlikely you'd be able to stop." His lips hitched upward. "That would have really made your wolf crazy."

"That meddlesome she-devil!" I ground out between my teeth. "She ruins everything."

"If you'd learned to control her better, you would've smelled the animals on him and stayed far away from him in the first place." His eyes twinkled as if laughing at an inside joke.

Before I could retort, Chel came out of the doors, her date trailing behind her. "Dalyn, will you start the car for me and bring it around?" She tossed him her keys before he responded.

"Sure." He eyed me with a mischievous glint. I felt Beast vibrate with an inaudible growl. I agreed. Dalyn's look sent chills up my spine, like he was assessing a hooker or something. *Yuck!* I was definitely telling Chel to stay away from that one.

With Dalyn in the SUV and out of hearing, Chel demanded answers. "What just happened?"

I scowled at my knees. "He must've slaughtered a cow or something yesterday because his stench was so much stronger today, and my wolf got the better of me."

"But you bit him?"

"It's her! I would never do that. Eww. He must think I'm a freak." I groaned, placing my head in my hands. "He was so perfect, too."

Chel patted my shoulder, but it wasn't soothing; nothing was, with this wolf in my head.

"You know what the worst part is?" I asked, looking up to see Chel raise her eyebrow. "She tricked me. She used my memory of Aunt Lily's jello cake to convince me to bite him. I didn't even know she could do that!"

"Jello?" Chel asked.

Beast cleared his voice.

"What?" I demanded.

"That isn't exactly true," he said. I lifted a disbelieving eyebrow at him. "Just hear me out. The smell, it was delicious to you?"

"Only after she tricked me into thinking it was cake. If I had consciously thought of it as blood, animal, whatever, I never..." I couldn't say the rest.

"That is where you are wrong." Beast paused until I looked up at him. "To your wolf, animal scent and blood are delicious, and so the best way you could understand those feelings was to relate it to cake." His voice lost its teacher tone when he got to the last word and turned more playful. "It must've been some delectable cake. Maybe my blood lust would curb a bit if you made it for me." He winked.

"Shut up." I smacked him in the leg, but couldn't resist the smile that spread across my lips. I had my wolfish friend back and was determined to side-step as many rift-creating topics as possible.

Chel bit her bottom lip. "I'm not sure I can fix this, Tay. A little drool I could explain away, but..."

My frown was back. I'd lost Brayden. "Thanks for trying. I guess we should stay away from cowboys." I gave Chel a rueful grin.

Chel puffed out air and rubbed her temples. "Friday night is a cancel then."

"Oh?" *Why did things always go to crap?*

"Yeah, one of Brayden's roping buddies. But after he hears Brayden's story, he'll be canceling before I get a chance to do it." She gave my shoulder a squeeze. "I'll find a replacement."

"Ah!" I buried my face in my hands. "Why did she have to bite him? Stupid wolf." She growled at me and nipped at my mind, causing a throbbing headache.

Beast crouched down to my level and tucked a finger under my chin. His touch held soothing warmth, but I fought it. I deserved to feel the crushing weight of my actions. The pressure on my chin increased until I could no longer resist his strength. My face tilted up to him, but I refused to look him in the eyes. At least, in that I still had the power to defy.

"Stupid is the last word I'd use to describe you." As if by its own accord, my gaze lifted and was met by the warmth coming from his eyes. His thumb grazed my jaw, and both my wolf and I trembled ever so slightly. He noticed my reaction, and his eyes lit with mischief. "And if he had been a werewolf, I guarantee you would've gotten a different response."

I couldn't breathe. What he implied was too direct to misinterpret. A horn blasted, and I jerked, breaking the spell. Beast lifted his head to look at Dalyn, giving me the needed release to breathe.

Honk! Honk!

Chel rolled her eyes. "We need to go, Tay. I think Dalyn is going to break my horn."

I shifted to move, but Beast spoke, stopping me. "I'll drive her home. It only seems sensible."

Chel's gaze shifted to mine as if asking if this was what I wanted. I nodded. "Just be careful with that one." I jerked my head toward Dalyn. "There is something that just doesn't feel right about him."

Beast grunted. "Better yet, we'll follow you until you drop him off. I haven't liked the smell of him all night."

"Oh, guys. That isn't necessary. I can't imagine him hurting me." She gave a giggle. "He plays the cello. The cello, Tay. Can't get any gentler than that."

"Maybe he won't do anything tonight, but that doesn't mean he won't in the future." Beast turned a stern look on her. "We'll be following you, Chel. Arguing with me is fruitless."

14

WOLF
PROBLEMS

Saturday, April 21

It was Saturday, and I wasn't sure I could handle another date. The Brayden Disaster had just been the beginning of my dating problems. I had hoped I could control my wolf better, but she kept rearing her ugly head. On Thursday, I'd gone on a date with Alex, a basketball player who smelled so offensively of gym socks that I had to end the date early. My eyes watered so badly I couldn't keep them open, like someone had rubbed onions in them.

Then last night my luck had changed, or so I'd thought. Michael Midlon took me miniature golfing and then to a pizza joint downtown. Chel was giving me hidden thumbs up while our dates calculated the perfect putting angle. He smelled clean and inviting enough that my wolf senses allowed me to finally make it through a date. But she sure did sulk in my mind the whole time. That only added to my hope that this guy had a chance.

He'd walked me up to my door, and just before I finally landed a goodnight kiss, possibly breaking my wolf's hold for good, Michael parted his lips and I was hit with the most revolting smell. One breath and the smell drifted into my mouth, curdling my dinner. I swear he had the worst case of halitosis I'd ever experienced. There was no way pizza could ever smell that bad. I gagged right in front of him. I couldn't help it. Humiliation flashed through his eyes, and I knew he wouldn't ask for another date. In fact, he hadn't even said goodbye. He'd just left me there, staring after him.

I truly was cursed.

I sighed heavily, my hands now braced against the bathroom countertop. My hopeless green eyes stared back from the mirror as I forced myself to get ready for my fourth date. I had little faith that tonight's date would be any better than the previous three. It was like fate had it in for me. The magical rose had already wilted a handful of petals. My time as a human was already half over and tonight was just my fourth date! Despair gripped me. I pled with all my heart that I would love this guy and prayed he didn't repulse my wolf somehow. Applying the last touches of mascara, I took a last look at the form-fitting midnight-blue blouse and designer jeans Chel had dropped off at the house the night before. She'd be here any minute with my blind date. It still amazed me how fast she could find these guys in such a small town. I was surprised after date number two that word hadn't spread about the crazy homeschooled girl.

A horn blasted, and I walked to the front door, taking deep breaths along the way. Anxiety knotted my stomach and giddy bubbles of hope tickled my heart, warring with each other. Which would win? I mentally gave my wolf's cage an added lock.

You are staying put. Her blue eyes flashed in my mind, and chills crept down my spine. Wasn't finding true love hard enough without her defiance and interference?

My body was changing. Soon I wouldn't be able to subdue my wolf sense at all. When angry, she could spike my senses to levels that left me hopeless in their power. I rounded the corner to the front door. My gaze fell on Beast's trenchcoated figure leaning beside the front door. His swirling caramel eyes stroked the length of my body until his gaze stopped to hold mine.

My breath caught of its own accord, and an electric current seemed to arc between us, drawing us closer. My wolf bit the locks off her cage easily, urging me closer. I had no power to resist, nor did I want to. I stepped in an almost elegant glide. He didn't move, just held my gaze in a hypnotic dance. My pulse raced. The distance between our bodies narrowed.

My hand rose, intent on cradling his cheek, but as my fingers brushed his stubbly chin, the horn blasted again. I jerked back, shaking my head to clear the fog. I pushed at my wolf. She growled menacingly, slicing my head with a flick of pain, but I got her caged.

Beast's truck keys jingled, and I found him with a lazy smile on his face as if nothing intense had just happened. "You're going to be late," he said as if baiting me.

I growled and stomped by him, careful not to brush against him on my way out. *The nerve!* He knew what he was doing to me, how to affect my wolf, and yet he taunted me like it was my choice. Like I could have controlled her. The more I rambled in my head, the more I realized that it hadn't been just my wolf. I wanted him more with every encounter, had wanted him for a long time, but I wasn't going to become a wolf for him. Even though the thought did have some allure, it wasn't worth losing my humanity over.

I neared Chel's SUV, thankful that at least one of us had a nice car. It was decked out with all the best technology. She even had a GPS and cop detector, not to mention the iPod dock and HD speakers. It would've been humiliating picking up dates in my beat-up heater-less van.

Even in the dark, Chel's Lexus sparkled a mica color that matched her favorite nail polish. I think that was one of the draws the car held for her. They could be twins.

The car door opened.

Steve Dales slid out of the backseat and held the door open for me. I smiled my best and brightest as I neared. He wasn't particularly attractive, but with all of the limitations my wolf put on me, I couldn't afford to be picky. Steve was six foot four and the classic beanpole, with blond hair buzzed to a crew-cut. His bones were easy to spot on his thin frame and his face was sharp and angular without an ounce of meat on him.

Good. Maybe I wouldn't bite this one. He looks so...breakable. My wolf snickered as the thought flittered across my mind. Without conscious thought, my mind wandered back to the electricity pulsing between Beast and me. And as forbidden as the thought was, I knew his arms weren't scrawny or weak, but strong and commanding. The very thought of me wrapped in those arms threatened to weaken my knees. Heat rose to my cheeks.

Enough. He isn't for you! I yelled at myself internally. Even if I did decide to brave the change and be with him, I wouldn't be the one running the show—my wolf would, and that truth snapped me out of my reverie and back to the stark reality of the wolf growing inside me. I would never trade places with her to ride shotgun to my own mind and body.

I stepped closer to my date, the guy I desperately needed to fall in love with, and I smiled up at him. "Hi."

He returned my smile with a thin one of his own. "Hey, I'm Steve."

"I'm Tayla." I held my hand out and he shook it. His bony fingers wrapped around mine. They felt all wrong and cold, like an old man's hands, but I didn't pull away. I knew I was comparing them to Beast's hands. I turned the wattage up on my smile, pushing Beast from my mind. But he was always there, lurking in the shadows.

Without being obvious, I looked out my peripheral vision. Beast had just about reached his truck. He just needed another minute to get situated. The routine was fixed: Beast drove inconspicuously behind us, and I would signal Chel whenever the distance between us began to tug our bond too far apart. Yesterday, we were almost separated by a stoplight, but Chel's quick reflexes saved us as she swerved off the road to wait for the light to turn green.

I turned my focus back on my date. "So how do you know Chel?"

"I run the lights for the theater department."

"That's you?" I was impressed. "The lights are always so amazingly in sync. I thought they hired a professional."

His smile grew into appreciation, the one that comes when you stroke an ego. "Thanks," he said. "I love doing it."

He stepped to the side and gallantly waved for me to climb into the SUV, as if he was one of the actors he lit the stage for. "Shall we start this date?"

A small giggle escaped my amused lips. I was starting to like this Steve. Maybe I was vain, prejudging a guy on his looks alone. Kyle, the most attractive guy at the high school, was first in line when it came to horrendous mistakes. Thankfully, he was still on vacation with his family, and I pushed him clean out of my mind.

"Yes, let's." I crawled into the back seat, and Steve walked around to the other side. Chel and her date Ivan said hello to me from the front seat, before continuing with their conversation.

As soon as Steve entered the car, a burning itch assaulted my nose. I tried breathing through my mouth, but the Old Spice clinging to his skin was like a thick cloud around my face. It was impossible not to smell or taste it.

I sneezed. "Sorry. Allergies." *I wish.*

I held my breath until my eyes watered and another sneeze exploded from me. I ducked my head in embarrassment, and rolled down my window. The fresh air helped, some, but it was freezing. Chel gave me a worried glance and mouthed, "Are you okay?"

I nodded, intent on making this work. I was simply running out of time.

As soon as we reached the bowling alley, I hopped out of the car before Steve had unbuckled. I caught the frown on his face, but if I'd waited for him to open my door, I might have sneezed all over him.

The clanging of bowling balls hitting the lane was deafening from the front door. Before entering, I quickly ran through filtering out the louder sounds like Beast had taught me.

Steve's smell wasn't as concentrated in the bowling alley, but the smell of secondhand smoke and old shoes clogged my throat, choking me. In my panic, my concentration on filtering sounds broke, and they came thundering at me like crashing brass symbols hitting my eardrum. I cried out in agony, and my knees buckled beneath me, sending me to the floor. Chel rushed to my side. With a hand clutching my throat, I pointed to the exit.

"Steve. Ivan. Help me get her out of here. She can't breathe." Chel hooked me around the middle and struggled to lift me. I tried to help but black spots danced around my vision. Then there was a stronger tug and soon fresh air filled my lungs. Well, almost fresh.

The spicy hot of Steve's deodorant sent me into a coughing fit, but I was breathing!

"Is she all right?" Ivan asked. He was also a beanpole, with startling amber eyes.

"She'll be fine." I heard Chel's response through my coughing.

"I think she might need a doctor," Steve said.

Beast's humor was clear through the bond, and he whispered, "Your lessons, Tayla."

I wanted to growl at him, but he was right. I need to learn to control my senses, since my wolf was determined to ruin everything. I thought back to my mandatory lessons. But nothing I'd experienced was this strong and pressing. No, I'd have to mask it, and try to make it home. I pressed my nose into Chel's wrist, knowing she used an all-natural perfume. The scent was heavenly, but it didn't keep Steve's scent from tainting everything around him. I looked up to see worry in his opal eyes.

"No." I coughed out. "It was just the smoke in there." I gave a weak smile between coughs. I took a deep breath of Chel's natural scent before adding. "Sorry. Want to hang out somewhere else?"

The group looked at me like I was nuts, but Steve finally said, "I guess we could just skip to dinner."

"Sounds great," I said, using up the last of my air. I stepped in the car's direction and gulped air before Steve could contaminate it. When I heard no one following me, I looked back at three confused faces. "Come on, I'm starving."

Steve finally broke the staring contest and shrugged. "Let's go."

Too soon, Steve was there opening my door and making my eyes water. I leaned as far away from him as I could without being too noticeable and breathed deeply the sweet outside air, before plunging into the fiery furnace of nostril torment. Steve climbed in the other side and shut the door. I grimaced as his scent swirled like scorching tentacles burning me. I pushed my wolf as far into her cage as I could, but she was already there. It was the venom in my blood that was changing my body to be more like her. And that scent was too powerful for me to ignore it.

Crap!

If I ever went out with him again, I'd have to either have him stop using that deodorant or I'd have to wear a respirator. That'd put the romance in the moment. I snorted. A shot of fire-scented air singed my nose hairs. My face scrunched, holding back a cry of pain.

In the rearview mirror, I saw Chel's eyebrow rise at my grimace. But I signaled I was fine. Our gazes held. She was probably debating whether or not to end the date. I shook my head. She gave me an irritated look, but started the car. I knew she hated to see me suffer.

We didn't even make it to dinner before I felt like I had snorted a whole bottle of cayenne pepper. My eyes watered like a broken dam, and I couldn't stop my thunderous sneezes from announcing my losing battle. After a while, Chel stopped accepting my reassurances that I was okay and looked over her shoulder. I must have looked pretty pathetic because she instantly turned the car toward Grandma's house.

"I'm really sorry!" I hollered over my shoulder as I bolted from the car.

My nose burned so badly I wanted to stuff ice chips up it. Stepping into Grandma's house, I found Beast leaning against the kitchen wall as if he hadn't seen every terrible incident tonight. I aimed for the ice in the freezer, but skidded to a halt when my nose directed me in another direction—to Beast.

His soothing smell coated my nose like a liquid Band-Aid, filling my senses with sweet relief. I stepped closer to him, breathing deeply until my body brushed his and my nose hovered inches from his aroma saturated neck. I closed my eyes, reveling in his heavenly scent. I barely heard Beast's intake of breath, but I did notice his slight shiver and low satisfied growl. My wolf rumbled with pleasure.

"You smell so good." I inhaled the cool earthen scent, and the burning in my nose dulled completely. I closed my eyes and took another deep breath, moaning as the tang of musky wildness permeated my surroundings. My cheeks flushed, but I couldn't step away from him. His scent called to me. My nose brushed his skin and my hands found the small of his back. A tickle of breath warmed my face, as he leaned his head toward mine, his hold on his emotions slipping as well. Not that I minded one bit.

"Control your wolf, Tayla," Beast commanded in a husky voice, taking a small step back. "Look at me."

I shook my head, unsure what I would do next if I did. The desire to wrap myself in his arms was too great. Maybe biting a werewolf wasn't such a bad idea...

"Look at me!" The alpha authority in his voice vibrated through my head and wolf, and my eyes shot up to meet his.

He let out a slow, controlled breath, taking another step backward. "Your eyes are streaked ice blue."

"What?" My eyes had always been green.

"Your wolf is taking more control of you. The change is close." Beast's face was strained, and his eyes held ancient sadness. He turned to face the moon shining through the window.

My mind reeled. No, I needed more time. Despair swam through me for only a second, before it was pushed aside by much stronger sensations—attraction and the need to be comforted. My wolf encouraged me to act on my desire, and my resolve to leave crumbled. Boldly, I stepped in front of him, blocking the moon's light, demanding his attention. My hands moved to his chest, exploring the fine lines of his muscles. His body tensed under my touch, but it was his eyes that caught my attention.

"Your eyes are streaked silver." My voice was silky and coy, and I felt my self-control slip. My body ached for him to hold me back, and I longed for his full lips on mine. I wrapped my arms around his neck and reached up on tiptoe. His heart thrummed like a hummingbird against mine. Our lips touched for a teasing second before he jerked his head to the side, shattering the moment.

"Tayla, you need to go to bed." He untangled my arms from his neck, and they slid back to his chest. "Now."

"What?" My senses picked up on the spicy scent of his arousal, heightening mine. I laid my head against his chest, enjoying the swish of blood through his heart.

"Tayla, please." He groaned softly and his hands lifted my chin so our eyes could meet. Fear squeezed my heart. If he pushed me away, I was sure it would break me. His internal struggle played out in his churning eyes. His lips pursed in a hard, determined line, and I couldn't breathe. He was rejecting me. My eyes misted and while his face said one thing, his hands revolted, weaving his fingers through mine, tugging me close.

"No." His mouth whispered his reluctance, but I knew he wanted me and that alone triggered my determination.

I leaned into him, allowing his smell to wash over me again. Closing my eyes, I nuzzled my way up his chest to the hairy flesh of his neck, stopping just below his jaw. Beast trembled ever so slightly, sending a zing through my hyperactive nerves. I opened my mouth to kiss his neck, but my wolf seized control, licking the underside of his jaw instead and nipping it quickly with my teeth.

His pleasure jolted through the bond, and I purred, pressing my lips into the soft underside of his jaw. He jerked back as if my lips had burned him. The cool air hit my overly flushed body like a wet towel. I gasped.

His molten honey eyes, swirled with decadent silver strands, gazed into mine, and I ached to have him pressed against me again. "Tay, this isn't you. I can feel your wolf calling mine."

I smiled seductively, taking a step closer. My voice a silky purr. "Give in." I gazed up at him through my eyelashes. "We'll make you happy you did."

"Enough." He harshly growled and walked toward the door.

With Beast at a distance, my mind finally caught up to my actions, and I slammed my wolf back into her prison. Had I really just licked him? Nipped him? My cheeks reddened and my eyes sought the ground, as the ramification of my actions become clear.

I wanted to die.

"Forgive me, I should've told you this sooner. I just didn't know how to tell you without it being—awkward." Beast stumbled for words.

Surprised that *he* was apologizing, I peeked up through my eyelashes and found him staring out at the moon lit sky.

"What're you saying?" My voice came out timid, afraid of more rejection. It was silly, since on some level I was glad he'd stopped me, but the pain of his rejection was still raw in my chest.

He ran a hand through his dark hair in a very human gesture. "From the very beginning, our bond has been stronger than I've experienced with anyone else. I didn't know why at first, but now…" He trailed off.

The suspense was killing me. "Spit it out already."

"My wolf…he…" Beast fidgeted uneasily, turning slightly to face me. I would've found it comical, had my heart not stopped beating. "He's claimed you as his mate." He finished in one hurried breath. "I didn't even know he could do that. With the other girls it was only the curse that linked us."

I stood paralyzed to the spot, staring at his half-turned chest. *Claimed?* The shock blanked my mind. The silence seemed to stretch into eternity. Finally, he stepped back toward me and lifted my head to his worried eyes, breaking me from my frozen state. I was hyperaware of his warm hand under my chin, like the touch of a lost lover. Was none of it real? My heart pulsed with pain.

"No," I said, to both myself and Beast, shaking his hand off. "I'm not even a wolf yet! And even if I was, I'm no one's to *claim.*"

His face clouded with sorrow. "I'm sorry, Tayla."

There was a part of me that still wanted him, needed his arms around me and his warmth once again seeping into my flesh, but the non-wolf part of me reeled. Being property might be acceptable to my wolf, but not to me. I wouldn't be trapped, caged, or forced to be some animal's mate, even if I was attracted to him. I wasn't even sure how much of that was actually me. I glared at him, infuriated by the chauvinistic claim, yet my wolf found her mate mouthwatering, and that part of me was now almost impossible to control. I'd just witnessed that. I refused to be a wolf forever, even if my refusal meant I couldn't be with Beast.

15

PROBLEMS WITH SHAVING

Monday, April 23

I hated that I wasn't twenty-one and allowed to bar hop. Sunday was wasted, no dates. Seriously, I needed a fake ID. Maybe if Beast took me they wouldn't card me. Hmm...the thought had possibilities.

The quiet purr of Chel's SUV pulled up the driveway. *Hopefully, Chel has some tricks up her sleeves other than this list of available guys she emailed me.* I stared at the computer screen and sighed. It just felt wrong, like I was judging them according to their online dating profile. Which I was, but I couldn't shake the feeling that I was looking for a mail-order date or something equally shallow. *How do I really get to know someone from just a photo or Chel's quick notes?*

Chel burst in to my room. "Good news!"

"Geez, Chel." I covered my ears like she'd just fired a gun next to my head. "Do you have to yell?"

She slapped a hand over her mouth. "Sorry," she muffled between her fingers before removing her hand.

"It's fine. It was my fault really. I loosened my hold on my wolf to hear you pull up and forgot to rein her back when you came through the door." I got up from my desk.

"Will that always be a problem? Because, I'm not naturally a quiet person." Chel's lips pinched together in a frown.

I laughed. "Boy, do I know that."

"Shut up." She pushed me, grinning.

"No, Beast said I'll get better at controlling it. But I'm hoping this date thing works and I don't have to learn how to control it, y'know?" I shoved my hands in my jean pockets.

Chel gave me a coy smile. "Hence my loud entrance. I found you a date for tonight!"

I squealed and threw my arms around her. "You're the best!"

"I know." Chel's blue eyes sparkled under the praise.

"So when's the date?" I released her from the hug and sat on the bed with my feet tucked to the side.

"Seven thirty."

"Perfect."

She flung her school bag on my bed, pinching my feet under her ton of books.

"Ouch!" I pulled my feet out from under the crushing weight.

"Sorry." She placed the pack farther from me and sat down.

"So." She turned her back and fumbled in her bag. "We have to pick him up in forty-five minutes. Time to prep." She turned holding up a large makeup bag in one hand and a lacy push-up bra in the other.

"Whoa." I pushed the hand holding the bra away. "For one, I don't need that, and for two, can't I just be me?" Flashes of the disaster at the party and the horror of last week's dates crept into my mind. I had to admit that Beast had a point: dressing like a slut hadn't worked—especially since Beast's wolf obviously had a problem with his mate attracting other males. My mood instantly soured.

Mate. I scoffed in my mind. Could this freak show get any more complicated?

"It will still be you, just with a little more perk." She winked.

Heat flushed my cheeks—the subject had to change. "So who's your date?" Every disastrous date replayed in my mind. I didn't want to jinx myself by asking about this one.

Her smirk faded, and she shifted uncomfortably. "I don't have one."

"What?" My heart flipped and pumped into overdrive. "I can't do this alone! You have to come." Panic made my tone sharp. "What if my wolf does something weird again and I can't control her? You won't be there to laugh it off as nothing."

She winced. "I'm sorry. I had one, but Taren bailed. Something about unexpected family coming into town." She rolled her eyes, conveying she thought he was lying through his teeth. She flipped her hair over her shoulder as if it was nothing, but I knew my best friend well enough to know the rejection hurt.

"He wasn't worth your time anyway." I knocked shoulders with her. "Doesn't he play the trumpet or something? Those guys always spray spit when they talk," I said in my best Daffy Duck impersonation.

"Eww!" She wiped spittle off her cheek and pushed me away with a laugh. "You're so gross!"

"Seriously, though, there has to be someone else. I've never seen you unable to snag a date." I pled with my eyes.

She smiled thoughtfully. "That's true on the weekends, but it's Monday. Do you have any idea how hard it is to get a date during the week? Studying for the Thursday, Friday test load is brutal." She smacked her backpack for emphasis.

Worrying about school. It felt like a different life-time for me. Had it only been a little over three weeks since the day Beast showed up and ruined my life? My head throbbed with the beginning of a headache. My brows puckered together as if that could stop the pain. *I'm so out of my league. How did I ever think I could do this? I don't have Chel's seductress skills. Even Chel knows I need the stupid bra just to have a chance. I've blown every other chance.*

Chel's soft arm wrapped around my shoulder, pulling me from my growing despair. "Don't look like that. Andy is really nice. You'll have a great date."

I jerked my head up. "Andy wasn't on the list. Where did you find him?"

"Geez, Tayla you make it sound like I grabbed the first bum I saw." She stood, appalled, with hands on her hips. "You know it wouldn't kill you to say thank you."

I shrunk away like I was the worst friend ever. "Sorry" was on the tip of my tongue when intuition kicked in and her over-reaction made sense. She was hiding something.

My brow rose and I apprehensively asked, "Who exactly is this *Andy?*"

Chel rubbed her arm, carefully avoiding my eyes. "He's really nice, and—"

"Chel," I said sternly, my patience gone.

"You have to understand." She shifted her weight from foot to foot. "I didn't really have a lot to choose from."

I glared at her timid expression. "Spill it, Chel."

"It's Cindy Flatterson's twin." She slapped her mouth close.

My eyes went wide and she flinched. A spark of an image flashed in my head of a dark haired girl with ponytails and thick bottle glasses resting on a freckled nose standing by a male who looked just like her."Oh, no, no, no!" My hands waved as if to ward off a repugnant animal. "He's a *freshman*, probably just turned fifteen. And have you seen how greasy his hair is? And those glasses, you could start a fire with them."

"Come on, Tay. He's really nice and you never know where your true love is hiding." She tried to keep a straight face, but it crumbled behind her hand in a giggle. "I mean, look at Beast. You'd never know he was yummy unless you looked a little closer."

I smacked her. "This is serious." Not to mention that my wolf's hackles went up at her mere reference to Beast.

Chel struggled to look contrite, but failed as her lips curled into a smile.

"You're impossible!" I stood and paced the room, pulling on a lock of my hair.

"I'm sorry, Tay." She walked to me, putting a hand out to stop me, but I jerked away. "Really, it was the best I could do. You should've seen his face light up when I asked him."

"Probably because it's his first date, *ever*." I glared at her.

"And it's only your fifth." She glared back, her foot tapping in exasperation. "You have no room to judge."

I exhaled a ragged breath. *How bad could it be?* I couldn't fool myself. It would be like taking a little brother to the park. My eyes landed on the white bra.

I snorted. "What were you trying to do, give him a heart attack with that thing?" I pointed to the unmentionable.

The sly smile on her face said it all.

"I can't believe you!" I threw my hands in the air.

"A little excitement never hurt anyone." Her eyebrow rose, clearly exasperated.

"Arrgg!" I plunked down on one of the chairs I stole from the kitchen. "You can forget it. I'm not going."

"You can't break his heart like that." She gave me her puppy-dog eyes, but even that didn't work.

"No." I crossed my arms. "I'd rather date the mummies at the museum!"

"He'll never date again. How can you ruin him like that?" Her teeth teased her bottom lip. "And it will be all my fault for trying to help you. Come on, isn't it at least worth a try?"

I felt my irritation dissipate to guilt. She wasn't playing fair.

"Fine, but you have to go with me. I don't care if you are the third wheel." I leveled an I'm-not-budging-on-this look at her. "I refuse to be alone with him."

"I'm hurt." Beast's voice came from behind me. I jumped, spinning around to face the door. "How could you forget me? And after everything we've been through together? Did it all mean nothing to you?" He winked, and his hinting at me crawling into his bed, licking him, and other moments I wanted to forget made my cheeks blaze with heat. He wasn't going to let me live those moments down.

There was no way I wanted Chel hearing about any of that.

"Oh, don't you start!" I pushed him toward the door. "Now get out of my room."

He chuckled. "Oh, but you can come into mine?"

I glanced back at Chel, whose eyes widened. "It's not like it sounds," I said.

"From that blush, I know you're lying," Chel said.

I sighed, knowing I'd have to spill the details or she'd badger me all night. "I walked in my sleep, and my stupid wolf had me climb into bed with him."

"How did you miss telling me this?" Her eyes twinkled.

"Nothing happened. No one needed to know." I gave Beast a pointed glare. His smile broadened, and Chel let out a muffled laugh.

"Ah! You both are impossible! Fine. Laugh all you want, I'm out of here." I stomped out of the room to start doing my hair for the stupid date.

"Oh come on, Tay," Chel said as she trailed me into the bathroom. "It *was* funny."

"No, it's mortifying." I ripped a brush through my hair, not caring how many spilt ends it produced.

She rolled her eyes at me. "It couldn't have been that bad. All those muscles..." A dreamy look draped her eyes.

"If you think he's so hot, why don't you try being chained to him!" I clutched the counter. If I was a dragon, I'd be snorting steam. She didn't get it! I *couldn't* fall in love with Beast. And my attraction for him was only jeopardizing my chances of stopping the she-wolf from taking over my body—my body! All Chel saw was muscles, not the curse that had stolen my life. I yanked on the brush, now tangled in my hair.

"That's perfect!" Chel clasped her hands in front of her.

"My hair isn't even done." I gestured to the tangled mess.

"Not your hair, silly." Chel's eyes sparkled, and she went to work on freeing the brush. "Beast has to be around on your date, so why not have him stand in as my date?"

I whipped around, ripping the brush from my hair and pulling a chunk free. I didn't even flinch. "You have got to be kidding!"

"It's a perfect solution." Her stubborn lips pressed together.

We glared at each other. My wolf snarled in my mind, and the jealousy coursing through my veins was like black poison. This was a horribly bad idea. I opened my mouth to tell her so, but Beast's voice startled me.

"I'd be honored." Beast reached around me and took her hand. Chel giggled and batted her eyelashes in a shy-flirtatious way. My hackles rose.

"This is wrong on so many levels."

"Just because you don't want him, doesn't mean he can never date." Chel flashed me a what's-your-problem look.

I felt like a semi-truck had just plowed into me. I looked from Chel, whose lips curled seductively, to Beast, whose handsome smile would melt any girl.

"Are you crazy! Have you looked at his face? You can't take him out in public like that." My angry words sliced the air. Chel looked like I'd just slapped her across the face, and Beast's knowing grin was maddening. He knew this was driving my wolf crazy. *Stupid bond!*

Chel straightened her spine. "Don't be rude. It isn't like he asked for these deformities." She pulled Beast past me, to the toilet where she pointed for him to sit. "A nice warm shave, and I'll be the envy of every girl in the town."

I knew I'd hurt her if I said anything else, but this just didn't feel right. Wrongness stirred in my gut like a witch's brew. Chel pulled a towel from the cupboard to her left and draped it around Beast. She leaned her chest into him to clip the towel behind his neck. White-knuckled, I gripped the counter like I was hanging from a cliff. Chel's finger skimmed his jaw as she leaned back, and my wolf snarled. A sound escaped my lips, low enough that only Beast noticed. He flicked me a sideways glance, probably wondering if I was about to tackle my best friend. I closed my eyes, realizing how close I was to doing just that.

"I do this for my dad all the time. So don't be scared." She winked at him.

"It won't last more than a few hours, but no, I'm not scared." Beast chuckled, and the sound made me nearly deranged. Those were my chuckles! I sucked in a painful lung-full of air. It burned as I held my breath.

I heard shaving cream squirting into Chel's hand, and my eyes popped open. I had to stop this. "I'd be scared. Her dad became a tissue face after all the nicks she inflicted." I'd seen the pictures in her photo album.

"Ah!" Her mouth popped open, aghast. "I was ten. And it was my first attempt!"

The irrational waves of anger continued to roll off me, and my wolf rammed out of her cage. "And why do you have all your dad's shaving supplies?" I demanded. "You planned this! You betrayed me. He is *mine* and you're trying to steal him, you...you...slut."

Her face reddened like a traffic light and her breath hitched. "How dare you call me that! Maybe I was prepared to shave your hairy pits. Ever thought of that? I've worked hard to get you dates, you..." her frame shook and her hands fisted into balls, "...selfish dog."

My hold on my wolf snapped, and I lunged at her, my nails ready to claw her eyes out. But my face slammed into the stone chest of Beast before I could reach her.

"Get out of my way!" I struggled to get out of his steel-like arms, my wolf thrashing in my head.

"Tayla," he said in a commanding voice. "She isn't a threat."

I clawed at his arms. His words slowly trickled through the fury clouding my mind. I disagreed.

"She touched you." My wolf and I growled through clenched teeth. "No one touches you but me!"

"She isn't a threat!" His alpha power slammed into me like high-pressured water, knocking the wind out of me. This time, his words stopped my struggling. His power caused my wolf to bow—mate or not.

I whimpered like a dog afraid of a beating, and slumped in his arms. My head pounded like a spiked ball bounced around in my skull.

"It hurts."

"I'm sorry, Tay." He cradled me to his chest in a standing hug, stroking my hair. "I shouldn't have baited you."

The sound of quick intakes of breath reached my ears. I tilted my head to see around Beast's bulk. Chel was huddled against the tub, tears streaming out of her wide eyes.

Her chalk white face pierced my heart. *I did that.*

"Chel." My voice broke. "I'm so sorry. I...I..." nothing excused my behavior, even if it was mostly my wolf. I knew I'd been jealous, too. I reached a hand out to her, but a strangled sound came from her lips and she pressed harder against the tub. I closed my eyes against the pain, and my hand fell back to my side.

I'm a monster. How could I have wanted to hurt her?

"Forgive me, Chel," Beast said, in a soothing voice. "I shouldn't have acted like I did. It was wrong and selfish of me to want to see the fire in her eyes and know it was for me."

"You used me?" Chel's voice was so sad that I bit the inside of my cheek to keep the sob at bay.

"It wasn't my intention. Tayla is my mate, and my wolf is...jealous." Beast hung his head, pressing it into the top of mine. Did he need to calm his wolf, too?

Chel pulled out of her fetal position. "What do you mean mate? Like you know...sex?"

I blushed. "His wolf has only put a claim on me. It isn't like that, yet."

Her brow arched. "Yet. As in, in the future you will consummate it or something?"

"Chel!" I blanched.

"I'm just curious. After all you nearly ripped off my head just for touching him."

My gaze fell to the ground. "I'm so sorry. I didn't mean those things I said. You're like my sister. I would do anything to keep from hurting you. But my wolf is stronger when it comes to Beast.

She...likes her mate choice and will fight to keep him. And if she wins and I become a wolf, I won't have a say in who she mates with—not a real say anyway."

I pressed into Beast, needing his strength. His arms tightened in response. My wolf was still restless, but having his body pressed against mine was calming her down. I had to get her back into her cage before I could go to Chel.

"That...kind of sucks." Her eyes met mine. "But why didn't you tell me?" There was a trace of hurt in her voice. "And why are your eyes a freaky blue?"

"They're her eyes."

Her lips made an "oh" shape.

I didn't want to linger on my color-shifting eyes, so I answered her other question. "And I didn't know how to tell you." My lips twisted into a rude grin. "I was hoping it wouldn't be an issue. Obviously, I was wrong."

She chuckled darkly. "Obviously." She stood and brushed off her butt. "Well, I think I better let you shave him, if you still want to do this double date. And I promise to keep my hands to myself. I'd like to keep them attached."

I grimaced but nodded. "Thanks, Chel. I really am sorry."

"Don't worry. We are still working out this whole werewolf thing. Accidents are bound to happen, right?" She tried for a brave front, but her hands still shook and I heard her heart race.

"There's orange juice in the fridge. I think you need the whole quart. You look like you're going into shock," I said.

"Yeah, I think you're right." She walked out the door, leaving me alone with Beast.

I squeezed Beast's torso with my arms, burrowing my head into the security I found there. I was going to fail. I was already losing my hold over my wolf. The change was coming. *How was I going to find true love when I couldn't even find a guy to ask me on a second date?* A single tear rolled down my cheek.

What if there wasn't a cure, and I was just endangering everyone

16
STALEMATE

I sat in the back of Chel's SUV. We were almost to my date's house, but I couldn't shake the foreboding cloud dampening my mood. Deep down I knew this night was a mistake. I'd lost control and was still shaken about it. I looked at Chel in the driver's seat, chatting away with Beast. She always amazed me in how fast she could bounce back. After I'd calmed my wolf, I had gone to the kitchen and apologized again, but she cut me off, and insisted we get ready for the date—a date that for some odd reason required tennis shoes instead of flip flops or high heels. But Chel refused to spill the details, saying, "You'll have fun. Trust me."

Beast chuckled. He looked so relaxed with his arm resting on the console between them. He wore a ball cap instead of his hooded coat, and except for his flattened nose, he looked almost normal now that he was shaved. That had been a daunting task.

Thankfully, after the first three nicks I inflicted on his chin, he'd eagerly snatched the razor from me and finished it himself. I didn't blame him. I couldn't hold my hand steady after what had happened.

Chel gave me fleeting glances in the rearview mirror. Someone who didn't know her well would think she was her normal bubbly self, but I noticed how she leaned as far away from Beast as possible, nervous I might attack again.

Geez. What kind of person attacks her best friend over a guy? Wolf or no, nothing excuses that. Maybe I should just let the change take me. If I'm dead, I won't endanger the people I love, and this silly parade of dates would end—permanently.

"Tayla." Beast's harsh voice reverberated through the vehicle. He looked over his shoulder with silver streaked eyes. "Never think that."

I couldn't bring myself to care that he had just tapped into my suicidal emotions. "You know it's the truth."

Beast growled and the vein in his neck bulged from the strain to keep his wolf under control. Chel gave me worried glances as we weaved through town.

"That isn't the girl I know. The girl who stood up to a werewolf to keep her life. Now you are willing to throw it away? Kill yourself just like that?"

Chel gasped. "Tay, no. How could you even think that?"

I snorted my internal disgust. My eyes brimmed with tears as I thought about what could have happened. "She would have killed you," I barely whispered as I referenced the wolf inside me.

"That would never happen." Beast's low voice was full of promise. "I'd never allow it."

"But even you lose control. How will you stop me from losing control as the full moon approaches and you yourself are struggling to dominate your wolf?" I sagged with the weight of how easily a wolf could kill.

"You take precautions, Tayla. Now stop this," Beast commanded.

Chel threw me an encouraging smile. "Besides, Tay, you're going to break out of this. I know you will. I'll just keep finding you dates!"

The sincerity of her pleading eyes touched me. "I don't know what I'd do without you, Chel."

"We will conquer this together. Sisters forever." She pulled up to my date's house. "And smile, this could be your dream guy."

Beast and I snorted at the same time. That sent Chel and me into laughter, and Beast smirked. When the laugher quieted, Chel honked, and my stomach knotted in dread. I reminded myself that Beast was here and would stop me if my wolf got out of control again. I had to trust him.

Andy Flatterson walked out of his house. My night vision didn't miss that his dark hair was slicked back and his stride was confident. He wore a crisp button-up shirt tucked into jeans that were two sizes too big and held up with a belt that barely kept them on his nonexistent hips. Had his mom taken him shopping for a new wardrobe just for this date? He wasn't even wearing his glasses. Was he blind or did he get contacts, too?

I was slightly in shock when he opened the door and slid in. "Hey guys."

From the grin on his face, I knew Chel had been right; not going on this date would've crushed him. Little did he know that his date was turning into a werewolf and was likely to bite him before the night was over.

"Hey Andy! Wow, you look...nice." Chel turned in her seat to see him better.

"You don't look too bad yourself." He gave her a wink.

I rolled my eyes. *Oh man, this is going to be a long night.* It was like he'd watched *Grease* and *Dangerous Minds* too many times and thought the perfect style was a mixture of the two. Someone really needed to help the poor kid with some fashion sense.

To Chel's credit, she didn't release the chortle she struggled to swallow. "You know Tayla." Chel gestured to me as an introduction. He took that as a cue to check me out.

His lips tilted in an overconfident smile. "Hey, babe."

"Tayla, not babe." I wanted to slap him back to normal, but I promised Chel I'd behave. Thankfully, I still had at least that much self-control left.

His cocky act slipped into doubt for a brief second, until he plastered it back on. "You got it, *Tayla.*"

My lips tugged into a tight smile. A small giggle escaped Chel before she could hide it under a cough. "And this is my date, B...Ben." She stumbled but recovered nicely. Beast gave her a raised eyebrow, and she blushed slightly with embarrassment. But she was right. We couldn't introduce him as Beast. That was just a little too weird for this small town.

"I haven't seen you around. Do you go to Northwest?" Andy buckled, and Chel pulled away from the curb.

Beast briefly glanced over his shoulder at Andy, showing his profile in the light of the streetlamps. "No, just visiting."

"Dude, what happened to your nose?"

Did this guy have no common courtesy? I opened my mouth to defend Beast, but to my surprise, Beast answered. "Snowboarding accident. As you can see, the mountain got the better of me."

"That's harsh. Must've been a nasty wipeout." Andy sat forward, eager for the details, but Beast shrugged like it was no big deal.

"Not much of a story. I fell and there just happened to be a rock there to break my fall." Beast lied so smoothly he almost had me believing.

"Don't they have plastic surgery for that?" Andy asked, and Beast's jaw twitched as if he gritted his teeth.

My wolf's hackles went up, mirroring my own feelings. This little brat was getting on my nerves and the night had barely started.

"So are you going to tell me what we are doing?" I directed my question to Chel, interrupting the boys' conversation.

She flashed me a teasing grin in the rearview mirror. "It's going to be so fun. You have on your tennis shoes, right?"

I arched a brow at her. She knew I had them on. She'd forced my feet into them and tied the laces. But before I could snap at that stupid question, Andy spoke.

"If you don't, I'll happily carry you." He winked at me, as if the notion was exactly what he wanted. I doubted he could even lift me.

I picked up my foot. "Got them right here. See?"

There was no way I could love him, but maybe that wasn't required. Maybe I only needed him to fall in love with me? I peeked sideways at him. Nope, there was no way even the hope of a spark between us existed. He was just a fun lovin' kid, out for a good time and possibly a kiss or two. My wolf lounged in her mental cage, giving no indication that she even saw Andy. That right there proved that he was as close to eliminating her as I was to jumping to the moon.

Andy didn't miss a beat in responding. "Awesome, now we'll be the first to catch the flag."

"The what?"

"Andy!" Chel chided, and it only piqued my interest.

"What?" He raised his hands in mock innocence. "My partner has to get her head in the game if we're going to beat the other team."

"I thought we were going to the movies?" I asked, even though I had no desire to ever step back into that movie house again. I was sure it was jinxed with bad karma after the first two incidents.

"You don't really want to see a boring movie over—"

"Do I turn here?" Chel interrupted.

Andy nodded his head. "Yup, and then you go for about a quarter of a mile before turning left."

I glanced around, noticing we were on the edge of town. "Why are we outside of town?"

I trusted Chel, but I couldn't handle surprises right now. My hands clutched the seat. Predictable was good, especially today when I needed to know what was coming in order to gauge my wolf's response.

"Not knowing is half the fun," Chel said as she turned behind the airport. Beast's face twitched as if he held back a smile.

I folded my arms, annoyed that I was the only one that didn't know what we were doing. "I'm not getting out of this car until someone explains what we're doing." No one answered, and my anxiety built. I needed to know—to prepare myself for my wolf's reaction. "I mean it. Someone had better tell me *right now.*"

Beast swiveled in his seat to look at me. "Tayla. You'll be fine." His rich voice leeched away my anxiety and I relaxed into the seat.

I caught a glimpse of the silver in Beast's eyes, and suddenly I felt betrayed. "Stop that!" I hissed through my teeth.

Beast had the good sense to look guilty about using his alpha powers on me. He nodded once in acknowledgment before turning his full attention to the road. But now I had Chel tapping a nervous beat on the steering wheel with her fingernails, and Andy looking at me like I'd lost my mind. Maybe I wouldn't have to endure a kiss from him after all. Who'd want to fall in love with a paranoid lunatic? Because that's what I looked like.

"Sorry. I just don't like surprises," I lied, my words directed toward Andy, unwilling to speak freely about my wolf issues.

No one said anything, except for when Chel asked Andy for further instructions that had us circling around to the backside of Beacon Hill. It was easy to remember the name since a metal tower sat atop it, supporting a large twirling light that warned planes of the hill.

Soon we were pulling up in a long line of vehicles all centered around one house.

"That's my friend Chuck's house." Andy pointed to the doublewide home.

Chel parked, and we all approached the house, but Andy didn't head for the door. Instead he grabbed my hand and raced us around back. At the first whiff of horses, I stopped breathing. Beast brushed my arm. I sent him a panicked look. My wolf senses were on high alert.

"Just focus on something else. Push the animals away from your mind," Beast coached me as we entered the corral. My wolf panted with the eagerness of the hunt, and my empty stomach ached for relief. My free hand went to my stomach, and I licked my lips. Instantly, I knew there were five horses around me, a full pigeon coop at the side of the house, three dogs in the backyard, and ten teenagers at the base of Beacon Hill.

"Don't think of your hunger. You have to distract yourself." Beast's voice was no more than the sound of a shoe rubbing against carpet, but I heard it clearly.

I focused on Andy's grip on my hand and the excited bumping of his heart. The swoosh of blood filled my ears and saliva pooled in my mouth. My body trembled from my wolf asserting her will on mine. Just when I felt my control slip, Beast's large finger parted my lips and purposely grazed my teeth—hard. Several drops of tangy, sweet blood coated my tongue and I quickly wrapped my tongue around the bleeding finger. I swallowed, and the blood jolted through my system like a mega dose of protein, silencing my hunger. The finger ripped from my closed lips as fast as it had entered.

The loss was so intense and fast that I whimpered.

"Tayla?" Andy stopped to look at me, releasing my hand. "Are you hurt?"

Yes. I wanted to say. It was like part of my soul had been ripped away. I shook my head. "I just need to tie my shoe. You go on ahead. I'll catch up."

"Make sure I'm on a good team." Chel teased from right beside me. "Because I'm going steal that flag right out from under their noses."

"Ha! You can try." He flashed a huge grin before heading toward the group of kids picking teams for a game of Capture the Flag.

With Andy far away and the horses huddled against the far fence, my mind cleared. I shuddered with repulsion and closed my eyes, counting to thirty before opening them again.

I knew Beast and Chel were staring at me, waiting for me to act. "Please tell me I didn't just drink your blood," I pled.

Beast didn't respond right away, and I was sure Chel was too horrified to speak, because I could hear her heart skip beats. I dared to glance up at Beast. He stood rigid. The only thing moving was his swirling eyes.

"Beast, please say something." I touched his arm covered in a long black tee.

"You want a lie?" He shook his head. "You know what happened." Beast's voice was low. He stepped closer, turning his back to Beacon Hill to stand right in front of me. "I had to distract you. Your self-control is sorely lacking."

I felt like I'd been slapped.

"What is he talking about?" Chel couldn't hold her curiosity any longer.

"It was the horses, at first," I breathed out, unable to believe I'd almost done it again. I'd almost bitten Andy. "Then, I tried to turn my focus on something else, but Andy's hand in mine was too much for me to ignore. If Beast hadn't *intervened* the moment he did, I'm afraid it would've been Andy's blood in my mouth and not Beast's."

Chel gagged and wiped at herself as if thousands of spiders crawled over her skin. "Ah. Tay! That is seriously nasty. How could you even swallow?"

I didn't want to admit how easy that part was, how intoxicating his blood tasted, or how soul wrenching it was to have it taken away. "What's wrong with me?"

"Nothing. It's normal for werewolves to share their blood to strengthen each other. Though, it is rare for the alpha to share his blood. I haven't done it since Jerome got tangled in a nasty bear trap last winter."

My eyes went wide. "You never mentioned the wolves in your pack by name." Except my mom. "Who's Jerome?"

"He was in the old alpha's pack and is older than I in both human and wolf terms." A thoughtful expression covered his face as if remembering good times. The silver in his eyes edged back before disappearing completely.

"I wasn't hurt, so why do it to me?"

"Think, Tayla. You know the answer."

I didn't want to admit how utterly distracting Beast's blood had been. And there was no way I was admitting it in front of Chel. She would probably dry heave. Thankfully, there were half-truths I could say in front of Chel, while still weaseling answers from Beast.

"Yes, but why did it zing through me? And I felt an incredible loneliness and despair, like my Uncle had died all over again."

"My blood is more powerful than a non-alpha. And you felt the loss more acutely because you are still human and unable to handle the intensity of it," Beast explained.

"Whoa, hold on. No one ever told me that you were an alpha." Chel eyed Beast as if she'd just seen him for the first time.

"It wasn't important." I gave her a look that said drop it, but that didn't stop her motor-mouth.

"Not important! You, like, rule a whole pack of wolves?" Chel stared at Beast, mouth slightly open.

"I don't sit on a throne and order people around." He smiled at her. "It is more responsibility than I ever wanted."

"Hey, guys, come on," Andy yelled from a good twenty yards away. "We're ready to start." The teams were comprised of both girls and boys, all freshmen from the look of it, and each team stood around the person holding their team's flag. I didn't mind that they were younger than me. In fact, it was refreshing that I didn't know any of them.

"Coming!" Chel shouted back.

So we played. The oscillating light messed with my night vision, but coupled with my other wolf senses I expertly dodged and hid from the other team until I captured their orange flag. I raced it back to my team's territory just as Beast carried our lime-green flag back to his territory.

Whoops from both teams filled the night air until it was discovered that we had a tie. So we started another round. This time, I was in charge of guarding the flag. The game progressed, and I enjoyed using my special "skills" to guard our flag. I tagged anyone who got too close and my teammates hauled them off to our "prison." I wondered why Beast hadn't tried for the flag yet, and I scanned the night for sounds of him. It wasn't long before I honed in on his steady heartbeat. He was far away, deep in his own territory. His breathing was even and I didn't notice any strong movement in this direction. He was no doubt guarding the other flag about twenty yards away.

Great, a stalemate.

Because I didn't want to stay on the hill all night, I tried to clamp down on my wolf senses, but it was just too easy to hear people tromping through sagebrush or cursing when they jumped over a bush just to land in a hole.

Boredom quickly set in. I listened to a couple of girls that were captured in my team's prison area. I was pretty sure one of their teammates had tagged them, and they were free to escape, but they sat there chatting instead—obviously bored with the game as well. It really wasn't a bad idea. I was about ready to holler for Andy to take my place when the girls switched topics from who dumped who to Danny.

"Did you see Danny this morning?" The louder girl's voice crackled in my ear. My jaw flexed under the grating noise.

"No, but I heard about how awful he looked," the other girl whispered in a soothing voice.

I stepped closer, drawn in by their conversation. What was wrong with Danny?

"It was awful. His eye was swollen shut with a nasty purple bruise."

The quiet girl shook her head. "Why would Kyle do something like that to his best friend? It's just horrible."

"I heard they were fighting over some girl." The loud girl scooted closer to whisper. "You know that one Kyle's all crazy for. What's her name?"

"Tayla," the quiet one supplied.

Hearing my name was like a sucker punch to the gut. They were talking about me. Obviously, they hadn't connected two and two together and realized I was here. But how did Kyle find out about the party? Did he have someone spying on me?

"Yeah, that's the one. I've never met her before, but she must be something to have two of the most popular boys in school fighting over her."

"Didn't she drop out of school, or something?" the quiet one asked.

Anger rumbled in my gut. "I didn't drop out," I hissed under my breath, too low for them to hear.

Suddenly, cheers erupted from the enemy's base. I jerked my head around to find my team's flag paraded above the head of a guy from the other team. *Crap!* I'd gotten distracted and someone had snatched the flag without my notice.

"Way to go, Scott!" Chel yelled, whooping with the rest of her teammates. Steam flared inside my rumbling stomach. Why hadn't Chel said anything about Danny and Kyle? I found her and led her away from the crowd.

"Why didn't you tell me Kyle was back?"

Her smile faded. "I was going to, but you went all wolf on me and I forgot."

I lowered my accusing eyes to her shoulders. "I'm sorry. I thought I'd have some warning. Did he really punch Danny?"

"Yeah, gave him a nasty black eye. I don't know why Danny puts up with it."

"I can bet Danny didn't tell him about the party. So how did he find out?" I asked.

Chel bit her lips, and I knew I wouldn't like what she was about to say. "Someone had a camera and posted pictures of you and Danny. Kyle flipped."

Natalie's vengeful eyes flashed into my mind. "That conniving, evil witch," I growled. "Natalie must have posted them."

"Sounds like her."

I rubbed my temples. "Chel, we have to get those photos off the internet." I was mortified someone had captured me parading around like a slut. The memories were bad enough, and now Kyle had seen them.

"I'm sorry, Tay." She put a hand on my arm. "They've been reposted so many times there's no way to get them all." Chel frowned with pity.

Right then Andy swung his arm over my shoulder. "Let's go get some ice cream. Winners have to pay." He grinned at Chel.

"Oh, no way, buddy." Chel pushed his shoulder, releasing me. "Losers pay and you so lost!"

Ice cream was the best idea ever. I poured hot fudge over my self-serve turtle sundae, craving a chocolate fix. Andy stepped up to the register.

"What is your order?" the lady behind the counter asked.

"We have a large pineapple sundae, a medium turtle sundae, and whatever those two are having," Andy said, digging his wallet from his back pocket. I was surprised it hadn't fallen out of those baggy jeans while we played Capture the Flag.

The lady turned her attention to Chel and Beast. Before she could ask, Beast spoke. "Thanks Andy, but I'll get ours." His lip curved into a crooked smile, and his gaze settled on me for a moment before turning to Chel. "It is a date, after all."

My wolf clawed at her cage, needing to claim what was hers. Was he intentionally making this difficult? My lips pressed hard against the growl building in my throat. I focused on fortifying the bars of the cage, but she pushed hard against me, and my temples throbbed from the effort. I scrunched my nose for only a second, but Beast noticed. The bridge between his eyes wrinkled, as if he regretted his words. I hoped that was the case. I wasn't sure how much more my wolf could take before she broke free of my restraints and tackled Chel, frightening her again.

"We'll find a seat." I took Andy by the arm as he completed the transaction and found a booth by the far window. My first bite zinged my tongue with sugar and the sweet calming taste of fudge. "Oh, this is so good. Thanks, Andy."

"No problem." He gave me a smile. "But you haven't tasted nothin' until you try this." He pointed his spoon at his ice cream. I laughed. *He really is a nice guy. Too bad I don't have romantic feelings for him, but that doesn't mean I can't have fun.*

"Get over here and let me have a bite of pineapple." I waved him over with my spoon.

He rounded the table, sliding in next to me. "You'll have to fight me for it."

I stared at him, unprepared for that comment, wondering if he meant it. He grinned and held up his spoon as if to fence with mine.

"I don't think you can snag a bite before I stop you." His boyish brown eyes laughed at me, daring me to play.

I held my spoon harder, and grinned. "Oh, I think you'll lose more than just one bite."

Spoons thunked in a plastic battle of which spoon would break first. We were laughing so hard that when we did get past each other's meager defenses and scooped ice cream we couldn't eat it, so I smashed my spoon onto his lips. His eyes widened briefly before my lips met with the same fate. Our next breaths of laughter sent ice cream flying into our hands and onto Chel and Beast who were sliding into the bench across from us.

Chel's eyes widened. "What are you, like two years old?" She dabbed her napkin at the sticky mess dotting her shirt.

Beast simply looked down at the ice cream splattered on him before looking up with a mischievous glint in his eye. "Amateurs."

He spooned some of his ice cream and catapulted it at me. I shrieked, holding my hands up to block it. The large blob hit my arm, running off it and landing on my jeans.

"You're so going to pay for that." I scooped ammunition into my spoon.

Chel's hand flew between us. "Oh, no you don't! Any messier and everyone is walking home. Besides, that," she pointed at my loaded spoon, "is good ice cream."

I glided the spoon purposely into my mouth, keeping my eyes on Beast. "You might just wake up one morning to shaving cream on your face."

He flashed me a wickedly amused grin. "You can try." His caramel eyes smoldered with intensity. "But I'd catch you." Electricity crackled between us and my wolf gnawed at the bars of her cage.

"Soooo, Andy." Chel's voice broke the connection. Thankfully. I was one breath from climbing over the table and into Beast's lap. "Have you seen any good movies lately?"

Keeping my gaze away from Beast, I listened to Andy talk about the latest video game turned blockbuster and wiped at the mess on my jeans. My cheeks hurt from smiling so much, but it was the kindling warmth in my chest that held my attention. The thought of Beast catching me in those arms and spooning me against his naked chest...

"Tayla?" A surprised voiced asked.

My head jerked up to find Kyle. The surprise in his voice didn't reach his calculating hazel eyes.

"I thought that was you." He strode over to us, dragging a chair to the end of the table where the boys sat. I was suddenly very thankful for my window seat. I turned my gaze on him. How did he always find me? It was like he had tagged me with a locater device. Movement outside the window caught my eye. A tall figure crossed the road. There was something familiar about him. He stepped onto the far sidewalk and glanced over his shoulder with icy promise in his eyes.

Danny! His face was swollen on the side that sported a black eye. I sucked in a breath, and Danny moved quickly out of view.

"Tayla?" Kyle tapped my hand on the table. I quickly snatched it off the table and into my lap.

I glared at Kyle. Somehow, I was not afraid. The wolf inside me ached to tear him apart. "You're not wanted here. Go away."

A twitch of his lips was the only indicator that he'd heard my harsh words. "Come on, Tay. You can't still be mad at me. I said I was sorry about our last date, and I meant it."

"Oh, and what about Danny?" I threw my barb. He was never going to get his hooks in me again. Kyle flinched and his eyes dropped to the table. But I wasn't going to fall for his act. "And don't act like you care."

His head snapped up, eyes hard with anger. "Danny is my best friend! Of course I care."

"Cared enough to hit him?" My wolf's hackles were up, responding to my unease.

"It was an accident." Kyle leaned back on his chair, reclaiming his relaxed posture, but he wasn't fooling anyone. I could hear his heart hammering like a bongo drum. "Danny knows that. Besides, he knew the risks when he touched you."

I saw Beast's hand clench the table and knew Kyle had better leave before one or the other of us made him.

"Don't make it sound like you were defending my honor or something stupid like that." My body tensed. *So much for relaxing.* "You fooled me once with Todd, but you'll not fool me again, ever."

"And I suppose I have competition now? Don't tell me I have to worry about this pup?" He gestured to Andy, who stiffened at the offense.

I ground my teeth and Beast growled a warning. If only Kyle knew who his real competition was.

"Geez, Tay, if you were this desperate, you should have come back to me. At least you would've had a real man to keep you company instead of an acne-ridden boy still in training pants."

He eyed Andy like the younger boy was an undesirable slug. Andy swallowed hard, his face turning beat red.

Enough!

I threaded my arm though Andy's and leaned into him. "Don't listen to him, Andy. He is nothing but a creepy stalker, hunting the streets for something to torture." I looked straight at Kyle. "How could someone love a person like that?"

Kyle's face reddened, and he rose to his feet. "When you stop lying to yourself, I might take you back." He walked a few steps away before glancing over his shoulder. "That is *if* you grow up enough to handle a real man."

Beast growled again, and I swear his fingers were denting the table. Silver swam in his eyes and I knew I only had seconds to calm him down. So I did the only thing I could think off, I leaned over the table and grabbed his arm, hopping my touch would placate his wolf. His gaze shifted to me; his wolf was so near the surface that his skin vibrated under my hand. His other hand came over mine, anchoring my hand to his arm—staking his claim. Was my touch calming to his wolf, like his was to me? My traitor heart fluttered at the notion. Andy stiffened next to me. I could smell the hurt and anger rolling off him like conflicting scents of tree sap and fire. A twinge of guilt slithered through me and I couldn't look at him.

Beast turned to glare at Kyle and, in a deep, guttural voice, said, "Leave, before I make you." His tone was so threatening that Kyle didn't respond right away. My pride in Beast's protective nature washed through me. Kyle eyed him for several moments, as if he considered challenging the threat, but Beast's stature and the confident air about him seemed to be enough to convince him otherwise.

"Whatever." He strode out the door and slammed it shut, making me jump.

Beast shifted my hand from his arm to his hand. "It is time to call it a night," he said in a near whisper. I understood the warning. His wolf was too near the surface to be safe. I dared a glance at Andy. Guilt curdled in my stomach. His lips were pressed tight as his eyes flicked from Beast's hand in mine and back to me. Chel fidgeted.

"Andy, I know how this must look." I looked down. "I can't imagine what you are feeling."

"No, you can't." He paused. "So what, was this whole date a joke to you? Did you only ask me so I could take the brunt of Kyle's words so you could make out with him?" He thrust a hand at Beast.

My head snapped up. "No, Andy. It was nothing like that. I really enjoyed myself tonight—with you."

"And that is why you are still holding his hand." His jaw flexed.

"Well, I... um." I bit my lower lip. "That's a little harder to explain." Seeing the hurt in his eyes made me feel like the scum of the Earth, but there was no explaining why my arm was stretched across the table in a rather uncomfortable position.

"Whatever, I'm out of here." He stood. "I should have listened to Brian when he said you weren't worth my time."

The words were like a slap, and I winced, knowing I deserved the anger coming from him. Beast's fingers tightened on mine, but I turned from him and called after Andy's retreating form. "Andy, please."

"I'll go after him." Chel grabbed her purse. "Do you need me to swing back by and pick you two up?"

I just shook my head, and she took off. With both of them gone, guilt set in. Nothing was fair in life. Not really. I had never wanted to lie to anyone, and yet I'd just ruined a boy's first date, seemingly snubbing him for another man. He didn't deserve a crappy first date like this. Even though he was immature, he wasn't bad once I got to know him. He was like a cool kid brother.

Beast squeezed my hand, and I snorted trying not to cry. "So...that was fun." Sarcasm dripped from my words.

"Tayla," Beast said.

I knew that tone and I couldn't handle a lecture on how it was out of my control. "Just don't, please." I rested my head on my arm stretched across the table. Beast still hummed from his near-change, and I was pretty sure the fastest way to settle his wolf required me by his side. Not that he was going to let me out of the reach of his arms, and I was traitorously okay with that.

What I really needed was my bed. I sat up straight and rubbed my neck. "I guess we should start walking back. It's going to take us a good half hour."

Beast's only response was to tug me gently out of the booth and outside. We walked in silence for three blocks before Beast spoke.

"Thanks for this." He swung our finger-woven hands between us. "I'm sorry that it cost you a date and hurt Andy."

"I'm sorry to hurt Andy, too." I looked up at the half moon. "He would've been a really fun friend."

"Hmm," Beast said, and we finished the walk in companionable silence, each understanding the other's need to calm our inner wolves, woven together in the silence of our interlaced fingers.

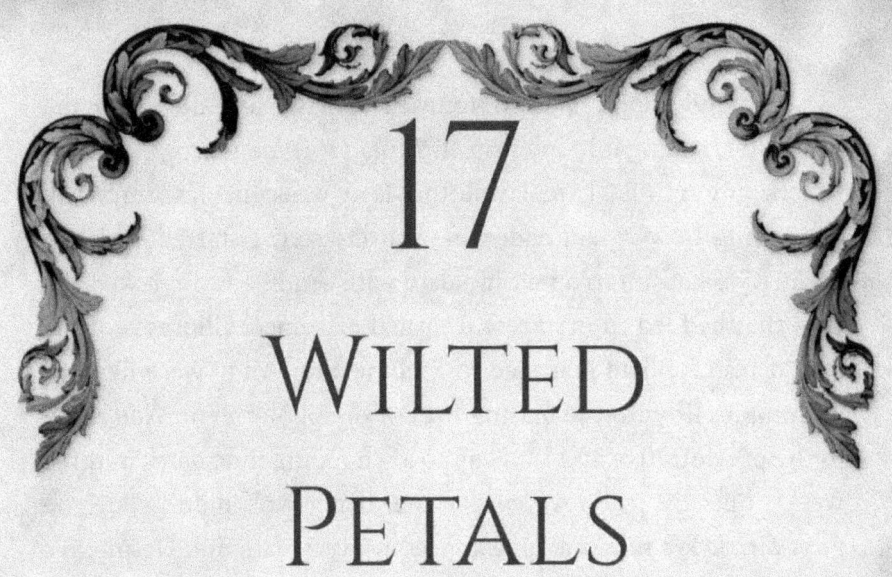

17
WILTED
PETALS

I sat like a statue on the edge of my bed in my star-print pajamas. We'd all received them from Uncle Stan the Christmas before he died in the mining accident. My vision blurred the pile of dried petals into a berry-red haze. They were shriveled reminders of so many wasted moments. A whole week had passed since my date with Andy.

Now only seven limp petals remained attached, still glowing faintly on the crinkled rose skeleton. I'd kept a journal of how many petals fell each day, trying to decipher a pattern, but it was as sporadic as falling autumn leaves. Some days only one petal fell, other days four at once. Even if only one petal fell each day from now on, Beast was certain I wouldn't make it past the full moon. Its call would be too strong for my wolf to resist, and the change would come.

The full moon was in four days. My nails dug into the comforter, balling it in my fists. *Why had it come to this?*

In my mind, I replayed the last week in fast forward, wondering how it had ended in such disaster. I started with the night Kyle had interrupted my date with Andy and reviewed the days that had led to my present dismal existence. Glimpses of the four dates Chel had managed to find me after Andy were like bad nightmares lit with the blazing fires of disappointment. Add those to the previous five and I was up to a whopping nine dates in three weeks, but still true love evaded me. If my wolf didn't scare the guys off, Kyle's random appearances at every date did. Despite his words at the ice cream shop, Kyle would sidle up to me and quickly try to steal me away with his flattering words and disarming smile, but I would never forget our first date. The way he'd attacked me, bruising my arm and shredding any thoughts of trust I had toward him.

When he'd realize I wasn't going to leave my date-of-the-day for him, he'd verbally harpoon them before leaving. It shouldn't have surprised me that Kyle would act this way. In reality, I should have expected it. I'd gotten lax with him gone and let my guard down. But the way he knew exactly where we'd be every time was beyond creepy. It was a small town, but not that small. Chel was having an increasingly hard time finding me dates—Kyle's handiwork no doubt. He was obsessively controlling, and I hadn't fallen into his posse of puppets. His determination equally scared me and puzzled me. What drove him to keep trying for me when rejection was all I dished out?

A crazy thought hit me. Could his obsession and domineering behavior be a misplaced form of love? Maybe he was never taught how to treat someone he loved with respect, instead of like an object to be owned and controlled?

The thought was too foreign and disturbing to consider, so I shook it from my head. My eyes focused on my pitiful rose, the symbol of my human life fading away.

I threw the covers over my head, blocking out the cheery afternoon sun. I sagged into the embrace of the mattress, wishing it could transport me away into some other world. I was so tired of trying, of failing. I wanted, no needed, to be someone else right now. I slipped my hand over the stack of books I'd recently been sleeping with, and picked up the largest. I lost myself in a different reality—a fantasy world—a world where I could forget my real life and pretend I'd actually come out victorious and still very much a human.

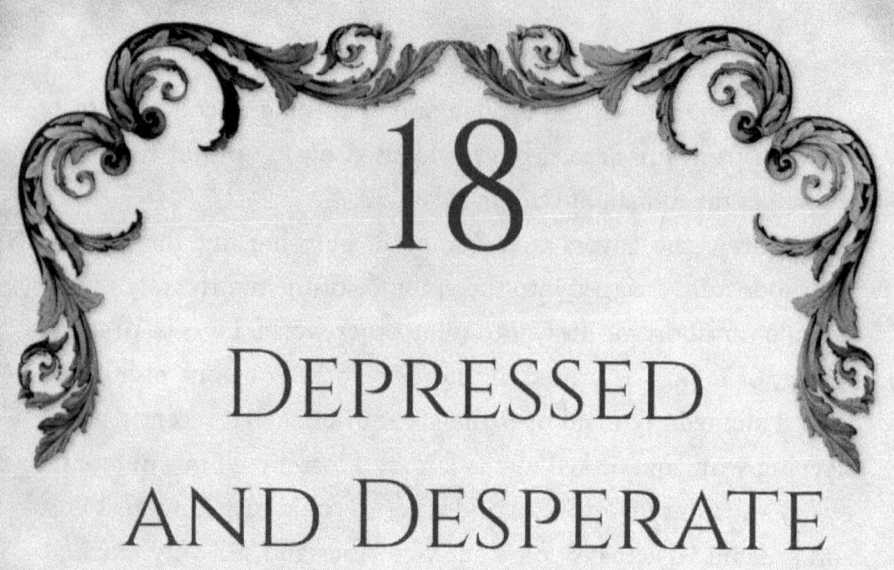

18

DEPRESSED AND DESPERATE

Wednesday, May 2

"Up!" Grandma shouted way too cheerfully for this early in the morning. I threw my blankets over my head with a groan. I was barely coherent from my all-night novel-reading marathon.

"Oh, no you don't." Grandma yanked the blanket from my head. "I'll not have you moping."

"Go away." I shielded my eyes from the blinding sunlight streaming through my now-open shades. Okay, so maybe it was close to noon, but still, it's not like I had anywhere to be.

Clunk. Clunk.

"You won't be needing these today."

My eyes sprang open, and my hands flew to the armload of books in Grandma's arms. "Those are mine!" I tugged on the top book, but she just held it tight.

Her lips pressed firm. "I'll not let you give up and just roll over for that she-wolf. I've already lost one daughter. I'll not lose you too."

Her words were like whiplash, and my hold on the books slackened. I had told Beast that same thing. Wide eyed, I stared at Grandma's turquoise eyes, unable to stop my swirling thoughts. How could I face the end, let alone another date? Everything felt so off, so—wasted. Nothing I did made a difference. My wolf was getting stronger, and the only male she'd allow me to be around for more than an hour was not human.

I scoffed. Yeah, she didn't mind forcing me into Beast's arms. Anger tickled my numb system, slowly bringing me out of my stupor.

Grandma's hands were empty. Somehow I'd missed where she'd stashed my books. *Crap.* She was notorious for finding the best hiding places. "You'd better remember where you put them." I narrowed my eyes with meaning.

"Don't you give me that look. I know exactly where they are, and if you don't get out of that bed, I might just douse them in turpentine and strike a match!" Her hands were on her hips.

I sat up with a gasp. "You wouldn't!"

"Oh?" Grandma's eyes hardened with promise. "Are you sure you want to test that theory?"

Ugly emotions bubbled into my heart, and my wolf fed on them, heightening her grip on me. Anger burned like lava, threatening to erupt from my mouth.

No one touches my books!

I growled. "Give them back."

Grandma took a minuscule step back. Her heart skipped a beat, but stood her ground. "No."

Her refusal snapped across the room, and suddenly my vision went red with fury. I launched off the bed, tackling her with a snarl. For a brief moment I was staring into her horrified eyes, then I was on my back. Large paws held me firm against the carpet and silver eyes swirled metallic. Beast's teeth bared down at me. Instinct kicked in, and I thrashed to throw him off me without success. A deep growl emanated from his chest and a wave of alpha power slammed into me. Instantly, I stilled, my brain slowly registering what I'd done.

Horror seized my lungs.

"Grandma," I choked. I couldn't see her. Had I knocked her out? "Grandma!" I yelled.

"I'm here." She stepped into my line of sight with a slight limp.

Tears welled in my eyes. "I'm so sorry. Did I...did I hurt you badly?"

Beast nuzzled my cheek, and I exposed my neck to his demand for submission. He licked the bottom of my chin; I didn't care that he'd just slobbered on me, I was only thankful when he lifted his heavy body off me.

"You're limping," I said to Grandma. I stood, but didn't approach, afraid Grandma would bolt.

A rueful smile tugged at her lips. "You'd have to do more than tackle me to put this old bird out of commission."

I slumped on the bed, holding my head. "I'm a monster."

The bed sagged as Grandma sat next to me and put an arm around my shoulders. A sob broke free from my mouth.

"Shhh." Grandma rubbed my back as if I hadn't just tried to kill her over a pile of stupid books.

"I don't deserve you." I hiccupped. "I...I can't do this anymore. I can't live like this."

She grabbed my shoulder and shook me. "Never—ever—let me hear you say that again." Her whole face was taut with seriousness, shocking my tears from me. "You are strong. No one else could've endured what you have. You knocked me over. So what? I'll not have you give up over such a silly thing. Now, get that head of yours back in the game. We fight until air fails to fill our lungs. You understand!"

Shell-shocked, I just nodded. Never had Grandma talked to me so forcefully before. Her arms drew me into a long, tight hug. Another thing Grandma didn't do often.

Releasing me, she said, "Good, now get dressed."

Grandma left, leaving me with Beast. "Thank you." I scratched the top of his head, and he licked my arm. A small smile lifted my lips. "Now, you get out too."

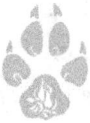

A few hours later, I sat on the lowest step of Chel's wooden porch, waiting for her to come home from school. Beast hid in the tangle of rose bushes and shrubbery in the backyard. Time ticked by as the sun beat down on me, making my skin uncomfortably warm. I thought about moving farther up the porch, but that would require energy I just didn't have. My vision blurred as I stared relentlessly at the gray rocks lining the flower bed to my right, fighting off the memories of attacking Grandma. Guilt rooted deep. I knew it would be a very long time before I could forgive myself for all the pain I was causing those I love.

The hum of Chel's SUV buzzed in my ears. My eyes flicked up, spotting red between the trees.

I waved halfheartedly as Chel hopped out, slinging her multi-colored, patchwork backpack over her shoulder. I was always impressed how she kept fixing that old thing. It was originally her mother's when she was a teen. When it got a hole, Chel patched it up with pieces of tents, old packs and other canvas-like material she saved from important childhood memories like camping trips or the diaper bag her mother used. She called it her usable memoir.

Chel sat on the step next to me. "Well, you look happy," she said sarcastically. I knew I looked like a walking zombie. I'd still be in bed if not for Grandma. In fact, I didn't think I'd even brushed my hair before I'd hopped in the van.

I rested my arms on my knees and cradled my head. "So who's the date for tonight?" I mumbled.

Silence was my only answer. It was so complete that I clearly heard the scuttle of ants in the flower bed. I tilted my head to peek up at her. Worry lines betrayed her true feelings.

When she caught my eye, she spoke. "I'm sorry Tay. I've found every guy I could. Kyle's got the rest of them so scared they crap their pants at the mention of your name."

I sighed. "It's not your fault, Chel."

"I got so desperate that I even asked Todd." Chel snorted, like that was a wasted effort.

Something inside me cracked, and I giggled helplessly. Breathing become difficult as I watched Chel's surprised face flash with concern for my mental wellbeing.

"Sorry." I breathed between fits of laughter. "I just pictured Todd's eyes popping at the mention of my name before he stumbled over himself to flee."

Chel scowled. "This is serious, Tay! I'm all out of guys."

"Not you. Never!" That sent me into another wave of giggles which I swallowed noisily. I knew I'd twisted her meaning and reflected it back on her.

Chel socked my arm. "Let me rephrase that. *You're* all out of guys."

"I know," I said, rubbing my arm in a mock show of hurt. "Wait. What about the college?" I asked, hoping she might know of a dance or something.

"Well," Chel bit her lip.

"Oh, no. What did you do?" My anxiety spiked.

"I kinda posted fliers around campus and..." Chel said. I gasped.

"You did what?" Humiliation rocked through me. "How is looking like a desperate psycho-chick going to get me a date? Obviously no one has responded. Have they?" I ran my hands through my tangled hair and Chel remained silent. Then something occurred to me. "You said and..."

Chel lowered her eyes. "I also posted an ad on craigslist."

I groaned.

"Hey, I was just trying to help." Chel looked at me. "If it makes you feel better, only weirdos responded. I wasn't even going to mention it."

I snorted. "Maybe only weirdos can love a wolf-infected freak." My mind went to Kyle, and I frowned down at the ground.

"Tay." Chel put a hand on my knee.

I dug my phone out of my pocket, and a knot formed in my stomach. "Maybe Kyle's right. We are perfect for each other."

Chel's eyes widened. "You can't be serious! Tay, we *will* figure this out."

I shook my head. "Chel, he *is* my last hope. Maybe I was too fast to write him off. He definitely wants me. That's a start, right?" I grimaced at my own words. It was a long shot, but it was the last one I had.

"Maybe there are too many maybes," she retorted, her face grim. "I can't believe you would even consider it! After all, the possessive jerk abused you the last time you dated him. And let's not forget that he gave Todd and Danny a black eye just for talking to you."

"Well, Danny did a little more than talk." My gaze traced the translucent silhouette of the nearly full moon in the clear blue sky. "I don't want to date Kyle, but I only have three days left and I'm out of options. Besides, if he gets out of hand this time, my wolf can take care of him."

Chel's gaze was on the ground, and she bit her lip. Sadness was like syrup in my throat, thick and hard to swallow. Had I been right to involve Chel in this craziness? It was too late for regrets now. At least she would know the truth if I disappeared. I shook myself from the hopeless thought. Neither death nor my wolf had me yet.

Enough stalling. I'd made my choice, and it was time to act. Holding Chel's hand, I flipped my phone open and scanned the list for the word 'desperate,' where I'd programmed Kyle's home phone number two days ago.

"No." Chel grabbed the phone and snapped it shut, shaking her head.

"What are you doing?"

"Give me until tomorrow. I'll find someone. If necessary, we'll go up to the campus and walk through the commons building..."

I touched her shoulder. "I couldn't ask for a better friend, but we are out of time. It will take a miracle to get this wolf out of me before the full moon. I believe Kyle loves me on some level, even if his version of love is a bit twisted. Maybe he just needs someone to teach him to be more gentle?" I swallowed hard. "I just hope it is enough."

"Tay, please don't."

"Chel, we've tried everything else. I have to give this one more shot," I said.

Chel traced her palm lines so intently I swear she was looking for the future in them. I held my breath, waiting for her to say something, to tell me I was doing the right thing. I was sure I'd lose my sanity if she didn't support me.

"I don't like it, but I'll stand by you." She glanced up at me, and my breath released with a sigh.

I tugged her into a hug. "Thank you."

"I'm sorry I couldn't do better." She squeezed me.

"Don't say that." I pulled back to look her in the eyes. "You were amazing. The fault is so not yours." I dropped my arms and fiddled with my phone.

"Hey, Tay." Chel's comforting hand curled around mine. My head lifted to see her face puckered in a frown. "Please be careful. Kyle is all sorts of unstable."

I scoffed. "Yeah, you don't have to remind me, but thanks."

Ending the embrace, I gripped Chel's hand for support. Ceremoniously, I held the phone between us, and before I could chicken out, I hit send and speaker.

One ring—two rings—every ring was torture. I wished I hadn't deleted Kyle's cell number the night of our first and only date. The thought of having his ice queen mother answer gave me more than the chills.

It rang a third time, and I feared no one would answer.

"Harrington residence, may I help you?" The man's British accent placed him as a likely candidate for the butler.

I brought the phone up closer to our faces. "Is Kyle there?"

"Master Kyle is here. Who's calling?"

I twirled a strand of my hair nervously before Chel slapped it out of my hand.

"Ow." I mouthed silently, shaking out my stinging hand.

"Tayla. Tayla Jonas."

"Very well, Miss Jonas. One moment."

The seconds ticked by in what felt like torturous minutes. I couldn't believe I was doing this. I almost hung up the phone when a familiar voice echoed through the receiver. My cell clattered to the pavement. I quickly grabbed it, jamming it tight to my ear.

"I knew you'd miss me." His voice vibrated in my ear, loud enough to make me cringe. I turned off the speaker, and Chel frowned.

Ignoring the pure satisfaction in his voice, I played my part in this sick game. "I just can't seem to get you off my mind," I said in my most sultry voice. I nearly gagged, but Chel was doing enough of it for the both of us. I licked my lips and swallowed my nausea. "In fact, I was hoping you'll still take me to prom."

"Would no one else ask you?" His voice was patronizingly sweet, with a hint of irritation.

My free hand balled into a fist, but I managed to keep my voice soft. "I turned them down, hoping you would forgive me for not seeing how perfectly matched we are." My mouth felt like it was full of cotton, and my skin crawled like snakes were slithering across it, posing to strike.

Staying human, staying human. I chanted in my mind, reminding me of why I was doing this.

Silence deadened the line for a few heartbeats until Kyle responded. "Why don't you ask me in person? Be here in an hour."

I wanted to throw a brick through his window or barf on him, not go to his house and woo him. *Why did boys have to be so difficult?* I wanted to grind my teeth.

Fine! I'll play his game if it means I can get this wolf out of my head.

"5:30 it is," I said in a sugary voice before snapping the phone shut.

19
CHINA DOLL

I knew where Kyle lived—everyone did—but I'd never traveled up the private drive to see his family's mansion. My hands were sticky with sweat as I gripped the worn steering wheel and turned up the steep road. The pine and aspens were thick on both sides, and I could only see a few well-groomed driveways branching off here and there. Fleeting images of large stone and wood houses peeked between the tree trunks. Flashes of Beast's home entered my mind—the solitude, the inescapability, the blood running down my wounded leg...

The van bounced along the rocky surface of the shoulder, and I swerved back onto the blacktop. An irritated snuff came from behind me. On impulse, I looked in the rearview mirror to see the massive wolf shaking himself like he'd jumped in ice water. In my nervousness, I chuckled, and his silver eyes glared at me, which only made me laugh harder. The image of him looking like a drowned cat was too funny. I wished a river was nearby to throw him in. Then he'd really have something to complain about.

"Oh, knock it off." I rolled my eyes for emphasis. "It's not like that little bump hurt you."

He snorted and curled back up on the floor with his backside to me.

I smirked.

Distracted by Beast, I'd almost forgotten why I was driving up Snob Hill when the road ended. A sandy-colored brick fence dwarfed my van. I felt like an ant about to be squashed by a giant shoe. Only the angular slope of the Harrington's Mansion roof was visible above it.

White-knuckled, I took a deep breath. "This is it."

I pulled up to the spiked iron gate and pushed the intercom button.

"The Harrington residence. May I help you?" The British accent of their butler was unmistakable.

"It's Tayla Jonas. I'm here to see Kyle." I tried not to sound as scared as I felt. I was in Kyle's territory now, and the only thing keeping me from shifting the van into reverse was my desperate desire to remain myself.

Staying human, I chanted one last time. The gate swung open silently, and I shivered. There was no turning back now.

Steering my van down the brick driveway, I took in the beauty of the landscape. Decorative trees flanked both sides of me, opening up into a courtyard. The driveway circled around a water fountain decorated in an assortment of colorful flowers. There were walkways meandering through the well-manicured grounds surrounding the mansion. The house glistened white like a polished mausoleum.

I watched as one groundskeeper polished the exterior walls and another squeegeed the floor to ceiling windows. It had to be freezing up there. A third worker threw something small into a garbage sack. Suddenly, I realized what it was. I wondered how many birds found their grave by smashing into those perfectly polished windows as they tried to find shelter and warmth. By risking a date with Kyle, would I be one of those casualties? I shivered.

The various angles of the jutting rooftops were strikingly different from anything else in Cody. Leave it to the Harringtons to stand out in a pine forest, forcing the landscape to bend its will to theirs instead of blending in like their neighbors.

I parked near the grand entryway just as the sun began to set. Beast whined with impatience at the setting sun, willing it to hurry into darkness so he could change. My hands stilled on the steering wheel. The last thing I needed was Beast's verbal banter after he made the change. It was hard enough to deal with the streaming disappointment he projected through the bond.

"Knock it off. I don't like this any more than you do. I'll be back in five." I quickly rolled down the window in an attempt to ease the wolf's nerves and cracked the door in case the bond prevented me from going inside the house.

I climbed the pristine granite steps edged with lilac, breathing in the heady perfume of the flowers mixed with pine. It calmed my nerves a little. I stopped on the welcome mat. *Am I welcomed?* I couldn't help but be nervous about what reception would greet me. Slowly, I lifted my hand to knock; before my knuckles touched the door, it swung open.

"This is a surprise." Kyle stood with a crooked grin on his perfectly chiseled face.

"You knew I was coming." I worked hard to keep my voice soft.

"So you said, but I wasn't sure if you meant it." He stepped closer. "Still don't."

I shifted my weight slightly back, my wolf growling at my slight retreat. "I know I have been...distant. But I really do want you to be my—"

His finger stopped my words. "Come with me." He dropped his hand from my lips to lead me by the hand. I suppressed the urge to pull away. "I have the perfect place for you to ask your question." A coy smile played on his soft lips.

My mouth opened to give a tart retort, but the inviting warm fragrance coming off him disarmed my tongue. It was nothing in comparison with Beast's musky scent, but it swirled into my lungs with pleasure, and I unconsciously leaned toward him. I took a deeper sniff, letting my wolf sense take over, and was surprised to find the flowery essences of jasmine and sandalwood. There was a warm citrusy smell of lemon, and something else I couldn't name. Together they transformed the smells into an alluring masculine cologne. Had he always worn that?

He chuckled as I straightened out of my slight lean. This peek into his playful side threw me off balance. I'd never seen him act this way without his signature leering look. I hoped this meant there was more to Kyle's teenage boyishness—something that I could love.

But the moment vanished, and like Dr Jekyll turning into Mr. Hyde, his boastful side returned with vengeance.

"Chicks dig the cologne," he said with a cocky air. "It's France's finest."

I mentally rolled my eyes. Yet, he had a point—it did smell good even to my wolf and that was a feat. He led me toward the corner of the house to a garden retreat. River rocks were arranged in meandering lines that varied in length, creating a lazy path. Verdant plants were spread out around me. Kyle finally released my hand. I stood where he'd left me and watched him take a seat on the oak bench zigzagging around the waist-high concrete planter boxes. His legs stretched out along the bench, the picture of ease, and I hated him for it. I was a bundle of knotted nerves, and my abdomen twisted uncomfortably from the distance between Beast and me. I wondered if he'd refused to leave the van just so I wouldn't go any farther. I silently pled for this not to be a repeat of the party.

Kyle was determined to wring every last drop of pleasure he could get out of my misery. Maybe I'd tricked myself into seeing something in Kyle that wasn't there. I looked back toward my van. This was a waste of time. He could never love anyone but himself. Yet I desperately held to that fleeting glimpse of what might exist behind the swagger. He was still young. Would he grow out of it? He had the potential to be everything I'd imagined I wanted in life, all wrapped in a snarled ball that dangled in front of me, daring me to reach for it and to untangle the mess. *At least he doesn't bite.*

I wasn't going to lose anything from trying. If I allowed myself to love Kyle, and he ended up being nothing more than the jerk I'd seen so far, I wouldn't be human long enough for it to matter, right? But what if time was all he needed to grow into the prince I so desperately needed?

Either way, I wasn't going to stand there much longer and take his smug attitude. His expectant hazel eyes were making me uncomfortable with the way they drank me in. My wolf clawed at her cage, wanting to rip his head off.

Role-play time.

Taking a breath, I curled my lips into a coy smile and got right to the point. "So will you be my prom date and make me the luckiest girl alive?" I was going to say the luckiest girl in Cody, but he would've taken offence if I didn't think his famed skills could get him any girl on Earth.

"Why the change of heart?" He tried for a disinterested tone, but his heart beat a little faster. Was he nervous? Excited?

207

"Maybe I just missed you?"

"So much that you kissed Danny?" His fist balled at his side and the softness he had shown was now gone.

"That's disgusting!" I shivered as if appalled, knowing I had to sell my performance. "Who would say something like that?"

"I have my informants." His eyes took in my every move, still not believing.

I worked hard to look affronted, placing my hand on my hips. "Well, I wouldn't believe anything *Natalie* says about me. These lips never touched his. It's insulting that you even believed her."

"Hmm." He stood. "So why all the dates, if you wanted me? Or am I last on your list of prospective dance partners?"

Ouch. My smile faltered and my gaze shifted to the daffodils in the planter over his shoulder. I desperately wanted to throw something at him, but I pasted on my best fake smile. Even the cheer captain would have been proud.

He was baiting me. He knew he was the reason none of the other guys would take me to prom, but I wasn't going to react—well, not the way he expected. I sifted through my mental catalogue of hot Hollywood stars and chose one. I'd imagine his image over Kyle's and maybe I would make it through this. Just like one of Chel's drama plays. But I was surprised when Beast's face popped in my mind instead—the night he'd given me the rose, the night he'd been most human.

Before I lost my nerve, I said, "How would I have known you were the best partner if I hadn't tried out a few others? There really is no comparison when it comes to you."

I could tell he liked my banter as his eyes drifted to my lips. My mental image of Beast began to waver, but I continued to uphold my alluring mask. I dropped my gaze to his lips and then back up to meet his eyes, inviting him over. And finally, that hint was all he needed to swallow the lie. His eyes twinkled and he stood. I suppressed a shiver. This was the response I had striven for, but that didn't mean his touch would be easy to bear.

He strolled over to me, standing so close I had to strain my neck to look up. "I accept your invitation, but remember who asked who first." He took my hand in his and lifted it to brush his lips over my fingertips. But he didn't stop there. His lips skimmed my cheek and down my neck. "It'll be the best night of your life."

I swallowed the mass forming in my throat and managed to keep my smile. Thankfully, Kyle's cologne seemed to be a mild sedative for my wolf as she lay contentedly in her cage.

His head bent towards mine, and the image of Beast vanished, forcing me to close my eyes and focus on the sweet scent rolling off his skin. It was the only way I was going to get through this. His lips brushed lightly across mine, teasing me, and I shivered again—this time from a mixture of fury, anxiety, and unexpected pleasure. I wasn't sure which one was winning, but suddenly the sedative wore off and I knew my wolf was pissed. If she could make me bite Brayden, Kyle was toast. I pushed the cage door closed with all my might, but it wouldn't be long before she freed herself. I was sure if Kyle didn't smell so good, I'd lost the war of wills at the front door.

Kyle's lips slid back to my ear. "Friday, I'll send a car for you at three sharp. Then I'll show you what a real kiss feels like."

"Three? That's a little early, don't you think?" I whispered, finding it difficult to draw a breath. Had he just played me? Again? A hurricane raged war inside my head as I struggled to keep my wolf at bay. She loathed Kyle more than I did and trembled with anticipation. She wanted nothing more than to rip into his flesh. Was it possible that she hated him so much because she sensed he could eradicate her from my body? I could only hope.

He leaned back to look at me in the eye. "I'm saving you money. My stylist will fix you up. Dress and all."

"What?" I breathed, startled back to the conversation. I shook my head. "No need to bother yourself with girly stuff. Chel will take care of it."

"Nothing against Chel, but Ian is renowned in his field." His finger curled around my brown lock of hair as if contemplating something. "You'll be amazing after he's finished."

I stiffened and my world tilted once more. I had prepared myself for the possibility that he would want his stylist to do my makeup and hair, but was he going to pick out my clothes, too? Was this how it would always be? Me, the brainless Barbie doll that would heel like a dog to her master? Happy just to have his attention? If I wanted that, I might as well just stay with Beast. I wanted to hit Kyle, to throw something, but most of all I wanted to run, and give in to the tears stinging my eyes.

Kyle shrugged, as if he hadn't noticed my rigid form and balled fists. "Ian guessed your size and has already ordered the dresses."

I picked up on the plural, and swallowed hard, holding on to anything positive. "Dresses?"

His fingers slipped from my hair, and he frowned a little. "Ian was emphatic that I let you pick your dress from several that he ordered."

My hands relaxed a little, and a grateful smile pulled at my lips. Maybe this Ian wasn't so bad after all.

"Okay." I tried playing it off as nothing, but my insides quaked with apprehension. I would much rather have Chel dress me up than a man I'd never met, but what choice did I have? Kyle held the cards in this game, and I would play my part, waiting for the outcome. There was no time left for another alternative. "I'll see you Friday."

"Let me walk you to your car." He offered me his arm like a gentleman.

Why did he have to be gallant now? I didn't want this moment to last any longer than it already had, so I trailed a finger down his cheek, before leaning in to kiss it. Bile rose in my throat and my wolf growled, but I managed to keep her from biting him and me from throwing up. "That's sweet, but I'll manage."

I sashayed away from him and to my relief he stayed put. With him out of sight, I relaxed my act. Old memories of his crazy possessive eyes and the terror of holding me against my will threatened to send me running back to my van to cancel the date. Yet, I knew I wouldn't. I had to see this through.

Please let Kyle be a changed man. If only for a little while.

A sinking feeling settled back over me, as if the earth wanted to swallow me whole. Kyle might break my inner-wolf's hold on me, but at what cost? I would be human, but would my freedom to make every day choices be sucked away from me? Would he want to control everything I said, wore, and did—like a China doll, set on a shelf and only taken down to make him look good? Maybe Beast's control over my life wasn't so bad...

Beast wouldn't tell me what to wear. But then again, he was alpha and I would be under his command and in no need of clothing. What would I rather be, a human slave who could at least still talk to my family without killing them, or with my mom and Beast, a wolf forever? Both options sucked, but being a human puppet would be better than being a wolf one, right? Either way, I'd be bound as a mate to one or the other. I just had to decide the form, and right now I knew human was the only option I could live with.

I found Beast waiting not so patiently in the back. We probably had no more than ten minutes before the change. I opened the door and climbed into the van, revving the engine to life as the sun dipped behind the trees. Kyle had walked to the shadowed veranda and was watching me. I waved, putting on a show of happiness. He waved back, but his attention was elsewhere, no doubt plotting our date. Flipping my lights on, I gave him a show of red taillights as I drove down his driveway. The wolf's war still raged inside me, heightened by the emotions rampaging through the bond from my furry companion, tempered only by the distance I put between Kyle and myself.

Beast's wolf nose brushed my shoulder, sniffing me. He snorted sharply, causing my loose hair to blow into my face. Kyle's scent still clung to my skin but was quickly fading under the stronger scent of Beast's natural odor.

"Do you mind? I'm driving here." I used my free hand to push his nose away, careful not to veer off the road. "I get it, you don't like this, but do you want me to wreck the van, too?"

He conceded, giving another snort, before resuming his position on the floor. When he changed, I was going to get an ear full. Every vibe rolling off him was negative. But my decision was final, and nothing Beast said or did would change that.

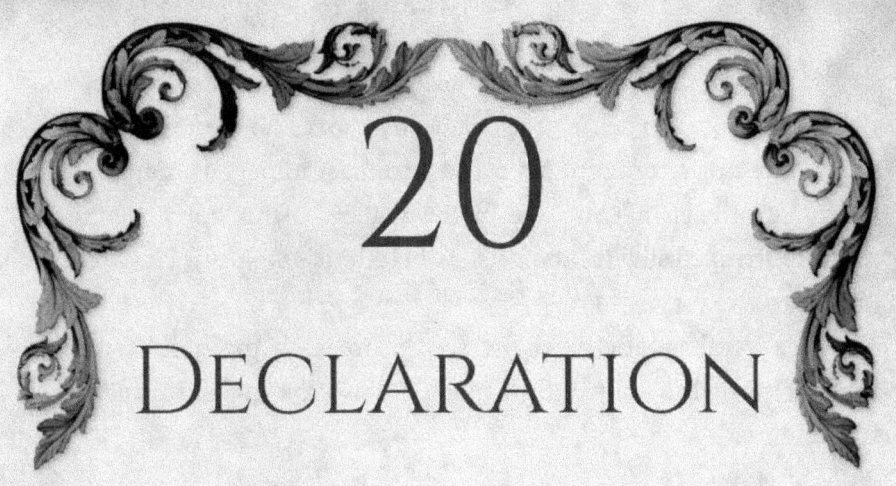

20
DECLARATION

I parked in front of Grandma's house and switched off the lights. I made my way to the back of the van, scraping my tennis shoes against the asphalt. I reached for the handle on the back door, but before my fingers could curl around it, the door swung open.

Beast, in human form, was draped in a long, black hooded trench coat and sweatpants that concealed his deformities and nakedness when in a hurry or shy on clothes. I gawked at him in disbelief. I hadn't felt him change—at all!

"But how?" I squeaked, shaking my head as if that would clear the illusion. "I didn't feel a thing!"

Ignoring my outburst, he stood like an immovable force before me.

"I don't like it." His voice was deep, like rumbling thunder.

It took me a moment to realize he was talking about Kyle, but I wasn't going to be sidetracked. "Why didn't I feel you change?"

He finally brought his eyes up to meet mine. His human eyes would've been hard to see in the shadow of his hood, but they were streaked silver. I took a slow breath. His wolf was close to the surface.

Several breaths later, he spoke, breaking the quiet tension. "I've learned to control how much I allow you to feel through the bond."

"How?"

I could feel the anger flaring across the bond as he spoke. "I picture squeezing the connection closed as if I'm squeezing the life out of Kyle's body." My wolf quivered with delight, but I ignored her.

Slowly, I felt his anger drift away as if struggling to reach me until it was cut off completely. The image of Kyle strangled to death made me nervous. Would he actually kill him?

"It's just prom." I walked past him, trying to brush off the moment, but he grabbed my wrist.

"Where do you think you're going?" he demanded.

His harsh voice made mine embarrassingly timid. "To bed?"

His laugh was dark, and his pointed teeth flashed through snarled lips. "No. It's time to take our lessons up several notches."

He gripped my wrist and pulled me across the yard. Fear curled in my gut, and my chest tightened. What was he going to make me do? I tugged at his iron-like grip, but I might as well have become a fly for all the notice he gave me. The instant my foot touched the backyard, the surroundings were filled with hushed sounds and shifting shadows that only my wolf senses could detect. I automatically shifted into the quiet meditation Beast had pounded into my skull, needing familiarity under Beast's unpredictable mood and the ongoing headache that would surely come if I didn't follow instructions.

He stopped under the ponderosa in the far corner, several yards away from the flowerbed we normally sat by. Unnerved, I looked up at him, waiting for the soothing tone of his lecture voice to fill the uneasy space between us, but it never came.

"Break free of my grasp." He taunted me by lifting the wrist he still held prisoner.

His grip pinched my skin and I bit back a cry. My fingertips tingled from loss of blood. Was this some sort of sick joke? I took too long to respond, and his eyes flashed silver.

"Now!"

Pain pricked my flesh, begging for relief. "You're breaking my wrist!"

He held up a hand to silence me. "Your wolf is strong, Tayla. You've seen that already, but you don't let her have more freedom. You're not calling on her strength. You should have twisted free of my grip out of reflex the moment I grabbed you."

He pointed to my heart hammering in my chest. "Her strength builds here. Close your eyes and feel it spread through your body. Call her forth."

Horror washed through me. I had been struggling to *restrain* my wolf, not drag her out on purpose!

"No way. I don't want any part of my wolf and you know it!" I wasn't going to let him win. I twisted my wrist upward, but was only rewarded with more pain. Where was my human adrenaline when I needed it?

His eyes narrowed. "What if I was Kyle? Would you let him have his way with you, just because you let your fear cage your wolf instincts?"

He began to twist my wrist to one side. The pain climbed up to my elbow. "No," I growled. "But he isn't here, and I *don't* need her. I can defend myself. Now, let go, you jerk!" I kicked at him with one foot. He deftly stepped to the side, but twisted my arm even further. I cried out in pain and tears stung my eyes. Was he going to break my arm before he relented?

"Make me," he said, his eyes filled with darkness that seeped into my bones. At the same time, an edge of alpha power clung to the words, calling directly to my wolf.

Cheater!

My wolf slammed out of her cage and before I knew it, my wrist was free, and the pain subsided to a burning ache. My legs trembled, and I jolted forward only to trip over my feet when I tried to regain control. Her desire to play was overpowering my resistance. I curled into the fetal position on the ground, focusing my whole soul on restraining her. She clawed at my mind, giving me a migraine that stole my vision and brought vomit to the back of my throat. I kept pushing her back with mental walls that smashed her flat.

This is my body, I hissed at her.

She snarled, but finally she was unable to resist the crushing weight of my consciousness.

Minutes passed before my body fully calmed. My face was damp with sweat. I closed my eyes, exhausted, but triumphant. My wolf was back in her place, and I once again had full control of my body. It was then that I felt the warmth from the large, firm hand on my shoulder. Opening my eyes, I found Beast's unreadable face above me.

"You're suffocating her, Tayla. It's no wonder she rebels so fast. If you'd just let her ease out, you could control her better." He stood with his hand out to me. "Now, get up and try again."

"Excuse me?" Anger boiled through my veins, and I clutched my fists. "It's my body! Forgive me for not wanting to share. You may be used to it, but I still have a choice!" I was screaming, but I didn't care if I woke the whole neighborhood.

"You're so blinded by this obsession to rid your body of the wolf that you can't see that she's gained even more control that way." His silver-streaked, caramel eyes were hard and unforgiving.

I lurched to my feet. "Well, at least I'm trying to fight back. You just roll over and let your wolf have his way."

The muscles in Beast's jaw tightened—his body rigid.

I tensed for a fight. It was a low blow, but I was too angry to take it back.

"And you think throwing yourself at a cad like Kyle is going to free you from your wolf? From this curse?" His laugh was harsh. "You wouldn't know love if it was standing right in front of you."

A tart response was poised on my lips, but something in his eyes stopped me. For a brief second, my heart stopped and emotions—not my own—flooded my system. In his anger, he'd lost control of the mate bond. Desire slammed into me, shaking me to my soul and igniting my repressed feelings. The memory of my hands under his shirt, on his hot skin, was like a tonic under the desire flickering in his smoldering caramel eyes.

I swallowed hard. Was it possible that not only did his wolf love mine, but that *he* could love the human part of me? My heart ached in response to my own undeniable attraction, but just as quickly, reason took the reins, and I scowled at myself for entertaining the thought. His wolf had claimed me as a mate, not him. Maybe he was just so used to feeling the mate bond that it affected his feelings too.

But even if he did have feelings for me, it didn't change anything. He wasn't human, so there was no point pursuing it—unless I wanted to do it as a meat-eating werewolf. I shuddered at the image of the two of us tearing apart a helpless animal.

However, there were other activities that I wouldn't mind at all. My gaze dropped to his full lips. Heat climbed up my neck. My heart rate soared and Beast shifted closer, his warm breath tickling my face. I ached to feel his lips on mine, to have his heat seep into my soul. My wolf thrummed with excitement. A sweet tangy smell filled the space between us, along with a fleeting feeling of companionship, and something even more desirable.

No...it couldn't be...He couldn't, could he?

As quickly as the emotions came through the bond they fled, leaving me wondering if what I'd felt was really love.

"I can't watch you do this anymore." His voice was barely audible as he nuzzled my cheek, sending my synapses into overdrive. "I'm trying to let you live your human life the way you want, but I can't see another man touch you any longer. To watch you give them permission to touch you," he trailed fingers down my bare throat, "like this." My wolf and I both shivered with pleasure and my eyes rolled back. "It's torture." His voice was husky.

The pain in his voice stole my already-laborious breath. His words tumbled in my mind. It had to be his wolf talking, he couldn't mean it. Before I could blink, he scooped me into his arms and brought us down to the ground with me across his lap. I clung to him, pressing my heated body eagerly into his.

My heart hammered in my chest. I was acutely aware of his strong arms around me and the beating of his heart thrumming in my ears. Fire roared in my belly, and I twisted and leaned into him better, inhaling the seductive smell of his skin.

He leaned back, searching my eyes with his. "*I* want you, and I want *you* to want me, not because your wolf calls to mine, but because you want *me*." He freed a hand to trace my lips with his fingertips. "I love you, Tayla Jonas."

His eyes were naked with love—yearning—fear. I'd never seen him so vulnerable, and it melted any defenses that remained. He lowered his head, brushed my wanting mouth with his electrifying lips before trailing, nibble by nibble, back to my ear. I closed my eyes, drinking in the feel of him. His teeth grabbed my ear, then moved to press a kiss below my jaw. I dug my fingers into his shoulders as longing raged through my veins like liquid fire.

"Stay with me." His warm breath caressed my neck with promise.

He was asking me to give up my human life, to be a wolf with him forever. And in that moment, oh how I wanted to. My heart ached for his arms to never release me; for him to kiss me until the world ceased to exist. I shifted my gaze to the shadows around us, fighting for a sane thought. How many days did I have left as a human? Three—maybe less—until the change came upon me? Yes, we could be together, but too soon I'd change to wolf form, never to be human again. How could he love me like this as an animal? And what of the curse? It would make him hunt another of Star's bloodline eventually.

Beast's hands moved over my back, massaging every inch with his skillful hands. How would I bear watching him with another girl, knowing I could never touch him like she could? The torture would be so complete that death would be a blissful release. No, I wouldn't live like that, but could I live without him either? I squeezed my eyes shut. I'd already made my choice the moment I'd come home. I had to keep fighting to stay human, but the choice shredded my insides, knowing I'd lose Beast either way. I couldn't have him and stay human, and it was killing us both. My wolf whimpered under the pain piercing both our hearts.

I buried my face into the coarse fabric of his cloak. Wrapping my arms around his torso, I let the tears come. He stroked my hair in silence.

"I can't become a wolf...I can't!" My voice was horse with emotions. His hand stilled and his chest stiffened. I released my hold on him and shifted out of his shocked arms. It felt like my heart was ripped from my chest. The cold air nipped my over-flushed skin, and I welcomed the pain as a necessary distraction. I knelt on the wet grass in front of him.

Unable to look him in the eye, I spoke at the ground. "Beast, I...I have to try to stay human. You can't love me forever...There will always be another girl."

I felt his shock course through the bond, but just as quickly an emotionless stone wall replaced it. "Even if I'm forced to Hunt, I'll never love another. You are my mate, now and forever."

"You can't promise me that. How will you love me as a wolf?"

"My love for you is eternal no matter what form you take. And yet you are the one rejecting it, rejecting me." In a slow and controlled movement, he stood. I grabbed his hand before he straightened to his full height, trying desperately to keep him with me, but he pulled me up to my feet.

"Please, Beast. This isn't an easy decision for me. You know this! I have to try. Please understand." My voice was unsteady and my eyes smarted. "I would never hurt you on purpose." My voice broke.

"I refuse to watch that excuse of a human touch you again." Beast took my hand off his arm. It dropped to my side, wounding my heart on impact.

"How are you going to refuse with the bond keeping us near each other?" I whispered. I stuffed my feelings away as much as possible and focused on his voice.

"The full moon is close. The bond will stretch enough that I won't be subjected to that rodent's presence ever again."

"Oh." The feeling of loss wrenched my stomach.

"It would be best if you stayed away from me, also." Without another word, he strode into the house, leaving my heart bleeding. Numb, I watched him go. What else could I do? Everything inside me screamed to stop him, especially my wolf, but I couldn't move.

What are you doing? He loves you! Why isn't that enough?

Misery swamped me, and my legs buckled, sending me to the grass. My wolf took her chance in my weakened state. She pulled me to my feet, and we started after him, but I froze mid-way as his words repeated in my mind. My wolf thrashed as my conscience weighed her down like a giant boulder.

Stop it! Leave me alone, you stupid wolf! If I can't have him, neither will you. Ever.

She surged forward, getting one more step out of me before I smashed her under my will and forced her, whimpering, back into her cage.

My wolf howled mournfully, the sound slicing through my body with such longing and despair that all my strength evaporated, and I crumpled to the ground. My sides screamed with pain as my body wracked with sobs. Eventually, I crawled red-eyed to my bed.

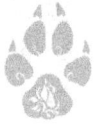

I woke with a numb heart and puffy eyes. I might have lost Beast and a piece of my soul, but I was resolved not to waste the last few days I had with my family. Gripping my phone, I called Aunt Lily and begged her to call in sick and excuse my cousins from school. She hesitated, afraid of the full moon and Beast. Sad, that she still thought he was the biggest threat here. If she knew I'd attacked Grandma, I'd never see the girls or her again.

"Please." The sheer desperation in my voice was heartbreaking, even to my ears. I needed every moment I could get with them before...

"All right, we'll be there in ten minutes."

I sighed in relief. My next call was Chel. She had no problems ditching her classes and forging a parent's note.

With all my family around me, including Chel, I felt almost normal. We played our favorite games: Scrabble, badminton, and charades. While munching kettle corn we watched Aunt Lily do her Elvis impression, and I laughed so hard my sides ached.

The sun's setting arrived too quickly, and Grandma pulled out a canvas for each of us so we could have a family painting party, something we hadn't done since I was ten. She told us all to paint whatever came into our minds first. Unfortunately, by the time mine was finished, the image of my mother in wolf form had morphed into a different wolf with fangs dripping with blood—my blood. My leg ached from the memory of the wolf bite I'd received that life-altering night. How had I let myself paint that?

I quickly shoved it into the reuse pile and cleaned my workstation. I didn't want to see what I would paint next, so I excused myself before Grandma and Chel had a chance to catch me.

The day had been wonderful, filled with laughter and uncertain tears, except for the times I couldn't ignore the distance Beast put between us. I searched for the bond every once in a while, but he had shut me out so completely I almost wondered if it was still there. It stung, seeing him in the shadows behind the house, his back to me, but I knew there was nothing I could do to ease his pain—or mine.

21
STYLIST

Friday, May 4

The morning dawned sunny. I growled at the cheerful rays and threw my comforter over my head. I felt sick. The last thing I wanted was some cheerful reminder that today's events would determine if I lived the rest of my life as a human or as a wolf—or maybe neither.

My heart thudded in my ears, and I took deep calming breaths, picking at my nails. After a few minutes, my panic ebbed to a tolerable level, leaving me feeling ill and with fingernails ripped to the quick. I climbed out of bed and ate something, but staring at the kitchen clock ticking painfully closer to 3:00 sent the knots in my stomach tumbling in an acrobatic performance.

If I couldn't ease my worries, I'd work myself into a stupor. I organized Grandma's sale's receipts for the last year according to month and balanced it against her bank statements. The monotonous work focused my mind on something other than

Kyle and my human life hanging in the balance. But it did little for my churning stomach. I felt like a swarm of angry hornets buzzed in my knotted gut.

I took a shower to wash off the sweat and, as water trickled over my bare skin, my thoughts reluctantly turned to Beast, opening my heart to the pain that accompanied them. What would I do with Beast when the car came to take me? I needed some way to transport him until night fell and he turned human. I didn't want him to have to run behind the limo, I was already torturing him enough just being bound to him. Besides, what if the car went too fast? Would the driver listen to me and slow down? It wasn't worth the risk. Chel was busy decorating the gym for prom. Though she'd offered to skip, I wouldn't let her. She had put so much into making this dance perfect for everyone. She needed to be there to see to the finishing touches.

Grandma was downtown at the art gallery that housed her paintings. She'd said it wouldn't take more than a couple hours, but there was no sign of her and it was already 2:30 p.m. For obvious reasons, Aunt Lily was out of the question, even if she was off work today. She could hardly stand to be in the same house as Beast, but in a car, there was bound to be a bloody fight, and I'm not sure if either would survive it.

I dressed and exited the confining house. I needed an excuse to shake my anxiety. With sneakers on, I ran, intent on cruising around the whole block, since Beast insisted the bond was lengthening. But the bond stopped me at the corner, two houses down. Turning around, I sprinted to the fifth house and back again. I used my wolf-hearing to listen for Grandma's old truck, but couldn't make out the truck's distinctive chug and clank. Personally, I was amazed it still ran. It had been Grandpa Jonas's, and Grandma wouldn't hear of selling it or buying a newer one.

On my seventh lap, a bright spot of red caught the corner of my eye, and I whipped around to see Chel coasting to a stop before me.

"Hey, Tay," she said, hopping out of the car.

"What are you doing here?" Out of habit, I tried to wipe sweat off my brow but couldn't find any. In fact, I wasn't even winded. The scariest part was, I hadn't even felt my wolf lend me her strength.

"You needed help." Chel shrugged her shoulders. "Besides, you need a good luck hug before Kyle's stylist sinks his claws into you."

I shivered. "Thanks for the image!"

She laughed, smiling huge. "So where is my hairy charge?"

Beast came around the corner with a huff. I couldn't help smiling at his high head and stiff tail, clearly showing his irritation.

"There you are, you handsome thing," Chel said as if she didn't care the wolf was really a man. He trotted across the yard and greeted her with a quiet woof.

It was easier, somehow, to be around Beast when he was in wolf form; thinking of him as human was too much for my sore heart. "Beast, you shouldn't have to run everywhere. Chel can only take you up to Kyle's anyway. She has to finish setting up and then get ready for the prom, too."

Beast didn't even glance my way as he went to stand next to Chel's car with his back to me. He would be trapped inside the SUV loaded with boxes. For the millionth time, I wished it didn't have to be night for him to change into his human form. But at least we'd dropped off his truck last night at the high school so he wouldn't have to turn wolf to run behind me, or in case I lost control over my wolf at prom and he needed to whisk me away like he'd done so many times before.

I suppressed a shudder at the thought that I needed a getaway car. The full moon was only two nights away, and there were only three petals left on my rose. What if I started turning wolf in front of everyone? Was it worth the risk? I realized I'd been gripping my fist too tightly and had left nail marks in my skin. I dropped my hands down and shook off the anxiety.

Stop it! I scolded myself. *I will make my heart love Kyle.*

Chel loaded Beast into the backseat and gave me a quick hug before she drove around the corner to wait. I was sure everyone who saw her either thought she was crazy or cruel to have a huge dog stuffed in the back with all those boxes, but I knew Beast would keep his head down. It couldn't be comfortable, and I urged the driver to arrive faster. Right at three, a sleek black limo stretched out in front of me as I sat on the porch steps. I hurriedly slung my small backpack holding a handful of personal items over my shoulder. A tall man in a crisp black suit and cabbie hat held the door open for me, like a bodyguard. I'm not sure that was too far off. He was well built with a broad chest and eyes hidden behind dark sunglasses. I climbed into a false sense of luxury, feeling more like a prisoner.

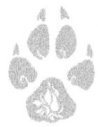

The butler greeted me in the entryway of Kyle's mansion. He was a tall man with a long, angular face. His gray-blue eyes held no emotion or spark of personality, like Lurch from *The Addam's Family*. I swear he even had the grunt down pat.

"Master Kyle is away. Ian is expecting you." The butler's voice was devoid of warmth, as if living with the Harringtons had squashed his spirits. That is if he had any to start with. I was starting to wonder if the Harringtons looked for hired help with emotionless qualities. "Wait here." He gestured me into a spacious two-story grand room off the entryway.

Light spilled in from the large windows forming the wall where the front door stood. The room was decorated in cold silvery tones with long couches paralleling each other. Between the two rectangular couches sat a stainless steel coffee table with a short disk-like vase holding two purple clematis flowers. The whole room was crisp and stark, like Kyle's mother's personality.

"Tayla!" I startled at the sudden burst. My eyes darted to my left, where a short, stocky man in his late forties descended the floating staircase. "How delightful," he said, clasping his hands in front of him. Each word he spoke was laced with joyful emotion, and he couldn't seem to keep his hands still, moving them with feminine elegance. He had too much excitement to live here at the Harringtons. Either that, or he hadn't lived here as long as the butler.

I was surprised he didn't have a Scottish accent, because he looked like he was going to pull out bagpipes from behind him. His shoulder-length, brick red hair held a slight curl, and his fair skin framed his moss-green colored eyes. He came to a stop in front of me. I could see the fine powder he used to blend his ruddy complexion into flawless skin.

He delicately held his hand out to me, and I shook it. His grip was feather light, and I couldn't help thinking he was gay. Stereotypical of me, but I couldn't stop the thought. It was rare to find someone who was openly gay in Cody's conservative community. Maybe he didn't live here at all and just flew in from New York when needed?

"Enchanté." His lips curved into a pleasant expression. His slip into French confused me. He was Scottish. I was sure of that. He looked me over like an artist does a mound of clay before he molds it. The scrutiny made me uncomfortable. "I'm Ian," he finally said.

My image of a tall lanky stylist with a French accent was shattered in wake of this flamboyant man, leaving me feeling a little unsteady as I stared up at him.

"Not what you expected?" He chuckled and winked at me. I felt embarrassment heat my cheeks. "No need to blush, my dear. Now spin and let me take in your beauty."

His bright eyes shone with unbridled happiness and excitement that I'd never expected to find in Kyle's home. Ian shared his heart through his eyes, and I relaxed, letting myself forget everything for a moment. Comfortable with Ian, I let him take my hand and twirl me around, making me giggle after a few turns.

I found his attention surprisingly flattering and fun. He made me feel beautiful and important, like there was no other place he'd rather be than right here with me. I wondered if this was his normal personality. If so, I could see why Mrs. Harrington liked having him around.

We halted, and he brought my hand to his lips. "You are indeed a rare gift." He placed my kissed hand on his well-defined arm before gesturing toward the stairs. "Shall we?"

"Let's." I grinned back at him, feeling joyfully carefree.

The floating stairs were adorned with glass panels and a slender metal handrail. It was like walking on clouds, and for the first time I was thankful Kyle was strange enough to have a stylist. Whether or not Ian was sincere, I didn't care. He treated me like a goddess, and the stark contrast felt fantastic after the month I'd had.

The whole house was decorated in an ultra-modern style with a few accents of bold color among all the white. It felt sterile and stiff, but that was what I'd come to expect from anything associated with the Harringtons. I wasn't even sure they liked living here.

Ian swept me into a bathroom as large as my bedroom in Beast's cabin. There was a long oval tub closed in with clear glass on one side. Flashes of bloody water haunted my vision, reminding me of the reason I was here. I shook the memory of that night from my head and focused on the vanity across the room. It had twin sinks and a large mirror that ran the full length of the countertop. The countertop was hard, textured glass with a wavy sea green tint. The sinks dipped seamlessly into the countertop. There was a large dressing area near the toilet, sectioned off with oriental rice-paper dividers. A small piece of maroon fabric poked out from around the dividers, piquing my interest. Was that one of the dresses Kyle had mentioned? Ian stopped my arm from untangling with his as I moved to find out.

"Oh, no you don't," he said with obvious satisfaction, humor dancing in his eyes. "We have to doll you up before you pick a dress."

I sighed with disappointment and sat on the plush bench with lower back support, subjecting myself to Ian's expert hands.

Intrigued, I watched him apply a series of foundations and powders, making my now-flawless complexion take on a soft glow. On my cheekbones, he brushed a hint of raspberry. His skilled hands made short work of turning my plain lips into fully seductive ones outlined in bronze and coated in a deep rose gloss.

My emerald eyes twinkled against the mixture of brown, gold, and green eye shadows, making my eyes shine with a bright luster, accented by the fake eyelashes that seemed to reach my eyebrows when I looked up. My wolf slumbered in boredom, and I wished I could lie down, too. My back ached from sitting straight for so long.

Then he attacked my hair. Curling and tugging it this way and that, he carefully arranged a mountain of curls atop my head. I was sure he used hundreds of bobby pins to keep it pinned just right, with only a few ringlets falling around my face. He placed a few rhinestone hair pins randomly in my hair, and I prayed that he would finish before my back gave out.

Next he grabbed my hands and *tsked* at my chewed nails. "This just won't do."

My brow crunched in guilt. "Sorry, nervous habit." I felt like a child caught doing something naughty, and to Ian, chewing nails was probably a cardinal sin.

His finger tapped my forehead. "No frowning with me in the room. Nails are fixable. I myself had the same habit."

"Really?" I was shocked.

He chuckled. "Oh, yes. I think my hands were permanently caked in cayenne pepper as a child."

I laughed, and he started filing my nails. He brushed layer after layer of nail gel on before curing the French manicure under the UV light. Once my nails were dried, he helped me stand and walked me to a hanging mirror.

"Whoa," I whispered, unable to believe it was me in the mirror.

Ian grinned, clasping his hands together. "Wait until you see the dresses."

He pushed the intercom button on the wall. "Sara, I'm ready for you."

Within moments, a robust woman in her early fifties entered the room. She wore tan slacks and an ivory blouse. Her face was stern and wrinkled in hard lines, presumably from hours working in the garden sun.

"Sara, you look more radiant every time I see you." Ian swept up Sara's work-worn hands in his, laying a kiss on each.

Sara's lips twitched as if trying to keep a smile off her stiff lips, but she soon lost the battle and gave the grinning Scottish man a small smile. "Oh, shoo, you big brute!"

"As you wish." Ian's teeth flashed even whiter as he winked at me and allowed Sara to push him from the room.

I found his infectious grin had spread to me. He was a ray of light in this gloomy house, and he made even this stern woman smile. If Ian lived here, maybe I could bear living in Kyle's world.

When Sara turned back to me, her smile had left with the man that conjured it. "Master Kyle is home, and we have less than an hour to finish here."

Kyle's home?

My heart pumped faster and nerves once again assaulted my stomach. Thankfully, I didn't have much time to dwell on him. Sara led me to the dressing room that held a whole row of the most exquisite dresses I'd ever seen. They must have cost a fortune! Sara quickly helped me into the first dress.

I swished the skirt of the plum dress with my hand. It had a Hispanic flare with ruffles up the leg split and strapless top. It was beautiful, but I didn't have time to admire it further as Sara skillfully zipped me out of it and slid another one on. The next one was a stunning, short teal dress with a layer of brown sheer fabric that shaped my body perfectly. Keeping it in mind, I let Sara yank me out of it.

I climbed into and out of so many dresses that I lost count. I had started to wonder if Kyle had bought a whole store by the time Sara brought me a dress that made all the others vanish from my thoughts. Zipping into the deep maroon gown, I ran my fingers over the clear crystal beads that formed a stream of roses that started at my left hip and flowed over the only shoulder strap.

Little flecks of green were sprinkled throughout the beaded design. The silky material ran under my fingers like wet polished stone, clinging to my modest curves. A high slit in the left side of the gown exposed my bare leg up to my thigh.

There was a delicate tap at the door, and I instantly stopped caressing the dress to look up. This interruption didn't seem unexpected to Sara. "She's dressed, Ian. Come see for yourself. She can't stop staring at this one."

My cheeks flushed with embarrassment. I heard the door swing open and shut as Ian entered.

"Do not hide, Beautè, come out and twirl for me." His voice was so sweet and coaxing that I did just that.

The form-fitting dress clung to my legs as I twirled self-consciously before Ian. His lips trembled and his eyes glistened with tears.

"Nothing to cry over," Sara scolded him.

"Exquisite beauty demands tears, my dear Sara. And she is exquisite!" Ian clapped his hands in front of him, and I blushed under his compliments.

"Now for the final touches!" He almost skipped to the vanity drawer and pulled out two elegantly designed jewelry boxes. I'd never been one to fuss over jewelry, but I gasped at the necklace he laid around my neck. Spaced evenly around the silver chain were small daisies studded with what could only be real diamonds. The same design was found on the dangling earrings he handed to me next.

Ian's hand rested on my shoulders. "Absolutely magnificent!"

His lip quivered slightly. Was he going to cry again? Before the tears could spill over, he waved a fanning hand to dry his misty eyes. "Sara, the shoes please," He said, his voice a little strained.

Kneeling, Ian slipped silver high heeled sandals on my feet and pronounced me a masterpiece.

Ian led me down the hallway back to the grand room. "Kyle and Mistress Vivian should already be there."

I tripped over my feet. Ian's arm flexed, catching me.

"Tayla, are you all right?" Ian's face was creased with worry as he steadied me. "Did you twist your ankle?"

"No. I'm fine. I just stumbled a bit." My chest clenched. How could I not realize she'd be here?

"Don't worry. Miss Vivian won't bite you with me around," and he winked.

I was so stupid. I should have seen this coming. Taking a deep breath, I started down the hall. Ian kept a firm hold on me. I smiled. He really was a sweet guy.

Suddenly, Ian halted our progress down the hall. "Twit! I forgot my camera. I'll be but a moment, my dear."

I stared at his back, feeling abandoned as he disappeared down the hall. Turning to look the way we were headed, I thought about my options. I could descend the stairs by myself and pray Kyle and his mother weren't there yet or I could just stand here and look stupid. Carefully, I leaned against the wall, choosing the lesser of two evils, or so I thought.

"I told you not to slouch!" A woman's voice snapped, making me jerk from the wall and look around the empty hallway.

"Mom, it's fine." Kyle's voice was muffled through the closed door I'd been standing near, sounding like a petulant child who'd sat still for too long. I tried to block my ears with my hands, but my wolf hearing tuned right in and the voices were as clear as if they were standing next to me.

"Tonight has to be perfect, Kyle. If we behave, your father might let us move back to L. A. and leave this hell hole," his mother said. I started creeping away, but I couldn't help noticing the determination and longing in her tone. Curiosity froze me in place. What *had* they done to land them here?

"It's not so bad. I've got friends, and now, my girl."

"Don't sass me," she snapped. "Now, hold still. Your tie isn't straight."

"Mother, just leave—it—alone!" His voice was strained with barely contained anger. My heart stirred with a tiny seed of compassion for Kyle.

"Have you forgotten you're a Harrington? The name demands perfection. Do you understand?" she scolded, making me glad the harsh words weren't directed at me. At least, not yet. Where was Ian?

"Yes, Mother," he said, defeated. "Tonight will be perfect, just like my date." The note of pride as he referred to me made me glow with hope. Maybe he already loved me. I wanted it to be true so badly my chest hurt. Time was running so short, and I still had to figure out how to convince my heart to love him in return.

"She will do. Thank Heavens for Ian. He can turn even the shabbiest country bumpkin into a movie star. Let's hope he can do the same for your date."

I felt like I'd been sucker punched. *That evil old hag!* I doubted she even remembered what I looked like. Unless she'd seen one of the pictures Kyle snapped of me while we were dating. I cringed, remembering the one in the lunch room where he'd caught me with my mouth full.

"Mother, she isn't a country girl. You have no idea how wonderful she is. She's not like the other girls." His tone was sharp, and I could have kissed him right then.

"Oh, I don't blame you, my son. Your choices were very limited in this Hicksville town. I would have picked that cheer captain. What is her name...Lacy? But oh well. Hopefully, Ian can work a miracle and still give the press something to sink their teeth into." Her voice was soft, as if this were an apology.

The press? We're going to prom, not walking down the red carpet in Hollywood!

"Open your eyes, Mother. The hicks are the press." He sounded exasperated. "This isn't going to magically patch things up with Dad and get us back to L.A."

"How do you know it won't? He'll be proud of the image you're setting here."

"Oh, I don't know, Mother." His tone was scornful. "Maybe because prom can't fix you having an affair with his L.A. Chief of Staff and possibly ruining his chance at becoming the next U.S. president?"

I heard a sharp crack and knew she'd slapped him. "Don't you *dare* use that tone with me." His mother's voice was low, threatening. "And never, *ever* bring that up again."

There was a moment of silence and then the sound of a chair scuffing the carpet, as someone stood.

"Shall we start the evening, *Mother?*" Kyle's voice was hard as he delivered a mocking show of respect.

Footsteps sounded as they approached the door, sending me scurrying to the end of the hall and into a shadowed doorway.

I crossed my fingers, praying they wouldn't look this way. My heart thrummed in my ears as a tall, elegant woman stepped out of the room. Her chestnut hair was straight, cut short in back and slowly lengthening to her jaw in the front. She walked stiffly, as if the world offended her just by existing.

I struggled to ease my breathing back to normal, but she didn't seem to hear me. Kyle followed on his mother's heels, offering her his arm, as Ian had for me only moments ago, and headed toward the great room opposite where I was hidden. Watching Kyle move to the end of the hall, I allowed myself to gaze at the black suede tux he wore. It gave his broad shoulders a crisper edge, complementing the soft wave of his dark brown hair that had been highlighted beige and tan. He didn't slouch like someone who'd just taken a verbal beating, but walked proudly. *Is that part of the Harrington act, too?* I was suddenly grateful my mother wasn't like that—neither of my mothers. One of them even had an excuse to be beastly, but fought it just to spend time with me. This lady was more beastly than any wolf I'd met yet.

I was so focused on Kyle that I jumped when a hand rested on my shoulder. Spinning around, I came eye to eye with Ian. So much for my superhuman senses.

"Eavesdropping, my little Beautè?" Ian's eyebrow rose in a mock show of disappointment.

My cheeks burned with embarrassment, and I bit my lower lip. "More like hiding."

Ian's lips curled slightly with humor. "Step out of the shadows, my dear. You have a dance to attend."

He held out his arm and bent at the waist in a slightly-bowed pose that made my lips crack a small smirk. I took a deep breath and hooked his proffered arm with mine. I couldn't hide any longer. It was time to see this to the end.

Cresting the top of the stairs, a soft gasp drew my attention to Kyle. His hazel eyes were glued on me as I descended the stairs. A warm buzz tickled my chest at the way Kyle stared at me, like he'd never seen anything more beautiful. Once again, I felt my cheeks warm under the flattery I was unused to. My wolf woke from her board stupor and paced her cage. My heels wiggled a little, reminding me to focus on where I was stepping or else I would end up rolling down the rest of the stairs.

I stopped in front of Kyle and his stern-looking mother, who scrutinized me with a critical eye.

Ian released my arm and turned to Kyle's mother. "My lady, Vivian, I hope you approve."

"You've done a suitable job considering what you had to work with."

My eyes fell to the plush carpet, indented by my sandals.

"Mother!" Kyle hissed, balling his fists.

She ignored him. "Your taste in fashion is, as always, worthy of the red carpet." Vivian smiled at Ian, stroking his ego.

My wolf bore her fangs, and I reciprocated the feeling. The urge to punch this woman's perfectly shaped nose was hard to subdue.

Ian smiled and turned to gaze at me. "She is a natural, a masterpiece," he said with pride. Ian seemed to lose himself in thought until his eyes drifted from me to Kyle.

"Don't just gawk at her, my boy! Tell her how beautiful she looks!" Ian ordered with a grin.

Kyle took my hand and drew me to his side. "Tay, you're stunning."

Gazing into his handsome face, it was easy to return the compliment. "So are you."

The next moment Kyle wrapped his arm around my waist. My wolf growled. I fought to keep her controlled, even resorting to imagining Kyle's hand was Beast's. That seemed to placate her for the moment, and I smiled for Ian's pictures. My vision was filled with bright spots by the time he was finished.

With pictures taken, I was anxious to get going before his mother decided to lecture me on the finer points of Harrington social law. Unnoticeably, I tugged Kyle's arm, signaling it was time to go. He was more than happy to comply and led me to the door. We had almost escaped when his mother's smooth voice stopped us in our tracks.

"What, no goodbye for your mother?" Her tone was light but carried an undercurrent of danger.

I felt Kyle flinch before releasing my hand to appease his mother with a quick hug and a kiss on the cheek she was tapping. He tried to avoid my eyes, but when our eyes met I could see how mortified he was. I was too distracted by Kyle to notice his mother had stepped around him and now stood beside me. She draped a dainty arm around my shoulder. The gesture made my body stiffen and my wolf's hackles stand up. Unsure of what to do, I gingerly side-hugged her in return.

She leaned her head close. "If you so much as blink wrong and ruin this night for Kyle," his mother whispered. "I'll make you wish you and your family had never moved to Cody." Her words were like icy tendrils in my ear. Then she held me at arm's length and gave me a false smile. "You two will have so much fun!"

Anger boiled like molten lava in my chest and my wolf growled, her fangs exposed. I stepped to the side, closer to the exit. I'd just subjected myself to being dressed and painted like some king's concubine, and she had the audacity to threaten me. Hadn't I already done enough? Did she think this was all roses and sunshine for me? The more she smiled, the more I wanted to bloody her lip. It took all my strength to control the urge to attack, and to keep the primal growl from exploding out of my mouth.

I had to get out of there. Without waiting for Kyle, I briskly walked out the front door. Halfway down the steps, Kyle caught up to me. "Sorry, my mom can be a bit intense and insulting."

"A little?" I scoffed at the understatement.

He shrugged as if to say, *There's nothing I can do about it.*

I came to an abrupt halt at the end of the stairs. "Where's the limo?"

His face brightened and he rattled some keys in front of me. I stopped to look at him and raised a questioning eyebrow.

"I have something better." Kyle pointed to a sleek black sports car, and my mouth fell open. "Maserati Gran Turismo," he said reverently.

I ran my hand over the smooth contours of the hood. Kyle opened the door for me, and I slid into the burnt-red leather seats. He slipped in and revved the engine to life. It purred with a power that vibrated pleasantly through me. Even my wolf thrummed along with it.

The car zipped as silky as cream down the mountain. The desire to go faster swelled in me, only to be quickly bitten off by the searing pain exploding in my gut.

I gasped.

Kyle looked at me, arching an eyebrow. "Too fast for you?"

I nodded and he laughed, but didn't slow down much. My gut twisted sharply, and black spots danced around my vision as the bond between Beast and me was stretched farther than it had ever been. Stupid! How could I have forgotten Beast?

Kyle had to slow down, before he killed me. "Pull over. I think I'm going to be sick!" It wasn't hard to fake the dry heave that slipped from my throat, since the pain nearly brought me there anyway.

"Oh geez!" Kyle slammed on the brakes. "My dad would kill me if you spewed in here."

"Keep it at a normal speed and I won't." My head spun. "Turn on the air please."

The blast of air helped and so did the reduction in our speed, giving Beast time to catch up. Fresh guilt swam through me as I envisioned Beast's sides heaving, his fur sticky from sweat, and his eyes filled with pain. My wolf growled at me, and I deserved it.

22

PROM

We parked in front of the school gym. It was about 6:30 and night had fallen. Kyle helped me out of the car. Already the car attracted a crowd of drooling teenagers, but I hardly noticed them. As soon as my feet touched the ground, I felt Beast's caramel eyes on me, and for a split second, the magnitude of his attraction for me leaked through our bond. The sheer intensity of it had my heart hammering and my feet walking toward the park where he hid.

I didn't get more than a few feet into the street before Kyle's hand caught mine. "Sorry about the guys. We can go in now."

Horrified that I'd almost ditched Kyle and my last chance at staying human, I let him lead me toward the small room adjacent to the gym, casting a confused look over my shoulder at the shadowed park.

I mentally prepared for the onslaught of noise and smells, using Beast's training. Tonight, I was definitely going to need it. I crossed my fingers and stepped through the door. The boom from the bass thrummed in my ears like surf beating upon the sand. It was bearable and under control, but my nose was a different matter. Perfume from the throngs of girls and cologne from the overeager teenage boys itched like fire licking the inside of my nose. My wolf pushed against my consciousness, begging for fresh air. Her pull was strong, but I had brought supplies. I fished in my purse for the dried lavender. I crushed the flower between my fingers and inconspicuously rubbed the oil under my nose.

Comfortable again, I smiled for more pictures, taken in front of a flowery arch with a starry night background that Chel had so masterfully created. Then Kyle swept me into the softly lit gym.

On the ceiling, twinkling lights were covered with billows of sheer blue fabric. Glittering silver and gold stars hung from the ceiling. Metal chairs lined the walls, and a few of my past dates sat in them. My heart skipped a beat in panic when my gaze rested on Brayden. My wolf licked her chops, and I belatedly registered the faint scent of old blood oozing off him.

Couldn't that boy take the week off from slaughtering innocent animals?

He turned my way, and I jerked around so I didn't have to see his accusing eyes. I felt the heat of his eyes on me, but after a few moments he moved farther away, taking his scent with him. But my wolf was agitated, and the desire to hunt made my mouth pool with saliva. I swallowed hard and focused on the décor. Clusters of balloons were scattered around the edges of the room, adding character to the otherwise dull walls. Silvery light sparkled from the disco ball, while the DJ kept the music going.

My eyes roamed over the faces, searching for Chel. It wasn't until I heard her laugh that I found her. She stood in a periwinkle dress that billowed out at her hips like a bell made of silk. Her date, Dean, was a full head taller than her, wearing a standard black tux.

I waved when she looked my way and she indicated for me to come over.

"Kyle, there's Chel." I started across the dance floor when his arm snaked around my waist, pulling me to him. My jaw flexed. His offensive hand was moments away from being ripped off, if he didn't unhand me.

"Hold up, Tay. I want you to meet Tom. He's one of our best linebackers," he said in a tone that commanded more than asked. My wolf clawed at my mind, demanding I let her out of her cage, but I held her tight and closed my eyes to center my will again. I had to stay vigilant tonight.

"Tay, did you hear me?" Kyle asked.

I slowly opened my eyes. "Yes, just a sudden headache. Give me a moment." With her mind attack finished, my wolf snorted with disgust and sat down on her haunches. I gave Chel the sign that I'd come as soon as I could, and turned to the stocky guy standing next to Kyle. I hated that I even needed Kyle. The pretenses were making me sick.

"Nice to meet you, Tom." I smiled, even though I felt more like screaming and decking Kyle.

I never made it to Chel. Kyle introduced me to what seemed like the whole football team before spinning me out on the dance floor. The song was slow. I wrapped my arms around his neck and leaned into his body, enjoying the same cologne he wore from the other day. It was like a drug to my wolf and I sighed from the reprieve as she finally lay down.

After a few dances, I thought Kyle would let me find Chel, but every time I tried, he dragged me onto the dance floor again. Finally, I convinced him to let me sit down after begging for some punch and complaining about blisters forming on my feet. The chair was hard, but my feet sighed happily. I hadn't realized how sore they were until I kicked my shoes off. I wasn't sure I'd be able to walk tomorrow. Maybe he wouldn't notice if I didn't slip them back on.

"Tay!" Chel squealed from the dance floor. Without Beast's training, my wolf hearing would have given me a migraine from the thumping of the music and the crowd of people if I wasn't blocking it out. It would've been tough to hear Chel's voice without knowing how to tune into different frequencies. I beamed at her and her date as they walked over to me.

"You look wonderful, Chel." I stood and hugged her, before acknowledging her partner. "Hey, Dean."

"Hey, Tayla. How's it going?" Dean eyed the dancing couples as if he would much rather be out there instead of standing here talking to me. That was Dean. He wasn't much of a talker, but he was a great dancer. He was lanky, not someone you'd picture dancing gracefully, but somehow he pulled it off.

"You look fabulous! I need to borrow this stylist of Kyle's." Chel gave me that *I'm-serious* look.

"I'll see what I can do," I said, before rolling my eyes at my best friend. "You guys did an awesome job decorating. What was the theme again?" I hated that my world was so off base from normal that I hadn't bothered to read the banner slung across the backdrop where the pictures were taken.

"Too wrapped up in Kyle to look around?" Chel teased, trying to gage my emotional state without calling attention to it. I shrugged and the corner of my mouth tugged upward, letting her know it was okay.

"I like the sound of that." Kyle joined us, handing me my punch. I gulped it down eagerly. Dean shifted his weight again, looking really uncomfortable now.

"Hey, Kyle." Chel greeted him with a smile, while her eyes assessed him. She was better than a guard dog.

Kyle went to say something when Chel squealed. "Ooo, ooo." She pointed excitedly at something or someone behind me. "Isn't that Toni Roloson?"

"Who?" I scanned the dance floor, waiting for some clue as to who she was talking about.

Chel snorted, and her hand found her hip. "Honestly, Tay, you haven't been out of school that long."

I dramatically rolled my eyes. "Just tell me."

"She just walked through the door. There." Chel pointed to the entrance connecting the gym to the side room where couples got their pictures taken. "The brunette in that sparkly emerald dress that I must get a better look at."

With that description it was easy to find the girl being escorted into the room by a tall blond guy. "She looks familiar," I said.

"The beading across the bodice is beautiful, and it goes up the straps. Where did she find it?"

"Chel." I waved my hand in front of her face to break the fashion trance. "Can we get to the *why* you are so excited?"

She scowled at me, her hand held out in the girl's direction. "*Toni.*" She said like merely repeating her name would spark my memory. When I didn't say anything she continued. "She's the head of the yearbook committee."

I arched my brow. "So?"

"So!" Chel pursed her lips and swallowed a retort that I was sure would've demeaned my intelligence. "If Toni takes your picture, you're almost guaranteed a spot in the yearbook pages."

"Well, then." Kyle winked at me. "We best get her over here."

Chel was beside herself with joy, tugging on Dean's arm.

In just a few minutes, Kyle had Toni snapping pictures of us. We grouped together for a goofy one and then Toni was swept away by her date for a dance.

"Now, that's what we should be doing." Dean grabbed Chel's hand, ready to lead her to the dance floor.

"Oh! I nearly forgot. Dean, will you grab me one of those mementos?" Chel pointed to the closest table with a basket centerpiece.

"Uh, Chel, you made these. Didn't you keep one?" Dean asked.

"No, I totally spaced it in all the excitement. Thanks!" She faked innocence.

With an exasperated sigh, Dean strode over to it.

Chel looked pointedly at Kyle. "They're going to announce the Royalty soon."

"I'm looking forward to it." Kyle's lips curved into a mischievous smile.

Of course he was, he was prom king every year.

"Here." Dean stopped next to Chel and placed a silver glitter-filled shot glass in her hand. "Now, let's go dance."

She handed it to me. "This is our theme," she managed to say before Dean spun her out onto the dance floor. I laughed.

"So what is it?" Kyle asked.

I smiled up at him, and then read the white lettering. "Dancing in Starlight."

"That's cool. Better than last year's: *Can't Stop the Moonlight.*" He rolled his eyes dramatically for emphasis.

My hand shook and a little cloud of sparkles tumbled out. I inhaled some and coughed violently for several seconds.

"Yeah, that one sucks," I said, when I finally stopped coughing.

Minutes later, the stage lights flicked on and the music faded to soft background noise. Mrs. Winworth, the music teacher, stood at the microphone in a bright orange blouse and purple skirt.

Her soft voice filled the room. "I'm pleased to announce this year's Prom King and Queen."

The gym erupted into applause and a few people hollered. Kyle stood beside me, clapping and hooting his enthusiasm like everyone else. On my other side, Chel's face was lit with excitement, making me smile. She would make a great Prom Queen. Next year, if I was around, I'd run her campaign.

Mrs. Winworth put up a hand and the noise from the crowd slowly trickled to a small hum of excitement. "For most of you, the Prom King won't come as a surprise. He's our star quarterback, Mr. Kyle Harrington."

The applause was thunderous. Kyle squeezed my hand in parting, and made his way through the crowd with his football buddies clapping him on the back as he went. He took the stage as if he was born to be in the spotlight. Beaming, he sat on his throne and received his crown.

"And now for our Prom Queen." Mrs. Winworth paused dramatically, and once again the room hushed. "Miss Tayla Jonas."

My chest squeezed like it was in a vice. I felt like the floor had just gaped open. The whole room was shocked and only a few claps filled the air. Chel grabbed my arm, pulling my stunned body forward. She had me almost to the stage before I snapped out of it.

"They made a mistake!" I hissed in hushed tones to Chel.

"Nope. Kyle's the king," she said, as if that made everything obvious.

"So?"

She rolled her eyes. "Did you really think he would have anyone but you for a queen?"

"You knew!" I whispered back as she prodded me up the stage.

"Just enjoy it."

Hearing the envy in her voice shut me up. My legs felt heavy as I climbed the last two stairs. Every eye was on me, but Kyle's warm gaze was the most distracting. Nervously, I sat next to Kyle and accepted my crown in front of the whole school. I wanted to pass out! That wasn't even the worst part. When Natalie took her place as a member of the royal court, she glared at me as if boring a hole in my skull. I was sure murder wasn't too far from her mind. Natalie had been Kyle's Queen last year, only adding insult to injury. Had Kyle paid someone off to rig the ballots, or had he just ordered the committee to make me queen, acting like the king he thought he was?

In fact, there were only a handful of girls *not* glaring at me. Of the girls who weren't upset, Chel was the brightest, with a huge grin on her face. I didn't blame the others. I would've glared at myself if I had the ability. As it was, my wolf filled my flesh with confidence, refusing to let my emotions make us look weak. But the truth remained; I was a fraud, and everyone knew it. I wasn't even a student anymore. Was there anything that Kyle and his mother couldn't influence?

Kyle nudged me to smile as we waved for the news reporters—reporters his mother had probably handpicked. It was all I could do not to throw up, let alone smile, but I gritted my teeth and attempted to play the part. Finally, the flashes stopped and Kyle curled his hand around mine. Grateful to be off the stage, I happily followed Kyle down the steps. But my relief was short lived as I belatedly realized a spotlight awaited us in the middle of the dance floor.

I swallowed hard, focusing only on Kyle and the confidence he radiated. He swept me around the floor, holding me tightly against him. His hand was low on my back and my wolf balked at his touch. My attention was too diverted to try and stop her from moving his hand up to the small of my back. Every time Kyle spun me around, Natalie's face seemed to be in my view, glaring at me with such loathing that I felt threatened. Her crush on Kyle made me her number one enemy, a fact she had backed up with action on more than one occasion. If I was honest with myself, Kyle and Natalie would make a perfect pair. But I couldn't afford to think that way. I needed to gain and return Kyle's love before tomorrow night.

I wasn't sure when the royal court joined us, but I was grateful that the attention wasn't just on me anymore and that Natalie wasn't shooting daggers at my back. Kyle twisted me out. He reeled me in fast. My dress caught on something and the sound of ripping fabric made several people gasp. I glanced behind me, even though my wolf sense had already confirmed my suspicions.

"Oops." Natalie put her long fingers over her lips. "Did I do that?" The quirk in her smile was proof her ways hadn't changed.

The rip was long, running up to my butt. Her stiletto heels said it all. My jaw locked in anger, and my wolf's presence fueled it. I narrowed my eyes at her. "You'll pay for that."

I lunged. Before my fist connected to her face, Kyle's arms wrapped round me, pulling me back. Natalie gave out a little shriek and stepped back, like the coward she was. The people around us stopped dancing and from across the gym I could see teachers making their way over to us.

"Get out of here, Natalie, because next time I won't stop her." The anger in Kyle's voice was unmistakable. He pulled me behind him. My wolf snarled at the insult. *We can take care of ourselves.*

"Please, Kyle. I'm the one you want. She," she pointed a shaky finger at me, "she's all wrong for you." Natalie reached out for him, but he deflected her hand with his.

Holding one of my hands now, he glared at Natalie. His jaw twitched. "I *know* who I want and it definitely isn't *you*."

I watched as each of his words hit her like a punch and her lip quivered. Kyle pulled me from the crying Natalie. I was very aware of the gap in my ruined dress as I walked, but I was too angry to care if the whole school saw my underwear. Whispers followed us as we passed. We were almost to the exit when I spotted Danny.

"Dude, that was crazy," he hollered over the loud music, matching pace with Kyle. I bristled at his relaxed tone. He sounded like he had already had a beer or two.

"Make sure Natalie knows she isn't invited to the bonfire," Kyle told Danny. "We'll meet you there later." Then we slipped out of the gym and into the night.

23

ESCAPE

Trees whizzed by in the dark as Kyle maneuvered through the curves of the canyon. I didn't care where Kyle was taking me, I was just thankful to be away from Natalie and all the whispers. I fingered my torn dress, and anger hissed through my veins. My wolf was still itching for a fight. I crushed more lavender between my fingers and breathed it in. The scent soothed my wolf enough that she lowered her hackles.

"You could have warned me about the prom queen thing." I glanced at Kyle, who was thankfully paying attention to the road and not to the struggle I was having with my wolf. It wasn't until I read the speedometer that I realized how fast he was going. *Eighty!* How was Beast keeping up? The side mirror confirmed a lone pair of headlights trailing in the distance. He must have grabbed his truck.

"I didn't want to spoil the surprise." Kyle gave me one of his devastatingly sexy smiles, sending slow warmth to tickle my insides. My wolf growled with loathing. He turned off the main road. "I am sorry that Natalie ruined it. You know she has nothing on you."

I shrugged and looked out the window.

"Tayla." His hand found mine and squeezed. "Since the first time I laid eyes on you, I knew you were for me. There was no one else, but you."

I smiled up at him, wanting to believe his words.

He grinned back at me. "You'll love the spot I'm taking you to. You can see all of Cody from up there."

My heart quickened as I finally recognized my surroundings. Lookout Point, or Make-Out Cliff as it was more commonly called, was only a few bends away. This was it. *Please, heart, let me love him.*

Sitting a little taller, I collected my courage. Kyle's cologne swirled into my lungs and helped drown out my wolf's objections as I let my body respond to the enticing smell. I gave Kyle my best come-and-get-me smile, and giggled softly at how fast he found a parking spot.

Only seconds after parking, his hand caressed my cheek, while the other one unbuckled our seatbelts. Nerves twisted in me, clouding my judgment. *This was what I wanted, wasn't it?* His warm hand on my skin was nothing in comparison to the electric zing Beast's touch sent through me. That thought was dangerous, and I pushed it far away. Kyle leaned in and pressed his lips hard on mine. My wolf rammed her cage and I winced, but Kyle didn't seem to notice. His lips were demanding, until all I could do was gasp for air. I clutched the edge of my seat fighting to subdue my furious wolf, but she was going to break free—and soon.

If I can hold on for just a few more seconds...

"Be mine, Tayla," he said, breathlessly, finally allowing me a full breath. "I love you." His voice was soft with sweet cadences of love. Although his idea of love might not be traditional, this was, I was sure, the closest thing he knew to love. But could I love him enough to break the wolf and cleanse it from my blood?

The moonlight streamed strongly through the windshield, tingling my skin. It penetrated deeper and deeper into my flesh as the full moon loomed closer. The call to my wolf was almost unbearable. The change was close. I clamped down harder on my wolf, pressing my consciousness on her like a suffocating landside. I was staying human.

"Why?" I looked intensely into Kyle's beautiful hazel eyes, only a short distance from mine. The cologne he wore was tantalizing as it mixed with another, more masculine scent coming from him. "Why do you love me?"

He looked startled at first by my question but recovered smoothly. Silently, he looked at me and skimmed his thumb over my jaw. He didn't answer right away, and I was sure that was my answer, but then he spoke.

"I've never met anyone like you, Tayla. You complete me." The honesty in his voice took me off guard. I wasn't sure I trusted him.

"What if you hurt me?" I asked quietly.

"I'll never hurt you again, Tay. You are too good—too beautiful." He stroked hair out of my face.

The words sent a chill through my blood as the "The Legend of the Beast" flooded my mind. The man had said those same words to the star and in the end he threw her away. I lowered my eyes, trying to keep the tears from falling.

"I'm sure what you're feeling is some form of love, Kyle. But what happens when I'm old and ugly?" I paused, letting my words sink in. "I need a stronger love, one that will last forever." I leaned out of his touch and rested my head against the seat. "I'm not sure that's a love you're capable of giving."

"I love you, Tayla." His voice was barely audible. I shook my head ever so slightly. I knew then, without any doubt, that he was not my true love. He'd never been taught how to love more than skin deep, and I was out of time.

Kyle's mood shifted as he recognized my refusal. His mouth set, and a protective wall went up around what little of his heart I'd been given. "I *am* capable of love. I'll prove it."

He was on me in the next breath, his mouth smashed against mine. My wolf slammed against her cage, clawing at my mind with a vengeance. My head exploded with pain. I winced but Kyle didn't care. I tried to make my lips move, knowing my wolf would soon break free and make me fight him back. My lips awkwardly tried to find a rhythm with his, hoping that it might still break the wolf's hold inside me, but the only thing I felt was pain. I struggled to keep a focused hold on my wolf. My head pressed deeply into the sharp chrome of the door frame, and the weight of his body crushed mine, sending waves of panic through my veins. My wolf slammed again into my consciousness, and my vision spotted. His tongue shot down my throat, closing my air, and I gagged.

I had to get away from him, before she completely broke free. He was easily twice my size, and even the extra strength I'd gained throughout the month wasn't enough. I screamed into his mouth, still pressed on mine. Finally, I bit his tongue and he cursed, jerking his head back. The cold determination in his eyes reminded me of a truly heartless beast, and suddenly I was very scared of what I saw there. He pinned my arm with his knee, freeing his hand to slide up my neck.

I used my legs and arms to twist my body, trying to throw him off me, but he was just too heavy and the constricted space only added to my panic. My wolf snarled in my head, rearing to ram into my consciousness again. Fear of changing drove me to call mentally for Beast. I just prayed he had the mate bond open enough to feel my distress.

"Stop fighting me." He growled.

"Get off!" I yelled back, but he just twined fingers tighter into my curls, pulling bobby pins free and forcing me to look into his eyes.

"You love me, Tayla. You love me! Stop fighting it!" The pitch of his voice rose as desperation crept into it.

I knew then that no words would convince him otherwise. My hold on my wolf slipped and she shoved her will on me. Using the only part of me not pinned down, I jerked my head straight into his face. Pain exploded through my nose, rocketing down my spine, and blood spewed from my broken nose. It hurt almost more than experiencing Beast's changes, but my whimper was cut short by a snarl that was purely my wolf's influence.

Kyle cursed, falling into his seat, taking a large clump of my hair with him, but I was finally free. My body shifted to attack him, fake fingernails drawn. Before I could move, the driver door was ripped off its hinges, metal grinding metal before it landed with a thud. Two large hairy arms seized Kyle by the shoulders and tore him from of the car. My wolf thrummed happily—proud of her mate.

"Beast." My voice was barely audible, but my relief was sweeter than any pain I had endured. *My beast had come for me, even after everything I'd put him through.* A warm, pleasant feeling settled over my heart, causing it to throb. With the little strength I had left, I whispered my gratitude to my wolf before reclaiming my body and slipping out of the car.

A terrible roar shook the air, sending a new feeling through me—fear. Not fear of my beast, but fear for Kyle's life. I didn't want

Beast to be forced to kill again, but he would to protect his pack—his mate.

Beast held a bloody Kyle by the lapels of his ripped tux. Kyle's eye was blackened and blood oozed from the cut above his eyebrow. Beast roared again, glaring murderously into Kyle's wide-eyes and pale face. Beast trembled, close to losing control of his wolf. His eyes changed to the light silvery-blue of his wolf, and I sucked in a breath. His wolf wanted blood. I couldn't let him change.

"Beast," I called, too softly. He barely acknowledged me with a slight twitch of his lips, keeping his eyes on the whimpering boy he held. I could feel the wolf inside him licking his chops, waiting to be unleashed. My wolf brimmed with pride, pacing eagerly for the kill.

No! He can't kill him. The pack will never be safe again. Please, help me protect him—protect them.

I wasn't sure if she understood my words, but I hoped she would feel my worry. I was no longer talking to Beast as a man but to the wolf slipping into control, and I needed my wolf's help. An image of her nodding gave me the courage I needed to step into Beast's direct line of sight, some distance from Kyle's back.

"Beast!" I commanded with force, and when his eyes flickered to mine, I held them. I felt my wolf's presence flash to the surface. A direct challenge, but I prayed Beast would recognize us and reclaim his control. His eyes were feverish with the need to hunt. I could smell the reek of fear rolling off Kyle that screamed "prey."

A growl escaped his snarling teeth. I was surprised when an answering snarl ripped from my throat. It sounded too *wolf* not to scare me, but I would deal with that later. I saw the glimmer of respect flash in his eyes, which morphed ever so slightly back to a caramel color.

"How badly are you hurt?" His voice was rougher than usual, like sandpaper.

"It's just my nose. I'll heal."

Beast studied me, making sure I wasn't lying. Slowly, painfully, he released Kyle from his grip, shuddering with the wolf's protests. Kyle stumbled backwards, falling into a muddy patch. He slid through the mud to get as far away as possible.

I stepped closer to Beast. "Beast, are you okay?" He shook with the effort to keep his wolf in check.

"I still smell your blood," he barely whispered.

"He's not okay. He's a freak!" Kyle's voice rang out, startling me. I'd been so intensely focusing on Beast that I'd forgotten about Kyle. My wolf growled in my mind. "He's dangerous, come on, Tayla. Let's get out of here."

Beast roared. "I didn't spill her blood, boy." His rough voice seethed with hate. "I didn't try to take advantage of her!" Beast quaked fiercely now.

"Kyle, get in your car and leave," I pled, unsure how much longer I could keep either of our wolves from tearing him apart.

"Not without you."

"No, Kyle." I turned to look at the boy I so foolishly had thought I could love. "I belong with him." The truth rang so clear it warmed my core, until my eyes focused on Kyle again. "Leave before you get killed." My voice was hard and commanding. Beast's eyes were changing to a more silvery color as his wolf started slipping to the surface again.

"You belong with me. Not this thing!" Kyle ranted insensibly, grabbing my arm.

As soon as Kyle touched my arm, Beast roared. *Snap! Crack!* His bones jutted at odd angles under his skin. Clothing shredded under his bulging body, falling off him like leaves from an autumn tree. Flesh ripped only to mend again in angry red lines that were soon covered in fur. Falling on all fours, my beast was now wolf, a gloriously handsome wolf, muscular and strong with tan, black and silver fur. My wolf and I drooled in our heads.

"What the—" Kyle's words died on his lips as he stared at the furious silver eyes of the wolf. Kyle's hand trembled, letting me go.

"You should've left, Kyle," I whispered, stepping between him and the wolf. "If you want to live…run."

I held my beast's eyes, and was relieved to hear Kyle's feet pounding the ground behind me. But it wasn't until I heard the car purr to life and drive off that I lowered my eyes submissively. "Forgive me, Beast. I should have listened to you about him. Thank you for rescuing me."

I waited for my punishment, unsure what it would be. What I didn't expect was for him to nuzzle the hand resting at my side. I felt my body begin to tremble as the adrenaline ebbed away and the horrors of the night crumpled me to the ground. My arms encircled the wolf's neck, and I buried my face in his soft fur, sobbing and bleeding into his coat. Streams of pleasure flowed from my wolf and my whole body vibrated with it. I held him tighter. He soothed me with a soft thrumming sound that resonated in his chest.

It was a while before I pulled away, tears gone, and pinched my nose with a scrap of Beast's shredded clothing. I used other pieces of cloth to get the worst of the blood off my face and hands. Beast found a nice patch of grass to roll in, cleaning his pelt.

I looked down at my torn and bloodstained dress. Tears welled in my eyes at the ruined silk. I rubbed at my eyes to stop the tears. There was no fixing the gown, just like there was no fixing my life.

"Time to go home, Beast." I knew my fate was sealed. Grandma, Aunt Lily, and the girls would lose another relative to the wolf, but there was nothing left to do but pray I would survive the change. Beast's home was my home now, and we walked side by side through the woods to his truck.

I went to open the passenger side door when Beast barked. I looked at him and he pointed with his nose to the driver's side. My eyebrow arched questioningly at him, but he growled and pointed again to the driver's side.

I gazed hard at the wolf and saw the signs I was missing. His hackles were raised and his body was tense. His silver eyes were still alight from the confrontation with Kyle. His wolf wasn't going to let Beast turn human, not until he calmed down. Holding a scrap of Beast's shredded clothing to my bleeding nose, I climbed in behind the wheel, and Beast jumped into the passenger side.

My fingers slid over the empty ignition. "Keys?"

Beast tapped my right leg with his snout demanding my attention before pointing it to the gas pedal. Obediently, I reached behind the rough pedal and snatched the keys. With Beast's head resting on my thigh, I drove to his cabin, only inquiring once which fork in the road to take.

The headlights brushed across the shadowed cabin before resting on the outside log wall between the windows. I killed the engine and nearly fell out of the truck. My exhaustion was complete. I needed to get inside before the moonlight's tingly beams gave my wolf enough strength to change me. I ran to the glass doors and flung them open.

I made it halfway across the grand room when a large figure streaked by, blocking my way to the stairs. Beast was faster than me, even after a recent change back to human form. He stood formidably in front of me, dressed in the long, black trench coat and sweats. I halted, barely in time to avoid colliding with Beast's solid form.

"What?" The exasperation in my voice was clear even to my ears.

"You're hurt. Let me see it." Beast made a move to cradle my face in his hands, but I brushed them aside.

"I'm fine. I just need time alone." I stepped around him to climb the stairs to my room.

Beast grabbed my arm, halting my progress up the first two stairs. I looked over my shoulder at him, preparing to argue.

"I need to fix your nose." His eyes were hard silver.

Baffled by his determination, I shook my head. All I wanted to do was curl up in a ball and hide from the moonlight. "It will heal," I whispered as I referred to my wolf powers.

"Even werewolves need to have bones set, before their bodies heal wrong. Now come." Beast headed down the hallway to his room.

What did it matter? It wasn't like I'd be human long enough to care.

The command in his voice sent chills down my spine, a premonition of the way things would be after the change. Even now his command pulled at my wolf to obey, but I still had enough power to resist him for one more day, and as long as I had a choice, I would take it. Beast halted, looked back at my still form, and raised an eyebrow.

My lips twitched slightly and warmth trickled through my chest from the bond. It was hard to take him serious when he made that face. "Tayla, it'll hurt more if I have to break it again to reset it," he said.

"What does it matter when I'll change tomorrow anyway?"

"It matters, Tayla. Please? I can't bear to feel you in pain."

The look in his pleading eyes was more than I could ignore. I sighed and followed him to the master bathroom. I let out a tired breath as I remembered the last time I was here. I'd been covered in blood then, too. It seemed pain and mending bloody wounds would be a large part of my life from now on. I sighed again, and Beast gave me an understanding look, but said nothing.

Perched on the edge of the vanity, I clutched the edge with white knuckles. Beast's large hands rested near my throbbing nose, and I flinched away.

"Hold still. This will only hurt for a second."

I didn't have time to prepare before he pinched my nose and twisted to one side, snapping it back into place. Needles of pain seared through my skull. I cried out, before my wolf could clench my teeth closed. She was disgusted by my show of weakness before her alpha and mate. I couldn't care less what she thought. It hurt!

Tears leaked from the corners of my tightly-shut eyes as black spots danced across the back of my eyelids. My world spun to the rhythm of my pounding head. A strong arm wrapped around me, keeping me from toppling off the vanity, while the other one held a towel to my hemorrhaging nose. My cheek rested on his chest and my arms wrapped around his torso, grabbing fistfuls of his heavy-duty trench coat. Every muscle in my body tensed as I rode the wave of pain zinging through my flesh.

Breath after breath. The throb in my nose dulled until my muscles relaxed enough to think again. Beast's large hand stroked my hair, pressing me to him. Tingles raced across my skin at his caress. I pressed harder into his muscular chest, enjoying the closeness. My heart swelled, and my eyes threatened to spill tears at his tender care. I'd rejected him and yet he'd stayed by me, even when it hurt him. *What would've happened if I'd lost his love when I'd chosen Kyle?* I shivered. The pain that accompanied the thought made me gasp.

"Tay?" Beast's deep voice was soft.

I pulled away enough to look at him, thankful that my nose had stopped bleeding for now. I opened my mouth, meaning to reassure him that I was fine, but I lost myself in the depths of his churning caramel eyes. His intense gaze made my insides melt and butterflies tumble in my chest. My eyes drifted down to his lips and my wolf thrummed with need. The desire to have his lips on mine was so palpable I could almost taste it. I let my hands run over the hard lines of his chest. My wolf shivered but wasn't pressing on my consciousness. I realized then that this was me— that my *human* lips burned for his, and it was not my wolf's instinct to lick him. Was that why I was unable to love the other boys, because my heart was already his? Was all the effort to break my wolf for nothing?

Being in Beast's arms, I couldn't deny the yearning pulsing through me. If this was wrong, I didn't care. I'd already lost my chance to cleanse myself of the wolf. I hadn't found a human love, but I had found Beast. I wanted to feel human one last time before the change came. I held him tight, fitting inside his arms like the missing half of a mold. His head leaned down, snuggling into my loose curls that had escaped Ian's bobby pins. Suddenly, the need to smell him with my wolf senses grew to unbearable levels, but my bloodied nose was out of commission and a small shudder of frustration zinged down my spine.

"Shhh." His hands circled in soothing patterns on my lower back. "No one will hurt you again. You are ours now." His voice was near a snarl at the end. His arms tightened protectively around me, effectively killing the moment. My temper bristled at the possessive tone he'd used, reminding me too much of Kyle and the horrible night that had brought me here. I pushed him away. But he only allowed me the length of his arms. His hands rested on my hips. I was angry enough to ignore the heat of his hands.

"I don't belong to anyone. Even if you are my alpha, I will always have power to choose my own way."

Silver flashed through his now-hard eyes. "You will respect your alpha and mate!"

I jumped off the vanity, ignoring the jolt of pain through my nose as I landed, and glared at him. It took all my strength not to slap him.

"Maybe I won't even survive the change. Maybe I don't want to! I'd rather die than be your sex slave for the rest of eternity!" Dark fury colored my words as I stormed out of the bathroom and up the stairs. I slammed my bedroom door, clicking the lock in place. It wouldn't stop a werewolf if he wanted to barge in, but the small act of defiance made me feel better.

Why did he have to open his stupid mouth and ruin everything? I folded my arms across my chest. My wolf whimpered at the space between herself and Beast. I echoed the sound before I clenched my teeth in determination. So many things had been ripped from my future. I couldn't even choose my own mate! It was beside the point that my heart was drawn so strongly toward Beast. I might have even chosen him when I changed, but the choice was never going to be mine, it was *hers*, and that was too suffocating to contemplate. *Would I become the backseat to her thoughts and actions, just as she was for me these last weeks? Would she stuff me in the same cage I'd locked her in so many times?* The thought sent a shiver of dread down my spine.

Stripping out of my ruined gown, I tossed it into the corner and grabbed black sweat pants and a solid blue t-shirt from the dresser. Now that I was alone, my anger dissipated into despair and my stomach ached with fear. I was trapped, lost to the wolf.

My life. My family. My freedom. All of it gone with one small bite.

My eyes stung and my knees trembled. I crawled under the comforting weight of the bed covers and let the tears fall in hot streams down my face until all I felt was the numbing power of oblivion.

24

BAIT

Saturday, May 5

Standing at the edge of a clearing, hidden in the shadows, I squinted up at the full moon glowing brightly in the star-speckled sky. The scent of pine sap wafted around me like a blanket of comfort, but my heart wouldn't slow. It pounded fiercely in my chest, threatening to break my sternum. My sweat-slicked skin glimmered as the silvery moonlight penetrated my flesh, entering my blood.

My back shot up in an arch, and I fell to the ground on all fours. Again my back jerked sharply upward, breaking my bones one by one. Unspeakable pain seared the very marrow of my bones, like stabs of a heated knife repeatedly thrust into my flesh. My skin shredded, giving way to dark mud-colored fur. With one last twist, the last of my bones snapped and molded themselves to the skeletal structure of a wolf.

I threw my head back, and a carnal howl ripped from my raw throat. Hunger consumed me. My stomach pinched with sharp twists and I feared I would collapse if I didn't feed soon. I sniffed the air, searching for prey. Soon the sweet scent of soft flesh filled my nose, and I howled, beginning the hunt.

The power in my muscular legs pounded adrenaline through my body as I ran. The blood scent grew stronger until I could see a willowy shadow running before me. It was slow and clumsy with its two legs. I ran ahead of it and crouched in the undergrowth— waiting. The weak human ran right to me. I leapt, sinking my teeth into its throat. Sweet warm blood oozed down my throat. The body fell and the face of my aunt stared back at me—pale and still in death.

I jolted awake, gasping for air. I wiped my sweaty brow with trembling hands. My damp clothes clung to my quivering body, and horror pounded through my rapidly beating heart.

White-knuckled, I gripped the sheets and rocked back and forth, chanting. "It was only a dream. It was only a dream. Aunt Lily is fine. It didn't really happen." Tears washed down my cheeks. I heard Beast bounding up the stairs.

He whined and clawed at the door.

"Go away." Then more to myself, I whispered, "Please, God." My eyes looked up at the dark ceiling. "I don't want to turn into a monster."

Beast whined, low and mournful, but I wouldn't allow myself the comfort he offered—it wouldn't last and I didn't need any more human memories to torture me. When I didn't answer again, Beast's padded footfalls receded down the stairs. I slumped back into my pillows. Next to me on the bed lay the letters to my family, securely in the envelopes I'd sealed weeks ago. I picked up the one to Chel. "She will never forgive me." I sniffed and placed it back in the pile.

I had slipped and fallen into the Shoshone River. At least, that was my cover story. Not a very original way to go, but it would be the easiest to stage. Even Beast couldn't complain about the simplicity of it. All he had to do was throw my dress into the river, sandals and all, and provide an eyewitness. I wiped at the tears running down my face and fingered the letters to Cammie and Sarah. They would take my death the hardest, having lost their dad only a few years earlier. My chin trembled and I turned, burying my sobs into the pillow. Soon, I succumbed to a mind-numbing sleep.

When I awoke again, the sky was the dusty rose color of evening turning into the dark violet of night, just like the end of my human life. Panicked, I rolled off the bed, taking the tangled mass of blankets and sheets with me, and crawled into the darkest corner of the room.

Wrapped in a blanket, I huddled in the shadow of my bed, afraid of the moonlight leaking through my window. Its call was strong and my body convulsed with the desire to bathe in it. But the nightmare was too clear in my mind. The shocked eyes in Aunt Lily's dead body still haunted my vision.

I clenched my teeth, determined to withstand the full moon's call until it ripped me from the shadows with its silvery claws. I trembled with fear. It had come too fast. I wasn't ready. I'd never be ready for this. A sob broke the silence—my sob. "No, I can't do this."

Suddenly, I wanted Mom with me, needing to hide my fears in her gray pelt. But tonight wasn't safe. Beast would have kept the pack close to him. Thinking of Beast sent guilt washing through me. I regretted overreacting, but the time for apologies had passed. He was a wolf now, and I might not survive the change swirling up inside me.

Were there no happy endings? There was a black hole of despair wherever I turned: the loss of my human self, the threat of my Beast dying at the fangs of another wolf, and the moonlight's constant reminder of the wolf gaining strength inside me. Overwhelmed, I leaned my aching head against the wall and curled up into a tighter ball, awaiting my fate with shaky limbs and heartache so strong it threatened to stop my heart before the change could.

When I woke again, the dark cloak of night encompassed the meadow. The force of the full moon had claimed dominance over the heavens. My wolf pushed her will over mine, inching me closer to the door. I fought her, squeezing my eyes shut and imagining a rope tying her down. My imaginary fingers burned from the rope sliding through my hands as my wolf stood. My control over her was slipping—her strength overpowering mine. She jerked and the rope slid from my hands. She wiggled free.

My wolf senses heightened, and I was helpless to rein them in. Smells fogged my now-healed nose, but the cedar wood bed frame was by far the most potent and annoying. It was so strong that I put it right up there with rotten eggs. Sounds of night chirped and buzzed around me, making me cover my ears. Thankfully, I didn't have a mirror to confirm my fears. I didn't want to look at my own eyes—icy blue—staring back at me.

The ruckus of a battered old engine clanged in the distance. I focused on it. Metal bounced against metal in a rhythm I knew well. Had my lonely, scared mind conjured up things that weren't real? But what if it wasn't an illusion? What if it really was Grandma?

The image of Aunt Lily's dead face flashed in my mind before morphing into Grandma's. Blood drained from my face and my hands grew clammy. Grandma shouldn't be here! It wasn't safe. Listening harder, I heard the chugging engine come to a halt close to the house. The truck door opened with squeaky protests and someone jumped out, slamming the door shut behind them. Footsteps ran through the forest and up the porch steps.

The warmth of happiness cooled as quickly as it shot through my veins. I could change any moment and kill her without thought!

"Tayla!" Grandma's voice was breathless with desperation as she threw the front doors open. The sour smell of fear wafted up to me from the swirling fans in the grand room.

Her fear fed my wolf and saliva dripped down my chin. I wiped it away, fighting to gain control. My will barely came out victorious. Praying I had enough control to warn Grandma away, I clutched the edges of the comforter I held around me and sprinted across the sliver of moonlight blocking me from the shadowed door. My heart hammered in my chest. I jerked the door open, sickened by the sound of ripping metal. The door hung crooked from having all but one hinge yanked from the frame. Horrified by my strength, I dropped the door as the top mangled hinge gave way. It crashed to the floor.

"Tayla!" Grandma's alarmed voice traveled up the stairs, closer now. "What was that?"

"You have to leave! It's not safe!" I yelled, but it did little good. Grandma's footsteps had reached the stairs.

"Not without you!" She went to say something more, but panic rose in my chest, and I cut her off.

"Please, Grandma, go...I'm changing." I shook from the effort of staying in the small patch of shadow my doorway provided. My wolf's desire to exit the house and soak in the moonlight was growing stronger.

Within two heartbeats, Grandma was at the top of the stairs. "You can't change here. Quickly, into the woods."

Nothing she said made sense. "Are you crazy? That's the last place I want to be on a full moon!"

Grandma's eyes flashed with urgency. "They're coming with guns. They might search the house first." She swallowed hard. "Tayla, I didn't know they were following me. Chel was frantic. I didn't think. I just left. I didn't mean to—"

The rest of her words became garbled as my ears perked up and the skin on the back of my neck tingled. More engines roared up the road, purring quietly like well-tuned, newer vehicles.

Kyle. Oh, this was bad.

Truck doors slammed closed. I counted at least six pairs of feet hitting the ground. It all happened so fast I wasn't sure if some of the thumps weren't two hitting at the same time. I let out a frustrated growl, wishing I'd listened to Beast and developed my werewolf senses more. My wolf agreed emphatically, and I felt her survival instinct war with the desire to save her pack, her alpha and mate.

My head throbbed from straining my hearing, but I had to catch more of what was going on. Grandma noticed my rigid form and stopped speaking, making it easier for me to focus on the group of humans shuffling about in the forest.

"Let's hunt!" Kyle's hard voice boomed, and the boys cheered.

I gasped. There had to be at least ten of them, if not more! Had he brought the whole football team?

The metallic ring of bullets sliding into rifle chambers created a sickening echo in my head. My heart jolted with each bullet loaded.

"Beast. Mom." My voice came out hollow with fear, and all thoughts of the change vanished from my mind. Reflexively, I pushed on the mate bond, trying to warn Beast, but he either didn't feel my efforts or was too busy with the pack to notice.

Impulsively, I dashed down the stairs, sparing Grandma a quick over-the-shoulder glance. She stayed at the top of the stairs wringing her hands, a gesture I knew well. She didn't have her paint brushes to busy her nervous hands and calm her anxiety.

Her eyes caught mine and an unspoken plea for safety passed between us. "There are letters on the bed, and...I love you." With that I was out the door and sprinting across the meadow toward the whispering voices. I threw my wolf's cage door wide open, needing her power. The moonlight burned like sunrays on a solar panel through my skin. The change was so close, my skin hummed with the knowledge. *Please just hold off until I can talk Kyle into leaving*, I begged the magic of the full moon. My wolf didn't fight me and for the first time our purpose was the same. Only two things mattered right now: Mom and Beast.

Entering the thick forest, I had the full power of my wolf's night vision. The dark shadows which had veiled my human eyes and caused me to trip over tree roots or rocks had no such effect on my wolf's eyes. Every plant, rock, and twig stood out easily, as if lit by the noon sun.

My wolf sang at the freedom she felt, and a sickening feeling settled like tar in my stomach. Her power hummed through me, tickling my skin. I rubbed my arms. Still smooth. I let out a shaky breath. No hair, yet. But I could feel the moonlight feeding my wolf, making her stronger. I sprinted faster than ever before, my lungs gulping in air as fear threatened to seize control. I knew my time was short now, but it would be worth it if I could save those I loved.

The forest flourished with sounds and smells so amazing that I floated on the high of my fully-unleashed werewolf powers. Tendrils of fear wrapped around that thought, whispering warnings that I was losing myself to my wolf too quickly and I'd be gone before I finished my task. What if I died in this very spot?

I swallowed hard, shaking my head. The action allowed reason to trickle back into my mind. If I only had minutes left, I was going to make them count. It took great effort not to let my senses overwhelm me again. I had to focus. Thinking back to Beast's lessons, I pushed the other sounds away, zeroing in on the soft footfalls of the practiced hunters.

Kyle and his posse were only a few yards ahead now, but I didn't slow my sprint. A new zing of fear rolled through me as I heard the distant sound of wolves snarling. My running stride faltered as the images of the last time I'd seen the pack flittered through my mind. My foot snagged on a root and I tumbled to the ground. I rolled into the fall and sprang back up gracefully. My wolf growled at my clumsiness, and I could feel her disgust at my weakness ooze through me.

Because of the distraction, I hadn't paid attention to the hunting party. Their footsteps were much louder now. My wolf pushed my legs to go faster. Her consciousness pressed in on my mind and I faltered, giving up precious ground. It was like arm wrestling an opponent of equal strength. I screamed in frustration.

Suddenly, I was right on top of the hunting party. I was going too fast to stop and ran right through the group of teenage boys, like a streak of color. A shot rang out as I reentered the foliage on the other side, and the bullet sliced across my upper arm. My wolf raged with fury, breaking her concentration. I dug my heels in, skidding to a halt and crouching in the underbrush to listen to the startled whispers.

I touched my stinging wound, my fingers pulling away dark with blood. Instinctively, I knew I was lucky. It wasn't deep enough to bleed much. Applying pressure, I held the wound with my hand. My wolf lashed at my mind, wanting to take control and attack. Her blood lust quaked through me. I held on to her rapidly-fraying leash with everything I had left.

"What was that?" one of the boys asked.

"I don't know, but I'm sure I hit it," another one responded.

I didn't instantly recognize the voices, but with my wolf fighting for control, I didn't have the focus to figure it out.

"Who shot?" Kyle's voice was hard, determined.

"Something streaked right in front of us, and Tom got it!" one of the guys explained.

Kyle growled. "Are you trying to lose me my trophy? You probably scared him away! And over what?"

"We're hunting wolves, Tom, not rabbits." Danny's unmistakable voice filled my ears.

"It *wasn't* a rabbit. It was too big for that. Just ask anyone." Tom's voice seethed with annoyance, and I was sure that if I tried I could've smelled it wafting off his skin.

"Anyone else see this thing?" Kyle asked, but no one spoke. Then, Kyle chuckled darkly. "Seems it was just your imagination."

"It was fast, but they saw it, even if they're too chicken to admit it." There was a tense moment of silence before Tom continued. "I'll prove it."

My wolf's bloodlust slammed into me, knocking the wind from my lungs. I trembled from the fight of wills, barely staying in control as a migraine pounded through my skull. I had to make them leave. And quickly.

My eyes darted to the escape route behind me. My wolf snarled at my cowardice and flooded my emotions. My heart thudded against my sternum. *They thought I was a rabbit!* Anger rolled through me. I was tempted to growl and give in to my wolf's desire to attack at the insult. *I'll show them that I'm no one's prey.* The violent impulse startled me. I tensed, refusing to let her win. I *was* going to save my pack and these idiots before she turned me forever.

I eased away from the rifle tip poking around in the bushes. There was no way I'd let him shoot me twice. I slipped far enough away to hide from him. A boy about eighteen, with a buzzed head and a hefty build, stepped through the foliage—Tom. I finally recognized him from prom.

He knelt by the skid marks in the dirt, where I had finally come to a stop and examined the few drops of blood that had dropped from my wound. He looked up with a confused expression on his face.

Energy built in my limbs and my wolf licked her lips for the kill. I bore my teeth. My actions slammed into my consciousness, and I took what little self-control I had left and backed further away. I had to talk to Kyle before I could no longer subdue my wolf. Her icy-blue eyes seemed to glow in my mind with a knowing empowerment. She knew I was growing weaker. My hands shook from fear of the uncontrolled feelings I'd had in the woods only moments ago—the feeling of losing myself to the wolf. The woods pressed in, suffocating the air from my lungs. I gasped for air as Danny called Tom back.

"So did you find the rabbit?" Danny taunted Tom when he emerged from the foliage with nothing to show for his rummaging.

"It wasn't a rabbit." Tom's fists balled.

I sucked in the night air, silently willing him to throw a punch. A fight would delay them and hopefully warn Beast of their presence. My chest panged. I didn't want anyone to die, and if the pack sensed them, there was no telling how many from both sides would die. Just the thought of Mom or Beast dead seared my heart. I wouldn't let that happen. The groups had to stay separate.

My heart hammered so loud in my chest that it hurt, but I stood from my crouch. My wolf snarled. Her essence bristled with unease. I forced my heavy legs forward, closer to the guns that would take my family away.

My wolf snarled and her razor claws slashed at my mind. I winced, eyes watering from the pain, but kept placing one foot in front of the other. I'd make them leave, drag them one by one back to their trucks if needed. My wolf glowered at me with narrowed eyes, crouched and prepared to extract vengeance for the many wounds Kyle had caused.

Please, just let me try it my way first. His parents will never give up the hunt if he is murdered. We have to protect the pack. Get them to leave before they discover too much.

My wolf snorted with disgust but grumpily lay back down.

Before I was visible to the group, I called out, trying to sound confident with my words. "You're right, Tom, I'm not a rabbit."

All eyes flew in the direction of my voice, and I stepped out from behind a tree, holding my wounded arm.

"Tayla?" Kyle and Danny both said in surprise.

"Yeah, and your friend there should watch what he shoots at." I moved my hand from my wound. It was healing fast and had already stopped bleeding, but old blood clung to my skin.

Tom's gaze fell to my bloody arm and the color drained from his face. "No, I didn't...I mean..."

"Philip, take that thing away from him." Kyle's angry voice bit the air.

I watched as Philip, a sandy-blond with a linebacker's build, walked over to Tom. "Way to go, hotshot. You could've killed her with that stupid stunt." He ripped Tom's rifle out of his hands, before the shocked Tom could protest.

"Rabbit? Yeah right," one of the other boys said. And another said, "He could've shot anyone of us."

Kyle's gaze flowed over my wound. "I have a first aid kit in the truck. It won't take long for Tom to lead you there and keep you safe."

"I'll be fine. What I need is for you to leave." I held his gaze hoping for a flicker of commonsense. Kyle glared at me through his non-puffy black eye.

Jerk. I wish now Beast had given him two black eyes!

"Where's the wolf?" He demanded.

I would've recoiled from the venom in his voice, but my wolf held me steady. Now that I'd forced her into enemy territory, she wasn't going to let me show weakness. My eyes gazed over the other boys in the group. Kyle knew something of what they were up against, but did the rest of them?

"Glad to see you're worried about your friends getting hurt, or didn't you tell them about the danger they're in?" I glared at him.

"We can handle ourselves." The look in his eyes said he'd like to strangle me until I broke to his will. "Isn't that right, boys?" He laughed and the others joined him, though a few of their voices were a little strained. My eyes hardened, and I clenched my fists until I felt the fake gel nails about to snap off.

I narrowed my eyes. "I was safely in the cabin until I heard you idiots tromping through the forest, trying to get yourselves killed."

"Is it his cabin, Tayla? What, does he hold you prisoner there, or do you dig freaks now?"

A snarl reverberated from my wolf and through my teeth. "These woods," I swept my arm wide, eying the other boys, "will—kill—you." I punctuated the last words, driving home my warning.

"And yet you are out here," Danny said. Whenever Kyle was around, Danny was his loyal puppet, though uncertainty was clearly etched in the pinch of his brow.

Spineless.

"Awe, isn't that sweet. Tayla's come to protect us from the big bad wolf." Kyle's mocking made my blood boil. A few of the guys darted their gaze about nervously.

My lips curled back in a snarl. "I remember saving your life not long ago." My wolf's energy buzzed through me, ready to fight. "But I'm not sure I'll do it again."

Kyle's lips twisted into a cruel smile. "My turn to save you. I'll stuff and mount that beast's head and then you'll be free of him."

I lunged forward, planting a right hook on his jaw. He fell hard to the ground. I kicked him in the gut and my wolf howled with pleasure. I went for another kick when something struck my head from the side, sending me sprawling. Pain exploded through my skull and the world spun. Someone lifted me from the ground, carrying me in a side hold. My vision came in and out, and my brain was slow. It took me several seconds to analyze the guy's smell. It was Danny.

I wanted to hit him too, but my limbs wouldn't respond. My head felt like shrapnel bounced around inside it, cutting my skull and everything in it. Blackness clouded my mind, but I pushed to stay awake. I couldn't pass out now. *Beast! Run! Get the pack out of here.* I grabbed for the mate bond, praying he'd hear my warning. But there was no response.

"What do we do with her?" Danny asked.

"Bring her. We'll use her to lure the wolf," Kyle said, his tone emotionless. "Let's go."

"Wait," a wavering voice spoke. "I didn't sign up for kidnapping or whatever you're going to do with her." The voice grew stronger. "I'm out of here."

"Yeah, me too." A few others chimed in, but the voices were starting to slur in my mind.

"Fine, you cowards, run home with your tails between your legs." Kyle's voice rang painfully in my ears. "Danny and I can handle this."

"I'll stay," Tom said, and another arm came around my waist. My head hit his shoulder and pain exploded through my skull. I whimpered and with the last drops of energy I called to Beast. *Run, please.*

The mate bond flew open and Beast's rage filled my senses. The world swirled black for a moment but my wolf stubbornly kept me conscious—barely.

25
STAR

Danny complained about my weight as they dragged me through the forest. I could feel Beast running, coming for me. I wanted to warn him off but my head hurt too much to think. I drifted in and out of consciousness. I was sure they dropped me a few times. My whole body ached. The silver moon's rays soaked into my skin, feeding my wolf strength, helping speed the healing process. Soon I'd be able to fight them again. I'd wait for the perfect moment. My wolf grumbled with frustration.

Then something slammed into us from behind. We tumbled to the ground. I heard Tom scream and Danny curse. I struggled to open my eyes, finally getting them open a crack. Beast's teeth were buried in Tom's flesh. The sound of a bullet being loaded curled my stomach.

"Beast"—my voice came out small and raw—"Watch out." His head jerked up and he leapt to the side, but not fast enough.

Crack!

The bullet hit and pain lurched across the mate bond. My heart rate spiked. *No!* With my wolf's help, I sat up. Pain sliced through my cranium and my hands flew to cradle it. The need to protect Beast surged through my veins, and I willed the world to stop spinning.

Murderous anger rolled across the open mate bond and a fierce growl thundered around me. I squinted at where Tom still whimpered in pain with Beast standing behind him.

"Beast," I whispered. *He was standing! Maybe the bullet missed him and struck a tree?* The tangy scent of blood—lots of blood—chased away my momentary relief and replaced it with fear. He stood only a few yards from me. My eyes searched Beast for wounds. Blood trickled down his back leg from a bullet wound high on his thigh.

I staggered to my feet, feeling my wolf's urgency to protect Beast, to be near him, but a large hand closed around my wounded bicep. I hissed from the pain that shot up my arm. My head swiveled and I glared at my captor. A white-faced Danny held a pistol against my back.

"Don't move. I don't want to hurt you, Tayla, but I will if I have to," Danny said.

"You're nothing but a coward," I spat. With inhuman speed I swiveled, knocking the gun out of his hand with my arm. Danny's eyes widened and he turned to dive for the pistol, but I caught him and drove my knee into his gut. He wheezed and hunched over.

"Danny, control her!" Kyle commanded.

I turned from Danny to the real threat here. Kyle stood only a few feet away. His hazel eyes were sulfuric with fury, his rifle aimed right at Beast.

A pained moan split the silent night, and my eyes focused on Tom, who was curled into a ball and lying on the crimson-stained grass at Beast's paws. My heart pounded against my ribcage. Beast's lips curled back in a snarl, baring his long fangs at Kyle.

It was a nightmare happening in fast forward, and I had come to the climax. I felt Beast's intentions before he leapt. Kyle squeezed the trigger. I screamed, and I lunged with werewolf speed for Kyle's rifle. My fingertips flicked the barrel the exact moment that a deafening bang cracked through the air. My Beast crashed to the ground, skidding to a stop at my feet.

"No!" My arms fell around him, cradling his furry head in my lap. His lungs rattled with each breath and fresh blood dripped from his mouth. I stroked his thick fur, telling him everything would be okay. His pain, love, and regret flowed unchecked into my soul through the bond. Tears flowed down my cheeks as my heart rent with anguish.

I was losing him.

"Ha! Told you I'd kill him." Kyle slapped a frozen Danny on the back. Kyle stooped, handing Danny his dropped pistol. "Better hold on to this." Danny's fingers curled around the gun.

Hatred flared like a bonfire, consuming me and my wolf. Kyle grinned down triumphantly at Beast. My hands clutched fistfuls of Beast's pelt.

A feral growl erupted from my throat, drawing Kyle's attention. Our eyes met, and his smugness faltered a little. My skin itched from the wolf raging just under the surface.

"You're eyes... They're...glowing blue." His shocked voice was barely a whisper.

I snarled, baring my teeth. Screw my eyes. Beast was dying because of *him*!

"I'm going to kill you." My voice was low and deadly. The pack howled, and I felt them close by.

Danny shifted uneasy. "Hey, man, Tom needs help. I—"

"Shut up, Danny!" Kyle's eyes danced with a crazy light. He cradled his gun, jamming another bullet into the chamber. "The freak is going to die! No one takes my girl and makes me look like an idiot! You'll see, Tayla. When he's gone, you'll love *me* again."

I moved my hand along the ground, ripping a good size rock out of the dirt. My hearing zeroed in on Kyle, who was driving the chamber home and cocking the gun. Adrenaline pumped through me, and I threw the rock so hard it sliced through my palm as it flew. The rock hit the barrel with a thunderous impact. The gun fired into the sky, knocking Kyle to the ground.

Suddenly, the pack broke the tree line, entering the small meadow. Danny yanked Kyle to his feet, dropping his pistol but not caring to retrieve it before they ran to their truck. Streaks of multi-toned fur coats ran past me. My wolf growled, wanting the bodies of those who hurt her mate to rot, fertilizing the forest floor forever with their corpses. I quaked with the need to make them pay for the blood oozing out of Beast's body. I pressed my hands into his wounds, desperately trying to stop the bleeding. I wanted to be on the hunt, but I couldn't leave Beast.

A wet nose nudged my arm. Sparing a quick glance, I found myself staring into my mother's wolf eyes, and her silent support caused fresh tears to fall.

At that moment, a calming sensation of peace rolled into me from the mate bond, making my throat burn with the emotions I held back. Beast still loved me. Even after all I'd put him through, he'd chosen to sacrifice his life for me.

The dim roar of engines reached my ears, and I hoped Kyle had been ripped to pieces before he could leave the forest. Beast's breathing hitched, and I clung to him fiercely.

My heart filled with a depth of love I didn't know could exist. I felt like I would die with him, not my wolf without her mate, but me, Tayla, without Beast. He was always good to me. Why had I fought it so viciously? Being mated to the alpha of all alphas wouldn't have been that bad. It would have been like being royalty, really. How had I been so selfish? My whole soul willed him to live. I wished could take back every hurtful thing I'd ever said or done to him.

"Stay with me, Beast." I stared into his silver eyes that began to droop closed. I shook his muzzle. "Fight it!" My voice was raspy with emotion as I cried. "I love you! Do you hear me? I love you. I can't live without you!"

Then I heard the sound of paws thrumming the ground. The pack was approaching the small glen where Beast's life hung by a thread. His eyes closed. Their alpha was easy prey for the strongest male now. My blood froze. Not two seconds later, they burst from the trees, approaching their fallen alpha, baring razor sharp teeth and ready to compete for the next alpha's place. Beast's ears flicked and anxiety flowed through our bond, urging me to run.

I cradled him closer, nuzzling his soft, furry head with my cheek. Kissing the top of his head, I squeezed back the tears. "Never," my wolf and I breathed out together.

The pack nipped at each other, fighting quick scrimmages for the right to be the first to feed upon the alpha's flesh and ascend as the next alpha. I trembled from their growling and yelping, but my wolf steeled my resolve. I would die with him, but fear nearly paralyzed me. I squeezed my eyes shut and clung on to Beast. The smell of blood coated the air with the sour smell of metal.

This couldn't be how it ended. Not after everything we'd been through. My mother's soft tail brushed my back as she stood guard. I realized there was something I could do.

I pulled my wolf out with all the strength I had. I needed to change, it was our only hope for survival; but my wolf whimpered in frustration, sending me impressions that she couldn't change—it was too early. She flashed me a picture of the moon at the zenith of its arch across the night sky. The moon still had to travel before she'd have enough power to change me fully.

I hung my head in defeat. Mom leaned against my back for reassurance. Even she didn't stand a chance against the huge black and white wolf that stalked forward ahead of the others to claim his prize.

"I love you, Mom."

The black and white wolf's yellow eyes burned with the desire to make the most powerful kill in his werewolf existence. My eye caught a glimmer off to my right. It was Danny's pistol. Adrenaline zinged through my veins, and I knew I only had moments. Using my wolf speed, I lunged for the gun. My hands curled around it. I swung it around. The wolf charged me, teeth bared and snarling. My slippery fingers struggled to cock the gun. The wolf leapt and I rolled out of the way but not before his claws raked my flesh. I screamed. The wounds burned my back. The wolf stalked forward again. I scooted back until my back pressed against Beast's body.

Growling, I pushed the cock down and aimed. "I won't let you have him."

The shot rang through the clearing. The wolf slammed into the ground. I sagged in momentary relief before the rattling sound of Beast jolted me back. My wolf sang with sorrow that matched my own.

I quickly cradled his head once again and applied pressure to his wound. My mom shook behind me and I looked up to see that the wolf I'd shot was back on his feet, looking more murderous than before. Blood coated his left side, just above his shoulder blade.

He growled a warning to the pack encroaching on us. They stopped, and he charged. Terror stopped my breathing and my hands fumbled to cock the gun again. His teeth grazed my shoulder.

A bright burst of light like the noon sun pierced the darkness, stinging my eyes blind. Teeth never sank into my flesh, though they should have. Or had they and I was already dead? I blinked several times, trying to rid my vision of light spots. Slowly, my eyes adjusted. The wolf that had charged me lay on the ground motionless. The whines of the pack echoed across the clearing as they slumped to the ground. A wolf body hit my back, sliding to the ground.

"Mom!" I reached a hand behind me. Warm breath hit my palm. She was still alive. Blood squirted into my face. I jerked around and jammed my hand back into Beast's wound to stem the flow. I cursed at myself for not taking more care. His chest heaved for air.

The light gathered together into a blur above the trees, shining like a strobe through the darkness. It advanced on where I sat, hypnotizing me with its shimmering whiteness. It lengthened into the shape of a person and stopped right before me, hovering just over the ground.

I hugged Beast closer, my blood soaked hands jarring me out of the beauty of the light. My chest tightened with panic. I wasn't letting anyone take him from me, even an angel.

"No! I won't let you go. I won't. They can't have you." If this was the end, they would have to take us both!

The light danced with sparkles, gathering shadows around the otherwise invisible form. I peeked through my lashes. The intensity stung my eyes, but I was too petrified someone would snatch Beast if I closed them. I reached for my wolf's strength to help me fight this being of light, but her consciousness was deeply asleep. I was truly alone. Tears brimmed in my eyes. Fear seized my body—fear that this ethereal being would rip my last reason for living right from my arms.

The light dimmed, now fully concentrated into the form of a woman floating above the ground. It was like she'd swallowed every ounce of light in the night sky into her body until the luster around her was no stronger than a fluorescent light bulb, and my eyes thanked her for the relief. She was dressed in a billowing white dress, and her face held an ethereal beauty. Her skin was as fair as the moon, framed by sun-dipped curls. I looked into her sapphire eyes that twinkled brighter than the stars.

I knew those eyes! Suddenly, it was hard to breathe.

"You're the Fallen Star," I whispered, unable to believe it. The painting in Beast's study did her little justice. It amazed me how any man could've thrown her away, when only a sprinkling of wrinkles lined her face.

"Yes." The woman's lips morphed into a sorrowful frown.

Beast's warm breath bathed my arm, and a mixture of love and resentment for my ancestor coursed through me. If she hadn't cursed her husband, Beast wouldn't be dying in my arms right now. But then he wouldn't have been turned a werewolf, and we never would have met. Was all the pain worth it? To find your true love and then have him ripped from you in the end?

Her pain mirrored my own. I felt it so deeply that my bones ached with sorrow.

My eyes drifted to the dimly glowing object in her hands.

A sad smile graced her lips. "Tayla, your love has broken the curse and given me the chance to finally end all of this pain."

I frowned. "I don't understand."

"Oh, Tayla." She smiled kindly down at me. "Your Beast didn't understand the true purpose of the curse. But your heart and his heart did."

I stared at her in confusion.

"You, Tayla," she pointed at me, "chose to see the man who hides beneath the beast and love him. Thousands of years have passed since that ill-fated night when I laid the curse. Many have suffered and none of my blood-line had the purity of heart to look past the monster and love the man." She looked at my face, searching for understanding that still wasn't there. "You are the human, Tayla. It was always a human that had to fall in love with the beast."

"But I've loved Beast for a long time now." My voice hitched as I looked down at my beloved. "Why didn't the curse break sooner?"

"Love must be tested before it can be true. You were willing to give your life for him. There is no greater test of love." Her eyes looked heavenward. "My torment has finally ended, and I can be forgiven for my sin upon this human race. Finally, my soul will be released from the moon to rejoin my ancestors in their resting place." She met my eyes. "Thank you, Dear One."

But what she said didn't erase my pain. "But he's dying. How could this end the curse and leave me mourning? Your torment might be ended, but what about mine? What about the man I love?"

The woman's gaze bore down on me, scrutinizing every detail. I felt transparent, like she saw my every thought and feeling.

Beast's chest wheezed and rattled. Fresh blood oozed from his wounds which struggled to heal, covering my hands with the reminder that he was dying.

Tears trickled from my eyes. "Please, save him. I can't lose him. I can't," I cried as my body trembled with grief and my tears once again soaked the top of Beast's head.

"Only you can save him," she simply replied.

"I—but what can I do?" I stuttered in unbelief.

"Your love is strong and has brought me here. I have heard your cries, and with the strength of your love I can offer you two choices, for that is all the power I have left to give." Her eyes showed her sympathy.

I nodded for her to continue.

"In a few minutes, your wolf will awaken and you will complete your transformation to become just like him." She held out her hand toward Beast. "You will lose much, if not all of your humanity."

I shuddered at her words.

"But I thought I broke the curse?" My voice was shaky. "Why am I still changing?"

"It isn't that simple." Star frowned. "You broke the curse—or, a better way to say it, the responsibility I laid on my bloodline. The original curse I cast, which created the creatures you call werewolves, can never be completely undone." Star's gaze fell to the rock she held. Her voice was heavy with sadness as she spoke. "But by coupling the power of love you two share and my life sacrifice, you have been given the power to choose between two different paths."

Her twisted explanations irritated me. Time was ticking. "Just tell me what I have to do. I don't care what happens to me. Just save him."

"Listen." Her eyes flicked to mine, quieting my rambling. "The first path will free both of you from the wolf forever and restore him to full health."

A small smile of hope curved my lips.

"But," the woman warned, "while you may both live happy, human lives, the other wolves will stay in their imprisoned forms and continue to struggle with their humanity forever, having no hope of redemption."

I felt the smile melt from my face. Mom was one of the imprisoned. I couldn't curse her to that forever...

"And the second choice?" I asked.

The woman's eyes sparkled, and her lips curled into a small smile. "The transformation will become complete and you will become a wolf." My heart fell, thinking of my fate. "But through exercising restraint, your human spirit will have the power to dominate the wolf. All werewolves around the world will be able to take their human form without restriction of pack position or time of day. But the moon's pull will never quiet." Her eyes clouded with deep trepidation, and I held my breath. "Those who cannot control their wolves will be devoured by them and die."

I gulped down a nervous breath. "You mean if I choose the second option we might all die anyway?"

"I doubt all will die, but there will be casualties." Her blue eyes dimmed with the heaviness of the choice before me. *I could die. My mother, Beast...*

Was the risk worth it?

I gazed down at Beast, and my wolf whined with worry. His breaths were further apart and my heart broke watching him fade from this life. I wished he could help me choose our fate. I knew how much grief being a werewolf caused him, but he knew and loved his wolves. They were his pack, his family; leaving them behind to suffer would never settle well with him. As I thought of my mom, whom I'd only known as a wolf, I knew I wouldn't be happy with that choice either.

"Time to choose, Tayla. He has but moments left, and I won't be able to save him if the light of life leaves his frame." Star's face was grim.

Looking up at the woman, I matched her sorrow with my own. Neither option would magically deliver us all to a happy ending, but I knew which one would give the most hope of happiness—*if* Beast and I survived.

"I choose to have the wolf come upon me," I said, praying that my body was strong enough to survive it. "I choose the second option."

"Then it is done. Beware of the strength of the full moon's call and strong, negative emotions. Humanity will triumph if you can exercise control. May you never be without love, my daughter." The woman held the glowing rock to the heavens. The last of the magic seeped out of the celestial rock and infused itself into the light around Star. Faster and faster the light swirled around her, growing so bright I had to shield my eyes with my bloody hand. When I thought I would bake in the heat of the light, it exploded. For a millisecond, it penetrated my entire being, waking my wolf and driving the darkness from every crevice around me before the black of night once again shrouded the glen.

Star was gone. Where she'd stood was a charred ember smoking on the spring grass.

Beast stirred in my arms. My eyes fell upon his wounds, and I gasped. Not a trace of blood remained, not even on my hands, but that wasn't what drew my attention. My beast was human. No wolfish deformities or excessive hair covered his perfect body. He was beautiful—alive. I stroked the golden tanned skin of his chiseled chest, running my hand up his neck and face to his wavy chocolate-colored hair, making sure he was really there. My wolf woke, vibrating with joy. Her mate was alive.

His caramel eyes fluttered open, dazed. I held him close to my chest, and his arm wove around my waist, holding me tight as his other arm propped his torso up so our faces were level. Our eyes met, and no words were necessary. Tears rolled down my cheeks and one of his hands threaded through my hair, resting on the bare skin of my neck.

"Tayla." He said my name with so much love, I thought I would burst. "I thought I'd lost you."

"Never." I caressed his smooth cheek. "I love you, Beast."

"Jameson," he said, and I raised my eyebrow at him. "My name is Jameson. Or James."

A mischievous smile pulled at my lips. "Well, James, you will always be my Beast." His name felt foreign to my lips.

He let out a low guttural growl that vibrated between us. It spoke to both my human body and my wolf, making it the sexiest thing I'd ever heard. My body pressed eagerly up against his in response. His arms tightened around me, and I melted into his touch, pressing my lips hard and urgently against his.

He returned my passion with his own. His strong lips moved in rhythm with mine, eager but gentle, like he was slowly devouring his favorite dessert. His arms kept me close, my hands intertwined in his hair. Every nerve in my body was on fire, and a small moan escaped my lips.

Beast trailed kisses down my jaw and neck, and I gulped in air. It was only then that I opened my eyes and ears to the meadow around me. I remembered we weren't alone and my cheeks flushed.

I tapped his bare shoulder. "James." His smoldering eyes met mine and I regretted opening mine. Somehow I managed to remember my reason for distracting him. "Look."

He turned reluctantly and stiffened at the sight around us. "The Choice."

Strewn around the meadow were naked humans, struggling into seated positions, and wolves lying motionless on the ground—dead.

I pulled away from him, suddenly sick at the sight of so many lives lost. "I tried to make the right choice. I'm so sorry." I hiccupped on a sob. They hadn't survived their wolves. I could die just like that. A hollow pit grew in my stomach, and my grip on Beast's shoulder tightened. His arm flexed, holding me close to him.

"It was the best choice, the only real choice in the end." His voice was weighted down with grief.

"Oh no, Mom! Please, Mom!" I sprang out of Beast's arms frantically, praying she wasn't one of the dead.

A movement close to me drew my gaze. A naked woman met my eyes. My mouth fell open. She looked only a few years older than the picture hanging in Grandma's hallway: the same warm brown eyes, long curly light brown hair, and fair skin.

"Mom!" I ran to her, wrapping her in a crushing hug. Tears stung my eyes and fell down my cheeks. "I thought I'd lost you."

"Oh, my Tayla." Mom's voice was unsure and rough coming from human lips once again. She held me tight. "Oh, my girl, my little girl. I'll always be here."

My mother sniffled, and I thanked the stars she hadn't died. Emotion squeezed my heart, and my sobs came out like strangled gasps, but I didn't care who heard them. I finally had my mother, human and alive, and nothing could ruin our moment.

Except perhaps the moon.

Bright moonlight burned my skin, and I could no longer hold back the change. I yelped in pain, releasing my mother to wipe at my bare arms. My skin crawled as though an army of ants marched under it, bulging and misshaping it. Repulsion overrode my horror. I dry heaved. But it wasn't bugs causing my skin to ripple. My wolf felt too happy for it to be anything other than the change. I tried to swallow the lump in my throat without success. The time had finally come, and I no longer felt so brave.

26
INTERTWINED

Monday, May 7

My eyes frantically slid over Mom's sorrowful gaze and landed on Beast's strong but compassionate eyes. I tried to find the mate bond, to plead with him for reassurance.

He must have seen the wild, panicked look in my eyes.

"The bond is not there, my love," he said, looking a little bewildered himself. "But the alpha's power surrounds you. As you change it will flood your mind, and you will be part of the pack."

What he was omitting, but was clearly in his worried eyes, was *if* I completed the transformation and didn't die. My stomach wrenched, and it wasn't all from seeing my arms start to sprout whitish-silver fur.

Beast's firm, warm hand tingled on my cheek. I leaned into it, needing his touch more than I realized.

"I'll never leave you, Tay. Fight and live. We *will* be together." His voice was hard with determination, but I couldn't take my eyes from the patches of fur on my skin. Fear clutched me so tightly, I wasn't sure I was even breathing. Pain lashed through my spine, arching it violently upward, bones cracking. I fell to the ground.

"Tayla!" My mother shouted. I wanted to comfort her, tell her I was okay, but all that came out was a scream, feral and desperate. White hot pulses shot through my flesh, ripping my muscles.

"Tay." Beast's agonized voice was both outside my ears and in my head. It must be the alpha bond forming, for I felt his call and listened even through the pain. "Engage your mind! Fight for control over your wolf. Don't let the wolf form strip you of your humanity. Do you hear me, Tayla? Fight!"

I gave a small whimper in reply as new waves of pain racked my body, breaking and reforming bones, muscles, tendons. Inside my mind, my wolf howled with excitement, pushing her essence through every vein in my body. Lightning fast, she rammed into my consciousness, fighting for dominance. I pushed back, but I knew she was suffocating me. My limbs, not human anymore, flailed in the air as I fought the pounding assault in my head. Soon all I could think about was the snarling wolf in my head and the fiery pain relentlessly pumping through my flesh.

Why was I fighting? I was sure that giving in would be a quick and easy way to erase the torment. As if in answer to my question, another wolf's presence pierced my cloud of despair and roared in fury. I winced from the jolt it sent through me. The sheer power of the voice gave me a shred of will to fight.

I pushed toward the presence. Confusion clouded my mind, but I had a strange feeling of belonging to that powerful voice. I trudged through the pressure of my she-wolf's attempt to keep me cornered in my mind. The closer I got to the powerful voice, the more I could smell a musky, wooden scent. It was tantalizingly earthen and heated my blood with a new fire. I reached out my mind to him, and the cloud oppressing me started to lift.

My would-be captor wailed and snarled, as if screaming, "Mine!"

At that moment, I knew myself again and Beast, who called my human self to the surface. Fury raced through my new wolf body, now free of pain from the transformation.

Yours? I hissed back at my wolf, in my mind. *He is mine!*

Her presence, battling me for dominance, buckled, but didn't relinquish. *Ours?* she cooed, like a spoiled child caught at her own game.

I didn't know how I knew it, but this felt right. He was ours, both his wolf and human selves. They matched us, two for two.

Ours, I agreed silently, and she submitted to me. Her wolf essence wove through me so thoroughly that we were a seamless unit with me in charge.

A wave of relief sent me springing onto all four of my wolf legs that twitched with the need to run—to hunt. Hunger stung my empty stomach and the need to fill it made me antsy.

My eyes found my alpha, still in human form, kneeling in front of me. Sweat ran down his face, but his silver-swirled caramel eyes shone with pride and a passion that made me shiver.

"You're exquisite." His hand reached out to touch me, and I stepped my whole wolf body into his bare arms. I tingled from the heat of his touch and the way his hands raked through my thick fur. The smell wafting off him made me light headed. I never wanted the embrace to end, but the need to hunt made saliva drip from my panting mouth.

He released me with a merry laugh. "You're right, Tay, it's time to go." He stood. "Change. We'll hunt tonight." He addressed the other humans as their alpha. From the corner of my eye, I watched them immediately bend their naked bodies to the ground and transform within seconds. I envied the speed of their change.

Mine had felt like an eternity, but maybe that was just because it was my first time.

There were so many different shades of gray, brown, and black that I found myself staring at the other wolves in awe. My wolf eyes enhanced everything. I could decipher the different shades and patterns of color on every wolf, the unique smells, distinguishing them from each other.

Mom came up to nuzzle my neck. I leaned into the gray wolf, surprised to find I was larger than her. I tried to speak with my throat, producing a strangled whine.

Mom grinned, baring her teeth, and her eyes danced with humor. I growled low, just enough for her to know I didn't think it was funny. Then in my mind, I heard her voice.

"We do not use our voices as humans do, Tayla. We use our alpha's magic to speak mind to mind. Try it. Find the silver thread in your mind that links us all to our alpha and to the pack, and direct your thoughts across the silver line connecting you to me." Mom's voice drifted into silence.

Searching, I found the complicated web of silver that seemed to go into every direction. I tried to trace the one that went to Mom, but I kept losing it in the snarled mess. Frustrated and angry, I thought of all the things I would tell Mom about her so-called directions, when a single strand glowed faintly brighter than the rest. Was thinking about the person the key to finding their link?

I thought harder about Mom: her gray fur and the lighter gray patch that covered her forehead and under her eyes. Suddenly, the line that had glowed dimly before, surged with bright light. It was like a door opened and Mom was there waiting.

"It took you long enough," she teased.

"It's not like you gave me much to go on," I snapped back half-heartedly.

I could feel her amusement through the link.

"Now, think of yourself again, and retreat back to yourself."

Intrigued, I did and found it was easy, now that I knew what I was doing. Mom nuzzled my chin and I could hear her telling me how proud she was. I nuzzled her back. It was then that I felt someone staring at me. Whipping my head around, my eyes locked with a sandy colored wolf with yellow eyes that glared daggers at me. I stiffened at the hostility in those sulfuric eyes. The primal wolf response overwhelmed me and I growled. She bore her teeth and stepped forward. My mother flanked me, hackles raised and her sharp canines exposed.

The wolf's eyes darted to my mother before flicking back to me. The hate in her eyes slammed into me like a baseball bat to the gut. I didn't know what I'd done to deserve that. I'd never even seen her before, but every part of her screamed enemy. Maybe I'd killed a wolf she loved when I made The Choice? I shivered at the thought.

The wolf turned then and left. If wolves could stick their noses up and sashay out of sight like a human, she'd have done it. She reminded me way too much of Natalie.

Without warning, the alpha's voice blazed through the lines, lighting them all. "Meet our newest members of the pack: Tayla, my mate." My doubts vanished, and warmth flooded through me that he still claimed me, even though our bond had been severed. I felt the searing eyes of the one wolf in this pack that wanted to rip my throat out. I clenched my teeth, determined not to let her ruin the sweet moment.

"And Tom," Beast continued.

Shocked, I looked at Beast, deciding Jameson or James just didn't work for me when he was in wolf form, and then quickly to the black wolf only slightly smaller than Beast himself.

"Tom? You mean that guy who shot me?" My wild thoughts found their way to Beast before I could stop them.

"He will not harm you, now, my love."

I wasn't afraid of him. I was shocked that another person had been changed so quickly. But then I remembered him ripped and bloody at Beast's feet, and realized the amount of alpha's venom would have been in too large a quantity not to change tonight. I winced, not envying him the painful change.

"What happened to the others hunting with Kyle?" I was reluctant to ask. How many died tonight? My heart was heavy with guilt. If I hadn't gone to prom with Kyle, Tom wouldn't be a wolf right now and the rest—

I gulped, shifting on my paws.

"Wounded, but most were already in their trucks or close to them before the pack caught up to them." Beast's silver eyes bore into mine and relief flooded me. Now that Beast was healed, I could think more forgivingly toward Kyle and his buddies. However, I wouldn't have minded Kyle being among the wounded.

Beast gave me a lopsided wolfish grin and licked my snout before I could skip out of the way. It tickled, making me sneeze, and laughter filled my mind. I would make him pay for that, but he was already at the front of the pack.

"We run." His quick command was met with howls of delight as wolves sprinted into the forest.

My own legs pumped after them, with Mom at my side. The pack was fast, but I kept up, enjoying the exhilaration of speed and agility that my wolf limbs gave me. It was like flying while keeping my feet on the ground.

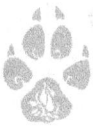

When morning dawned, I found myself exhausted as I handed the last pillow to a willowy girl who looked like she was about twenty. Her head nodded slightly as she took the pillow. Her hazel eyes were filled with so much uncertainty that I felt sorry for her.

Mom squeezed my shoulders. "This isn't a time for frowns."

I looked into her youthful chocolate eyes. We looked the same age; it was too weird. Her eyes were the only thing that gave away the years she'd lived.

"I am happy. I have you." I wove an arm around her waist and smiled.

"And you have us all." Grandma pulled us into a group hug. Our eyes misted with emotion. We had already called Aunt Lily. That phone call had been filled with tears, especially when Mom talked to her, thanking her for caring for me. My life was complete now. I had my family and my Beast. I could deal with anything now.

Grandma gave a final squeeze, before letting go. "Now, let's get this finished so we can sleep. I'm exhausted. " She went back to distributing hygiene supplies.

"I love you." Mom pulled me into a deep hug. "So much."

I hugged her back. "I love you too." My voice hitched at the end.

We stayed in the embrace for a long moment before Mom placed a kiss on my head and said, "I'd better go help Grandma."

She let me go, and my eyes landed on Beast right behind her. "Walk with me." Beast —I wasn't used to calling him James yet— held out his hand to me. I never thought I'd get tired of gazing at his face, free of deformities. His short chocolate brown hair complemented his warm caramel eyes. The strong cut of his jaw and nose gave him a ruggedly handsome look.

"But there is so much to do," I said, looking at the twenty-some people clothed in mismatched items found throughout the cabin. Grandma and Mom were busy distributing toothbrushes and towels, but there was barely enough for them all. The fires were burning bright, but the sight reminded me of a refugee camp. What were we going to do with all these people?

"Rose and Maria are taking care of things. Besides it's been too long since I felt the sun on my human skin." He tickled my fingers with his, and I finally allowed him to lead me out into the cool morning air, conceding to let Mom and Grandma handle the pack for a while.

We walked for several minutes without talking. It seemed that Beast was not only soaking in every particle of the morning sun, but also breathing it in as he wove through the forest, finding every shaft of light in our path. My heart was lighter, watching him enjoy something so simple and yet something he'd been deprived of for so long.

I stifled a yawn, unsure how long I could stay awake after last night's events. Plus my stomach was full from the several deer we'd killed. I was sure it would gross me out, but to my wolf, it was natural, and as a human, I could still honor my vegetarian tendencies. Maybe I could think of meat as a necessary medicine or something.

"James." His nickname rolled off my tongue with an odd feeling. Would I ever get used to using it? He turned his head in my direction. "What do you plan to do with the pack? They can't all stay in the house and lounge around for the rest of forever. They'll go crazy in a week."

He gave a tired nod. "Star changed so much all at once. It will take time for us to get our feet under us again."

I frowned at the ground. "But won't they have to live somewhere nearby? And what about identification papers? I'm sure they've all been pronounced dead or missing. They can't just go back to their former lives." I knew I was rambling but there was so much to think about, I couldn't slow my mind.

Beast stopped in a ray of sunlight, his face turned upward, soaking it in. I watched, memorizing the strong line of his jaw, the way the worry wrinkles relaxed into smooth skin. And my body relaxed. My eyes roamed over the man who had stolen my heart, amazed that he was mine. He was so perfect it was hard to take him all in. Even his nose was beautiful, begging me to run a finger down its arch to its strong base. Everything about him radiated strength, and I felt safer than I could ever remember being. But the two features that really stole my heart were his caramel eyes and the way his lips curved into a half smile, and both were hiding from me.

I stepped closer. My fingers brushed his sun-bathed cheek down to his cleft chin. His heart-stopping eyes opened, enveloping me in their swirling depths. His lips curled into a seductive smile under my exploring fingers. Zings of electricity shot through my veins as his strong arms encircled me, drawing me hard against him. The distant roar of the waterfall mingled with the rushing sound of my heated blood. I gazed into his smoldering eyes and my body molded once again to his. My wolf and I quivered with desire.

"We'll worry about all that soon enough. Right now, I'm going to kiss you." Beast dipped his head toward mine.

Heat flared through me as our lips met, deepening in intensity as our bodies pressed against each other. His hands teased lightly up my back and I shivered in pleasure. I fully embraced my love for Beast, melting into his touch. He filled the hole inside my heart with eternal bliss, and in that moment, all my concerns wafted away. It was just us and the love we shared.

27

HEADLINE

TWO INJURED IN CRASH SOUTH OF PAHASKA TEPEE

Two eighteen-year-old Cody boys were found unconscious in a crash south of Pahaska Tepee Saturday night.

Driving at reckless speeds, the driver lost control of his Toyota Tundra while on a back road. It rolled three times before slamming into a large pine. Both boys sustained head injuries, rendering them unconscious, according to information released by the Wyoming Highway Patrol.

A local resident reported the crash just after 11 p.m., about 9 miles south of Pahaska Tepee.

The passenger, Daniel Markner, is in critical condition and was life-flighted to St. Vincent Healthcare Hospital in Billings. The driver, Kyle Harrington, was taken to West Park Hospital, in Cody. He regained consciousness during the ambulance ride to the hospital.

The Highway Patrol said in a news release that the boys had a handful of unusual injuries that weren't caused by the crash. When asked about the claw marks that shredded Mr. Harrington's right bicep, he told police that a group of friends were out for a hike when a pack of wolves attacked them. He insisted they weren't regular wolves, but monstrous werewolves, who killed his football teammate, Thomas Bantmas.

The Cody Police Department investigated the crash scene, discovering shotguns and a pistol with empty bullet shells in the truck cab, suggesting the boys had shot several rounds from the truck.

Around 10 a.m. on Sunday, Thomas Bantmas was found at home with no injuries. He admitted that he was part of the group of boys that went hunting for wolves around Pahaska Tepee. "I never thought we would find any," Thomas said. "When the wolves attacked it was chaos, and a few of us were hurt. The pack chased us back to the trucks, and Kyle shot several."

The Wyoming Game and Fish Department has been notified and will search for signs of the wolf pack where the incident supposedly occurred. The Cody Police Department continues their investigation. According to Officer Tanner, three boys have been linked to the incident with a possibility of seven more.

Shortly after Mr. Harrington's claim of seeing werewolves and Thomas Bantmas being found unharmed at home, the Harrington family flew Kyle Harrington to California where he will be undergoing psychiatric and medical evaluations. His family will give no other statement other than to suggest that their son had sustained head trauma during the crash and that he was not mentally sound.

As of 2:00 this afternoon, Mr. Markner had not been released from the ICU and has yet to wake, but is in stable condition. A future court date has been set to address the boys' illegal hunting and gun use.

ACKNOWLEDGEMENTS

I love my support team. They range from my wonderful family to my awesome fans. With your enthusiasm and cheers, I have finished this book. Thank you!

A high five out goes to my new cover designer M.R. Polish! You always amaze me with your talents! My new covers are absolutely stunning!

A huge shout out to my editors, Jessica Drollette at Mystic Manuscripts LLC, Diane Yerka, and Lydia Ross, who have pushed me to write better and have spent hours combing through this novel making it shine. You guys rock!

Thank you to my wonderful beta readers: Jen Lattin, who found those homophones errors I can ever see. Angie Smith, whose rodeo expertise enhanced the book and kept me from embarrassing myself. M.R. Polish, Jeanette Hunter, Holly Millett, Anna Gonzalez, and Tawnya Meyer for your insights and awesome error catching skills!

Last but certainly not least, to all the bloggers that have helped me spread the word about my books. Especially to Lady Amber's Reviews, who has done so much to promote my books. You are just amazing!

Special Note: Thank you to my first cover artist Katt Amaral and model Brennan Winegar for making my old covers so amazing. Those covers will always have a special place in my heart.

ABOUT THE AUTHOR

Ashley Lavering loves to weave stories and see them come to life on paper. However, this wasn't always the case. She used to run screaming from writing assignments in school. The irony isn't lost on her now. Her love for writing may not have started when she was a child, but her passion for telling stories did. She enjoys the arts and the sciences. Exiting college with a Mathematics and Science Degree, she now uses her knowledge to world build and create exciting new stories.

Please support her by posting a review and recommending the novel to others. Ashley loves to hear from her readers, so drop her a line. You can visit her at www.ashleylavering.com

Thank you so much for reading Star Cursed!

I hope Tayla's struggle to break the curse—and to hold on to her humanity—kept you turning pages late into the night. Writing this installment has been such a rewarding journey, and I'm grateful you've shared it with me.

But their story isn't finished yet.

If you're ready to discover the final secrets, the hidden dangers, and the true strength of Tayla and James's bond, join them in the epic conclusion: After Star.

If you enjoyed this story, please consider leaving a review. Your support helps indie authors like me reach new readers and keep bringing these worlds to life.

With gratitude,

Ashley Lavering

www.ashleylavering.com

Books by Ashley Lavering

AFTER STAR
(SNEAK PEEK)

The Epic Conclusion to the Curse of the Beast Series

The curse is broken.
The bond remains.
And now... her mate is dying.

Life was supposed to be simple now that Tayla has chosen James—her alpha, her heart, her mate. Together, they flee to the remote mountains of Idaho to escape the growing wolf hunts stirred up by their old enemy.

But peace is short-lived.

Shadows from James's past threaten everything Tayla thought she knew. When he's struck down by a mysterious poison, she and her best friend Chel must unravel a deadly puzzle to save him—before the bond between them breaks forever.

With time running out and danger closing in, Tayla must face old enemies, hidden truths, and the wolf inside her.

Can she save the one she loves... or will she lose him to the
darkness that haunts them both?

After Star is the third book in the *Curse of the Beast* series—a clean YA paranormal romance full of fated mates, forbidden longing, and emotional twists.

www.ingramcontent.com/pod-product-compliance
Lightning Source LLC
Chambersburg PA
CBHW071535260626
47170CB00002B/643